M000081594

COUNTERATTACK!

When they got within sight of the Bisbee Municipal airport, its terminal building still ablaze, Curt Carson saw that the road ahead was crowded with the Herreronista invaders moving back toward the Mexican border.

"Tac Batt One, this is Tac Batt Leader!" Carson snapped. "Multiple targets, range one thousand meters. Deploy your warbots! Marching fire! Execute!"

The highway ahead suddenly erupted in gouts of explosions and clouds of dust as the Hairy Foxes, Mary Annes and jeeps fired at anything that was warm and moving, anything their radars or infrared sensors could spot that looked like a human being.

This is it, Carson thought to himself. The time to worry and the time to be scared was over. There was only time left to think about the battle that had just begun!

ACTION ADVENTURE

SILENT WARRIORS (1675, $3.95)
by Richard P. Henrick

The Red Star, Russia's newest, most technologically advanced submarine, outclasses anything in the U.S. fleet. But when the captain opens his sealed orders 24 hours early, he's staggered to read that he's to spearhead a massive nuclear first strike against the Americans!

THE PHOENIX ODYSSEY (1789, $3.95)
by Richard P. Henrick

All communications to the USS *Phoenix* suddenly and mysteriously vanish. Even the urgent message from the president cancelling the War Alert is not received. In six short hours the *Phoenix* will unleash its nuclear arsenal against the Russian mainland.

COUNTERFORCE (2013, $3.95)
Richard P. Henrick

In the silent deep, the chase is on to save a world from destruction. A single Russian Sub moves on a silent and sinister course for American shores. The men aboard the U.S.S. *Triton* must search for and destroy the Soviet killer Sub as an unsuspecting world races for the apocalypse.

EAGLE DOWN (1644, $3.75)
by William Mason

To western eyes, the Russian Bear appears to be in hibernation — but half a world away, a plot is unfolding that will unleash its awesome, deadly power. When the Russian Bear rises up, God help the Eagle.

DAGGER (1399, $3.50)
by William Mason

The President needs his help, but the CIA wants him dead. And for Dagger — war hero, survival expert, ladies man and mercenary extraordinaire — it will be a game played for keeps.

Available wherever paperbacks are sold, or order direct from the Publisher. Send cover price plus 50¢ per copy for mailing and handling to Zebra Books, Dept. 132, 475 Park Avenue South, New York, N.Y. 10016. Residents of New York, New Jersey and Pennsylvania must include sales tax. DO NOT SEND CASH.

G. HARRY STINE
#4 SIERRA MADRE

WARBOTS

PINNACLE BOOKS
WINDSOR PUBLISHING CORP.

PINNACLE BOOKS

are published by

Windsor Publishing Corp.
475 Park Avenue South
New York, NY 10016

Copyright © 1988 by G. Harry Stine

All rights reserved. No part of this book may be repro-
duced in any form or by any means without the prior
written consent of the Publisher, excepting brief quotes
used in reviews.

First printing: November, 1988

Printed in the United States of America

TO:
LCDR L. Sprague de Camp, USNR (Ret.)

"Rapidity is the essence of war; take advantage of the enemy's unreadiness, make your way by unexpected routes, and attack unguarded spots."
    —Sun Tzu, *The Art Of War*, ca 500 B.C.

CHAPTER ONE

Two aerodynes bearing the red-white-green triangle insigne of Mexico and the words "Fuerza Aerea" came in quickly from low altitude, skimming the tops of the trees as they climbed up the mountainside toward the large house tucked neatly into the trees near the top of the ridge.

The pilots didn't know their saucer-shaped craft were being tracked by the sensors of one of the most sophisticated air defense systems in the world.

"*Mi coronel,* the *federales* are almost here. May we open fire on them?"

The handsome, dark-eyed man with the trim mustache smiled. "No, Emilio, not while they may still be in radio communication with either Hermosillo or Chihuahua," he replied in Spanish. "Let them land. Let them power down. Francisco has his orders. There is no need to excite the *federales* at this point. They are no threat to me. None at all." He spoke with complete confidence.

And well he should.

Nearly a hundred members of his personal army, the Herreronistas, were deployed around the aerodyne landing stage. Each man was armed with the superb FABARMA M3A4 Novia rifle. The comm-intel people were using the magnificent Swiss digital pulse-width communications gear to keep in touch with each of those hundred riflemen, plus hundreds more grouped under infrared camouflage cover in the valleys and canyons of the Sierra Madre Occidental for 50 kilometers around the house. His own armed French-made DeLauny-Coanda *Vultur* attack aerodynes were ready to spool up and lift from their secluded, hidden *campos* positioned within 10 kilometers of the house. And no transport aerodynes were there; this visit had been anticipated, and all the cargo 'dynes were elsewhere. No sense in risking them if a fight broke out; the cargo 'dynes were a valuable part of the business.

And the house itself was merely the visible portion of a veritable fortress perched high in Mexico's Sierra Madre Occidental range, the extension of the Rocky Mountains and part of the cordillera that ran from Alaska to the southern tip of South America. The bastion contained enough food, ammunition, and other supplies to support almost a thousand people for several months. Built on the sides of 2,300-meter Cerro Caliente, both its water and electricity came from volcanic steam tapped from the mountain itself, one of many geological "hot spots" scattered along the length of the American cordillera.

Casa Fantasma — Ghost House — really wasn't there at all. Don't try to find it on maps or even on satellite images. It could be seen by the visual spectrum sensors of high-flying recon aircraft and satellites, but it looked like a motley collection of shacks and hovels, not a multimillion-dollar house and all of the support buildings that surrounded it. Most of it was underground, and various stealth technologies had made the aboveground complex virtually invisible to radar scanners and infrared sensors. It blended into the jumbled mass of the Sierra Madre Occidental, still a wilderness in the twenty-first century.

A few of the warehouses of the far-flung drug empire were to be found there. There was no way that they could possibly be emptied of *material* just because of a known visit by the *federales*. Casa Fantasma was a major accounting and distribution point. The *material* came in via aerodyne, was inventoried in, stored until ready to be inventoried out, and then transshipped north across the border into Arizona and New Mexico, whence it was further transshipped to other destinations in *los Estados Unidos de America*. However, nothing left Casa Fantasma without an exchange of hard cash. Even the aerodyne pilots and *troqueros* who took it north were part of the *hermanistas*. They operated on a cash basis.

10

The entire organization did. Accounting and inventory, what there was of it, was done with an extremely sophisticated high-speed computer complex also housed at the Casa Fantasma with remote links to other mainframes of the *hermanistas* operation.

This was part of an empire. And, like any empire, it required defense, an item considered by the businessmen of the *hermanistas* to be a necessary evil. Politicians and bureaucrats could be paid off and the bribes considered a business expense. But an army was necessary.

They did not need the army to defend them against politicians and bureaucrats, because the *hermanistas* dealt only with honest politicians—their definition of an "honest politician" being "one who stays bought." Although some politicians and their associates, the bureaucrats, often appeared publicly to be righteous, upstanding, and very serious moralists who believed it was their bounden duty to deny an individual the right to choose his own form of poison, the *hermanistas* knew that these had to have been bought by another association or syndicate. To the *hermanistas,* the concepts of idealism and altruism weren't really part of human nature. Their belief was unshakable: Anything worth doing was worth doing for money.

Thus, Casa Fantasma had its own army because it was merely one *capítulo* of the *hermanistas* under its own *cabo.*

And in the case of Casa Fantasma, the *cabo* was the tall, slender, handsomely dark-haired and dark-eyed man in the comfortable slacks, shirt, and *huaraches,* Colonel Luis Sebastian "Gordo" Herrero.

His rank was not facetious ego-puffery. The man had actually been a *coronel* in the Army of Mexico before events transpired to bring him into the *hermanistas.*

And he was still a *coronel* in charge of his own private army. But, unlike in the Army of Mexico, here he controlled his men completely because he was the one who paid them and exercised total discipline over them, often harsh when necessary but also compassionate in the manner of all who have learned the realities of good military leadership. The colonel took care of his men. There were no desertions

11

to the *federales*, but there were a few "unfortunate accidents" with firearms when required.

"Freddie," he said into the intercom on his ring finger, "the visitors we have been expecting have arrived. Please come to the reception area." Then he added in Swedish for security's sake, "I hope your appearance is quite sensual. I want you to keep Guillermo off balance, and you know what a macho stud he thinks he is."

A female voice came back to Herrero through the neuroelectronic transducer in his ring. Thus, he was the only one who heard it, because her voice sounded only in his head. "Shall I carry my social purpose weapon, Gordo?"

"If you're wearing what I think you should be, there is no place where you can hide it," he told her.

"I suspect I will surprise even you, *muchachito*. Are we well covered?" she asked. "Guillermo is often a vile-tempered hothead, especially when he has a little power and several men with guns to stand behind him."

"He will either be a little *gato* or . . ." Herrero promised.

"Or?"

"It is best that you do not know, Freddie."

"I require little imagination to guess," came the reply.

"Emilio," Herrero told his *teniente*, "let us prepare to welcome our guests. *Señora* Herrero will be here shortly."

"I'm already here," came the voice that the Colonel had heard from his intercom ring.

He turned to look. "Very good! Very good indeed, Freddie! But you could have hidden that social purpose weapon . . ."

Fredrica Nordenskold Herrero came down the curved steps into the living room and foyer. She had chosen a tight peasant blouse that stretched tautly over her firm breasts and left her fair shoulders bare. The swirling and colorful peasant skirt with its multitude of feminine ruffles and pleats hugged her slim hips and was gathered at her narrow waist with a silver *concho* belt. She looked very Mexican, except for her statuesque height and the long blond hair that fell freely and softly to her waist behind her, held out of her face by clasps of Mexican silver.

12

She was a stunning and sensual Nordic beauty. She always had been, Herrero told himself. In spite of the fact that she could never adopt all of the attributes of a Mexican woman because she was unable to shed the American ways acquired while growing up in Newburgh, New York, she was still an exciting and suitable mate insofar as Gordo Herrero was concerned.

And her appearance would certainly be enough to keep Guillermo Moreles y Herrero off guard and distract him from his official business. If it would do that for Guillermo—who the Colonel knew had always lusted after the woman—it would also distract the Mexican officers and troops who would accompany him.

"I took the precaution of bringing it anyway," Fredrica said, "but you would have to look to find it."

"I intend to do so with pleasure, much pleasure . . . after we dispatch our guests," Herrero promised her.

"If I allow it," she replied somewhat testily. "I'm growing weary of hiding in the mountains, Gordo."

"You don't like what I've given you?" he asked. "Isn't it better than being the wife of a mere Mexican army officer?"

"It is," she said with a nod. "But then I could go to Mexico City and back to New York without a bodyguard and without fearing for my life . . . or yours."

"Wealth has its price, Freddie," her husband reminded her.

"I sometimes wonder if it's worth the price," she muttered.

"A little late to back out now," he observed. A heavy pounding was heard on the massive front door. "Ah, our guests have arrived. Emilio, please get the door."

When the *teniente* unlatched and opened the heavy door, it was suddenly flung open from the outside by two *soldados* who quickly stepped through, their 9-millimeter Mendoza HM-11 submachine guns at the ready. Then a small, stocky young man in a military uniform stepped through into the foyer.

"Cousin, you have certainly chosen an uncivilized way to enter another man's home, especially in the family," Herrero remarked.

"If I had not been family, *primo,* I would not have known where to find you," the short man replied curtly without formality.

"Ah, I wondered how you were able to fly directly here!"

"You have certainly chosen an isolated place to live," Guillermo Morelos y Herrero snapped.

"Fredrica and I value our privacy. And this is a beautiful place to live."

"We know it is more than that, Gordo!"

"Many people, yourself included, have been advised of this for years, Guillermo," Herrero reminded his cousin. "So what is the problem now? Are you not satisfied with your consulting fees? Or is there more that you want?"

Guillermo Morelos was having a hard time keeping his eyes off Fredrica, and she was doing everything possible in the circumstances to draw attention to herself. "Yes and no, Gordo. As you know, the New Revolution and our new constitution have changed things in Mexico. President Alvaro has a new program that will get Mexico out of debt to the *gringo* banks and pay for defending our southern borders. . . ."

"I believe I've heard something of this," Herrero remarked. "I suspect you have come to discuss this with me and to make new arrangements. So, now that you are already in, *mi casa es tu casa.* Shall we go in and sit down? Your long flight must have been hot. It's summertime, after all. A drink, perhaps? For your *soldados* as well? And, Guillermo, we are the only ones here. You see no weapons. So please ask your companions to put away theirs."

"I know you, Gordo, so my soldiers will maintain their weapons at the ready. Now . . ."

Herrero ignored him. He turned his back on the armed men and gallantly took Fredrica's arm, telling her, *"Preciosa,* shall we?" Then he said over his shoulder, *"El que nada debe nada teme.* He who is guilty of nothing fears nothing. Please join us in a civilized manner, Guillermo."

The way Fredrica swayed her hips as she walked away into the living room raised Guillermo's excitement.

So he followed.

But he did not sit down when Herrero offered him a chair overlooking the patio, which in turn overlooked the Sierra Madres.

Herrero shrugged at his cousin's reluctance. Although he knew why the man was here, why he had come with soldiers, and all the details of Guillermo Morelos's defection to the *nuevo sinarquismos*, he was reluctant to blow the man away right at the start. After all, Guillermo was family. Perhaps some of Herrero's information had been wrong, or perhaps he hadn't been given all the information. Perhaps there was something more to his cousin's visit.

Herrero was in no hurry. He had time to sit and listen. No *material* had been scheduled to arrive, and none was scheduled to depart for the north. Furthermore, he'd learned that a wise commander does not make a decision or a move until it becomes necessary to do so. It wasn't necessary yet. And Herrero was ready whenever it became necessary to move.

"Please, cousin, what may I do for you? Why are you here?" Herrero asked unnecessarily.

Morelos placed his hands on his hips and announced, "I am here to make you legal!"

Herrero didn't answer at once. Finally, raising one eyebrow, he replied, "Oh? Am I not legal now? Look around. Am I not an ordinary citizen going about my business?"

"I am looking around. I see a home that could not possibly be within the means of a colonel in the Army of Mexico."

Herrero pursed his lips, then said, "You know our family, Guillermo. You married into its money. You also know that I had my small bit of legacy, which I prudently invested in opportunities made known to me while an army officer . . . as most officers are prone to do. Are you jealous of what I have been able to do? Or am I being presumptuous? Do *you* need help because you have perhaps not been as successful in investments?"

"Your business and your investments have not all been within the law, cousin Luis," Morelos told him bluntly. "You and I both know — and Ciudad Mexico knows — that you are

15

one of the largest drug lords in Mexico. That your operations include *amapolo de opio, mota,* cocaine, crack, angel dust, and psilocybin, designer drugs, neuroelectronic disks, and crysto-records . . . the latter from some of the finest houses of pain and pleasure in the world."

"You have forgotten to mention allopeptides," Herrero said, reminding his cousin that he now dealt in the most powerful of mind drugs, the ones that would allow a user to creatively hallucinate at will rather than suffer the vagaries of LSD and other hallucinogens.

"You . . . have . . . allopeptides . . . now?" Guillermo suddenly said in halting, almost reverent tones.

Herrero nodded, knowing for certain at that moment what he had expected for months: that Guillermo Morelos had become a slave to the most modern and stylish of the new substances. It disgusted him. Morelos had been part of the *hermanistas*. Now Herrero knew why his cousin had turned. It was bad enough that Morelos was a traitor. It was disgusting to learn that the man had become a hab-user. "Allopeptides are available, cousin, and it is my personal policy to give a liberal family discount . . . Now, what was it that you were saying about your ability to make me legal? For what?"

Guillermo Morelos swallowed hard, then tried to take his eyes off Fredrica Herrero and keep his mind on business. He was storing up visual memories. If he could not have that sensual, desirable woman, he would at least attempt to re-create her in his mind with the help of the chemical substances he had learned to use. *Why doesn't Herrero make disks or crystals of such a fantastic woman available?* he had often wondered. But he knew that Herrero, like most Mexican men, would not think for a moment of sharing such a woman with other men, even through the medium of neuroelectronics. Or would he? Guillermo might ask at the proper moment . . .

"You require a large and expensive army," Guillermo Morelos reminded his cousin. "President Alvaro has a new plan that will eliminate the need for you to maintain such a profit-eating organization to protect you. It is the Alvaro

Program."

The drug lord suddenly said in very cold and hard tones, "You do not need to explain the Alvaro Program to me. I know all about it." Indeed, Herrero did. One did not survive in his business without excellent intelligence sources. The Alvaro Program was announced publicly as a plan to license all Mexican drug dealers and transporters in order to provide an additional source of income which would help repay the Mexican foreign debt. However, Herrero harbored no illusions about the Alvaro Program. Most of the money would never be accounted for except in the secure computers of Swiss, Singaporean, Brunei, and Bahraini banks where someday Alvaro and his compatriots would be able to tap it to sustain their profligate life-styles in one of the ABC Allianza countries — Argentina, Brazil, or Chile. So Herrero went on pointedly, "Explain to me how *el Presidente* and his minions can provide me with defense and protection at a cost less than what I now expend for my own Herreronistas. And where will President Alvaro get the soldiers? The army is fully occupied on the southern borders. Even as we speak, a seventh invasion is being met. How then can Alvaro provide the *soldados* to replace my own?"

"If you know the Alvaro Program," Morelos broke in, "then you know that it is the policy of Mexico City to license all operators such as yourself . . ."

"For a fee."

"Of course, for a fee to cover the cost of the protection. The cost will be far less than what you now pay your Herreronistas."

"And I repeat my question: Where is Alvaro going to get the soldiers?"

"From your Herreronistas because you will no longer be requiring them."

"That is exactly what I thought." Gordo Herrero was silent for a moment. "And what will it cost me?"

"I am in full charge of the licensing program, cousin," Morelos explained.

"I know that."

"Therefore, I am willing to offer considerable discounts

17

to the fee structure in return for . . ."

"For? . . ."

"Certain favors, especially from you."

"Allopeptides?"

"No. I have a source."

Herrero knew his cousin's source. It was a competitor. And he knew the favor to be asked. And what his reply would be.

"Then what is your request? Your favor?"

Guillermo Morelos swallowed, then tried to say in a level tone the one word, "Fredrica."

Herrero started to turn his head to look at his wife.

He never got the chance.

Two sharp explosions went off right next to his ear.

Two very large, wet, red holes suddenly appeared in the khaki uniform of Guillermo Moralos while a red spray of blood exploded out of his back.

There was a third explosion, and Guillermo Morales suddenly had no face.

The living room then erupted with a maelstrom of the noise of many 9-millimeter submachine guns firing.

The two *soldados* with their own submachine guns suddenly were no more. They never had the chance to bring their guns up and into action. Each of them must have taken at least twenty rounds in the upper body and neck.

The sounds of gunfire also came through the walls from outside the house where the two aerodynes had landed. It lasted less than thirty seconds.

In spite of the fact that violence had been a part of his life for years, Gordo Herrero was shaken. His own Herreronistas had opened fire as they were supposed to if he, Fredrica, or Emilio got into trouble in the living room. And his other Herreronistas had taken care of the remaining *federales* in the government aerodynes outside. But the source of the initial three shots had taken him totally by surprise.

Fredrica sat with her MiniMax Magnum 9 in her hand. She was as cool and calm as her Viking forebears.

He knew she'd brought her "social purpose weapon." But it was for her protection, not for her to use offensively. And

18

it was apparent from the effects of the weapon that she had deliberately loaded it with Blitz MiniMax rapid-expansion hollow-point caseless rounds.

He was so surprised at her sudden bloodthirsty reaction that he could only ask, "Fredrica?"

Slowly and calmly, in English, she said, "He was a filthy pepto hally. I would never let that bastard touch me. Neither would you. So I made the job easier for you."

Gordo Herrero sighed. He tried to speak to her without anger because she was his wife. He did indeed love her. And she was even more beautiful now than when they'd walked out of the West Point Chapel together as man and wife those many years ago. But she was an American woman who would never, ever become a Mexican wife. She was too individualistic and strong-willed to make the change. So he told her, "Freddie, you spoiled my plans."

"How? You were going to kill him anyway," Fredrica replied coolly.

"Not exactly. His soldiers would have been killed. Guillermo would have been sent back to Mexico City alive—just barely alive—as a threat and warning."

"So? Alvaro and his people sent him. They know where we are. Now they'll just send more troops."

Herrero shook his head. "No, not if I activate Plan B."

"Plan B? You never told me about any Plan B."

"Freddie, sometimes I don't tell you everything. You shouldn't know everything if something happened and someone got you," Herrero told her frankly. "One of the things they taught me at West Point was always to have Plan B. So I do."

"What is it?" asked the Nordic beauty as she calmly put her small pistol away in a place where Herrero never would have thought she could have hidden it.

"I'm going to have to invade the United States of America."

CHAPTER TWO

"Sir, I'd appreciate it if you wouldn't leave just yet," Major Joanne Wilkinson remarked. "I have some additional reports that require your attention."

Major Curt Carson, temporary commander of the 3rd Robot Infantry Regiment (Special Combat)—popularly known by its historic name, the Washington Greys*—stopped halfway through the process of arising from his desk. It had been a hard day for Curt because he was temporarily wearing two hats and he didn't like one of them worth a damn. He'd been behind that desk all day. He hadn't even taken time for lunch.

He glanced at the clock. It said 1434. He had 26 minutes to join Carson's Companions, his regular company command, up on the range for two hours of practice live firing with their warbots.

It was important that he be there. He had a new platoon commander. Second Lieutenant Kathleen Clinton was fresh out of West Point and the Fort Benning Infantry School. She'd had her head filled with regular neuroelectronic warbot procedures at Benning, and it was going to take some time before she forgot all that and relearned her West Point personal combat skills. She couldn't be expected to replace Alexis Morgan for several months yet.

In fact, Curt doubted if anyone could replace Alexis. It wasn't that Alexis had been transferred out of the Greys; it was Army policy these days not to transfer individuals from unit to unit except on personal request or the recommenda-

*See *Regimental Roster, Operation Black Jack,* p. 389.

tions of the commanding officer. Keeping regiments together and building regimental morale was important in a high-tech volunteer military organization. Alexis had taken over what was left of Manny's Marauders.

In the past few months of temporary regimental command, Curt discovered he wasn't ready for such a thing yet. He learned he wasn't a desk officer. Eight years out of West Point, he was still a man of action who didn't really relish all the paperwork involved with higher command or a staff position. But since Operation Diamond Skeleton in Namibia had left the regiment leaderless when Colonel Belinda Hettrick had been wounded by a poison Bushman arrow that left her almost paralyzed, Curt had had no choice. The Greys had suffered a high number of casualties in the campaign, and he'd had to assume temporary command in the field because he'd been the most senior combat-rated officer.

After several months back in the 17th Iron Fist Division's casern at Diamond Point, Curt had come to the realization that commanding a regiment amounted to a hell of a lot more time with the computers than time with his troops. He was getting too far from his troops, and he didn't like it. He *had* to start spending more time with them.

But his chief of staff had more reports for him to look at.

"Dammit, Major!" he exploded, sitting back down. "Why the hell has the Regiment got a staff?"

"Major Carson," she reminded him, "if you knew half the crap that comes up on the terminals 'eyes only and for your immediate attention,' you'd realize that your staff protects the hell out of you. Sorry, sir, I don't mean to seem impertinent or petulant, but the recent cutback in the military budget plus the Emergency Military Expenditure Justification Act have created a whole new stack of status reports. If we didn't have computer data processing, we'd never work our way through them all."

"I thought I signed authorizations for you and the staff to sign off on most of them!"

"You did, sir." Joanne Wilkinson was a good staff officer, and she had Curt's respect because she'd been shot at in both Trinidad and Namibia . . . and had shot back. When it came right down to it, everyone in the Greys fought because they were the first Sierra Charlie regiment in the Army. And Wilkinson very much liked and admired this man who took care of his troopers and managed both his combat company and the regiment with a set of priorities that made sense to those serving under him but which were not normally in accord with regulations.

First in line came the regiment's ability to do what it was getting paid for: successfully carry out the orders of the civilian government in Washington when the regiment was required to take military action or be present to protect national interests.

Second on the list came the welfare of the regiment's officers and NCOs.

Everything else was low-priority make-work as far as Curt was concerned. Wilkinson knew her work was therefore Number Three on his priority list because, as chief of staff, she took care of the administrative details as well as being head honcho to the regimental staff.

"Sorry, Major, but the new regulations specifically required your personal perusal," Wilkinson reminded him and started ticking them off on her blunt fingers: "All status reports of regimental funds, pay, and allowances plus the status of all logistical items, especially expendables such as rations, fuel, and ammo . . ."

"Dammit, Joanne!" Curt lapsed back into a first-name basis with her. She, too, had recently been promoted, and they both had the same date of rank. Curt felt a little bit uncomfortable as her de facto commanding officer since both of them now wore gold oak leaves . . . and especially since they had fought together in Trinidad and Namibia. "I trust you. I trust the staff. And I trust my officers to report the straight skinny."

"Yes, sir, I know that. So do they. And so does General Carlisle's division staff. And we do a hell of a lot of covering for you. Uh, I never said that, of course."

Curt knew what she did; he'd spent extra time with the division's computer, "Georgie," checking what she'd done signing him off and covering her tracks. That was during the first few weeks after their return from Namibia, when the whole situation was a can of worms with endless reports and debriefings. They'd used up a lot of warbots, vehicles, ammo, and other supplies, all of which had to be accounted for in some manner other than stating, "Expended in combat." Casualties had to be processed. Some officers and NCOs had been transferred out, ostensibly because of severe wounds but also because the quiet inner circle of the officers and NCOs of the Greys believed the outfit would be better off without them. Replacements had to be requested, found, their Form 101s reviewed, and then placed where they would both be the most compatible and fulfill the requirements of the regiment.

In those weeks, Curt had confirmed Joanne's trustworthiness as the new chief of staff. As a result, he now made it a practice not to officially know about some of the things she had to do to keep the field clear. "Major, I appreciate your efforts to keep me from being up to my armpits in terminal data," Curt admitted.

"Thank you, sir. But there *are* some things that you *must* see. I don't want the Inspector General or some board of inquiry asking you about something you were supposed to know and have it come as a Big Surprise to you. Total trust sometimes stops at the horizon. That's why it's a different story at the Pentagon and, uh, with Congress," she said with hesitation. In the Army of the Robot Infantry, it was definitely improper to criticize "Dreamland on the Potomac," at least officially and on duty. This did not mean, of course, that a hell of a lot of bitching didn't go on during Stand-to on Friday night . . . but it never left the Club.

Curt knew what was behind all the new reports and double-checks. It wasn't just the budgetary cutbacks of the new administration in Washington, and it wasn't the new act of Congress. Running deep beneath it all was the recent inside scandal involving the clandestine black-market sale of Army weapons, ammunition, and other material to numerous small Middle East interests by officers on Persian Gulf duty with the Big L Division who thought they could get away with "expending" it in the occasional fracas that took place in that unstable part of the world. "Those bastards in the Gimlet Regiment have dishonored their regiment, the Army and all the rest of us! I hope to hell they get the goddamned book thrown at them," Curt muttered darkly.

"Yes, sir, I do too. They made life a hell of a lot more complicated for all of us. But I often wonder how many officers could withstand the temptations they had."

"Temptations be damned! Temptations are all around us all the time! That's the reason for esprit de corps and the honor of the regiment. That's the reason each of our commissions says that the government 'reposes special trust and confidence in the patriotism, valor, fidelity, and abilities' of us as officers." Curt looked at the clock again. "What's the deadline on this stuff?"

"Should have been in the database at fourteen hundred hours, Major."

"Well, it's not going to get there," Curt advised her. "Tomorrow by oh-nine-hundred for sure. I'll get to it first thing."

"Sir, you have a regimental commander's meeting at oh-eight-thirty with General Carlisle and his staff up on Level D," his chief of staff reminded him.

"So I'll be at this desk by oh-eight-hundred. And I expect to see you here bright and chipper with those reports on my terminal at that time, Major," Curt told her. "I have conflicting duties, and I can no longer postpone the ones I've neglected. So I really *must* be going!"

Major Joanne Wilkinson nodded. She understood. "I really don't envy you. It's a difficult conundrum. You shouldn't have to divide your time and efforts between two responsibilities, even though you've got an excellent second in Jerry Allen."

"Allen's showing promise, but he isn't all the way there yet. I have to depend a lot on Sergeant Kester," Curt admitted. "My big problem is that I've got a new brown bar, and we've got to get her up to speed. Goddammit, I miss Alexis Morgan!"

"Well, from all the reports I see—and I see them all as

chief of staff—Morgan's Marauders are shaping up fine in spite of the problems the company had with its former commander in Namibia," Wilkinson observed.

"Yeah, but Alexis has her hands full too," Curt observed as he pulled on his windbreaker combat jacket and equipment harness. "It's her first company command, and she's got an almost new company roster because of Namibian casualties. By the way, I'd like to see the latest sit-rep on our Namibian casualties who weren't reassigned or mustered out on medicals. I want to know when they're due to report back aboard."

"Yes, sir. Will do. And tell Alexis I think she looks great with those silver railroad tracks on her collar."

"I'll do that. That was a great make sheet, wasn't it?" Curt asked rhetorically, referring to the promotion list that had been released a few weeks ago. He picked up his M33A4 Novia rifle.* "And, Joanne, keep your ears tuned to rumor control headquarters. I want to know who's going to take command of the Greys . . . and when I'll get this monkey off my back."

"I have my network of Little Black Spies alerted up at Gee-One. But nothing yet," she told him. "I take it you're concerned about who it might be?"

"Yeah."

"That's good. A lot of us are. I hope our reasons for concern are the same as yours."

"Well, I tell you what my big worry is. Whoever takes over this outfit," Curt observed darkly, "won't be a Sierra Charlie. The new regimental commander will be a warbot brainy. Has to be. We're the first Sierra Charlie outfit, and we have no officers qualified for regimental command. So there can be no promotion from within the outfit as there should be. Whoever gets this job—and I don't want it any longer than I have to handle it—whoever gets it is going to have to do a lot of learning. . . ."

"We're still learning ourselves," Wilkinson added.

*See *Glossary of Robot Infantry Terms and Slang,* p. 396.

"Are you bragging or complaining about it?"

She raised her chin and stood straight. "Bragging, sir! And damned proud of it, sir! Everyone, man and woman, in a Sierra Charlie outfit fights instead of lying on their ass on a linkage couch! Damned if I liked the idea of being reassigned to a non-combat outfit just because I'm a woman! And damned glad we got the chance to show the high brass and the whole damned world that men and women could fight together in Namibia!"

For the last twenty-plus years, neuroelectronic robots had been the primary weapons of the United States Army. Because a single soldier could control up to a dozen war robots by remote linkage—seeing what the warbot saw, hearing what it heard, feeling what it felt, and commanding it by thoughts alone from a linkage control van sited to the rear of the action—the human being was removed from the deadly hazards of the modern battlefield.

The technophile American public had liked this idea twenty years ago, and therefore Congress liked it too and had been more than generous in funding the Robot Infantry. The war planners, strategists, tacticians, and doctrine experts loved the Robot Infantry not only because NE warbots were virtually immune to the potential problems of the nuclear battlefield, but also because warbots helped overcome the enormous imbalance of manpower and equipment that continued to exist in Europe. After more than a hundred years, the Soviet state had shown itself to be incredibly stable, built as it was on the foundations of internal and external fear. The troika of the Politburo, the KGB, and the Red Army worked because each element needed the other two; thus the political status quo could be maintained.

The Russians, being great chess players, found themselves stalemated in Europe by the warbots of the NATO allies. Therefore, the Big Red Tide had never broken through the Iron Curtain in its anticipated surprise "Friday night offensive" with hordes of tanks and armored personnel carriers. In the words of one NATO strategist, "Every morning, they looked westward, and checked their intelligence data and told each other, 'Nyet, Comrade, not today.' "

This hadn't kept the Soviets from playing games elsewhere in the world. Some were successful and some were not. But the Soviet state continued to stumble along with a marginal economy propped up only by its prisoner-mined gold. It was far from being an economic basket case; it was economically paralyzed from the waist down, so to speak. Like a disabled person, the Soviet Union was still capable of doing many things as long as it could get help from others.

Thus, unable to be used as originally intended in central Europe, the Robot Infantry regiments of the United States Army found themselves primarily engaged in security patrols, an occasional minor skirmish, and a lot of high-visibility public relations that were partly psych-war and partly to keep the folks at home happy, which in turn kept the Congresscritters approving budget requests for the visible, glitzy, awesome, and high-tech Robot Infantry.

The Army finally learned something from its own stepchild, the United States Air Force. Having gotten its hands on the ultimate technology of interfacing the human being with the computer, the Army had played it for all it was worth — until it became painfully obvious, after a series of worsening small brushfire conflicts, that warbots were *not* a total substitute for the forgotten mud-slogging infantry soldier, the doughboy, the GI, the grunt.

After almost losing the Washington Greys in a hostage rescue mission in the backwaters of Iran, the Army finally admitted — but only to itself — that warbots couldn't do it all. The human soldier had to be put back on the battlefield.

That was one tough job.

The Robot Infantry wasn't disbanded. The army never makes sudden, drastic changes. Although it was a slow change, some officers and NCOs couldn't hack it. Since the army takes care of its own until they get a chance to retire, none of the four Robot Infantry divisions and their regiments ceased to be RI. Instead, the Washington Greys had been selected to become the first Robot Infantry (Special Combat) Regiment, the Sierra Charlies, in a typical Army change that amounted to sidling slowly and gently alongside

27

the problem. The Army didn't want to lose the charisma of the Robot Infantry.

Yet it discovered to its amazement that the American public was ready again to embrace military heroes . . . on a limited scale and as long as too many people didn't get killed.

To become Sierra Charlies, not only did officers and soldiers have to learn how to shoot and be shot at again—an almost lost art after twenty years of warbots—but they had to do it with women in the combat units for the first time. The Robot Infantry had created a combat environment where women could fight warbots alongside men because battlefield hazard had become minimal. In short, the Robot Infantry meant that women were no longer restricted to "non-combat" duties where they could be shot at but never allowed to defend themselves.

When the Washington Greys converted to Sierra Charlies, the women stubbornly refused to give up the final equality: the right to fight alongside men as they had done in classical armies as well as on the American frontier. And the men of the Washington Greys didn't want them to go, either. Together as "warbot brainies" they'd learned to function as a team, an outfit, a unit. No one in such a taut organization wants to break up the people who make the team function.

As a result, the women of the Washington Greys stayed in, fought well, and were accepted by the high brass, Congress, and the public.

The women of the Washington Greys were something special.

The men of the Washington Greys liked that.

If there was any sense of difference in the Greys, it was one of mutual respect. The men and women were fiercely proud of one another because they'd achieved something *together* that was unique.

And both groups were meticulously adult and professional about observing Army Regulation 601-10, the infamous "Rule Ten" that prohibited physical contact between opposite sexes while on duty. No one in the Washington

Greys was going to mess up a good thing. . . .

In some ways, the personal and social environment of the Washington Greys was stodgy, formal, and even overpowering . . . if one did not look behind discreetly closed doors. In the Greys, there was a time and a place for everything.

And it was time for Curt to get the hell out of his temporary regimental commander's office and out with his troops. With his combat windbreaker, helmet, equipment harness, and rifle, he had suddenly metamorphosed into a combat officer. "Dammit, I'm going to be late!" he grumbled as he found his way out the door.

But not before quickly returning Major Joanne Wilkinson's departing salute as discipline and protocol required.

CHAPTER THREE

The border fence had been down since the Treaty of Nogales had been signed between the United States of America and the United States of Mexico. This controversial convention essentially opened the U.S.-Mexican border just as the U.S.-Canadian border had been for decades. But Congress, in a fit of budget cutting, also enacted a law that eliminated Mexican immigration controls in a series of phased programs. In short, the U.S. government stepped back from the Mexican border because it had not only become extremely expensive but also impossible to police. This didn't prevent the border states—California, Arizona, New Mexico, and Texas—from adopting statutes limiting employment opportunities and welfare services for Mexican nationals crossing the border into the United States.

At the time the treaty was signed, the law put into effect, and the fence torn down, no one north of the border believed it would work. But it did work . . . just barely, even over the opposition of many powerful American interests.

The only border watch maintained by the U.S. was an attempt to control the drug traffic.

Thus it was the Drug Enforcement Branch of the Border Patrol that first saw it.

The stretch of border between Naco and Douglas is open, flat high desert savannah. The infrared and microwave radar sensors operated by the DEB picked up the returns first. The border watchman seated in his control cubicle at Sierra Vista keyed the phone and reported it to his supervisor in Tucson just as the procedures manual told him.

"Turquoise Control, Sierra Victor Station reporting border penetration." The man was new to the job, a mere GS-4 hourly paid sensor monitor. It was his first week on watch at Sierra Vista.

The bored voice of the Tucson control center chief came back, "Where and what and how many, Richards?"

"Chief, it looks like about fifty people. They crossed this side of Paul Spur headed north."

"Look like they're headed toward Cecil Norman's place?"

"Uh, yeah."

"Goddammit, Richards, quit bothering me with that sort of shit! That's just another group of Mexican families coming north to Norman's ranch. They come up every week or so, and Norman gives them his surplus beef. Must feed a hundred families in Sonora from there. Let him do his thing. He's a charitable soul. Report when they cross back to Sonora. Should be about four hours."

"Okay, Chief. Sorry about that!"

"You'll learn, Richards, you'll learn. The real drug smugglers are a lot more subtle and covert. They bring the stuff across by the carload, not by the backpack."

So Richards went back to reading his comic book while the sensors kept their robotic watch for him.

The sensors were not programmed to pick up sounds or they would have heard the rifle and machine-gun fire at Cecil Norman's ranch.

Five hours later, Richards turned the station over to his relief, another young man in Border Patrol green. "About fifty or so Sonorans crossed about four klicks east of Benson Junction earlier tonight."

"Yeah, they come across and take advantage of Norman's surplus stuff," the relief man observed, checking the sensor records. "Okay, yeah, I see here when they crossed."

"Turquoise said to notify when they crossed back southbound."

The relief man, a considerably older and more experienced old-time U.S. Customs official who'd retired to Sierra Vista and found that a Border Patrol watch officer's job kept boredom from interfering with retirement, was suddenly alert. "They haven't gone back to Sonora yet?"

31

"No."

"That's damned funny! They usually don't stay very long. Border's been open for years, but the Sonorans still can't get it through their heads that we won't come looking for them as illegal aliens. Step aside; I think I'd better call Norman's place and make sure everything's copacetic."

"Uh, it's four in the morning. You'll wake up Norman."

The relief shook his head. "Not if he's got someone there who won't go home."

The relief man punched up Norman's telephone and waited while it rang.

And rang.

And rang.

"Shit!" the relief exploded. "He's either got the phone turned off or he's in trouble."

"Trouble?"

The relief let the phone continue to ring. "We haven't had any *banditos* around here since the border was opened. And I don't know why there might be a bunch here now. Maybe things have gotten bad down south in Sonora, and some of the bandit gangs have migrated north." He savagely punched off trying to call Norman and touched in another number instead. "Turquoise, this is Sierra Victor."

"Go ahead, Sierra Victor."

"Tell the Chief that the penetrators who went into Norman's ranch about four hours ago haven't come back out yet. I suspect trouble. Request Air Check send in an aerodyne to have a look at first light."

"This is Chief Evans. You mean the penetrators are still there?"

"That's what I reported, sir."

"Damn! Okay, you're authorized to request Air Check look in on it right away. Sunup's in about forty minutes anyway. By the time they get airborne and scoot down there, the sun will be coming up."

"Roger! Will do!"

"And keep me posted, dammit! Richards, are you still there?"

"Yessir."

32

"I told you to report to me when the penetrators came back out."

"They haven't come back out yet, sir."

"Well, you should have notified me anyway!"

"Uh . . . Yes, sir."

"Goddammit, I should have put you on watch as a trainee for a couple of months to learn the ropes! Would have done it, except the budget's been cut again and I don't have the manpower," the Chief explained, but not in apologetic tones. He was angry but didn't know exactly whom to direct his anger toward. He'd been the one who'd given a new man an incomplete order under the assumption that he was dealing with an experienced watchman.

The klaxon buzzer went off in the Zulu Alert shack. Pilot Officer Ken Anderson of the Border Patrol came awake in puzzlement. *That couldn't be the Zulu Alert horn!* he told himself. The alert horn *never* went off at night. In fact, it hardly went off at all any more. Border Patrol Air Check had deteriorated into a snap assignment: Go out for an hour or so and check the border every day, usually in late afternoon when it was cooler, just to keep the aerodyne in the air, log some air time, and find out if the squawks had been fixed by the maintenance crew.

It certainly didn't include intruder alerts these days.

But as Anderson heard the sound of people running down the hall outside his alert shack bedroom, he realized that something was up.

It took him five minutes to get dressed. No one on Zulu Alert slept in flight suits and body armor any longer; it was too damned uncomfortable, and they hadn't had a night alert in *years*. (Of course, all procedures were scrupulously followed when the inspectors were due to show up.)

Everything was ready for him in the hangar when he got there and scrambled up the boarding ladder into the patrol aerodyne.

As he slipped into the seat and pulled the neuroelectronic linkage helmet over his head, his crew chief was plugging his back and spinal harness into the proper terminals in the cockpit. With the biotech on one side and the crew chief on the other, Anderson ran through his preflight checks. The biotech was injecting him with accelerators and enhancers while watching his vital signs. Within minutes, Anderson was one with the aerodyne, and it was an extension of his mind and body.

He thought the orders for the slot valve checks and "felt" the blower slots cycle open and closed in sequence. Control of the craft was assured.

Communications check, he thought. *Turquoise Air Center, this is Ranger One. How do you read?*

Loud and clear, Ranger One, came the reply, which was voiced in his head although it was the voice signal from the controller in the Border Air Watch Center in Tucson. *Your code is Fearless Frank. Your beacon should be squawking zero-zero-one-three.*

Fearless Frank here. Roger. Confirming squawk. Is this for real?

You bet your sweet ass it is! Condition Yankee! Stand by for lift-off! What the hell took you so long, Ken?

Uh, minor glitch in the plumbing.

Sure it was. Damned body armor is rough to sleep in, isn't it? Okay, target coordinates coming up on your navigational system now!

Cecil Norman's place!

Yeah, check it out down low. Stay in linkage. We want real-time data and we want it fast. Norman may be in trouble.

Center didn't need to say more. The computer downloaded the brief history of the border crossing in zip-time, and the aerodyne's linkage computer time-shifted it into pilot-time so Ken Anderson could understand it. He "saw" the whole affair just as the sensors had, and he "heard" the conversations between Sierra Victor and Turquoise. He knew the background.

Spool up! Lift it! Clear to lift!

Roger! Anderson turned to his crew chief and biotech. "We're clean and linked! Button up and disconnect and get the hell out of here! I'm lifting as soon as I get thrust and flow!"

The biotech nodded and withdrew from sight over the edge of the cockpit. The crew chief gave the thumbs-up and pulled his plugs. Anderson sealed the canopy as he instructed the turbines to spool up.

The hangar roof rolled back to reveal the waning stars of a clear desert morning. A gibbous moon hung in the western sky. The eastern horizon was now barely visible in the coming light of day.

The nav system told him he had a little more than 58 kilometers to go. Flight time 17:14, including lift and climb to altitude to clear the Mule Mountains.

The aerodyne told him it was in a go condition. He ordered it to lift.

One of these days, Anderson told himself, shielding his brown thoughts from the aerodyne's system, *we'll get some good Army surplus warbot stuff, and I won't even have to leave the ground! Then we can send this frisbee out there all by itself for a look!*

Everyone in the Border Patrol knew the outfit got hind tit these days.

Once clear of the hangar, the aerodyne tilted and accelerated toward the southeast, climbing slightly to clear the 2,400-meter summits of the Mule Mountains 37 kilometers away on the skyline.

The rising sun caught him just as he was letting down to nap-of-the-earth flight beyond Bisbee. He flipped his visor over his eyes while the aerodyne dropped filters over its visual and infrared sensors.

Fearless Frank, this is Watch Center. Be advised that border sensors indicate that people are moving southbound across the border from Norman's place.

They're leaving?

Rog. But not all together. Still some of them at Norman's. We don't have a good visual on them yet because of the low sun angle, but we should get a teleoptical from the Douglas Watch Tower in a few minutes.

Okay, rog, tally-ho! I have them! Strung out between Norman's and the border! Want me to check them out?

Negatory! Get to Norman's place and report status of ranch and inhabitants.

As Anderson came in down-sun with the aerodyne, all hell broke loose.

Watch Center! Fearless Frank is picking up ground fire!

What? Say again!

I'm picking up ground fire . . . light automatic weapon fire mostly . . . coming from the ranch area as well as from some of the penetrators making their way back southward!

Okay, pull back out of range and come to hover! I'm scrambling the Nogales swat flight!

Watch Center, Fearless Frank here! The Norman ranch house has just been torched. I repeat: The Norman ranch house is now on fire!"

Roger, I confirm your report from your sensor data! We're notifying the Bisbee fire authorities now. Got enough fuel to remain on station in hover?

For how long? When will the Nogales flight get here?

Two-eight minutes.

Negatory! I'm putting it on the ground!

Withdraw to the Bisbee Airport and go to ground.

Roger. I guess that was no food trek to Norman's this time.

Guess not. Bandits again.

When you gonna let us put autocannons on these 'dynes?

Not until Congress says our patrol ships can shoot.

Goddammit, Center, can we call in the Air Force? Looks like someone raided Norman's and set fire to the place! They shouldn't be allowed to get away!

Patrolling the border isn't an Air Force mission, Fearless. But the Border Patrol swat flight is airborne!

The swats were a little faster than the patrol aerodyne. Anderson's sensors picked them up as a flight of three rounded the southern flank of the Mule Mountains less than a kilometer north of the border. They were flying nap-of-the-earth. If it hadn't been for the patrol aerodyne's surplus Air Force high-resolution doppler radar capable of picking up their wake turbulence, Anderson would never have seen them. He spooled up his aerodyne, got airborne, and followed them in order to complete his assigned mission of checking out the Norman ranch.

The swat flight apparently caught ten people between the ranch and the border. They landed between them and the border and unloaded four warbots out of each swat 'dyne. It surprised them when they were immediately shot at by the retiring bandit group.

Once the shock of encountering a heavily armed band was overcome, the swat team recovered the initiative. They had only surplus old Mark 3 warbots mounting quad 7.62-millimeter prolonged-fire machine guns, they were slow and clumsy, and this was the first real action some of the Border Patrol swats had encountered. But they were between the bandits and the border. They had superior firepower. And they were virtually indestructible because of their armor, which would stop the submachine-gun and light-rifle rounds of the bandits.

Normally, well-disciplined and well-led guerrilla troops and small units of light infantry had a fifty-fifty chance of beating the old warbots, which had been primarily designed to handle mass Soviet motor infantry assaults in Europe. But these bandits weren't disciplined. They were a gang, not a military unit. And they fought like they'd been smoking and sniffing and needling the primary export products of Mexico. They didn't seem to know the meaning of the word fear. And they didn't seem to care whether they lived or died.

So die they did.

The remaining bandits didn't surrender even when it became clear to them that they couldn't overcome the Border Patrol's antique warbots and get back across the border to safety. They continued to fight. And they fought to the death. The ten bandits who were caught in the open were killed. So were the ones who tried to hole up in the cover of the non-burning Norman ranch buildings.

It wasn't the usual sort of clash between the Border Patrol and the uncommon *banditos* who occasionally came across the border and were caught.

And this was the first time in a long time anything like this had happened this far west of the Big Bend country.

They weren't the only ones who were killed that morning.

When Ken Anderson grounded his aerodyne at the Norman ranch and sent his ground recon robot to look around, he was almost glad he couldn't do it in person. It was bad enough to sense it all neuroelectronically through linkage with the recon bot. And it was made bearable only because

37

Anderson knew he wasn't really there.

Cecil Norman and his wife Carmella had been tortured and murdered.

But the way it had been done was brutal. Anderson knew—and so did the Border Patrol people linked in with him from Tucson—that this wasn't just a cross-border raid.

It was terrorism.

Cecil and Carmella Norman had been dismembered. It was difficult to differentiate them from the hundred kilos of prime beef that they'd taken out of their freezer to give to what they thought would be hungry Sonorans.

In spite of the fact that Ken Anderson wasn't personally present with his recon robot and couldn't smell the scene, he became violently sick to his stomach.

CHAPTER FOUR

"Here's the situation," Major Curt Carson explained to his two lieutenants as he pointed out landmarks visible from where they sat under cover just below the hill's crest. "Our objective is to take and hold that hill at the road junction. The rest of the regiment will be moving up the road to the left, and we have to be able to hold this road junction and protect the regiment's right flank as it wheels the enemy. The enemy holds the fork of the road leading to the right. He's deployed in depth, although we're currently on his right flank at the moment and his attention is diverted elsewhere by the Cottonbalers. If he discovers the Washington Greys making this rapid sweep around his flank, he's likely to move reserves up the road and try to either cut us off or stop us at this junction. Now look to the right there, about a kilometer down the road. He's got a picket sentinel perched atop that other hill. We've got to take the road junction, preferably without having the enemy move in on us. I'll entertain suggestions at this point. How do we do it?"

The afternoon was getting soggy. Huge thunderheads were building up over the mountains to both the east and west. Curt knew that within an hour, they were going to get soaked by a gully-washer. Whatever action Carson's Companions took would have to account for fighting in a downpour.

Despite her diminutive size, Second Lieutenant Kathleen Clinton—known to her friends and colleagues as "Kitsy"—was slender and in superb physical condition after four years of West Point. Even her year of Robot Infantry training at Fort Benning hadn't affected her physical training.

She was a physical fitness addict. Although her short dark hair was hidden in her battle helmet, her elfin facial features betrayed the fact that she was a young woman although she was wearing the usual baggy cammies of a Sierra Charlie. And she was intense. "Sir, may I ask a question?" she snapped.

Curt told her easily, "Kitsy, while I appreciate your attention to military protocol, we're leading troops and warbots in the field at the moment. Ease up."

"Yes, sir, I'll try. Is it necessary that we take this road junction without the enemy knowing about it? In other words, sir, do we have to take out that sentinel before he can report us?" the new lieutenant asked earnestly.

"Do you think we can, Kitsy?" Curt replied by asking her a question in return.

"No, sir, I don't. Even if we smothered him with ECM, our very countermeasures would tip off the enemy to our presence."

"You're right," Curt told her. He knew what he'd do, but he was training a new officer and wanted to find out what she'd do. Kathleen Clinton was a different person from Alexis Morgan. Curt would have known precisely what Alexis would do, but his former lieutenant now wore captain's bars and had taken over the Marauders. So he not only had to train this new officer in the ways of his own thinking but learn how she thought as well. "Apparently you've got some plan in mind as a result of your recent Benning experience?"

"Uh, yes, Major." She couldn't yet bring herself to be on a first-name basis with Curt. Five years of living under strict military discipline had created habits not quickly broken. "I'd take Alpha Platoon and swing to the right along the west side of the road. Lieutenant Allen would then have time to register the guns of his Hairy Foxes on the sentinel. I'll leave my Saucy Cans with him to add to his firepower, because I want to move fast and won't need it. After an initial barrage, Alpha will take the sentinel out. Then Bravo can move to the company objective to occupy and hold it as a fire base. Alpha will remain at the sentinel's position

40

ready to move as necessary. If we move fast enough, we can cream the bastard before he can get a report out."

"Jerry?" Curt asked First Lieutenant Jerry Allen, commander of Bravo Platoon. "Comments?"

Allen grinned. "Good old Kitsy!" Jerry chuckled. "Bold and enthusiastic as ever! Look, Kitsy, there's a hell of a lot of open ground between here and that sentinel. Not much cover, especially for your platoon moving in the open across that low ground. Let me tell you something: Heavy fire even at this range may make him keep his head down so he won't fire back, but it probably won't keep him from reporting in. He'll see you coming. So he'll probably call down some artillery on you. We don't know what the enemy has emplaced on that ridge to the east. We have no recon reports that are less than a day old. So you're probably going to be shot at, Kitsy!"

"Probably!" Clinton snapped. "So? If we get incoming from that ridge, your Hairy Foxes can provide answering fire. It's within range of fifties. Besides, I don't intend to give the enemy enough time to react. I've got to advance only a kilometer. If you make him keep his head down with your fire, I can cover that ground in less than three minutes and bring him under fire with my Mary Annes."

"And in the meantime, I'll probably draw the enemy fire," Jerry pointed out.

"Not if you shag-ass for the objective when you see me begin my assault," the new lieutenant told him. "One thing I've learned so far as a Sierra Charlie: We've got firepower *and* mobility! I'm the mobile assault platoon; you've got the fire base. And if you do catch incoming that your fifties can't reach, you'll have the two Saucy Cans that can reach out to fifteen klicks' range."

Jerry Allen shrugged. "Might work."

"You got a better idea, Lieutenant?" she wanted to know.

He didn't. Kitsy Clinton had been one of his plebes; he knew very well that she was sharp and sassy. And she was gung-ho. When he'd found out she'd been posted to the Companions, it was only his sense of loyalty to Adonica Sweet, now in OCS, that prevented him from finding out how she arm-wrestled in bed.

Curt watched this interplay between his two lieutenants with interest. In Kitsy Clinton, he knew he had a terrier on his hands. She was perhaps overeager. But then again, she hadn't been shot at, and when this happened it tended to temper a lot of a new officer's overenthusiasm. Except in the case of Marty Kelly, who'd been a special case and a continuing problem . . . and was still recovering from Namibian wounds.

Curt also knew the ground and Clinton didn't. Along the west side of the road, the footing was relatively wet and a little swampy because it was at the headwaters of the lake spreading out to the south. She might take a little longer than three minutes to cover that soggy kilometer.

Curt was willing to let her try it. There was only one way a new eager-beaver officer could learn Sierra Charlie tactics and all the little wrinkles that went along with the new doctrines being worked out by the Washington Greys. Clinton's personal combat training at West Point was still fresh, although it had been overlaid by the neuroelectronic warbot training at the Infantry School. Eventually, she'd make a good Sierra Charlie officer. But she also had to be allowed to make mistakes in a field exercise such as this.

"I like it, Kitsy, and I'm going to try it with one minor change," Curt announced. "As soon as Bravo Platoon opens fire and you begin to move, I'm going to start toward our objective with one of the Saucy Cans and our three ACVs."

He didn't tell her why he wanted to do this, but Curt caught the quick look from Jerry Allen that indicated Bravo Platoon's commander understood. If Clinton bogged down in her assault, Curt would be able to establish a secondary fire base on the objective hill while Allen continued to function from where they now were. Spreading out the fire base would gain them some security and allow them to cover Alpha Platoon if it had to dig and push and pull itself out of the muck that Curt *knew* was out there.

And it was going to get worse because the thunderboomer building over the western ridge was going to dump rain on all of them like a cow pissing on a flat rock . . . and within 30 minutes. Clinton wasn't familiar with this climate; she was in a hurry and apparently not willing to wait out the thunderstorm. So she was going to get caught in it. And this would multiply her troubles.

"Any questions as to who's going to do what and when?" Curt asked.

"No, sir!" Clinton chirped.

"Simple enough, Major," Allen replied coolly.

"Okay, Bravo will open barrage at fifteen hundred hours. Alpha will depart this hill on the assault at fifteen-ten. Enough time?"

"Oh, more than enough, sir! We can move before that if you want!" the little second lieutenant chirped.

"I don't want to move before that, Lieutenant. Sergeant Kester and I have some work to do reprogramming your Saucy Cans for our voice signatures. And we've got to collect the ACVs of both platoons and give their warbot brains the instructions to follow us and to handle contingencies," Curt explained. "Lieutenant Allen? Will you be ready?"

Allen nodded. "Ready and willing, Major. We'll have the guns laid in well before that."

"Okay, time is short, so let's move!" Curt looked at his watch, but he was really checking the growing thunderstorm out of the corner of his eye. As a final warning, he remarked, "Don't open your muzzles until you're ready to act."

Allen understood him. Clinton apparently considered that warning to be merely a standard precaution. Normally in humid climates, the muzzle covers of the rifles and cannon wouldn't be removed until ready to fire if for no other reason than to keep moisture out of the small-caliber bores and water from running down the barrels of the heavies.

Lieutenant Clinton took off at the run for her platoon. Allen hung back only long enough to remark to Curt, "Major, that was a goddamned sneaky thing to do. We're going to get wetter than hell here just about the time she gets down into the bog."

Curt shrugged. "Jerry, I don't need to remind you that I

43

had to do something like this to you a couple of times, too. Some things can be learned only by blundering into them. That's why we subject ourselves to these training exercises." He knew that Lieutenant Kitsy Clinton was going to find herself and her platoon in real trouble because she hadn't taken all the combat factors into account — in this case, the weather. When you were working a neuroelectronic warbot from the warmth and dryness of a linkage command van, it didn't make too much difference what the weather outside was because the standard RI warbots were big and powerful enough to squish through damned near any kind of terrain. Not so the new voice-commanded warbotic grunts of the Sierra Charlies, the M60 Mobile Assault Robots or Mary Annes and the M44 Heavy Fire Robots or Hairy Foxes. They were smaller, lighter, and less powerful because smaller size gave them greater speed and mobility . . . which was what the Sierra Charlies were all about.

Master Sergeant First Class Henry Kester had been listening on the perimeter of the Orders sessions. He knew exactly what to do without being told. "Sergeant Gerard is going to be pissed off when Lieutenant Clinton gets him stuck up to his asshole in muck down there, Major," Kester warned.

Curt nodded. "I know. So we're going to learn how Lieutenant Clinton handles her troopers when the going turns to slime, aren't we? Pick up Clinton's Saucy Cans vehicle and let's saunter over to our objective once Allen opens fire."

"Are we gonna run this on the inside?" Kester asked.

"Hell, yes! I've been plenty wet before!" Curt wanted to appear dry and crisp when Lieutenant Clinton came back soaking wet. It would add to the effectiveness of this maneuver.

It was strictly a company maneuver with blank rounds and laser-fire designators, and the enemy was strictly imaginary. Roosevelt Lake shimmered in the distance while the thunderheads of the Arizona monsoon season continued to build around them.

At 1500, the 50-millimeters on Allen's Hairy Foxes opened up, and Curt watched as scintillating spots of red

44

light touched the target hill a kilometer to the south. Edie Sampson along with Sergeants Cole and Dillon were getting very good. At that point, Curt moved his ACV back down the reverse slope and onto the road, then moved toward the objective hill as fast as he could push his vehicles. He got there and secured the hilltop just in time.

Alpha Platoon's troopers and Mary Annes were down in the low ground now, and they certainly were not moving as rapidly as Clinton had anticipated.

"Companion Alpha, this is Companion Leader," Curt called on the company's tacomm. "Move it along! We can't maintain this rate of fire forever!"

"Companion Leader, this is Companion Alpha," came Kitsy Clinton's reply. "This is sloggy going down here!"

"Does your Platoon Sergeant have any suggestions?" Curt asked rhetorically, knowing damned good and well that Sergeant Nick Gerard was probably cursing up a storm at this point. Curt wanted to make sure that Clinton was listening to the voice of experience in her platoon.

"Uh . . . Wait one! . . . Uh, we're going to move left and onto firmer footing on the road!"

"Roger! We're covering you," Curt told her.

Then the skies opened up, following a bolt of lightning that arced down out of the overbearing thunderstorm cloud into the swarm of troopers and warbots of Alpha Platoon down in the marshy ground. This was followed by the crash of thunder. The lightning stroke created the necessary ionic trail to trigger rain which began to fall heavily.

"Companion Alpha, this is Companion Leader!" Curt asked anxiously. "Did that lightning strike hit anyone?"

"Uh, affirmative! Got one of my Mary Annes!" came the hasty reply.

"Roger, push on, Companion Alpha."

"They ain't gonna make it, Major," Kester observed quietly. "Want I should call for warbot recovery vehicles?"

"Probably wouldn't be a bad idea," Curt opined.

"Take them about an hour to get here from Diamond Point," Kester remarked.

Curt nodded. "Roger, I know that. Lieutenant Clinton's

outfit is going to muck around down there for a little longer than she thought. Excellent lesson."

"Yessir, but Gerard is going to be pissed."

"Yeah, I'm sorry about that, but he can do as much or more than I can to educate Lieutenant Clinton about the realities of Sierra Charlie warfare," Curt said.

It was a hell of a thunderstorm, with lots of lightning and about 3 centimeters of heavy rain that fell within thirty minutes. The dirt road in turn became a sea of mud. To attempt to move on it now would mire anything. Curt knew the ground was so porous that the water would soak into the soil within thirty minutes after the thunderstorm was over, so he wasn't worrying about getting back to Diamond Point in time for Retreat and chow call. Kathleen Clinton and her platoon might be a bit longer than that getting back.

But Major Curt Carson wasn't going to be given the luxury of finishing this exercise.

"Grey One to Grey Head," chirped the voice of Major Joanne Wilkinson over the regimental frequency.

Curt reached up to the ACV's comm console and touched the switch. "Grey Head here."

"Major, I've just received the orders posting our new regimental commander. He's on his way back from Bahrain at this time, and his ETA is expected to be oh-eight-hundred tomorrow.

"Thank you, Major," Curt told her, somewhat relieved to know that his temporary command was about over and he could then devote his full attention to his company again.

"Major, I'd suggest you get back to Diamond Point ASAP, sir." There was a note of concern in Wilkinson's voice.

"Problem, Joanne?"

"Maybe. Maybe not. I hope not. Our new commanding officer is a fresh-issue light colonel and former company commander in the Gimlet Regiment from the Gulf."

He suddenly understood her concern. The Gimlet Regiment of the 50th Big L Division was the one just racked by the arms-selling scandal that was causing the United States Army a lot of grief at the moment.

Yes, he had to get back to regimental headquarters. He had to know whether or not this new regimental commander was being assigned to the Washington Greys because of a post-scandal breakup of the Gimlet or whether it was because whoever was coming happened to be the best available for the command.

Either way, the Washington Greys could be in trouble from the morale standpoint, depending on who the new commander was.

CHAPTER FIVE

Even at 0800, the weather was already warm and somewhat humid on the landing stage of Diamond Point. Curt
removed his service cap, wiped the sweat from his brow and
from the cap's sweatband, then searched the cloud-speckled
eastern sky for an incoming aerodyne.

Nine other officers of the Washington Greys were clus-
tered together on the landing stage, waiting to greet their
new regimental commander.

"Damned Air Farce missed its ETA again!" Major Wade
Hampton muttered.

"Yes, and if the Greys happened to show up late for a
pickup, we'd never hear the end of it from the trash haulers," Major Frederick Benteen pointed out.

The officers stood around uncomfortably, making small
talk and shop talk to keep busy. They were people of action;
they didn't like standing around.

They were also nervous. Some of them had had the
chance to look at the new colonel's 101 File; others hadn't
had time. Regardless, they were anxious to meet this new
person who would lead them. Army policy was intended to
ameliorate this sort of thing because it was standard procedure to promote to command from within a unit. However,
it was impossible in this situation. Major Curt Carson was
the senior combat-rated officer in the Washington Greys,
and he'd just been given an outstanding officer promotion
to major two years ahead of the time when he'd actually
qualify. Most of the Greys felt that Curt should be their
CO, but there was no way that the TO&E and the regulations could be bent enough to allow a fresh-caught major to

command a regiment. And no one else in the regiment could be promoted to lieutenant colonel. The same situation held true for the available officers within the 17th Iron Fist Division at Diamond Point.

"That's for sure. The Air Force doesn't like to be kept waiting, but they always seem to have a built-in headwind when it comes to meeting a sked," Major Patrick "Pappy" Gratton added tentatively. He was new to the regiment, having been assigned from the 52nd "Ready Rifles" of the 26th "R.U.R." Division to fill the S-1 adjutant slot vacated when Joanne Wilkinson was promoted and bucked up to chief of staff. He was also new to the Sierra Charlie concept, and he was feeling his way along there as well . . . and not so sure he was going to make it. An older man — hence his nickname among the younger staff officers of the Greys — he'd been following the career track of a Class 42 Administrative and Personnel Systems Management Officer and hadn't been expected to become involved in combat in the Robot Infantry. But now he'd been posted to the Washington Greys because Curt had picked him from among three others suggested for the slot by the Pentagon. And Pappy Gratton had then learned that *everyone* in a Sierra Charlie outfit had to know how to fight, shoot, and be shot at. There was no rear echelon in the Greys. Curt hoped Gratton could make the grade; the man was conscientious, a pro, a person with the love of the military life ingrained in his personality. Anyone who could make it through Texas A&M, then climb to the rank of major in the Regular Army, had to have a lot on the ball, especially in a noncombat specialty. But whether Gratton could hack it as a Sierra Charlie was something else. Curt knew of no way to find this out by examination or study of a 101 File.

"Have you gotten any additional data on our new commander since we got the news last night?" Captain Joan Ward asked of Joanne Wilkinson.

The new COS fielded the faux pas gracefully by asking the new regimental adjutant, "Pappy?"

Gratton had detected Ward's slip. He forgave her for it. He was the new man on the staff, and it would be habitual

49

for a while yet before personnel questions were no longer delivered to the former adjutant. "I pulled his One-Oh-One File last night and spent a little time studying it before I hit the sack," Gratton replied. "Bellamack, William Donald, Lieutenant Colonel, Army of the United States. Outstanding promotion on a special order released yesterday. The Colonel formerly commanded 'Bellamack's Bearcats,' Second Company, Twenty-first Gimlet Regiment, Fiftieth Big L Division, on station in Bahrain. Distinguished Service Medal. Silver Star with oak leaf cluster. Just awarded the Meritorious Service Medal . . ."

"Interesting," Captain Alexis Morgan observed. "And from the Gimlet Regiment. Any note concerning the citation on that last decoration, Major?"

"Yes. Bellamack led the three officers who blew the whistle on the arms scam over there," Gratton said quietly. "He laid his career on the line. His colonel and five other officers are probably going to get Dishonorables when the court-martial records are reviewed by the Pentagon."

Curt had glanced at Bellamack's 101 File about an hour before. The man was apparently a stickler for procedures, protocol, and regulations. Curt understood Bellamack's reasons for whistle-blowing; he was a West Point graduate several years before Curt's time and obviously still operated under the cadet honor code. So did Curt. But it's a tough decision for a mere major commanding a company to blow the whistle on a bird colonel and most of a regimental staff, plus several close colleagues. If it backfires because of *any* reason such as incomplete substantiating data, it means the end of a service career. Takes guts. Curt thought he was probably going to get along with his new regimental commander.

He'd soon know.

"Diamond Point Tower, Air Force Iron Man One with you, landing Diamond Point with protocol and landing information Romeo," came the sound from the loudspeaker mounted on a ramp pole and hooked into the air traffic control net.

"Iron Man One, Diamond Point. Ident. Radar contact

50

three-two east of Diamond Point inbound. Make straight-in approach. Clear to land, Pad Oscar," came the reply. "Attention, ramp personnel, stand by for inbound Air Force transport aerodyne with Class A Protocol, Level Three personnel aboard. Ramp honors to alert!"

Curt looked around at the nine officers—his regimental staff plus his company commanders. It was the first time in many, many months that they'd had an occasion to wear Army Green Type B uniforms with service caps, ribbons, and unit badges. Save for Curt, who'd had to shave his head to work recon birdbots over Otjomuise in Namibia a short time before, the rest of the officers didn't look like shaved-head warbot brainies even though they wore the light blue and yellow colors of the Robot Infantry on their shoulder boards. They'd allowed their hair to grow, a distinctive badge all in itself because no special beret or insignia had yet been authorized for the Sierra Charlies.

Curt was proud of these people. They'd closed ranks behind him when he'd had to take command on the field of battle. In spite of the additional administrative duties he was forced to handle as temporary regimental commander, Curt had inwardly enjoyed the job of leading these outstanding people. In due course of time, when he was ready for it, he hoped he'd have a regiment of his own. "Ladies and gentlemen, it's been a pleasure commanding you, however temporary it was. And however traumatic it's been since Namibia. Let's look sharp to greet our new colonel!"

The distinctive bright shape of a large Military Airlift Command aerodyne with its high-observable colors—in direct contrast to the low-observable "stealth" colors of tactical aircraft—appeared over the trees to the east. With its bottom tilted toward them in deceleration, it was a huge object.

A landing control warbot with its brightly flashing strobe lights dashed to the touchdown site, stopped, and raised its blinking wands.

The standby fire-suppression robots came to standby alert status around the pad. Pilots detested these safety measures which, to some extent, tended to question their abilities to land an aerodyne without crashing and burning . . . or so they said. But regulations required fire-suppression crews.

A band robot rolled out of a shed and positioned itself to one side of Curt's group.

A colors robot wheeled into position and unfurled the national colors along with the ribbon- and streamer-bedecked regimental colors.

Downwash barriers rose from the surface of the pad to deflect the landing blast of the aerodyne away from Curt and his officers.

The huge round shape came to hover over the pad while its turbines whined and the lifting blasts of air over its upper surface bent down to splash over the deck. It slowly settled until its three landing legs touched and compressed to take up the weight of the craft. The landing downwash died away as the turbines spooled down.

The downwash barriers slipped back into their stowed positions on the deck. The personnel ramp swung slowly down from the bottom surface of the aerodyne until its end touched the ground.

And Lieutenant Colonel William Donald Bellamack descended into the bright Arizona morning sunlight.

He was a tall, lean man with a horselike face. His eyes were hidden in the shadows of the visor on his service cap. It looked like a new cap because the gold braid of the oak leaves on the visor, the "scrambled eggs," was still bright. In fact, Bellamack seemed to be wearing a new Army Green Class A uniform complete with jacket. Three rows of service ribbons spread across the left breast of the jacket. He began to walk the short ten meters across the ramp toward Curt.

"Detail, 'ten-*hut!*" Curt snapped and came to attention. He brought his right arm and hand up in salute. The other nine officers merely snapped to attention. It wasn't proper for them to also salute. The protocols said otherwise.

The band robot began broadcasting the last thirty-two bars of Sousa's "Stars and Stripes Forever," the proper protocol music for a colonel.

The colors robot dipped the regimental colors briefly but without allowing them to touch the landing deck.

The military profession is a sentimental one, and its members rely on protocol and other formal actions so that proper honors and respect can be shown to superiors who have greater responsibilities or experience. Some of the functions are traditional, with deep roots in military history. Knowledge of the protocols also means that an officer is never at a loss for what to do or how to respond to any situation. It's all codified in the military and social customs of the service. Thus, an officer can more easily conform to the policy that "an officer is a gentleperson who is never unintentionally rude to anyone." Any military person with the awesome license to utilize physical power to take lives *must* be a civilized person who's been taught to act under great personal restraint and control. It dates back even beyond the code of chivalry, which the Crusaders learned from the infidels and which separates the age of squalid military butchery from the age of codified warfare exemplified in the Hague, Geneva, and Manila treaties.

Eleven people, only ten of whom knew each other, thus met on the landing stage of the Diamond Point casern that morning, and no one was at a loss concerning how to act or what to say, even the new colonel, who'd just arrived from the other side of the world. It put everyone more at ease in what might have otherwise been an awkward situation.

General Jacob O. Carlisle, CO of the 17th Iron Fist Division, wasn't there, nor were any members of the division staff. But Carlisle was watching via video pickup. It would not have been proper to Carlisle to be there. It was up to the new colonel to visit the division commander later to report on board and pay his respects.

Bellamack stopped in front of Curt and returned the salute.

Curt said, "Colonel Bellamack, I'm Major Curt Carson, temporary regimental commander and commanding officer of First Company. Welcome to the Washington Greys and to the Diamond Point casern! I hope your trip was a pleasant one."

Bellamack extended a long hand to Curt, who reached out and shook it. Bellamack's grip was strong, firm, and

53

warm. "Major. I'm a little bushed because my circadian rhythm is screwed up! I'm ten hours ahead of all of you, and it's past time for Tattoo. Thank you for turning out to greet me. I'm sure you've done an excellent job filling Colonel Belinda Hettrick's shoes until the Pentagon got around to assigning me to the Greys. By the way, have you heard from her recently?" he inquired.

"Yes, sir. Colonel Hettrick's recovering on schedule now that they found the poison's antidote," Curt replied.

"Good! She's a friend, and one hates to see a friend become a casualty," Bellamack replied, then paused.

"Colonel, may I introduce your regimental staff officers and company commanders?" Curt interjected following the signal of the brief pause. He turned and guided Bellamack toward the group now standing at attention.

"Major Wade Hampton, commanding Headquarters Company."

"Major Joanne Wilkinson, chief of staff."

"Major Patrick Gratton, adjutant."

"Captain John Gibbon, intelcomm."

"Captain Hensley Atkinson, operations."

"Major Frerick Benteen, commanding the service company as well as serving as your staff officer for logistics."

"Captain Joan Ward, commanding Ward's Warriors."

"Captain Alexis Morgan, commanding Morgan's Marauders."

"Captain Russell Frazier, commanding Frazier's Ferrets."

It was all quite formal and relaxed with greetings and replies of "Major . . . Colonel . . . Captain . . . Colonel . . . Major . . ." and so forth.

This done, Curt rejoined the ranks of officers. His regimental command was effectively over, although there were a few details to take care of in the regimental commander's office — administrative items such as transfer of organizational records including classified documents, accounting for property as shown in the Regimental Property Book, handing over of funds and allowances, accounting for property purchased from funds, and complete briefing by Curt concerning the level of readiness and training of the Greys.

54

The Army used to run on paperwork. Now it was mercifully assisted by computers and data bases.

"Stand at ease, ladies and gentlemen," Bellamack said as he faced them. "I'll be talking to each of you in the coming days. And I'll be visiting your companies and units. I want to get to know each of you and your people. Most importantly, I have a lot to learn about the Sierra Charlies. And although I've read and studied everything available, especially in the professional literature, I'm sure you'll agree that it isn't all in the books yet by any means. Major Wilkinson, please make the necessary arrangement and inform all officers to Stand-to tomorrow at eighteen-hundred hours in the Club; the first round is on me, of course. Then we'll have a little private dinner together afterwards. Please return to your duties. Majors Wilkinson and Carson, I request you show me to the regimental commander's offices so that we can immediately commence transfer of command. And, Major Wilkinson, if you please, have a robot get my personal effects off the ship and down to my quarters. Thank you for coming. Dismissed!"

Wilkinson keyed something into the communications set, the "brick," which she carried, and two robots moved out of the marge of the landing deck and into the aerodyne. Then she and Curt escorted Bellamack from the landing stage.

As they were riding down on the lift to the Greys' command level, Bellamack remarked to Joanne Wilkinson, "By the way, Major, the officers I just met all need haircuts . . . except Major Carson here, and he'll need one shortly. If the Greys look anything like the officers I just met, they're the sort of ragtag outfit that I won't put up with! Have everyone get their heads shaved pronto!"

Oh, boy! Curt thought. *Here we go!* So he spoke up, "Colonel, it's no longer necessary that the Greys shave their heads."

"Then how do you get good contact with the electrodes of the neuroelectronic equipment to control your warbots?" Bellamack wanted to know.

"Sir, the Washington Greys are the first Special Combat regiment," Wilkinson explained. "We don't use neuroelectronic linkage any longer. Our warbots are voice commanded."

"So? You should keep your heads shaved according to the RI regulations," Bellamack said.

"Colonel, the Greys are a pretty proud outfit, and we're pioneering the new Sierra Charlie doctrines and procedures," Curt told the new commander in explanation. "The Sierra Charlies have no special unit badge or insignia yet, no distinctive cap or beret, nothing that sets us apart as the special new troops we are. Therefore, since we no longer needed to shave our heads, we stopped doing that in my company shortly before Trinidad. The rest of the regiment started to let their hair grow before Namibia."

"Colonel Hettrick put a standing order into the Order Book about it," Wilkinson added. "A head of hair has become our badge as Sierra Charlies."

"Of course, Colonel, you may rescind that order if you wish," Curt reminded him.

Bellamack took off his new service cap. His head was shaved smooth. But he ran his hand over his shiny pate and grinned infectiously as he remarked, "The Good Book says a new commander shouldn't change things right away. Navy used to require that a new watch never reset the sails for thirty minutes after coming on deck. Sorry, Majors, I didn't realize the significance of the Sierra Charlies not shaving their heads. I guess I'd better start letting my hair grow again. Maybe by the time it gets long enough to trim, I'll rate as a Sierra Charlie. But, Major Wilkinson, as a woman, perhaps you can therefore advise me concerning appearance matters from a woman's point of view. Tell me: Should I cover up with a toupee until it grows out?"

CHAPTER SIX

Lane Hay Lansing III, the American ambassador to Mexico City, was angry.

At least, he was as angry as a diplomat was supposed to be when delivering a note of protest.

Mostly, he was angry that his boss, the secretary of state, had instructed him to deliver a note of protest to his friend, Mexican foreign minister Sebastian Madera y Francisco. A protest note spelled trouble, and Lansing didn't like trouble. He wanted the smoothest of all possible relationships between the United States of America and the United States of Mexico. Otherwise, he might have to do some work or risk finding himself in a decidedly dangerous embassy post such as Brasilia.

Lansing, the third generation of a family that had contributed lavishly to the campaigns of liberals of both political parties in the States, had claimed the patronage spoils resulting from the recent election of their bought-and-paid-for candidate for the United States' presidency: a foreign ambassadorial post. His only qualifications for the position were that both he and his father had been educated in Political Science at Princeton, he spoke Spanish, his family had business interests in Mexico, and he'd spent irregular periods in the foreign service of the United States when not involved in Boston merchant banking.

As a result, Lane Lansing's diplomatic training had taught him not to lose his temper. In fact, he'd had to spend several hours psyching himself up to the point where he might appear to be suitably disturbed when he delivered the secretary of state's protest letter to Madera. And such a trivial matter, too! Only some *banditos* of questionable origin and in an unknowable drug condition who had penetrated the Arizona border and engaged in an orgy of killing two retired Americans on their little ranch. Twenty-three of the estimated fifty *banditos* had been killed; the rest had escaped back into Mexico. Lansing felt that suitable justice had already been done because of the casualty ratio.

Besides, Lansing found it very difficult to be angry with Sebastian Madera; the Mexican foreign minister had arranged for Lansing to play polo with the foreign ministry's team.

But nonetheless, Lansing knew it was part of the job he had to do, and he approached it from that viewpoint.

It was actually a game that had to be played out. Madera knew why Lansing was coming. Indeed, the Mexican foreign minister already had a copy of the protest letter obtained covertly if opportunistically by a Chilean ELINT operation housed quite legitimately in the Pan-American Union building in the heart of Washington not a kilometer from the spot where the message had been transmitted via satellite to Mexico City.

Lansing knew that Madera knew. They'd discussed it quite privately over dinner the night before.

However, Lansing believed that no big fuss would result from the protest note. The banks wouldn't allow anything to go too far. For the last two hundred years, the American and British banks had kept the government of Mexico mired in debt. But the banks kept on loaning Mexico money because most of it never went to Mexico in the first place; it never left New York or Boston or London where it was on deposit for several Mexican holding companies— held, of course, by both Mexican government personnel and various international banking interests.

Something had to pay for the Mexican polo ponies and Lane Lansing's hand-tailored polo shirts.

However, the official visit wasn't a charade; both sides knew exactly what was going on. It was, instead, a sham.

But the meeting would be recorded by the Mexican secret police, the *Securidad,* so both men had to go through the motions.

"The foreign minister is expecting you, *señor*," the aide said solicitously, opening the 5-meter-high solid oak door to the minister's cavernous official office. (His actual working office was smaller, very private, and equipped with the latest computer and telecommunications equipment.)

"*Gracias, señor,*" Lansing replied, as fluent in both formal and colloquial Spanish as he was in both formal and vulgar American English. In fact, the whole discussion thereafter took place in Mexican Spanish.

Sebastian Madera y Francisco was as small, wiry, and swarthy as Lansing was thin, tall, and preppy. He rose and came around his huge desk as Lansing walked in. "Good day, Mister Ambassador! A pleasure to see you again!"

Acting out the part of the injured party, Lansing did not smile and shook the foreign minister's hand in a perfunctory manner. "Good day, Mister Minister! I wish indeed it was a pleasant matter that I must bring to your attention today. . . ."

"Please sit down, my friend." Madera indicated an ornate chair before the huge desk as he returned to his own chair behind it.

Madera's chair was slightly higher than the chair for his guest. Lansing had to look up at Madera. It didn't bother the American diplomat. This was just the way things were done in Mexico City.

"May I offer you refreshment?" Madera went on.

"Not today, thank you," Lansing replied in strained, flat tones. He set his attaché case on his lap and snapped open the two latches. "My government has instructed me to deliver a note to your government." He removed a document carefully and formally bound in a folder with the Great Seal of the United States of America in silver on its blue cover.

Madera reached across the desk and took it. "A note?"

"Yes, a note of protest and a demand for an apology and reparation."

Madera pursed his lips and made a show of studying the document, which was many pages long. After a minute he said smoothly, "This is a tragic incident that took place at the Norman ranch in Arizona. I'm sorry that two of your citizens were killed and their house burned. But how can your government be so certain that Mexican citizens were involved in this admittedly heinous crime?"

"Our Border Patrol recorded the passage of the bandits northward across the border," Lansing explained for the hidden microphones.

"Ah, yes! But the citizens of our respective nations have been freely crossing the border in both directions since the Treaty of Nogales was signed and the border opened. Have you positive identification of the culprits as Mexican citizens?"

"We do, Mister Minister. Our Border Patrol interdicted the return of most of the bandit band. Regrettably, none of the intruders that our Border Patrol intercepted were taken alive. They chose to fight to the death. Why? Because a postmortem medical examination indicated they were strongly under the influence of narcotic drugs."

"I see. How sad. But how were your officials able to identify them as Mexican citizens?"

"They were carrying Mexican small arms, Mister Minister."

"Is that *all?* Mister Ambassador, even your army now carries Mexican assault rifles, the excellent Novias!"

"Nonetheless, Mister Minister, appended to the note from my secretary of state you will find supporting data that indicates beyond a shadow of reasonable doubt that the band of about fifty intruders were indeed Mexican citizens, that they entered the United States of America with intent of malice, that they murdered two American citizens, and that they subsequently set fire to the ranch once they had looted it of everything of value to them."

"I shall have my people study your secretary of state's message."

"My government demands an immediate apology and a monetary indemnification for the damage caused and the lives taken." Lansing tried to sound adamant. "My government also requests that your government take the necessary steps to assure the security of the common border as set forth in the Treaty of Nogales."

"My government shall take the matter under advisement, Mister Ambassador," Madera told him smoothly. "We may be able to issue an apology if the circumstances warrant. However, because of the debt situation with the American banks, we may not be able to pay any reparations or damages." He paused, and then pointed out, "As for providing additional security on my government's side of the border, please be advised that the Army of Mexico is fully occupied at this time in the defense of our southern borders with Guatemala against the continuing and increasing intrusions of the Marxist powers of Central America. And, as you should be aware, the requests of my government for military aid and assistance — as well as American troops — have not met with a sanguine reception by your Congress."

"As a result, you are being lavishly supported by the ABC Allianza," Lansing couldn't help but point out.

"At a price, Mister Ambassador. At a price. In any event, I am certain that my colleague, the minister of defense, will report that it is not possible to withdraw troops from our southern border and move them to our northern border just because one bandit group happened to make a drug-crazed foray into your territory."

Lansing had expected this, and since his meeting with Madera last night, he'd had further information come in via very secure diplomatic means — a State Department courier with a sealed diplomatic pouch. Lansing didn't really want to spring the surprise on Madera. But he had been instructed to do so, and, if the information ever got back to State that he hadn't, it might mean his recall. The people in Washington were pissed.

"Then if your government will not take steps to control the penetration of your northern border by bands of brigands and bandits, my government will have to act to protect its citizens who are threatened. I must inform you, Mister Minister, that my government will move United States Army robot infantry and robot armored units to positions along the border."

This *was* a surprise to Madera. He really didn't believe

61

the Americans were serious. The American military and naval forces had been kept at a ridiculously low level of manning and equipment ever since the warbots had made it possible for machines to do the fighting instead of humans. And, although the Americans had conquered Trinidad with surprising speed and agility, Madera and others believed it was only a quirk, because Operation Steel Band had been expensive in terms of both money and politics; it had cost an American president the next election when the news media and the opposing liberals got through mounting their political attacks.

So although the Americans *might* deploy some army units along the border, Madera believed it would be merely a show of force. It would mean little or nothing in terms of Mexican-American relations. The Americans wouldn't disturb excellent trade relations and access to the low-cost manpower of Mexico for their repetitive production-line industrial operations. It would take time, but the Mexican-American border would eventually become as tenuous as the American-Canadian border.

Besides, Madera didn't know where that bandit group had come from or why it had crossed the border to kill and loot and burn. Mexican government forces were so lean in northern Sonora and Chihuahua that this American diplomatic protest note contained far more information about what had happened than the Mexican government itself knew!

Or was this some signal, some advanced warning, that American intelligence activities had gotten word of a concentrated push north into Mexico by the Central American Marxists? Were the Americans unobtrusively moving military units to their southern borders in anticipation of either a swift Marxist campaign through Mexico or a potential collapse of the Mexican government under the increasing pressure?

Madera made a mental note to bring this possibility to the attention of the cabinet in its closed session later in the week. In the meantime, the *Securidad* might well be advised to look into the possibilities. . . .

On the other hand, the bandit raid could have been merely some ploy of the drug lords in their constant mini-wars with one another . . . but that was one area that the foreign ministry was well paid to stay out of.

"Of course, your government has the perfect right to move troops wherever it pleased in your country," Madera finally replied.

"Then please don't be upset when we do it," Lansing advised his friend.

"We shall not be. In the meantime, I shall discuss your government's protest and concerns with my government. I suspect that you can anticipate at the minimum an expression of regret. . . ."

"I should hope so!" Lansing exclaimed in an exceedingly rare raising of his voice. He had to be careful. He was becoming rather upset about the matter himself, mostly because of the cavalier treatment Madera had given it during the meeting.

"I feel reasonably certain of that. After all, our two great nations have lived side by side in peace for over a century," Madera pointed out, holding back his own Mexican feelings about what the United States had done in 1848 and subsequent years when "Manifest Destiny" was the ruling policy of the Giant of the North. He stood up, signaling that the appointment was over. "Please report to your government that my government will give this matter its immediate attention. You will be hearing from me in the very near future."

Lansing snapped his attaché case closed and stood up as well. When Madera came around the huge desk and extended his hand to the American, it was difficult for Lansing to realize that they were from totally different cultures. In spite of the fact that there was an occasional rough spot between their two governments, the two men managed to get along quite well. This was, after all, part of Lansing's own personal philosophy: "All human beings are alike if we'd just get to know one another better."

He didn't know how wrong he was, because he was at the leading edge of international relations, where only talking took place. When diplomacy failed, there were other people ready to step in. There was the military, and Lansing really didn't understand the military mind. Save for the Marine guard at his embassy, he'd had practically no contact with the military at all.

In spite of the fact that Army units would be moving into positions along the border, Lansing ignored the possibility that it could come to anything more than just a show of force. . . .

CHAPTER SEVEN

"Well, Allie, we all knew that the new regimental commander couldn't possibly replace Belinda Hettrick. And we knew the transition wasn't going to be easy," Major Curt Carson remarked to Captain Alexis Morgan as the two of them were having supper off-post in Payson.

"I know that, Curt. But, honest to God, I never thought it would be so damned difficult. Or that we'd have to go off-post if we really wanted to talk to each other about it. I'm worried. Deeply worried," Alexis admitted, toying with her main course.

The two officers of the Washington Greys were in a little steak house in an out-of-the-way place by the airport, an unpretentious establishment housed in six semi-trailer rigs jacked up on concrete piers with doors cut through the sides for interior access and the required exits to the outside. It was quite "truck-driver ethnic," and most of the Army people didn't come there in spite of the good food; when the personnel of the 17th Iron Fist went into town, they wanted something more than "Arizona primitive" decor and surroundings. As a result, Alexis and Curt had come there often of late because they could talk privately.

Both of them were concerned about the Washington Greys.

"It would sure as hell be better if Colonel 'Wild Bill' Bellamack wasn't such a virtual unknown even up at division level," Alexis went on.

"Well, his mystery is certainly understandable," Curt noted. "Like you and me, he's been with a single unit for his entire service career because of the Army's policy of keeping combat units together. About the only objective thing we know about him is his promotion record. He must have something on the ball; he successfully rose through the ranks in the Gimlets to the point where he commanded Bellamack's Bearcats."

"I suppose so, judging from our own experience in the Greys. But his One-Oh-One File is fairly sterile stuff, even with all his evalreps." Alexis sounded frustrated, although there was little reason for it. Evaluation reports rarely told the whole story about any person because, even with continuing Army efforts to improve them and to instill in evaluating officers the need to be as absolutely objective as possible, evalreps were by their very nature only highly subjective observations.

Curt raised his eyebrows. Army policy allowed access to the evaluation reports in another person's 101 File only to commanding officers and their staffs. However, the so-called "Rumor Control Headquarters" activity within the tightly knit Washington Greys meant that nearly any officer who wanted any data could get it sub rosa. And Alexis Morgan, as a new company commander, had apparently developed her own channel into Rumor Control.

"Yeah, interesting. Bellamack's never received an overall point score less than three-point-eight, which is pretty damned good," Curt had to admit.

"Yup," Alexis replied, adding, "and he's consistently been rated in the eighty-fifth percentile or above by both intermediate and senior raters. In that respect, his evalreps look like yours, Curt."

Curt didn't care that she'd gotten access to his evalreps now that she was also a company commander with the ability to probe certain nooks and crannies of Rumor Control Headquarters. He was much too close to his former subordinate to be bothered about it. He didn't care. In fact, if one of his own sergeants had asked to see his evalreps, Curt would have pulled a copy. Curt obviously didn't place much faith or credence in evalreps. It was to him unfortunate that the Army hierarchy was forced by circumstances to depend on them. In the long run, it was actual performance that really counted, especially in a close-knit outfit where everyone moved up the ladder together.

"Snooping again, I see," he said.

"There isn't very much that I don't know about you."

"May I point out, my dear, that it's mutual?"

"You don't need to. And if you think I'm hiding anything from you, I'm sure we can rectify that later . . . say out at the Star Valley Inn."

"I'd never consider taking a fellow officer to a mere motel. You forget: I bought a little A-frame up by Pine when we got back from Trinidad. . . ."

"Sir," Alexis said in mock indignation, "I wouldn't consider accepting the invitation of a superior officer to accompany him to his off-post digs unless he was more than a close friend and even then not without suitable and proper persuasion. . . ."

"I'm glad you qualified that."

"So persuade me," she added.

"That's exactly what I'm doing at this moment by plying you with good food and hard liquor. Eat up. Drink up."

"I shall. I realize I'm being plied. And I happen to be pliable tonight." With her curly mop of hair that announced to all that she was a Sierra Charlie, she looked good to Curt all of the time. And especially tonight, since both were not in uniform. Alexis had the knack of choosing and wearing civilian clothes that were both feminine and extremely attractive on her. To Curt, they were also highly provocative. And so was she that night in the dim light of the little café. True, Alexis Morgan was no stunning beauty, but she had an attractiveness all her own. The world had few women combat officers, and she was one of the first. Physically fit, mentally disciplined, and one of those who'd been shot at and survived, she bore her femininity proudly and with assurance. She was in control of herself at all times, even in battle and especially when she'd recently faced sure and certain death in Namibia. She'd stood up to the unknown, not without fear, and had defeated it . . . and it showed. As a result, she had a virtual glow about her, an essence, an aura that gave her a beauty all her own.

"Apparently" she went on between bites, "some discreet inquiries were made by Joanne Wilkinson with one of her classmates in the Big L. She pulled a big zero. Even Pappy Gratton struck out working a tortuous channel through the R.U.R. Have you heard anything from the division staff as a result of some of the snooping that's been going on there?"

Curt shook his head. When circumstances required that a commander be brought in from the outside instead of up from within, it was usually possible to make discreet inquiries among personnel of the officer's former unit. "Nope. They hit the wall, too. No one can get to his former regimental commander, several regimental staff officers, and some of his contemporary company commanders in the Gimlet Regiment waiting out higher authority review of the findings of their court martials. . . . Well, their opinions probably couldn't be counted on as reliable or objective anyway, considering what Bellamack did to them."

"So what do you think?"

"About what?"

"About Wild Bill?"

"He's different from Belinda Hettrick."

Alexis whistled softly and shook her head. "He sure as hell is! Hettrick always knew what was going on. Bellamack has to be told. His daily morning reports and evening progress reports are driving me right up the goddamned wall! And every time I turn around, there he is, watching me and the Marauders either in the battle sims or the classrooms or out in the field! It's spooky! And it's one hell of a lot of work! This is the first time in a couple of weeks that I've managed to sneak an evening away from work to go off-post with you!"

"Yeah, I know, and I don't especially like it, either. But it can't last. And don't forget," Curt reminded her gently, "that Belinda Hettrick climbed the greasy pole of promotion within the Greys. Only Henry Kester has been in the regiment longer than she was. Hettrick knew everyone. She was here when we reported aboard. And she was right at the top of everything we were doing in pioneering the Sierra Charlie doctrines and operations."

"Belinda Hettrick made this outfit!" Alexis said firmly.

"No, we all did. She just led us by telling us what needed to be done, then kept sweeping the upper echelon horseshit out of way so we could do it," Curt told her. "On the other hand, Wild Bill Bellamack is totally new to this outfit and to the Sierra Charlies. He's trying like hell to get up to speed as quickly as he can. Yeah, I bitch about all the time I have to spend at the terminals making reports, but I think I know why he's requiring it. Furthermore, he isn't depending on Georgie to get him out of the slime. So be happy he's sticking his nose into everything the Marauders are doing. He's been doing the same thing with the Companions."

"Speaking of the Companions, how's Kitsy Clinton doing?" There was a touch of jealousy in her tone.

"Making all the new-johnnie mistakes. Not making the critical mistakes. Getting mad as hell at me for allowing her to get wet or muddy or stuck. Wanting me to solve the problems she's got to solve. And somewhat upset with me when I make her solve them herself . . ." Curt grinned, then added, "Just like you once did, Allie!"

"I think I'd better drop the subject."

"Company command suit you?"

"Yes and no," Alexis admitted. "Yes because it's what I've got to do and what I want to do. But no because I've got no one except my first sergeant to rely on for help when I get in a bind and have to drain the swamp."

"Carol Head's an experienced man."

"True. And I count on him a lot."

"You should. You've got to learn to count on your first sergeant. I couldn't run the Companions without Henry Kester."

"I know," she said, nodding. "But that isn't it. When I was in the Companions, I not only relied on Nick Gerard and Henry Kester, but also on *you*. Now I have no one above me I can turn to when I get into a situation where my NCOs can't help."

"That means you've got to go to Bellamack just as I went to Hettrick."

She sighed heavily. "Wild Bill Bellamack is an inscrutable, unapproachable, very private man. He acts like he has a wall around him."

Curt paused before asking her, "Have you tried to approach him with your problems, Allie?"

"No."

"Why not? Are you afraid of him?" Curt suddenly asked.

"Not really," Alexis came back quickly and firmly. "Intimidated by him, perhaps. He's imposing. He radiates confidence. And he seems friendly enough. But . . . I don't know what it is. He's strange."

"No, Allie, he's not strange. He's a stranger. We're not used to strangers among us. Our world is the Washington Greys. Everything and everyone else belongs to the outside world." He paused, then went on, "I've got my troubles with this man, too. But they're *my* troubles! They're troubles I've made."

"Maybe. But Bellamack demands a lot . . ."

"What were you trained and educated to do at West Point? What was I trained and educated to do?" he asked rhetorically. "I'll answer that: Be a military professional, a career Army officer, with the concepts of honor and duty and country above all. And the discipline required to submerge our own desires and fears so we can follow the orders of our superiors—not without question when we honestly believe the orders are questionable, but on the bounce and to the letter once we'd questioned, had our concerns listened to, and then been told to proceed. Our regimental commander gives orders, and we're bound by oath and our personal honor to obey them. Our new regimental commander doesn't make demands any more than I made demands of you when you first joined Carson's Companions as a raw brown-bar right out of West Point. . . ."

Alexis Morgan didn't reply immediately. She looked down at her plate. Finally, without raising her head, she looked up at Curt and smiled coyly. "Well, there's a great deal to what you say. Thank you for reminding me of some important principles I may have overlooked because of the stress of taking on greater responsibilities and a new regimental commander at the same time. *However,* Major Car-

70

son, you gave me orders which I often questioned but always followed. And, incidentally, you always made demands of me . . . some of which I thought were unreasonable and most of which I complied with because I saw they'd make me a better officer . . ." She softened and added, "And often simply because I wanted to, especially when Rule Ten wasn't in effect. The real joys of a military career can be few and far between . . . and it was a hell of a lot better than going to bed alone when it was cold or lonely or scary outside. One hell of a lot better, I might add."

"It's not cold outside tonight," Curt pointed out.

"No, but it's wet . . . and like any soldier I yearn to be warm and dry in such weather."

"I suspect your yearnings can be accommodated. Another soldier has the same yearnings."

"In that case, why are we just sitting here idly stuffing our faces with food and drink?"

"I don't know either. But I think I can do something about it."

At that moment, the wrist comm units of both officers beeped.

"Goddammit!" Alexis breathed.

"Shit!" was Curt's expletive. He touched the receive stud on its edge.

"All Grey personnel! Recall! Recall!" came the voice of Captain Russell Frazier, the regiment's officer of the day at Diamond Point. "Oscar brief at twenty-one-hundred hours! Signal your receipt! Repeating: All Grey personnel! Recall! Recall! . . ."

Curt touched the silencing stud and pressed the receipt stud.

"What the hell?" Alexis asked.

"Bellamack wants an Orders briefing," Curt explained unnecessarily.

"Why?"

"Damned if I know! I suspect we'll find out in the snake pit at twenty-one-hundred."

"OhmyGawd!" Alexis breathed. "Orders briefing means we go do something nasty to someone. Here we are with a

71

fresh-caught regimental commander, and we have to piss on another deadly brush fire somewhere!"

"Well, if we have to, we have to. But I don't know any better way to bring Wild Bill Bellamack up to speed with the Sierra Charlies in one big, fast hurry, do you?"

CHAPTER EIGHT

Lieutenant Colonel William Bellamack found himself faced with doing something he had not done since he graduated from West Point: conducting an operational briefing at the regimental level in person without the aid of neuroelectronic equipment.

The job fell into his lap because Major General Jacob O. Carlisle could no longer conduct massive briefings of the 17th Iron Fist Division (Robot Infantry). The Iron Fist was an outfit in transition.

Following the path pioneered by the Washington Greys, the other regiments of the 17th Iron Fist — the Cottonbalers, Can-Do, and Wolfhounds — were now undergoing their initial phase-over from full RI units to new Special Combat status. The Cottonbalers were furthest along, having come up to the point where the Greys were a few months before Namibia; they were posted to the Diamond Point casern but were spending most of their time in the field getting used to the new world of being shot at. The Can-Do regiment was in Charlotte Amalie where two of their companies were transitioning, using instructors from the War College Annex who had picked up the basics of Sierra Charlie operations from the Greys. Because of the Gimlet mess in Bahrain, the Wolfhounds had had their initial Sierra Charlie indoctrination in the Virgin Islands cut short in order to move quickly to Bahrain and cover for the demoralized and temporarily disorganized Gimlets.

So the 17th Iron Fist was essentially down to the Greys and the Cottonbalers at Diamond Point.

With the transition in progress — and the Iron Fist was

the only division scheduled to become a Special Combat (RI) division; the Army was still enamored with warbots—most of the division's neuroelectronic linkage equipment had been removed from Diamond Point. It was no longer being used by the division and it was needed elsewhere as replacements or parts for other NE equipment in the Army. Most of it was more than five years old and therefore obsolete in the commercial world, and few vendors made the parts any more, much less outright replacements for the "old" stuff.

So it was no longer possible to hold the standard RI division-level Orders or Oscar briefing with full neuroelectronic hookup to all officers. In addition, the Greys had discovered that full division briefings weren't effective in letting commanders down to the company level get specific questions answered or for these same commanders to make suggestions and provide other input. It had also been discovered that it was better to let the familiar regimental commander carry the briefing because the presence of a general officer seemed to be overwhelming.

Therefore, Oscar briefings occurred after command briefings had taken place at the division level. Regimental commanders then held Oscar briefings with *all* their officers and NCOs.

Thus, Lieutenant Colonel William Bellamack found himself stepping into the center of the briefing theater or "snake pit" to present the first non-neuroelectronic briefing he'd given since leaving West Point. The room had been cut in half, converting it from a "theater-in-the-round" to an amphitheater with a holographic projection tank behind the briefer.

Bellamack found it almost oppressively personal. The actual faces of his officers and NCOs stared at him from very close range. No longer was it merely a mental projection through the NE equipment into their minds; he had to do it face-to-face in the old way. Bellamack wasn't sure he liked it. On the other hand, he was forced to admit that most of the great military commanders of the past had operated this way, so it had to be effective if history was right.

74

"Good evening," Bellamack said briefly and curtly, surprised to hear his own voice echoing from the back wall of the snake pit. He decided this might take some getting used to unless he had the 17th Iron Fist engineering battalion sound-deaden that back wall. "Although apologies aren't really necessary because we're RI, I would like to offer them anyway for this apparent strange and unusual meeting called at a late hour after a hard day of training. No choice was available. I was called to the divisional briefing by General Carlisle at eighteen hundred hours on zero time notice. Missed chow call, but I probably didn't need it in the first place."

He looked around slowly at each of them. Curt thought the colonel's eyes rested on his for a split second. Curt decided that Bellamack was a consummate actor. He was making eye contact with everyone in the room. He was projecting himself effectively to each person *without* the use of NE equipment. Curt was forced to ask himself, *And this is the man who just came from a full warbot brainy outfit? Jeez, he learns fast! Or he has the talent to begin with!*

"First, I have a few questions. Did anyone watch Phoenix or satdish video tonight? Please raise your hand if you did."

It was a surprising question. Tentatively, a few officers raised their hands, not really certain what their new commander was leading up to.

"Did you watch telenews programming? Hands, please."

A fewer number of hands went up.

"Did you see or hear of any incident occurring around Bisbee, Arizona? Hands again, please, if your answer is affirmative."

No hands went up.

"Good! The news blackout was effective! Or I presume that the Gold Dust Dancers or Goldconda were far more interesting. Yes, I know: A glimpse of a highly salacious and fantastic nonmilitary world is both exciting and relaxing at the same time! As for myself, I much prefer the real thing . . . when I can find it. . . ." An appreciative flutter of laughter went around the room, indicative of the sudden realization that Wild Bill Bellamack might be somewhat

75

more of a human being than many of his officers and NCOs had previously thought.

But Bellamack was suddenly deadly serious again as his piercing dark eyes looked quickly at various members of his audience. "This briefing," he went on slowly, "is classified Secret. Its subject and data are not to be discussed with anyone outside this briefing theater. Because of the security classification and the subsequent operations that will take place, all leaves and passes are herewith canceled. No member of the regiment will leave the regimental compound in the Diamond Point casern until it becomes time to do so. You will not speak of this or discuss it with anyone outside the regiment. Those of you with families living off-post in the area will not be allowed to communicate with them as of this moment. The reasons for this will become clear as I proceed. Your dependents will be notified by the regimental staff and told that conditions have arisen that will not allow you to communicate with them for a few days at least. They will be advised that this is not an emergency and that you will probably not be exposed to combat or danger."

A mutter went around the snake pit.

"Again, you'll understand these draconian measures when the full story comes out," Bellamack tried to explain.

Colonel Bellamack raised his head, which was now covered with the short stubble of his growing black hair. He called to the 17th Iron Fist Division's megacomputer, "Georgie, show me the Operation Quick Cactus three-dee chart."

In the holotank behind Bellamack, a computer-generated holographic map of the area between Sierra Vista and Douglas in the southeastern part of Arizona appeared in three dimensions.

"Georgie, as I describe locations, show me their position by means of a projected arrow symbol with highlighting," Bellamack further instructed.

"Last night at about this time," the regimental commander continued, "the United States Border Patrol sensors feeding into the Sierra Vista monitoring station here detected and reported a group of about fifty intruders crossing

76

the open border east of Bisbee proceeding northward in this highlighted location. The BP didn't feel this was unusual. Many Sonorans cross the border to take advantage of the charity of some of the ranchers and retired people living in the area. However, such family and village groups rarely remain north of the border for more than a few hours because of old fears of being caught and detained by the BP. But when this group didn't return by first light, a BP aerodyne — an old surplus Air Force piloted recon model — went to check things out. It ran into a group of armed bandits. A BP swat flight was called in, a firefight ensued, and none of the intruders survived."

Bellamack paused. Then he said slowly, "Literally, there were no survivors. The intruders attacked and murdered two retirees who owned a small ranch within five klicks of the border. I do not intend to show you the video images of what remained. I looked at them, but I'd missed dinner beforehand, which was a good thing. It wasn't pleasant. The assault and the killings appeared to be acts of terrorism on the part of the intruders.

"You didn't see anything about it in the news because the BP got control of the situation before the newshawks and newsharpies heard about it. The BP got what was left of the two American retirees under cover before the Bisbee Fire Department arrived to attempt to save what was left of the ranch. Officially, Cecil Norman and his wife perished in the holocaust of their burning ranch home. A reporter from the Bisbee newspaper showed up after the Fire Department had reduced the fire. So it was a local news story, nothing more.

"However, our ambassador in Mexico City presented a note of protest to the Mexican government today. No action has been taken by the Mexicans. No apology or expression of regret has come forth. Our ambassador did confirm what our recon satellites and intelligence operations have already told us: The Mexican Army is totally committed on its southern borders. It cannot carry out its treaty obligations to prevent bandit groups from crossing the border into the United States."

Bellamack paused for emphasis and effect, then went on,

"Therefore, the President in his role as commander-in-chief has ordered the United States Army to move various units into bivouac at existing facilities close to the Mexican border. These units will assist the BP in patrol functions and prevention of intrusion of armed bandit or terrorist groups into the United States.

"Here's the full picture. Georgie, show me a chart of the border between the United States and Mexico."

Another holochart replaced the one of southeastern Arizona. Regions of the U.S.-Mexican border lit up in highlight as Bellamack spoke.

"The One Hundred and First Screaming Eagle Airbot Division is moving to Fort Sam Houston, Texas. They will deploy rapid-response battalion-sized air-mobile forces along the border between Brownsville and the Big Bend Area.

"The Second Robot Armor Division is deploying to Fort Bliss, Texas, and will maintain roving patrols along the border from the Big Bend area to the Arizona-New Mexico line. Their major effort will cover the border west of El Paso.

"The Iron Fist will headquarter at Fort Huachuca with its three remaining regiments. We can't bring the Wolfhounds back from Bahrain at this point. I can tell you from recent experience that the Gimlets stationed there will have to be recalled to the ZI and completely reformed. So General Carlisle has told me that we must make do with what we've got . . . and that's really nothing new to us, is it? I don't complain about being consistently short of manpower and equipment to do the job right; the only time the Army gets everything it wants is in wartime, and too many people get killed when that occurs.

"So General Carlisle has made regimental assignments as follows: The Washington Greys will have the responsibility of the border from the Arizona-New Mexico state line west to Nogales. The Cottonbalers will cover from Nogales to Yuma, and the Can-Do will handle the area from Yuma to San Diego. . . ."

There was dead silence in the snake pit. Every Grey

except for some of the newcomers like Lieutenant Kitsy Clinton knew that the Greys had gotten the most rugged terrain but a high desert climate where it was perhaps a little bit cooler than elsewhere. The Cottonbalers had been shafted with the rugged low desert environment, a type of biome that the Greys had had more than their fill of in Namibia. The Can-Do people were going to have their Caribbean assignment abruptly terminated, but the Yuma-San Diego stretch wasn't too bad.

"The Washington Greys will headquarter at Fort Huachuca along with the division headquarters. The Cottonbalers will work out of beautiful downtown Ajo. the Can-Do will take over an old naval facility at El Centro, so they got the best deal on that," Bellamack told them, editorializing a little bit.

"That's the background. Now here's what we've got to do:

"The Regiment will begin deployment to Fort Huachuca at oh-eight-hundred on the day after tomorrow. We will move by road. We will not go through either Phoenix or Tucson because of the traffic problems our convoys would create. Therefore, we shall move along Roosevelt Lake to Globe, thence south to Benson, and then to Sierra Vista. It's a little over four hundred kilometers, so we'll need to stop to refuel near Globe or Winkleman. We'll overnight at the refueling point.

"Our first job: Assist Corps of Engineers and Quartermaster Corps personnel to reactivate Fort Huachuca. Engineers and QM forces are being airlifted into Libby Army Airfield from Fort Leonard Wood and Fort Ord. They won't be there for about four days, so we'll have to do the initial work with the civilian caretaker to bring Huachuca up to active status again. I understand five or six hundred buildings are available, so we won't have to sleep in our vehicles very long.

"Our second job: Be prepared to assist the Border Patrol in maintaining law and order. We shall move quickly to the scene of any intrusion by Mexican nationals.

"Our third task: Continue our training and maintain our readiness."

79

"Question, sir." Curt spoke up because he spotted the fact that the colonel hadn't covered one important aspect. "Will you please inform us concerning the rules of engagement?"

"I was given none, Major Carson."

"May I respectfully request that division staff provide us with them, sir? For example, may we engage in hot pursuit across the border into Mexico? Do we shoot to kill or do we merely shoot to deter, and under what conditions?"

Bellamack didn't hesitate in his reply. "I'm going under the assumption that we'll operate with the same ROE that are in effect in the Persian Gulf area where I just came from. We will not engage in hot pursuit across the border. We will act as a defensive deterrent. We will not shoot unless fired upon."

"Yes, sir. I understand. Not hot pursuit. Basically guard duty," Curt replied respectfully. "However, Colonel, the Greys are not neuroelectronic. In the RI, if the warbot takes incoming from an ambush, the warbot gets written off and the warbot brainy switches to another bot. When the Sierra Charlies are out there in the field and get bush-whacked, the voice-commanded warbots may take some of it but if any of us intercepts the Golden BB without body armor or heavier than body armor, we're customers for Major Gydesen's biotechs or Major Gratton's graves registration. Our experience in Trinidad and Namibia says there are times when we've got to shoot first to keep from being creamed."

"Major, thank you for bringing the matter to my attention. I'll check into it," Bellamack replied quickly. As far as Curt was concerned, that was a cop-out on the colonel's part. Or maybe it was Curt's fault for bringing it up and embarrassing Bellamack. It was obvious that the regimental commander had no Sierra Charlie experience, and Curt's comment might have caught the man the wrong way. *Well, I had to ask it,* Curt told himself.

"Colonel Bellamack?" Major Joanne Wilkinson raised her hand. The regimental commander nodded at her, so she went on. "Sir, we're a Sierra Charlie outfit. We're mobile. We have a very fast response. We responded in less than

80

twenty-four hours to the situation on Trinidad, and we were on our way to St. Helena within hours of the activation of Operation Diamond Skeleton. As your chief of staff, I believe it's my responsibility to inform you that the Washington Greys are in a position to be on the road at oh-eight-hundred tomorrow morning. Furthermore, we travel faster than a regular RI regiment. A lot faster. We can be in Fort Huachuca by dinnertime tomorrow. Sir, may we show you what we can really do?"

This really surprised the new regimental commander. He'd predicated his timing on his own experience with the slower-moving regular RI units that used slower leapfrog procedures.

"Are you telling me, Major, that a hundred and four people, a hundred and twenty warbots, and a hundred and six vehicles loaded with logistical support can move more than four hundred kilometers in eight hours?" He obviously didn't believe her.

"Yes, sir! And we've done it under combat conditions!" Wilkinson responded with zeal.

"Major Hampton, how about that?" Bellamack asked his second in command, the man in charge of Headquarters Company.

Wade Hampton quietly replied, "Sir, the Washington Greys are capable of bugging out on eight hours' notice and operating independently in the field for ninety-six hours without logistical support. We can move faster and go longer than that in terms of time and distance if the movement isn't under combat conditions."

Wild Bill Bellamack was beginning to understand that he had a tiger by the tail as a commander of the Washington Greys. "May I entertain candid comments from other officers present, please?"

"Sir!" It was the little voice of Captain Joan Ward, a 7-year veteran of the Greys, a plain young woman whose small voice could suddenly erupt into an astounding parade-ground bellow when necessary. "I don't know what we'd do, sitting around here all day tomorrow and unable to leave the casern! Let's get to Huachuca tomorrow night and be on hand to welcome the bridge builders and the log haulers when they drag themselves in! We're the fastest, smoothest, deadliest outfit in the Army, and it's time more people knew it, sir!"

A quiet chorus of affirmatives and support welled up from the officers and NCOs of the Washington Greys: "Yes sir! Let's do it, Colonel! We can sleep on the road tomorrow, sir!"

Colonel Wild Bill Bellamack grinned, his long face lighting up with the realization that the morale in this outfit left little to be desired. Furthermore, if he wanted to keep that morale as high as it was, he had to let these troops show their pride and abilities. It was an outfit at nearly its full state of readiness; he was the one who wasn't. He realized he was going to have to go like hell to really lead this regiment; if he didn't lead, he'd never get the chance to follow because they'd roll right over him. "Major Wilkinson, you and your staff just bought yourself a pile of work! And all of you have deprived yourselves of a night's sleep! We're not going to roll at oh-eight-hundred day after tomorrow. Hell no! We're going to roll at oh-six-hundred tomorrow morning and beat the traffic! Everybody, shag ass! Briefing dismissed!"

CHAPTER NINE

The high-speed military convoy of the Washington Greys roared out of Payson, thundered down the hill on the Bee Line Highway, turned off at the Highway 188 junction, dusted Punkin Center, and joined Highway 88, the Apache Trail, as it crossed the broad new top of Roosevelt Dam.

It was a line of vehicles more than 3 kilometers long. If they hadn't been painted in low-visibility chameleon and infrared absorbing camouflage colors, one might have mistaken the various vehicles for GMC Turbo-18s with live-in cabs and hauling two box trailers, D88 tracked Cats, and double-length high-bay Greyhound long-range SenicSleepers. However, a closer look would have revealed that they were standard Army ATVs, RTVs, LAMVs, CTVs, OCVs, and BSVs. They may have *looked* like civilian vehicles, but they'd been built to different and more stringent military specifications which made them more rugged and covered them with Chobham or Exman armor. Their robot autopilots were set to maintain ten meters' separation between vehicles. Even on a two-lane back highway in the wilds of Arizona, the robotic driving computer of the lead vehicle was maintaining an average speed of 60 kilometers per hour.

It had been a night without sleep for Curt and everyone else in the Washington Greys. But Joan Ward had been right. The Greys were an action outfit. They would have gone ape sitting around on their buns at Diamond Point for a full day when they were primed and ready to move on 8 hours' notice. The Greys had moved faster before,

83

and going into combat to boot. This was a snap in comparison to the preparations for St. Helena and Namibia for Operation Diamond Skeleton. And an absolute bed of roses compared to riding the submersible Navy landing ships into Trinidad in the hot, damp hulls.

The warm morning sunlight made Curt sleepy after a night with no rest, but it was his turn on watch in the turret of his ACV while Master Sergeant First Class Henry Kester rested below. However, it wasn't a Zulu-type alert. This was a non-combat environment and midweek as well. No one was going to shoot at them, and Curt didn't expect much civilian traffic. The worst thing they might encounter would be some civilian boating enthusiast towing a 5-meter sailboat behind his pickup truck, an incongruous sight against the desert terrain if it hadn't been for the huge expanse of Roosevelt Lake alongside the road.

And this trek was a good training exercise for the Washington Greys, Curt thought. It was the first overland road trip they'd taken as a regiment since they'd gone overland in southwest Africa's Namib Desert.

The road trek was making Second Lieutenant Kitsy Clinton work hard because, as commander of Alpha Platoon, she was on point and charged with moving along the right road and maintaining 60 klicks. In this environment, she couldn't simply commandeer the road, either. At every intersection, she had to send convoy traffic control robots out ahead to secure the right of way, then recover them once the convoy started through. The navigational computers had all the right data in them, so she couldn't easily make a mistake and take the wrong turn. But Curt kept an eye on things anyway. Sometimes there was no telling what a fresh brown-bar might do in a momentary panic when a whole regiment was pounding along the road for more than 3 kilometers behind the lead vehicle.

At least the Sierra Charlie vehicles had brakes. He chuckled when he remembered trying to follow the *Legion Robotique* convoy out of Otjomuise to Strijdom Airport for airlift home. The French had an interesting convoy system. It was a matter of tradition to them, he guessed, because the terror of a French convoy had been mentioned in many books about the two World Wars in the last century. The French drivers, human and robotic, simply stopped by running into the vehicle ahead of them, and their robotic military vehicles were apparently made to take that sort of treatment. But it had been rough on the American contingent, the Washington Greys, who had to follow the *Legion*. Curt hadn't enjoyed having to write off three vehicles totaled as a result of French panic stops with no signals.

Yeah, he decided, this was a snap. And Lieutenant Harriet Dearborn of Supply had worked it out to refuel the convoy on the fly coming out of Globe; her POL tankers had gone out ahead of the convoy and were waiting this side of Globe to refuel on the roll. Precision robot driving systems made it easy to refuel on the go using a system adopted from the old Navy alongside replenishment methods.

A vehicle was roaring up alongside the convoy even now. Curt couldn't see it in detail yet, but it appeared to be an ATV.

I'll bet it's Wild Bill Bellamack checking things out and getting a feel for this fast-moving outfit, Curt said to himself. He waited for the radio call to come up.

And it did. "Companion Leader, this is Grey Head in an Alpha Tango Victor!" the tacomm spoke with Bellamack's voice. "I'd like to come aboard your Alpha Charlie Victor and pay you a visit."

Curt settled his helmet on his head and keyed the tacomm. "Grey Head, this is Companion Leader. The latch string is out!"

"Say again, Companion Leader?"

"Come aboard at will, Grey Head. Looks like a straight stretch of smooth road up ahead that would be perfect for the transfer."

The ATV pulled alongside and its robot driving circuits precisely matched speeds and maintained a separation of exactly 30 centimeters between the two vehicles. The top hatch disgorged Colonel Bill Bellamack. With ease and

85

grace, he stepped between the two speeding vehicles onto Curt's Armored Command Vehicle. Curt motioned for him to drop through the turret's aux hatch.

"Sergeant Kester," Curt called, "I hate to disturb you, but I've got a visitor and I need you to take the conn."

Kester's voice wasn't sleepy-sounding. Curt knew the old sergeant was up to his old tricks, just dozing lightly and prepared for immediate action if required. Kester was an old soldier who knew more than Curt ever thought he could learn. "Okay, Major, I'm up and monitoring. Coffee's hot if you want it."

"Henry, someday you're going to make some lucky girl a great housekeeper!" Curt told him as he exchanged places with the Master Sergeant.

"What do you think I've been doing with this outfit for more than twenty years?" Kester replied with a smile touching the corners of his mouth.

Curt dropped into the innards of his ACV and took off his helmet. Bellamack had done the same. "Henry says coffee's ready, Colonel. Be my guest!"

"Thanks, but my body thinks caffeine is uric acid, and I've filled up two piddle packs already today," the colonel replied and sat down. "Take the load off your feet, Major."

"Thank you, sir." Curt sat down, wondering what the man wanted.

"This outfit works so well and so smoothly," Bellamack began, "that sometimes I think I'm really not needed. . . ."

"Colonel, I was temporary regimental commander before you took that monkey off my back. I think I can truly say that Headquarters Company and the staff sure as hell kept me jumping while I was in the hot seat you're presently occupying," Curt told him.

"What I mean, Curt, is that I'm not really needed in order to monitor every little move and watch every action," Bellamack explained. "This convoy's a good example. The Greys know how to move!"

"We've had some practice, Colonel."

"That's obvious both from the regimental records and the way this operation is balling along. Working fine with-

86

out me. So for the first time in quite a while, I've got a few minutes to do something I've wanted to do for weeks: Chat with you."

This surprised Curt. "Sir, all you had to do was call me, and I'd be there on the bounce!"

"No time, plus the fact that I wanted to talk privately with you."

"The walls at Diamond Point don't have ears."

"I guess I came from a regiment that was on the slide . . . and the walls often had ears . . ."

"From what I hear, Colonel, the unit pride was allowed to slip in the Gimlets. I can't imagine any other reason why the scandal happened." Curt danced gently around what might have been a touchy subject for his new colonel.

"You nailed it! Anyway, it's time you and I had a chat, just between the two of us, nothing official, strictly between two West Pointers. With the robots and subordinates running things, this seemed like a good time."

"Yes, sir." That was about all that Curt could think of to say at the moment.

"I'm the new kid on the block, Curt," Bellamack admitted privately. "The Greys should have gotten a regimental commander promoted from within the unit."

"It didn't work out that way because Major Ed Canby caught it in Namibia," Curt pointed out, perhaps unnecessarily.

Bellamack shook his head sadly. "Ed always looked forward to commanding a regiment. He never got his chance. God rest his soul; he was a good friend and my roommate in my Third Class year."

"Colonel, he was a good friend of mine, too."

"I'm sure he was. The Greys seem to be a tight unit; I suspect everyone's a friend of everyone else. . . ."

"Not always, sir," Curt admitted carefully. "I've had some personal problems with others in the regiment. Unhappily he was wounded in Namibia. I wouldn't wish that sort of thing on anyone in the Greys, even those I didn't like," Curt had to admit. "But he recovered and was posted to the Wolfhounds as a Sierra Charlie instructor. He'll do all right. He's just the sort of person to get soldiers up off their butts and converted to Sierra Charlies. . . ."

"As I said, I'm new to the regiment, and I'm having to learn not only your unwritten traditions but also your totally new combat doctrine. But I can hack it," Bellamack admitted with surprising candor. However, he paused for a moment before he said, "Maybe I'll appear to be revealing a weakness a regimental commander shouldn't have, but I decided it would be a hell of a lot easier if I had some help from an old-line Grey like yourself to keep me from making a goddamned fool of myself."

"Colonel, you and I both know from running a company that a CO who doesn't ask for the advice and support of his troops is heading for Big Trouble. But Major Benteen has been Greys longer than I have and Major Hampton's your second in command . . ." Curt started to point out.

Bellamack waved his hand and shook his head. "Fred's a good man. So's Wade. They're tops in their specialties. But they're not West Pointers, or the former temporary regimental commander."

"I don't think I understand, sir." Curt did, but he wanted to hear more so that he knew exactly and precisely the ground on which he stood.

"Think about it," Bill Bellamack urged. "When you were running the Greys, your subordinates were also your friends. You'd known them for years. You'd worked and played with them. You'd been shot at along with them. You'd led them and you'd followed them. You could call on them for help, and you probably did."

Curt nodded. "You're right, Colonel. Something I never thought about because it was just something everyone in the Greys did naturally. All COs do that in good, tight outfits. . . ."

"You could also bend elbows with them at the Club without others thinking they were brown-nosing," Bellamack added suddenly.

The figurative light bulb lit up in Curt's head. The colonel had just come from a demoralized, disintegrating regiment that had lost its pride because some of its critical officers had forgotten personal honor and integrity. In that sort of organization, internal politics ran rampant. So Curt replied easily, "This is a different outfit, Colonel. The Greys would never think anyone was bootlicking or ass-kissing just because the CO happened to be friendly to-ward them. Hells bells, Belinda Hettrick was one of us! She was *always* the colonel, but she was also one of us. She was a good friend. We had a lot of fun together."

"I'm sure you did. Belinda was a pistol. She was my batt commander at West Point," Bellamack replied coolly and urbanely, leaving a lot unsaid. "She left me a damned sharp outfit, by the way. She also left me a tough act to follow. I know damned good and well I'll never fill her shoes. . . ."

Curt nodded. "We know that, Colonel. You're going to run this outfit your way. We have no heartburn over that."

"I do."

"Sir?"

"Goddamn it, Curt, it will never be *my* regiment! It will always be the Washington Greys! It's up to me to conform to the regimental traditions and quirks while leading it. I'll hack it. But I've got to clear up something between you and me. *You're* the ex officio regimental commander, not Wade Hampton. If I happened to catch the Golden BB or go KIA, Wade would step in and stand on my marks, but the rest of the troops would actually follow *you*. And Wade knows it. So I've got to make my contract with *you*, Carson."

"Colonel," Curt said slowly and carefully, looking his commanding officer straight in the eyes, "I'll tell you straight to your face now and anytime that I haven't the *slightest* interest in doing or participating in *anything* that would undermine your authority. I don't play those games! I don't know anyone in the Greys who plays those games, either! Whoever tried it just wouldn't last. The Washington Greys have a history and traditions that date back to the Revolutionary War, and no one wants to be the person who brings dishonor to the regiment after more than two centuries. As for me, I don't *want* the goddamned regimental command! I had it on a temporary basis, and you'll never known how fucking glad I was to give it to you and get the administrative monkey off my back! You're my commanding officer. And as you get settled in, I hope to get to know you better, because we're probably going to go through hell together a lot of times. In fact, although I've studied your One-Oh-One, I feel I know you much better now."

Bellamack's eyebrows went up. "Well, I also looked at your One-Oh-One . . . in an official capacity, Curt. I liked what I saw, and I like what I've heard this morning."

Curt shook his head slowly. "Jesus, serving in the Gimlets must have been pure hell!"

Bellmack nodded. "Just hope to God you never have such an experience! I saw my regiment go on the skids. The infighting and internal politics got vicious toward the end. I could do nothing to save the regiment. I had to destroy it by going to the inspector general."

"Colonel, I don't believe you were the one who destroyed the Gimlets. The officers you reported to the IG were responsible for that. You only did what both you and I have been taught to do. It was the only thing an honorable person could do. You earned far more than a Meritorious Service Medal."

Bellamack said nothing for a moment, then remarked, "Thank you. I thought I was doing the right thing or I wouldn't have done it. I'm glad you understand."

"You'll find the Greys are a hell of a lot different."

"As I said, Belinda left me a great outfit."

"That she did, and I'll help you keep it that way, Colonel."

In spite of rules, regulations, laws, and codes, when it comes right down to the personal level there is nothing as binding in the world as an unwritten and often unvoiced agreement between two people. It has existed for centuries among military people. In the days of fighter pilots, who had to control fragile machines in an already hostile environment while trying to kill and keep from being killed, it emerged as "the contract" between a flight leader and his wingman or a pilot and his backseat partner.

Another contract was silently and powerfully formed between two men inside that ACV that morning on a back road in Arizona.

Both men met one another's eyes. In a spontaneous movement, both thrust out their right hands. And the contract was sealed.

It would in time cost lives.

CHAPTER TEN

Coronel Luis Sebastian Herrero allowed his close friends and even his wife to use his nickname, "Gordo." However, the *coronel* certainly wasn't fat; he was lean and trim and healthy. The sobriquet had been hung on him during his plebe year at West Point. When he'd arrived at that gray granite fortress on the Hudson as a foreign honor graduate of the New Mexico Military Institute, he'd been a fleshy, overfed teenager who was indeed pudgy from his last two years as a lazy upperclassman with his corps of "rats" to do everything for him. After the traumatic months of Beast Barracks, he'd never allowed himself to get out of shape again. But his nickname, "Gordo," stuck. Now he relished it because he certainly wasn't fat.

One of those who was privileged to call the drug lord by his nickname was Herrero's colleague, an older man many steps up the ladder in the "brotherhood" or *hermanistas* whom Herrero knew only as Carlos Mota or *Tío*, his "uncle." Herrero and *Tío* Mota had been even closer after Herrero's father had died and the *coronel* had left the Mexican Army to take over the family's part of the *hermanistas* business. "Mota" was the Mexican name for marijuana, but Herrero had only known his uncle by the man's *hermanistas* name. Among the *hermanistas,* real names were rarely used. Herrero was an exception.

"Gordo, your raid was a disaster!" Mota told him as the two men sat on the patio overlooking the deep canyon below and the high peaks of the Sierra Madre around Cerro Caliente.

"On the contrary, Uncle," the drug lord replied casually,

sipping the fine Scotch in his glass. "It went exactly and precisely as I'd planned."

Mota also appreciated his young friend's Scotch. But he sounded like he was mildly scolding Herrero. "You lost thirty-two men!"

"While I agree that a sixty-four percent loss rate would be considered unreasonably high by a former general such as yourself, Uncle, I was prepared to lose the entire group of fifty," Herrero explained diffidently. "It was not necessary that *any* of them survive the raid!"

"Even a personal *ejercito* depends upon men," Mota reminded him. "That level of casualties is too high. It's the way the Russians operate. They've got lots of people. We don't. Good and loyal soldiers are not easy to find, train, and keep."

"The men I used were neither good or loyal, Uncle. And they were easy to find. They were starving farmers, truck drivers, and miners. They required little training. Anyone can shoot the Brazilian submachine guns which are the children of the Soviet Kalashnikovs. The few old Mondragons I had for them were nearly worn out, and it mattered little if the *sembradors* could shoot them accurately or not. In any case, the guns were as expendable as the poor souls that Pancho was able to hire. He stuffed their stomachs, filled them with peyote and other hallucinogens, and sent them to cause trouble beyond the border. But be assured that their families were paid, because I'm an honorable man who doesn't force others to do things for nothing."

"Your raid did not cause the planned trouble for President Alvaro," Mota reminded his subordinate. "The *hermanistas* approved of your invasion plan only because it would reveal the weakness of Alvaro's government. It was also calculated to prompt the United States to apply diplomatic pressure which would cause Alvaro's government to collapse. It has perhaps done the first, but it has not accomplished the second."

"Patience, Uncle, patience!" Herrero urged smoothly.

"The invasion has only reached its first goal. The second intrusion will be even sharper. It will embarrass the United States as well."

"We expected results that were more dramatic . . . and sooner."

"Mi tío, the results will be very dramatic. . . ."

"And more expensive?"

Herrero shook his head. "Another drink, Uncle? I'm glad you decided to visit me today. I'm expecting my *capitán* Pancho Garcia to arrive within the hour with a report of what actually occurred. I hope you will listen. And Pancho will also tell us of the progress on the next phase of the operation. . . ."

"Again, I say that the *hermanistas* believe you suffered an expensive early failure," Mota kept pushing on the subject. "And here I discover just now that even you must depend upon a personal report from a subordinate to find out what happened — you, with all your high-technology communications equipment and expensive technicians to keep it running. Perhaps you can tell me then why *nothing* about your invasion has appeared in the American newspapers or television?"

"I don't know," Herrero admitted. "It might have been too little in a place that was too remote. It might have taken place on what the American news media calls a 'fast day' with many other stories breaking quickly. It may have been too thorough with very little visual impact, which is important for television. In short, it took place a long way from everyone else and resulted only in some burned buildings, two dead old people, thirty-two dead *banditos* who couldn't talk and no clear and present danger to a lot of other people." Herrero shrugged. "That's why I'm waiting for a report from Garcia. I'll find out. And the next attack will benefit from what I learned on this one . . . and at a very low relative price, I might add."

"Madera brushed it off, the cabinet refused to accept responsibility, and Lansing is too friendly with Madera to push very hard to get an apology for the Americans,"

Mota grumbled, then added, "much less embarrass Alvaro by pushing the American demands for reparations."

"Ah, yes! But we *do* know as a result of the meeting yesterday that the United States government does indeed know what happened! *Capitán* Garcia may be able to tell us whether or not the American government hushed up the news media. . . ."

Mota shook his head. "Gordo, in spite of the fact that the American news media are in love with the new American president, American journalism has a tradition of refusing to be gagged by the government."

"Uncle, we can sit here and speculate all day. We'll find out soon what the real story is. Again, may I offer you a refill?"

"I suppose so. Are shipments passing through on schedule?"

"Of course. But I must ask you to complain to the *hermanistas*. They have not delivered some products as scheduled. It affects my cash flow and outshipping schedules when items are back-ordered with no anticipated shipment date." Herrero looked at the watch on his ring finger. "Garcia is late. That's unusual."

"It's a long way from Nacozari," Mota muttered, swirling his Scotch and ice cubes. "Perhaps he ran afoul of a *troquero* again. . . ."

"He's supposed to be coming by air. I sent an aerodyne for him."

Mota raised his eyebrows slightly. He, too, had arrived by aerodyne. He'd been surprised to see another one sitting exposed on the landing pad. Mota knew Herrero's practice of never leaving an aerodyne exposed; American recon satellites would be quick to pick it up and thus compromise the location of Ghost House. He had the feeling that Pancho Garcia had already arrived. Why the *capitán* had not reported was unknown to Mota. He never snooped on the internal affairs of his subordinates; he was concerned only with their performance. But two thoughts came to his mind.

He surreptitiously felt for his pistol; it was still discreetly hidden in his armpit under the folds of his shirt.

As for the second possibility, that was something of concern only to Herrero, for even an *hermanisto* never raised the question of a brother possibly being cuckolded; one never questioned another's *macho*.

He didn't have to, because his question was answered by the appearance of Fredrica Herrero, that striking, long-limbed, blond Nordic beauty. Who always dressed to impress her husband's visitors, and today was no exception. Her jeans were about as tight as jeans could be, emphasizing her long legs and slender hips. She wore a full silk blouse with butterfly sleeves and the front unzipped beyond the point of being merely provocative. Today she had her hip-length blond hair gathered into a swinging ponytail behind her.

"Hello, Uncle!" she greeted him brightly, kissing him on the forehead before he had the chance to rise. "I thought I heard you arrive! What brings you to the wilderness of Ghost House? Certainly not the beauty of the Sierra Madres . . ."

"Would it delight you, Freddie, if I told you I came to enjoy the beauty of you?" he told her, rising to kiss her hand.

"You are a dear! Flattery will get you *almost* anything you want," she told him coyly.

"What would happen if I offered to take you away from all this?" Mota asked, waving his arm around to indicate the incredible luxury of this mansion hidden in the Sierra Madre Occidentals.

"I think there might be an unfortunate accident," Gordo Herrero put in quickly with only a *touch* of coldness in his voice.

"Oh, come on, Gordo!" Fredrica told him playfully, kissing him on the cheek. "Uncle Mota is old enough to be my father! Besides, it would be fun to get out of this back country and be squired around Ciudad Mexico by Uncle! I need some new clothes!" She stopped, then turned and said, "Oh, yes! I almost forgot! Pancho Garcia is here!"

Fredrica had so dominated the scene with her beauty and vivacious manner that neither man had noticed a smaller mustached man wearing a wide-brimmed straw hat and packing two pearl-handled revolvers. He stepped into the sunlight, went up to Herrero, and saluted in a perfunctory manner. "*Coronel,* I am here to report! General Mota, I am please to see you again!"

Mota noticed that Garcia had had a shower although his clothes were rumpled, sweat-stained, and dusty.

Herrero didn't notice or didn't comment if he did. "Long flight?"

"*Sí.* We had to come around from the south. We were warned that an American recon satellite was making a pass, so we deviated to allow it to go be before we approached," Garcia explained.

"Sit down, Pancho," Herrero told him. "Fredrica, see to it that Pancho receives a drink, please. Now, Pancho, tell us why the American news media aren't paying any attention to the first raid."

Garcia settled himself into a chair, being careful to keep his back to one of the walls of the patio. "I went to Tucson to check it out. I discovered that none of the newspapers, radio stations, or television stations there knew anything about it. I found one story in the Bisbee newspaper reporting the deaths of the two old people in an accidental fire at their ranch house."

Herrero pursed his lips. "There was no report of the raid at all?"

"None, *Colonel.*"

"Why?"

"Our contact in the Border Patrol said that the story of the raid was not revealed to the press but kept confidential. *Gracias, señora,*" he said to Fredrica as she handed him a tall, cool glass. She smiled at him and sat down on the rock ledge behind her husband.

"Yet the United States government knows of all the

details and is so scared of the consequences that it's embargoed the information," Herrero mused. He'd not only heard the tape made of the meeting between Madera and Lansing but had a copy of the American diplomatic note and all its attachments. *"Bueno!"*

"Eh?" Mota spoke up. "What's good about it? We want pressure on Alvaro and his government! It is difficult to create that without a climate of outrage in the United States!"

Herrero shook his head. "At this point, it makes little difference. The pressure is already on Alvaro and his stooges in Washington. If we can bring about the failure of his government without upsetting our customers north of the border, so much the better . . ."

"Coronel, the United States government has reacted beyond a mere diplomatic note to Ciudad Mexico," Garcia suddenly revealed. "They have moved three divisions of United States Army warbot troops to cover the border from Brownsville to San Diego!" He handed his *coronel* a slip of paper listing the divisions and their new postings.

"Aha!" Herrero yelped as he read the note. "I was hoping for this! And they did it! They can't hide a major engagement between my Herreronistas and the United States Army!"

"Gordo, I don't quite understand your strategy here," Mota admitted. "Now you stand to lose even more men and equipment in your raids into the United States."

"But now it's costing the United States money to maintain their troops on the border. And three divisions of them! Hah! Only three divisions! How can they possibly police more than three thousand kilometers of border with only three divisions? I can go into the United States with a thousand men, do a little looting and burning, and be out again before the United States Army can react!" Herrero was almost ecstatic.

"So?" Mota wanted to know.

"So this doesn't stop anything but keeps it from being hidden from the news media," Herrero explained. "You can't hide three warbot divisions! They require food, water, petrol, and other supplies. These are either procured locally, if possible, or flown in . . . which means a lot of air activity which can't be hidden. Questions concerning why the American army moved the divisions to the border will be asked. The news media will be primed to cover any actions the Army takes, and that will bring our activities to their attention. And this allows us to carry out the original function of my invasions of the United States: to discredit the Alvaro regime and cause it to fall. The United States will not put up with military raids across its border, regardless of whether the troops are Mexican Army or not. The United States will demand that Mexico do something. And Alvaro can't! His government will collapse!"

Mota didn't say anything for a moment. "Since the very beginning, one thing has worried me about your program, Gordo. One may tickle a tiger and get away with it if the tiger is busy eating something else. But if one annoys the tiger, one may get clawed regardless of what the tiger is doing. What do you plan to do when the United States Army engages in hot pursuit of the Herreronistas into Mexico?"

"They won't do it," Herrero stated confidently. *"Mi tío,* I was educated by American military people. I know them. I know their national guilts and fears and restrictions. They will not engage in hot pursuit of the Herreronistas into Mexico."

"The Americans have entered Mexico in hot pursuit in the past," Mota reminded him.

"Not for a hundred years."

"But they have crossed borders in hot pursuit . . . Cambodia, for example. And lately they have shown no hesitation to go into Iran, Trinidad, and Namibia." Mota recalled his lessons in military history as well as his knowledge of current events.

"And they had both world opinion and international sanction on their side when they did . . . more than a hundred passengers of many nationalities in the Zahedan hostage affair. Four Caribbean nations with them in Trinidad. And four national military contingents with them in Namibia. Here they are alone," Herrero pointed out. "The new American president will not permit it; he seeks 'peace and diplomacy,' according to his inaugural address. The United Nations Security Council will react against the Americans, even with the American veto. World opinion will be against any American invasion of Mexico. So the Americans won't do it. They haven't got the national will."

"Gordo, one of the reasons I came today," Carlos Mota admitted, "was to tell you that the *hermanistas* believe you must consider the worst-case scenario: an American expeditionary force coming into Mexico to chase down, catch, and punish those who attacked the United States. What are your contingency plans for this worst-case situation?"

Herrero smiled. He was bluffing because he hadn't thought it out in its entirety. "Uncle, if the Americans do engage in hot pursuit, they are in *our* neighborhood, where we know the land and speak the language. If they invade Mexico and if the government of General Juan Alvaro de Mendoza y Alvarez cannot reassign troops from the southern border to halt the invasion, how long do you think President Alvaro will remain president of Mexico? How long do you think the Americans will allow him to remain president of Mexico? How long before there are riots in the streets of Ciudad Mexico? How long before the Army stages a coup? Certainly, it should take very little effort on the part of the *hermanistas* to encourage that."

Carlos Mota said nothing in reply. He thought for a moment, then stood up and said, "I shall take your reply back to the *hermanistas*, Gordo. I cannot say whether or not they will agree with you. But, on the other hand, they did not give me the authority to order you to stop your program."

"Do you agree with me, Uncle?" Herrero wanted to know.

"From a military standpoint, what you have to say is probably valid. From a political and diplomatic point of view, I don't know because I am not a politician or diplomat. Insofar as business goes, it makes little difference as long as the shipments continue to go through to our customers in the United States. *You* are bearing the expense of your operation. You will have to determine its impact on your own business." He walked over to Fredrica, took her hand, and kissed it. *"Adios, señora.* It is always a pleasure to see you again."

Without saying farewell to Herrero, he walked off the patio toward the hangar where his aerodyne and pilot were waiting.

Pancho Garcia had come to his feet with Carlos Mota and remained standing. He looked at his *comandante* and asked, "Any change in plans, *Colonel?*"

"No, we shall proceed as scheduled, Pancho. Please stay tonight. I need to discuss some details of the operation with you," Herrero told him, rising to his feet. "You may retire to your quarters. I will call you after dinner."

Pancho gave his perfunctory salute and left.

Herrero found his wife standing in front of him. "Gordo, I don't like this," she told him firmly.

"What don't you like, Freddie? This is only part of business."

"Business is business, but what you're doing is war and killing."

"So? I'm a military man. You knew that when you married me at West Point. You grew up with military people all around you."

"Yes, but you were once an officer whose military activity was in defense of his country. In your case, Mexico, which has been a very non-aggressive nation since the nineteenth century," she told him in steely tones. "Now you're deliberately killing people."

"Freddie, my dear, you've never had any qualms whatsoever about killing people," he reminded her. "In fact, you gunned down Guillermo Morelos before I could."

101

"I couldn't stand the thought of that pep-head staying alive and wanting my body!" she snapped. "And I know you must occasionally do some selective elimination of colleagues and employees. Some of them are better dead, anyway. That's part of this business."

"And you're not upset that drugs probably kill more people in the United States than anything else?"

She shook her head, causing her long, blond ponytail to swing back and forth. "What they do to themselves with drugs is voluntary. Every person should be allowed to choose their own form of poison. You know my feeling about that. Drugs help eliminate the weaklings, the ones without willpower, the people who should never be allowed to breed anyway. But what you're doing is murder. It's senseless warfare in which innocent people are going to be killed just because they happen to be in the way. Furthermore, it *is* possible that the American army could come into Mexico chasing your Herreronistas. They could even get this far and destroy this place, my home, much as I hate being out here in the wilderness without friends."

"So what do you want me to do, Freddie?"

She did something that no Mexican wife would do. She reached out and took him by both shoulders. "Gordo, I don't like what your bandit gang did in Arizona, I don't like what you plan to do. I want you to stop it right now."

"The business may collapse if I do that, Freddie," he warned her.

"Let it! You've stacked enough money away in Zurich and Singapore to keep us in luxury for the rest of our lives! Let's pull out now before you kill innocent people."

He took her hands off his shoulders and told her bluntly, "If I quit now, there is no place in the whole world where you and I would be safe from the *hermanistas*. We wouldn't be given the chance to enjoy that money. We would be vulnerable to government police, and the *hermanistas* would never allow us to live long enough to be spotted and picked up. I must carry this thing through. One does not 'retire' from this business."

102

"Your father retired," she reminded him.

"And turned it over to his heir, me. You have not given me an heir, Freddie."

"Not because we haven't tried! But even then, I wouldn't want to raise children *here*. Gordo, I love you, and I want us to have children! But I want us to be in Ciudad Mexico where there are good hospitals and stores and schools and other children for ours to play with. . . ."

"When this is over and business gets back to normal and we can safely relocate to Ciudad Mexico, I'll discuss this again with you," he promised her. "In the meantime, I have to overthrow a government. So stay the hell out of my way, Freddie!"

CHAPTER ELEVEN

For several years, the Washington Greys hadn't come down off the hill at Diamond Point to Fort Huachuca for desert training exercises. The oldest of all the army posts in Arizona, "Fort Watch" had been activated originally in 1877 and suffered a continual series of deactivations and reactivations as the military situation in the United States changed.

As Curt looked out of his ACV's turret hatch at the old post in the late afternoon sunlight, he wondered why its buildings never seemed to grow old. He'd seen photos of the Fort taken in 1890; the old buildings arrayed around the parade ground were still there. Under the care of a civilian caretaker contractor for the last quarter of a century save for a few weeks every summer when the Arizona National Guard trained there, Fort Huachuca had basked in sleepy fashion under the sun, patiently waiting the time when the Army needed it again.

Except that afternoon it had rained like hell when a typical Arizona monsoon thunderstorm dumped 3 centimeters of rain on the post in 30 minutes. Some of the storm drains hadn't been cleared of winter debris, and pools of standing water were everywhere.

Because the post was currently in a deactivated state, no flag flew from the old flagpole.

Captain Hensley Atkinson and her operations staff had pulled ahead of the three-kilometer convoy after they'd passed Interstate 10, and she was now on the parade ground ready to direct units to parking positions. As the convoy pulled in, she was very busy getting the first night's bivouac organized. She'd borrowed the traffic control warbots Kitsy Clinton had used during the trek, but even using them plus Sergeants Forest Barnes, Andrea Carrington, and Albert Johnson of her staff, they were busy.

In the first place, the parade ground was still wet from the thunderstorm. Although there wasn't very much mud because of the sandy soil, the vehicles churned up the short grass, leaving deep ruts and generally making a mess out of things. The ground would dry out in a few hours and become hard as rock. But in the meantime, the Greys were tearing up Fort Huachuca's parade ground.

Someone was obviously very upset about it. As Curt parked his ACV in the line designated for 1st Company, he saw Captain Hensley Atkinson in apparent verbal altercation with a large, beefy civilian wearing a jacket and a baseball cap advertising a well-known western brand of beer. Over the tacomm, Curt heard her message: "Grey Leader, this is Grey Ops. I've got an irate civilian contractor here. I need either Colonel Bellamack or Major Hampton or both, preferably with a copy of our march and relocation orders. I could also use any other help I could get at the moment. This man isn't very cooperative or friendly."

"Henry," Curt called down to his first sergeant, "take over and see to it that the company is properly emplaced in bivouac. Don't nail anything down until you get the word from topside. I have the sneaky feeling that we were either unexpected or that the caretakers haven't had time to cover up the neglect of a couple months with no military here."

"Always some poor sonofabitch who don't get the word" was Kester's brief reply. "Major, we're going to need to dump the honey tanks before we settle into bivouac for the night."

"We may end up having to dump the onboard sewage down a storm drain somewhere," Curt observed.

105

"Not in the United States, Major. Got to be dumped into a holding tank or a proper waste management system," Kester reminded him.

"Shit!" Curt growled in disgust.

"Yes, sir. That's what it is."

"Well, we may have to dig latrines."

"Jesus Christ, Major, I don't think any of the Companions have ever done that. . . ."

"Then you'll have to teach them, Henry. Don't sweat it. Keep a cool stool and a hot pot, and I'll go find out what the drill is." He clamped his combat helmet on his head not because they were in a combat area but because of all the comm equipment in it that would allow him to stay in contact with Kester. Sliding down the glacis plate of his ACV, he walked over to where Hensley Atkinson was in confrontation with the civilian. He saw Bellamack and Hampton also heading that way, so he slowed his pace in order to arrive when they did.

When all of them were together, Atkinson said, "Colonel Bellamack, this is Mister Frank Rogers. He's in charge of the civilian caretaker contract operation here."

Bellamack extended his hand. The big, fat man took it. "Colonel, I didn't expect you all until tomorrow night. I got nothing turned on for you. No water—especially no hot water so your women can take showers and wash their hair. No crappers or latrines. No electric power. No waste and sewage disposal. And no food service or supply."

"Mister Rogers, you should have been expecting us, and you should have notified Diamond Point if you weren't going to be ready. The division comm-intel unit would have passed the word on to me. I don't like surprises such as this, and I don't understand why you aren't ready for us," Bellamack told him bluntly. "I had Captain Atkinson here hard-copy you at twenty-two-hundred hours last night telling you we'd be here before eighteen-hundred today. Major, where's our hard copy of that message?"

Major Wade Hampton handed over the piece of paper

protected in its clear plastic envelope.

"Yeah, I know. I saw it. But I didn't find out about it until noon today," Rogers admitted.

"Noon!" Bellamack exclaimed, then wanted to know, "Don't you keep watch on your comm terminal? Don't you read your mail?"

"No, I don't, 'specially when there's no reason to. And I can't do it when I'm out supervising my crews and getting the base ready for the arrival of a regiment tomorrow night and a whole division within a week! As it is, it's just damned lucky I happened to check the terminal last night before we buttoned up and set the night watchmen out; I wouldn't even have caught the mail from your division commander until this morning. I never even looked at the comm terminal before lunch today."

"Well, why not, Mister Rogers?" Bellamack wanted to know. "You're the caretaker. . . ."

"This ain't Phoenix or Tucson," Rogers pointed out. "Nothing happens very fast down here. In fact, nothing really ever happens much. We're out in the boonies. Things take longer to do, and we don't rush things. Besides, since I got the first message last night, I've been too damned busy to recheck the comm terminal. As it was, I was up most of last night trying to round up my people to get them out here." Rogers was obviously annoyed. Then he added, "By the way, overtime is time and a half and more than eight hours is triple time. Some of my people have been at it since six o'clock this morning, and looks like we'll be at it all night. Your finance people going to be able to cover that? I got payday coming up Friday, and my crew is going to want their overtime in addition to their regular checks. . . ."

"We have no authorization to pay your overtime, Mister Rogers," Wade Hampton told him bluntly.

Frank Rogers shrugged. "Okay, no skin off my nose. So we'll quit and go home in about an hour, then. Tough luck. You and your troops sure ought to be able to fend for yourselves after that."

"We'll live," Curt put in. "Colonel, we're stocked ninety-six hours of combat self-sufficiency . . . except for dumping our honey tanks. My company can make do in bivouac if we can unload our vehicle waste management systems."

"How would you do that in a combat situation?" Bellamack asked. He knew how the robot linkage vehicles of the regular RI did it, but he wasn't yet sure how this new mixed-mode regiment of Sierra Charlies had worked it out.

"We'd just dump our load by the side of the road and go our merry way," Curt advised him.

"You can't do that here," Rogers advised. "You just can't dump it even down the storm drains. I'd have both state and federal health, sanitation, and environmental control people all over my ass for that. I'd get cited and fined, and they'd cause trouble for you, too."

"Okay, we can keep our honey tanks sealed until you're prepared to service them," Bellamack agreed. "But let's go for the alternates: temporary crappers, portable latrines. Can you get some? Who in Sierra Vista handles the portable field latrine concession?"

"Well, there's one outfit," Rogers admitted but didn't tell them he was a partner. "But they're closed down for the day by now. And they have to bring them in from Tucson where they're stored. They haul in truckloads of them when the Guard is on two-week encampment here, but we know about that about a month or more in advance. No matter what I do, I can't get any of them here before tomorrow night. Got some of them on the way for delivery tomorrow because I planned for you to get here then. So your vehicle systems and holding tanks are going to have to handle it until then. I'll have water turned on in most of these surrounding buildings by tomorrow noon, even though the plumbing is rusted and needs to be replaced in some of the toilets. By then, I oughta have the problems with the sewage system solved, too. Don't worry; we can handle the division when it gets here. But

I can't get you porta-crappers by tonight! Or do much else for you. I've already gone over my current budget. . . ."

"The post's sewage disposal system doesn't work?" Wade Hampton asked in disbelief.

"Some parts of it. Pretty old system. Got a request for parts and funds in to both Army Engineers and GSA. I'm on the list but it'll be about three months yet before the stuff gets here. . . ."

"Do you have any shovels in a warehouse?" Bellamack suddenly asked the civilian caretaker.

"Yeah. Got lots of D-handle shovels. Why?"

"Any toilet paper?"

"Some." Rogers had far more than he actually needed. He had a lot. It kept him personally supplied, and he took care of his employees, too. It was an expendable item. So were soap, toothpaste, paper towels, sheets, and other everyday items. He had a great little business going for himself. No one questioned his requisitions through General Service Administration channels. Great Southwest Paper Products in Tucson loved him; he was their biggest customer.

"Any straight-handle shovels?"

"You can dig fine with the D-handle shovels," Rogers advised.

"Straight-handle shovels are better. Toilet paper can be stored on the shaft of a straight-handle shovel and kept out of the dirt," Bellamack said. "Get me all the straight-handle shovels you've got, a couple of cases of toilet paper, and we'll give the troops their head. . . ."

Rogers shook his head. "Can't do it, Colonel, unless your TO&E shows a listing for straight-handled shovels. I got my orders, and I got my contract to follow, and I gotta account for all them tools and supplies."

Curt thought for a moment that Bellamack was going to blow his cool and deck this pompous asshole. Instead, he proved his was an officer and a gentleman. He merely took one step closer to the big, paunchy civilian. Bella-

109

mack's tall and slender body suddenly became even more pronounced; he may have drawn himself up a little bit. But now he towered over the civilian caretaker. "Mister Rogers, this is a government military post. I have military orders to be here. I am assuming the position of temporary post commander and placing Fort Huachuca under martial law as of this time." He turned to Curt. "Major Carson, I request you form a detail to survey the warehouses and other logistical dumps, locate whatever material is necessary for the health and well-being of the regiment, take possession of same, and report your findings to me. You may utilize any cooperative civilian contractor employee as well, and be sure to get names and pay numbers of those who are helpful. Any civilian who attempts to obstruct your mission will be placed in custody and brought to me. Use discretion in your treatment of civilian contractors, of course."

Curt saluted with a grin. "Yes, sir!"

Bellamack turned and looked down at Hensley Atkinson, who looked like a teenage girl in uniform beside him. "Captain Atkinson, I want you to form a detail of as many personnel as you require for the purpose of setting up housekeeping here, including making provisions for water, food, and sanitation beyond that which we have in our vehicles. I'm sure we have personnel in the Greys who know such mundane technology as how to turn on water and get the electricity and plumbing to work."

Atkinson saluted. She was smiling also. "Yes, sir!"

The colonel didn't tower over his second-in-command quite as much. So he could look him in the eye as he said, "Major Hampton, please run the national colors up the post flagpole at once. Then see to it that these two officers have what they need to carry out their assignments."

Hampton saluted. He didn't smile, but his expression was one of relief, and there was a twinkle in his eyes. "Yes, sir!"

Bellamack turned to the astounded Frank Rogers and

110

in spite of the civilian's size and girth managed to look imposingly larger and stronger than the beefy man. "As for you, Mister Rogers, you will immediately be escorted to the main gate and you will not be permitted across to this post again pending my report of this to both the Inspector General and the Judge Advocate General. If the IG, the JAG, or Major General Carlisle of the Iron Fist Division wants to let you back, that's their prerogative. But I will not have you in this base while I am in command, and I don't care what your contract says! You have refused to cooperate, and I hereby cancel your contract."

"You can't throw me out of here, Colonel! I have a right to be here! I am legally in charge of this post!" Rogers objected, his voice rising.

"No, Mister Rogers, this is a military base and the property of the Unites States government. I have assumed command as the highest ranking military officer present. I am acting under the authority of my orders to transfer my unit here. As the new base commander, I will not suffer the obstructions of a civilian contractor in matters relating to the health and welfare of my troops. Captain Atkinson, get an ATV and two armed troopers over here and get this man off-post before he does something he'll later regret — as he's presently considering — or before I forget it's my duty to protect the rights of citizens such as he."

Lieutenant Colonel Wild Bill Bellamack had not raised his voice in the slightest during the entire conversation, although his attitude had become harder and more controlled. There was no doubt in Curt's mind that Wild Bill Bellamack was pissed off, that he knew exactly what he was doing, and that he knew he had his regiment behind him.

The "Fort Huachuca Latrine Battle" would go on to become a favorite legend of the Washington Greys. It was the first time their new commanding officer stuck his neck out for his troops, going far beyond his orders and perhaps his authority in the process, but acting well within

111

his responsibilities as the regimental commander.

It was going to be another night of little or no sleep and lots of hard work, but Major Curt Carson felt a lot better. Colonel Bellamack was quickly becoming the leader of the Washington Greys.

CHAPTER TWELVE

The Herreronista irregulars penetrated the border south of Bisbee, Arizona, at 0600. The first unit to cross was Colonel Herrero's version of the United States Army's old, deactivated Delta Force, his *especialistas*.

Herrero had studied the OSS, Green Berets, Delta Force, the British SAS, and the Soviet *speznatz* histories and field manuals while he was a West Point cadet. These outfits had been of particular interest to him because he knew he'd be going back to Mexico to serve in an army that was partly an internal police force and partly an external defense organization whose fighting, if any, would be of a counterinsurgency and counterterrorist nature. Even a decade ago, when Guatemala was still an ostensible democracy, the eventual Central American Marxist covert invasion of Mexico could be foreseen. Herrero knew that the nonrobotic Mexican Army couldn't operate in the mountains and jungles of Chiapas and Campeche with American warbot doctrines. So he'd studied the old pre-warbot tactics while he did what he was supposed to do as a West Point cadet: learn how to be an officer and how to fight with warbots. So he knew both worlds.

However, in recent times he'd given only cursory attention to the articles in the professional journals that described the development of the United States Army's new Special Combat troops within the Robot Infantry. He was no longer a professional military officer; he was a businessman.

Herrero's *especialistas* were his best men set apart from his irregular infantry of peasants, ranchers, miners, and other rough, hungry, and ready-to-fight poor people from Sonora and Chihuahua. They were his technologists, the ones who kept his high-tech communications and computer networks up and running.

The *especialistas* were accompanied by the cream of his personal bodyguard, his elite *caballeros,* all former officers and NCOs with whom he'd served in the Mexican Army.

On this day, the job of the *especialistas* was to spoof the U.S. Border Patrol sensors with high technology. This they did by hooking little black boxes full of nanochip circuits across the sensor outputs, then disconnecting the sensors themselves. The equipment downstream of the sensors was thereafter fed a constant series of sensor signals which looked real but which did not report the movement of the Herreronistas across the border. Those sensors the *especialistas* couldn't get to because the security fences were spoofed externally.

There weren't many sensors to spoof, nor were they very sophisticated. The Border Patrol had inherited many of the intrusion systems the Air Force had removed from ballistic missile silos a long time ago. These were sensitive but also relatively low-tech in the twenty-first century. The *especialistas* took care of them quickly and quite covertly. According to plans, the Border Patrol wouldn't find out until it was too late.

Once that was accomplished, the *especialistas* with the *caballero* security escort moved into the Mule Mountains and took care of the commercial telecommunications systems linking Bisbee to the rest of the world—the microwave towers, the fiber optic cables, and even the old hard-wire copper telephone lines. What they did to these systems wouldn't cause America West Communications or the various cable TV and computer networks or suspect there was anything wrong for hours. When they did discover something was really wrong, their remote tests from Tucson and Wilcox would give them such ambiguous data that they'd have to send repair teams to find out what was wrong . . . and a specific company of Herreronistas would be waiting for them.

114

Colonel Luis Sebastian Herrero had learned his lessons well at West Point. He knew how to plan a mission, how to establish an operational staff to take care of all the details, and how to use the principles of war to support Operation Mulas, the surgical terrorist strike on Bisbee. It was planned quite simply: take Bisbee, raise hell, do a little looting, stay as long as possible in order to achieve the maximum level of terror, then get out when his intelligence system told him the Americans had found out and were responding. His Herreronistas would vanish back across the border without a trace, leaving only death and destruction behind in the retirement and tourist town of Bisbee.

So he sat back five kilometers south of the border like any army commander and watched his plan unfold under the field command of his *capitános*, Pancho Garcia handling the looting and terrorism in Bisbee and Vasco Gomez leading the *especialistas* and *caballeros*.

In Sierra Vista, the Border Patrol sensor watch changed at 8:00 A.M.

"Anything to report?" the new watchman asked as he came in and put his lunch box in the fridge and his coffee container near the microwave.

The on-watch BP man shook his head. "Quietest morning we've had in a long time. Not even any trucks crossing between Naco and Bisbee Junction. Normal traffic at Douglas and some small but otherwise normal activity over by Duquense."

The new man checked the sensor record charts. "You have a power glitch about six-thirty this morning?"

"Yeah, looks like someone shot a hawk off a power line and the hawk got partly fried as it fell across the lines on the way down. At least, that's the way I'd read the glitch. Or it coulda been that freakish thunderstorm we had last night. I checked the sensors right after that; they were normal."

"Okay, shove off, Mike. I'll take her from here."

About the same time, the America West Communications rural lines supervisor in Tucson coming on duty for the morning noticed something strange: There had been no communications traffic into Bisbee either on the microwave or the old hard-wire landline since about six-thirty that morning. When he tried checking on this, he couldn't get through to Bisbee; all lines reported busy. A spot check on the board indicated voice and data transmissions occupied all circuits. But it was strange, because all the transmissions were *originating* from Bisbee. He called his engineers at Sierra Vista, Benson, Tombstone, and Douglas; they reported the same situation.

"Could be the Army," his Sierra Vista engineer told him. "They moved a warbot regiment into Fort Huachuca yesterday. Rumor Control has it that a full warbot infantry division is coming in later from Diamond Point up north. The boss military man fired the civilian caretaker, and it's been Rat Race City for the soldiers getting the base reactivated on their own. The telecomm system could be busy because of that."

"Yeah, that could be it," the Tucson super decided. "If we start getting customer complaints, would you send your line crew over to the Mule Mountain relay to check it out?"

"Sure, once they get back from Huachuca where they've been activating circuits for the military all night."

"Okay, I'll have the Tombstone office send their lineman down. Sounds just like another busy day like when the Guard comes in."

But it hadn't been just another busy day in Bisbee.

Although the rest of the world didn't know what had happened in the old mining town until later, it didn't even dawn on the inhabitants themselves that they were being invaded.

Tom Buck had arisen at sunup and turned off the airport rotating beacon. He was frying up a plate of eggs Sam Ogg had brought over the day before in appreciation for Buck's help in changing the tires on Ogg's old Socata

Trinidad. As he washed off the spatula, he happened to look out the window over the sink.

The two-lane asphalt road running north from the border to the town of Bisbee itself was suddenly full of armed, uniformed, somewhat ragtag soldiers.

"Holy shit!" Tom Buck exclaimed and reached for the telephone. He dialed 911. It rang once. Deputy Ben Lewis answered up at the Town Marshal's office.

All that Buck was able to get out was "Ben, the goddamned Mexicans are invading!"

Then the front door of the airport office banged open, six armed men stormed in, and three of them rushed through the door into Buck's living quarters.

They shot him on the spot and tore the telephone off the wall.

Sam Ogg, a retired American Airlines pilot, was out in his hangar preflighting his ancient fixed-wing propeller-driven aircraft in preparation for a flight to Williams to go dove hunting. He heard the noise of the Herreronistas on the road, heard the shots in the airport office, and peered around the partly opened hangar door to find out what the hell was going on. What he saw made him grab his Weatherby Eighty-Eight Auto Magnum 12-gauge, pull the plug out of the magazine, shove five shells into it, load one in the chamber and open the choke to make a scatter gun. He'd bought the shotgun because he'd be able to use it as a riot weapon if things ever went to hell down here near the border.

This morning, he knew the men on the road and coming into the airport weren't on a little foray. This wasn't just an incident involving a few Mexican bandits; he could see the line of marching men stretching southward back along the road to Mexico. Furthermore, he watched as they set fire to the airport office. Other armed men had also come onto the field and started smashing airplanes. They also broke the window of his pickup truck parked alongside the office when they couldn't defeat the antitheft ignition system by hot-wiring.

117

As a group of the ragged men approached his hangar, he knew he had no place to run. It was too late for that. He also knew they'd killed Tom Buck. So he waited until five men got within a few meters of the hangar door. He might only have five shots in the gun and no time to load more, he told himself, but he was going to take at least five of these bastards with him.

He did. He blew the heads off two of them and put very large holes in the chests of three more.

But the sheet metal of his hangar couldn't stop the hail of high-velocity 5.56-millimeter rounds from dozens of automatic weapons that quickly raked the building. He was the second American to die in the Battle of Bisbee.

But he wasn't the last.

A Town Marshal's pickup came roaring down the road southbound, its flashing colored lights and strobes frantically blinking in the morning sunlight and its siren screaming. Only when the Deputy Marshal saw the cordon of men on the road did he realize he'd made a big mistake. He tried to turn the car around in a high-speed skid. As he did so, a Brazilian 73-millimeter antitank rocket came through the windshield; the glass wasn't tough enough to trigger the warhead, so it went off when the round hit the back right corner of the pickup's cab. The Deputy was later identified only by some of his parts.

The Herreronistas continued their march into Bisbee.

They counted on taking the town with little opposition. Their first move was to hit the police station with a series of 73-millimeter rockets. No one was in the City Hall yet. They went into the fire station, pulled the alarm, and shot the firemen off the pole one by one as they slid down from their sleeping quarters upstairs; then a squad went upstairs and shot the rest.

By this time, it was 8:30 A.M., and most of the townspeople were awake.

When Paul Metzger (Lt. Col. AUS, Ret.) stepped out of his front door, coffee cup in hand, to get the morning paper, he heard familiar sounds: automatic-rifle fire com-

118

ing from down the street and the sounds of firing and exploding 73-millimeter antitank rockets. He wasn't a warbot brainy; he'd retired out of the regular grunt infantry just before his old outfit, the 52nd Infantry Regiment (the Ready Rifles), started conversion to a warbot outfit fifteen years before. He'd heard about the bandit raid on Norman's ranch. So he didn't wait to ask questions or to find out what was causing the ruckus. He went back inside without picking up the newspaper.

"Carolyn," he told his wife, "get down in the basement."

Carolyn Metzger had been a major in the Ordnance Corps and had taken early retirement when her husband had been mustered out. She'd been a small-arms ballistics expert specializing in self-guided munitions. She'd learned to shoot every small arm in the inventory of every army in the world. "Basement? What the hell's going on, Paul?"

"Sounds like a Mexican bandit outfit just came into town. Get down in the basement." He unlocked his gun cabinet and took out his surplus M22A3 5.56-millimeter assault rifle and four boxes of caseless ammunition. "I'm going to put the street under fire if necessary. Likely to get a little deadly around here if I'm right."

"Basement, hell, sweetie," she told him in no uncertain terms. "Lemme tell Hilda next door if she hasn't heard it already. And damned if I'm going to cower in the basement when I know she'll be out there with her little submachine gun looking for the chance to brag to everyone that she's still as much of a marksman as she was in Signal Corps." Before her husband could shut the cabinet door, she pulled out the old M16A2 which sprayed brass casings as it fired but still was a street-fighting weapon with real stopping power out to 300 meters.

Thus when the first Herreronistas tried to come down that curving street, they ran into something they hadn't counted on.

Although Bisbee was an old mining town and the open pits were still a very definite part of the landscape, it had become a tourist attraction and, more important, a retire-

119

ment community. Some of the Herreronistas who'd been there in the past had tried to warn Pancho Garcia that the place wasn't full of creaking old men and frail white-haired grandmothers.

Some of the retirees were former military like Paul and Carolyn Metzger.

Those who weren't were active people who liked the hunting in southeastern Arizona.

Almost all the citizens in Bisbee had guns in their homes.

And they knew how to use them.

Furthermore, once the initial shock of the Herreronista assault wore off, they weren't hesitant about using them, either.

Back in the days of the Cold War in the last century, some people feared the possibility of a Soviet invasion of the United States by airborne units of the Red Army. In fact, several movies had used that theme. Anyone who knew anything at all about the United States of America also knew that such a move on the part of the Soviets would lead to the bloodiest and most costly invasion imaginable. It would be even worse than Afghanistan. Millions of people in the United States had millions of guns. They'd always had guns. They were an unofficial *de facto* irregular militia.

The Herreronistas found that out the hard way that day in Bisbee.

They even discovered that what they'd been told about Americans not being allowed to own automatic weapons was wrong. Nobody realized that a $400 license and a clean police record were all that were required to get ATF permit to buy and own an automatic weapon. Most ex-military people and gun collectors had automatic weapons.

The Herreronistas encountered not only submachine-gun fire at close range in house-to-house fighting but came under sustained long-range fire from general-purpose machine guns of every imaginable type that swept

120

the streets and made life very hazardous for them.

Every crooked, twisting street through the narrow valley of the town of Bisbee became a death trap for the Herreronistas.

It wasn't a walk-through like they'd been told.

The narrow streets provided lanes of fire for retired military people who knew how to use such things and hunters whose deer, elk, bear, and javelina rifles were just as accurate. Furthermore, the hunters had an abundant supply of soft-point and hollow-point hunting ammo of the sort that various treaties prevented the military from using; these could not only stop a large bear, but they did a particularly effective job of blowing very large holes in unarmored Herreronistas.

The old stone buildings of Bisbee were nearly impervious to bullets and surrendered their structural integrity only to the rare and expensive Brazilian antitank rockets. The Herreronistas quickly ran out of antitank rockets.

And, in spite of the fact that the *especialistas* had cut all the commercial communications links between Bisbee and the rest of the world, they'd forgotten some things that were uniquely American.

Bisbee had about a dozen ham radio operators, and they had portable emergency electric generators to run their rigs because they wanted to be operational in emergencies.

This was an emergency, and the radio hams got the word out. "CQ, CQ, CQ, this is Kay-Nine-Five-Zed-Ju-liet-Romeo calling CQ. Specially CQ Tucson or Wilcox or Douglas! Hey, if any of you guys in the Chicken House Gang haven't gone to bed yet, listen up! We got ourselves a small war going on down here in Bisbee! CQ, CQ, CQ!"

The hams weren't alone. Marti Mitchell heard the gun-fire and the explosions downtown, which wasn't more than a couple of blocks away. She looked out to see the column of smoke from the burning police headquarters building. She punched her husband. "Mike, dammit, wake up!"

121

"Huh! Jesus, Marti, I didn't get in until midnight and you wouldn't let me get to sleep until three! I'm not due out until tomorrow night! So lemme sleep!" Mike Mitchell was a trucker and he'd drive a load anywhere. He was licensed for Mexico as well as the United States. Bisbee happened to be convenient not only to Interstate 10 in the USA but also to Mexican Highways 2 and 15.

"Get up!" she told him. "Damned Mexicans are attacking! Get out and get the rig warmed up!"

He sat up in bed and heard the gunfire and saw the smoke. Without bothering to dress, he dashed out of their small house to where his rig was parked. A quick twist of his wrist turned on his CB radio. "Hey, anybody who's listing, this is Big Mike in Bisbee! Anybody on Channel Thirty? Break, break!"

"Hey, hey, Big Mike! Howyah! Dirty Edna here passing through Benson! What's up, Big Mike! Breaker breaker!"

"Pass the word, Dirty Edna! We've got a bunch of rowdies in town shooting up the place. May be a bandit bunch from Mexico like shot up Norman's a while back! Call Smoky!"

"Big Mike, this is Speedy Gonzales east of Bisbee on Highway Eighty! Hell, I see the smoke down by the airport! Need some help?"

"No, no, Speedy! Stay out of here! It's deadly! Turn around and get the hell out! Looks like a thousand of them from here! They're still coming over the border! Christalmighty, don't just call the laser-tag boys. Call out the goddamned army!"

CHAPTER THIRTEEN

Major Curt Carson was bone-weary tired. He hadn't gotten much sleep for two nights in a row. Quick catnaps in his ACV hadn't eliminated the fatigue that gripped his body. The Companions were even late getting lunch, which arrived early in the afternoon because there were only a couple of fast-food outfits in Sierra Vista that could handle an order for 106 hamburgers with fries. It had also taken time to get the food out to Fort Huachuca. When it did get there, some of it had gotten lukewarm and had to be reheated in the vehicle microwave ovens normally used to prepare combat field rations. But Bellamack was wise when he decided not to allow the Greys to draw down from their combat reserves when local food sources could be utilized, however overburdened and slow they were. When plastic bags of food were delivered to the Companions by Supply Sergeant Mariette Ireland, Curt deliberately ordered the company to knock off whatever they happened to be doing, gather together in the shade of his ACV aligned with the rest of the company's equipment on the parade ground, and relax for an hour. They'd all been working hard, and a brief break was needed. Curt knew his people, and he could see the fatigue in all of them.

His two platoon leaders—Lieutenants Jerry Allen and Kitsy Clinton—looked as tired as he was. But they were young and should be able to take it after the months of training, physical conditioning, and rehab he'd put them through following the return from Namibia.

Master Sergeant Henry Kester *did* look tired but didn't act that way. Kester hadn't complained to Curt; that

123

wasn't his way. The Master Sergeant knew how to pace himself. He also knew how and when to grab some sack time during periods he wasn't needed or wouldn't be missed. As usual, however, Henry Kester didn't say much during lunch. He was obviously conserving energy.

It was hard for Curt to tell whether or not Platoon Sergeant Edie Sampson had reached the end of her rope. She, too, was an experienced soldier, and she had the sort of personality that wouldn't let her admit she was bushed. Hard as nails and able to whip her weight in infuriated wildcats, Sampson would drive hard right up to the moment when she crapped out completely. Curt could sometimes predict that point; often he could not. Today was one of those times when he didn't know how far she was from exhaustion, and it worried him. He knew he could test it if he wanted to risk it; he could continue the running joke between them by complaining about the fact she still packed a 9-millimeter Beretta pistol with questionable stopping power.

But Curt was mostly worried about Platoon Sergeant Nick Gerard. According to the medics and biotechs at Beaumont Army Medical Center in El Paso, Nick had completely recovered from the wounds he'd suffered in action in Namibia and was fit to return to duty. But the experience of being actually hurt on the battlefield had been traumatic in many ways, and it had taken a lot of out of Nick Gerard. Curt knew it had only been within the past few weeks that the sergeant's gaunt face had begun to fill out again and that the give-'em-hell gleam had returned to his eyes. That gleam was gone today. Nick Gerard was tired, and he showed it. Part to if was due to the fact he was breaking in and educating Lieutenant Kathleen Clinton. Although Gerard had never mentioned it to Curt—and it would have been improper to do so even in the familiar comradeship of Carson's Companions—Platoon Sergeant Nick Gerard was torn between his loyalty to Curt Carson and his devotion to his former platoon leader, Alexis Morgan. Gerard really wanted to be with now-Captain Morgan, but he felt he had a duty to Curt to hold together Alpha Platoon while its new platoon leader got her feet on the ground.

"After this morning, I'm the Army's most experienced combat-rated plumber," Gerard griped as they ate in the shade of Curt's ACV. "The galvanized iron pipe in some of these buildings has to be more than a hundred years old! It's a goddamed miracle it survived the hard water here!"

"It didn't," Jerry Allen corrected him. "The stuff I saw you working on wasn't galvanized pipe; it was a tube of hard water corrosion that had dissolved the pipe and was acting as a low-pressure conduit for the water."

"You think the plumbing's corroded?" Edie Sampson put in. "The swamp coolers are even worse! Cole and I got one fixed after working on it all morning. Even with new pads, it won't blow cool air . . . and that building is a damned oven! I don't know how we can sleep in it!"

"Humidity's up," Sergeant Elliot pointed out. "When the dew point gets above fifty-five degrees, it's monsoon season here. And when the humidity gets up above forty percent with this heat, evaporative cooling just doesn't haul down the temperature enough to be comfortable."

"How'd you get to be such an expert?" Sergeant Charlie Koslowski wanted to know.

"He's right," Sergeant Tracy Dillon commented. "That's why our vehicles use refrigerated air for their environmental control system. Evaps would be simpler, and they'd work great in the Persian Gulf theater. But not in the tropics . . ."

"Yeah, and sometimes even the fridge systems can't handle the load, as we found out on Trinidad," Gerard remarked. "At least Signal Corps found a way to keep the green stuff from growing on our electronic gear. . . ."

"What's this about a monsoon? In the desert?" Kitsy Clinton wanted to know.

"It's from the Arabic word *mausim* which means 'season,' " Jerry Allen told her.

"Where'd you learn Arabic?" Clinton asked.

"My second language at West Point. Thought I'd be spending most of my career where I'd need it," Allen remarked. "Looks like I should have studied Spanish instead. Anyway, a lot of places besides India have monsoons—even Europe."

"In Europe, it's the mistral and levanter," Clinton pointed out.

"Those are winds," Allen told her.

The discussion didn't get much further. Curt's beeper went off. He picked up his portable tacomm brick. "Companion Leader on the net."

Silence followed for a moment before Alexis Morgan's voice said, "Marauder Leader here."

"Greys all, report to Grey Head at once. All companies, all personnel, report to Grey Head at once." It was Major Joanne Wilkinson's voice, and it had a note of urgency in it.

Curt stood up and wolfed down the last of lunch. "Okay, Companions, trash what's left of chow if you haven't swallowed it by now. That message was an imperative. And Major Wilkinson meant *right now*." He tossed the disposable mess gear into a plastic trash sack. "Follow me."

"The *whole company?*" Kitsy was nonplussed by that.

"Sure thing, Lieutenant," Nick Gerard told her. "That's SOP in the Greys, especially when a unit's going into the field and combat's a possibility."

"Combat? Here?" she wondered.

"Remember why we're here," Curt said, picking up his Novia and helmet. "I suspect we're going to be sent to either check out another bandit raid or prevent one."

No unit marches around in formation any longer. It wasn't necessary to move large bodies of troops in ancient and obsolete battle formations. But the Companions and the other Washington Grey companies had a tradition of walking in what they called "semi-formation." Curt and Henry Kester led, the old sergeant keeping two paces to the rear and one pace to the left. Behind came Alpha Platoon with Lieutenant Clinton leading, followed by Sergeant Gerard and then Sergeants Koslowski and Elliott. Bravo Platoon with Lieutenant Allen, Platoon Sergeant Sampson, and Sergeants Cole and Dillon followed. They naturally marched in step; it was easier to do it that way.

Headquarters Company was busily putting together the equipment for an open-air Oscar briefing alongside Colonel Bellamack's van. The Companions were soon joined by Morgan's Marauders, Ward's Warriors, and Frazier's Ferrets. All companies stood quietly, awaiting the regimental commander.

Alexis Morgan stepped over to Curt. "Any rumors?" she asked cryptically.

Curt shook his head. "I suspect a battalion-strength patrol coming up."

She nodded. "Beats the hell out of fixing up quarters the civilian contractor should have kept livable in the first place."

Bellamack stepped out of the van into the sunlight and walked down the short set of access steps to the ground. Everyone came to attention.

"At ease," Bellamack told them easily. "In fact, sit down and be comfortable. No need to stand up unless you have to. You don't have to. I do. We've got problems. This is a field Oscar briefing. I'm told that in the Sierra Charlies all involved officers and NCOs participate. So be it. For those of you who don't have tacomm displays, Captains Atkinson and Gibbons have arranged to project the briefing data."

A map of Cochise County appeared on the side of the regimental OCV.

"The Greys came down here to protect American citizens living near the southern border of the United States," Bellamack began. "Captain Gibbon just got word down from division headquarters at Diamond Point that about fifteen hundred bandits attacked Bisbee this morning at about oh-six-hundred. Yeah, I know: How come it took

127

this long for us to get the word when Bisbee is just over the hill to the east? Answer: It was a planned terrorist strike against Bisbee; all commercial communications media were cut. Why wasn't it detected by the Border Patrol? We don't know, but I suspect this strike was so well planned that whoever did it managed to spoof the BP sensors. Word got out via radio hams and truckers on their CBs. The Arizona Department of Public Safety was first alerted. Two Arizona DPS vehicles sent to check from Benson and Douglas were stopped and their occupants pinned down by heavy rifle fire. The BP swat team has been alerted and will be moving in to check Bisbee within the hour. We just heard of it because it took time for the word to get to the Arizona governor in Phoenix, who called Washington. It took this long before the Pentagon reacted and issued the necessary orders to Diamond Point, which relayed them to us. I'm madder than hell. If we're supposed to help out down here, we've *got* to clean up the communications procedures."

He turned and indicated the projected map. "I'm splitting the Greys into two tactical battalions for this operation. The reason will become clear in a moment. The First Tactical Battalion will consist of Carson's Companions and Morgan's Marauders. It will be under the command of Major Carson. He is the most senior company commander and has the greatest amount of experience in this sort of thing at this time. So he'll command the First. The Second Tac Batt will consist of the Warriors and the Ferrets with Captain Joan Ward, in command. The Second will follow in support to act as reserves and a fire base. The Intelligence Unit at Headquarters Company will bring up the rear and be ready to deploy birdbots on recon. I will accompany Major Carson. Both Tac Batts will depart Fort Huachuca immediately this briefing is completed. Major Carson, you will proceed as rapidly as feasible via Highway Ninety-Two to Nicksville, Palominas, and into Bisbee from the south."

"Sir?" Curt raised both his hand and his voice.

"Question, Major?"

"Yes, sir. We can get there quicker on Highway Ninety to the Mule Mountains and then into Bisbee via Federal Highway Eighty."

"True, except for the fact that the Mule Mountain tunnel on Highway Eighty is reported to have been blocked by an intruder demolition team," Bellamack explained. "In addition, that would put the regiment into Bisbee, and that's *not* where I want us to be! It's too late to protect Bisbee; the intruders are already in there. And, by the way, they're not having easy going, according to reports. The citizens of Bisbee are fighting back."

"Way to go!" Lieutenant Kitsy Clinton exclaimed.

"Yes, Lieutenant," Bellamack told her gently, not wanting to dampen the obvious enthusiasm of this new officer even though one does *not* interrupt the regimental commander except for a question during an Oscar briefing. "We will move around the south end of the Mule Mountains and engage the intruders from their western flank along their line of support into Mexico. The First Tac Batt under Major Carson will be on point because there isn't room to maneuver the whole regiment between Naco and Bisbee without crossing the border into Mexico. The rules of engagement say that we shall not—repeat, *not*—penetrate the Mexican border either in maneuvers or in hot pursuit. Anyway, I don't want to chase these bastards; I want to cut them off and then cut them down."

He looked up at the sky, which was full of the towering cumulonimbus clouds of the Arizona monsoon. It was going to rain like hell again in an hour or so, and it was going to be sloggy going even on the blacktop road of State Highway 92. "We've got sixty kilometers to move, so I want us to move at the same rate we did coming down here. When we cross the railroad track leading south to Naco, I want the regiment to come to full Zulu Alert. Stand by to dismount and deploy your warbots with you. We'll probably have to work off-road eastward from that point, and we could make contact with the intruders at any time. With any luck at all, we may pick up some tacair support from the Border Patrol's swat flight, but they may elect to support us instead because they're badly outnumbered unless they join with us. That's going to be a coordination problem I'll have to solve. I've requested tacair support from Luke Air Force Base, but I don't know if we'll get it or when we'll get it. But if we do get it, Captain Gibbon will serve as our communications node for air-to-ground communications. Major Carson, you will be in charge of forward ground observers and calling down any tacair strikes if we get any air support at all." He looked at his watch. "We've got an hour or a little more on the road, then about three hours of sunlight with the sun behind us. Any questions?"

There were none.

Bellamack looked around, a man very much in command of his unit now although this was his first Sierra Charlie combat experience. He was trying to recall everything he'd learned about personal combat years ago at West Point. To that he was trying to add what he was picking up very quickly from these experienced officers and NCOs. "Okay, Sierra Charlies are supposed to be mobile as a roadrunner and meaner than a javelina. Colonel Hettrick told me on the phone the other day that your specialty was to hold 'em by the nose with firepower and kick them in the ass with movement. Major Carson, the Greys will move out behind you. Dismissed!"

130

CHAPTER FOURTEEN

"There's the railroad!" Colonel Wild Bill Bellamack exclaimed, pointing ahead along the road through the dense downpour of rain.

A lightning bolt snapped down out of the sky, hitting an old wooden telephone pole alongside Highway 92. It was so close that it didn't bang, it cracked. The electrostatic ionization of the air was so great that Curt felt the hairs on his head stand up under his helmet.

"Colonel, we just crossed the San Pedro River," Curt objected. "We're too far from the Mule Mountains! That's the first railroad track. The second one is about six and a half kilometers farther east."

"Goddamn, it's raining so fucking hard I can't see those mountains!" Bellamack complained, his voice on edge.

Curt knew what it was; he felt the same things gnawing at his insides. And the same worries were running through his mind. It was precombat stress, the nagging questions of when and where and how it was going to start, who might get hurt, would I come out with everything intact, will I run? Even the most experienced combat soldiers suffered from it. In a way, Curt was glad to know that Bellamack was no different. "Uh, yeah, sure, Colonel. And would you please pull that poncho a little bit more around the hatch coaming so we can keep as much water as possible out of the ACV?"

Bellamack's dark eyes darted about under his helmet while rain poured off. He turned his head jerkily. "Damned if I want to blunder into those Mexican intruders in this crap! We'll stop here until we've located

131

ourselves," he suddenly decided.

It wasn't lack of guts, but the usual supercaution of the unknown before a fight. Curt told his regimental commander, "Sir, I know where the hell we are! Call up the inertial system coordinates on your helmet visor!"

Curt had already done so. Bellamack, who wasn't yet quite as familiar with this new-to-him piece of Sierra Charlie equipment, took a few seconds finding the proper command switch for his helmet visor display. The readout showed 31° 24' N × 110° 3' W."

"Now overlay the chart, Colonel. You'll see we haven't even crossed hundred-ten west longitude yet!" Curt explained.

"Yeah, but are you sure your system hasn't lost alignment?"

"Yes, sir! I set it at the benchmark back at the Fort Huachuca parade ground. This system doesn't drift even a thousandth of a second of arc in twenty-four hours! And, Colonel, don't worry about blundering into the intruders! They're under cover in this thunderstorm, too . . . if any of them are this far west of Bisbee, which they probably aren't because there's no reason for them to be out here."

"Well, I hope to God it stops raining damned soon!" Bellamack voiced his concern, still sounding very touchy. "Gibbon can't put up our recon birdbots until this storm is over. On top of which, we won't get any air cover because of this storm."

"We can fight without either, Colonel. We've done it before. We'll do it again," Curt promised him. It was frankly a pain in the ass having the regimental commander riding the point with him, but Bellamack wasn't going to learn Sierra Charlie operations by riding warm and dry back in his OCV.

And the colonel himself was thinking how much neater and drier regular warbot operations were. No one had to expose himself to the rigors of the weather; they lay on their linkage couches and let the warbots get wet. Thus

132

far, except for the phenomenal speed with which the Washington Greys could move on the road, Bellamack hadn't seen where this couldn't be done with neuroelectronic warbots. This was gut-tearing with suspense, not knowing where or how they'd contact the enemy, when the shooting might start, how the enemy might be deployed, how the enemy might fight. . . .

Eight minutes later, they crossed another railroad track. At the same time, the downpour ceased. Lightning bolts still struck down in the Mule Mountains to the north and thunder rattled the ACV. But the huge dark cloud with its skirt of rain was to the north of them now.

It was finally time to take some action other than speeding along the asphalt road. Curt didn't wait for Bellamack to issue orders. Bellamack didn't have to. Curt knew from the Oscar briefing what needed to be done now. "Tac Batt One, this is Tac Batt Leader! Exit the road to the right. Maintain roadway heading. Objective is the Bisbee Municipal Airport. Once off the road, Companion Alpha and Marauder Alpha deploy vehicles in skirmish line with Companion Leader as center, Companion Alpha to the left, Marauder Alpha to the right. Companion Bravo and Marauder Bravo, deploy vehicles as skirmishers three hundred meters behind Companion Alpha and Marauder Alpha. All units be prepared to halt, dismount, and deploy warbots on command."

As they were rolling down the shoulders of the road, Curt pointed to the northeast. "Colonel, may I suggest that Tac Batt Two break up and send Frazier's Ferrets with me over to the airport. Have Ward's Warriors continue along the road and take up a position to the west of the tailings pile. That will put Tac Batt One plus one company astride the main escape route with the Warriors covering the other."

Bellamack shook his head. "No, I wouldn't like to do that. Compromises the principle of mass. I'm splitting my force as it is, and that's a choke point over there. I'll need strength over there. They'll put the pressure on Ward to

133

break through when they learn she's only at company strength. And she has no room to maneuver," Bellamack pointed out.

"Colonel, if I read these intruders right, they aren't really looking for a fight. They aren't regular Mexican army troops; they're bandits . . . or peasants and miners hired by some local bandit chief to stir up trouble for God knows what reasons. They came in here with the idea of a quick, painless looting expedition. Except for their special units that cut the communications, they're probably undisciplined. When they find out we're between them and the safety of the border, they're going to break and run. If they run into Joan's outfit, she'll have them pinned against the Mule Mountains, probably with some locals behind them shooting up a storm. They won't want to take her on. If they do, we can reinforce quickly or even lay in artillery to help her. The main mass of enemy is going to try to go straight south toward the safety of the border. If they're blocked by Tac Batt One, they may try to go cross-country east of the airport, but I won't chase them. When I get Tac Batt One to the airport, that's our strong point. I'll put the road under fire. If they go east, I can lay the fifties and the Saucy Cans on them with air bursts. In either case, we can provide artillery support for each other because we'll be only about five klicks apart."

"Goddamn it, Carson, you've made this sound just like a field exercise at West Point!"

"Yes, sir! I haven't forgotten them. Those old field exercises work just great for Sierra Charlies," Curt told him. "Too bad they bear little relationship to Robot Infantry operations, but thank God the Sierra Charlies can profit from them!"

Bellamack looked around. "Damn if I don't think you're right, Carson! That sounds like a reasonable plan. Do it! But I'm going to get on my ATV and join Ward's Warriors. I think I should be there to help her out when the shit hits the impeller. . . ."

"Sir, Joan Ward is an experienced Sierra Charlie. She

can hack it," Curt advised him. "Stick here and see how your regiment really handles a fight!"

It was fairly flat country covered with creosote bush, a few shallow runoff ravines that had a little standing water in them from the thunderstorm, and little else to impede the cross-country progress of a Sierra Charlie outfit in its vehicles.

When they got within sight of the Bisbee Municipal Airport with its still-burning airport terminal building Curt could see that the road already had men on foot walking back toward the border. The Herreronistas both saw and heard the Greys coming across the flatland about a kilometer away.

Several of them turned and started to shoot. But even a 5.56-millimeter Penetrator round doesn't have very much energy left at a range of a thousand meters. Neither does a 7.62-millimeter NATO round, although its bullet is heavier. And both were fired at the Sierra Charlies.

The rest started to run toward the south.

"Hot damn!" was Jerry Allen's elated cry. "We caught them on the flank!"

"Tac Batt One and Ferrets all, this is Tac Batt Leader!" Curt snapped at once. "Multiple targets, dispersed troops, range one thousand meters. All vehicle units, open fire! Saucy Cans, open fire! All troops dismount, fight on foot, deploy your warbots! Hairy Foxes and Mary Annes, fire at will! Proceed eastward! Marching fire! Execute!"

This was it. The time for worry was over. The time to be scared shitless was over. There was little time left to think about it, only time to think about the fight itself. As Curt slid down the back end of his ACV to the ground, he heard Joan Ward call on the tacomm, "Grey Head, Warrior Leader here! I am encountering no resistance on the road. Request permission to occupy the high ground to my left where I can dominate the route out of town!"

Surprisingly, he heard Bellamack's reply: "Grey Head to Warrior Leader! Request confirmed! Take it! If you hold the high ground and can see us from up there when you

135

get there, you can also act as artillery spotter for us!"

With Henry Kester on one side of him, Colonel Bill Bellamack on the other, and the three of them flanked by the two M33 General Purpose warbots firing their 7.62-millimeter machine guns, Curt began to move toward the road dodging from bush to bush and trying to create as small a target as possible while he fired his Novia from his hip.

Curt heard rounds snapping past him, fired from the road. He didn't have time to be scared now. Besides, he knew that if he heard the snap of the bullet's shock wave, the round was already past him and it had missed.

Someone was shooting at him, but he didn't have time to worry about it. All he was concerned about was shooting to keep the other bastard's head down.

He had a lot of help from his robots and robot vehicles.

His ACV was firing its robotic 15-millimeter heavy machine gun over their heads.

The rounds from six Saucy Cans tore overhead, their 75-millimeter projectiles making noises like a velcro seam being ripped open. Alongside them in the fire support base were three companies' ACVs and RTVs, their 15-millimeter weapons also firing on robot command.

The highway ahead erupted in gouts of explosions and clouds of dust as thirty-six Hairy Foxes, thirty-six Mary Annes, and nine jeeps fired at anything that was warm and moving in that maelstrom, anything their radars or infrared sensors could spot that looked like a human being.

As this was going on, three old tac strike aerodynes bearing the Border Patrol identification marks wheeled in from the south and began to strafe the road. Curt saw six more overfly the airport and land to the east. The Border Patrol swat flight had arrived and was moving into position to help them out.

Amidst the confusion, smoke, noise, and dust, he heard a muffled "Uhf!" He turned to see Bellamack start to double over.

The colonel straightened up with a surprised look on his face, then started moving forward again. "Caught a round on my body armor!" he yelled to Curt. He was okay. He was walking and firing.

Within a few minutes, they were astride the road. The place was a mess. Dead and wounded lay everywhere. Curt had been right; the intruders were just peasant irregulars. They wore no uniforms, only the ragged shirts, trousers, straw cowboy hats, and leather *huaraches* of Sonoran peasants. They'd been armed with anything that would shoot. Some of them had been carrying loot from Bisbee.

"Grey Biotech, this is Tac Batt One Leader!" Curt called on the tacomm back to the support units. "We have no wounded, but the enemy does. Send the biotechs up as soon as I tell you the shooting's stopped." He wasn't going to expose his valuable noncombatant biotechs to enemy fire when he had no wounded of his own. Without waiting for an answer, he switched frequencies and told his unit, "Tac Batt One, this is Tac Batt Leader! Deploy along each side of the road! All Alpha units on the east, Bravo units on the west. Target anything coming south along the road. Ferret Leader, deploy into the airport, check for snipers in the hangars, recon to the east, and establish contact with the Border Patrol swat flight on the ground. Grey Intel, keep your birdbots on the ground. We've established contact."

The battalion's fire was now directed along the road toward Herreronistas trying to escape back toward the border from Bisbee.

"Grey Head, this is Warrior Leader," came Joan Ward's call. "We are established on the high ground to the west of the highway. We can target them coming out of town now! We can see targets moving to the east of the airport attempting to get around your roadblock. The BP is picking them off."

But at that point, all hell broke loose alongside the road. Curt looked up to see a flight of two USAF tac

137

strike aerodynes coming in from the south and firing directly into his units. They roared overhead and started to turn, obviously picking up ground fire from the intruders.

"Goddamn fucking Air Force! Why the hell didn't they check in before firing into us?" Bellamack suddenly yelled and punched up the air-ground control freak. His helmet visor displayed the tacomm call code. "Heavy Hedy Leader, this is Grey Head! You're firing into my troops along the road abeam the airport! Knock it off, you bastards!"

"Grey Head, this is Heavy Hedy One. Can you authenticate a Victor Mike?" The Air Force flight leader was asking for the usual code confirmation of a forward air controller's communication.

"You never gave me any goddamned Victor Mike code! Your wing commander at Luke said we didn't need one because we'd be the only ground controller here!" Bellamack fired back.

"Sorry, Grey Head! We need a Victor Mike confirmation!" The aerodynes were lining up for another pass. Two more skipped in over the hills to the northwest.

"Screw your Victor Mike!" Bellamack replied. "If you come back in over us shooting, I'll shoot your goddamned ass off! Curt, get a couple of your Hairy Foxes tracking those frisbees!"

"Please stand aside, Colonel," Master Sergeant Henry Kester said quietly as he popped the end caps off a 50-millimeter M100 Tube Rocket. "I'll try to miss the bastard when he comes over, but I'd kinda like to scare a little shit out of him without hurting him. After all, he's supposed to be on our side. . . ."

Bellamack permitted himself a quick grin. "Goddamn, now we've got to fight the fucking Air Force as well as the Battle of Bisbee! Curt, when your sergeant launches, have one of your Hairy Foxes put some tracer across the bastard's nose."

"Yes, sir! Got that, Jerry?"

"Roger! Edie Sampson's command tracking for a Hairy

Fox on override so it doesn't shoot him down."

"Heavy Hedy One, be advised that if you make another pass at us on the road abeam the airport, I've authorized my personnel to put some fifties tracer across your nose and ram a rocket up your ass! I hope to hell it doesn't hit you. I'd hate to kill you, but better you than me," Bellamack snarled into his tacomm headset.

"Oh, this should be fun . . ." the pilot started to say just as Kester fired.

Kester had deliberately aimed at the aerodyne's exhaust trail and told the M100 that was the target. He fired. The pilot saw the rocket coming. So did the wingman. The warhead detonated behind the aerodyne, peppering its upper side with fragments.

The sky ahead of the incoming aerodyne was then laced with bright tracers.

"Jesus H.P. Christ! You weren't kidding!" yelled the pilot.

"Goddamned right! You shoot at us, we shoot back," Bellamack told him calmly. "But if you don't shoot at us, we won't shoot at you. Agreed? Now, shall we get down to business? I have targets for you . . ."

"Roger, Grey Head, spot 'em for us, please!"

"Warrior Leader, this is Tac Batt One Leader," Curt called to Joan Ward on an impulse. "Are you in a position up there to direct some tacair strikes for us?"

"Roger, roger!" Joan Ward's voice was suddenly a little strained and urgent. "And I've got some targets up here that are giving us hell! A company-sized group on the ridge alongside us. These guys are wearing uniforms and trying to cover another group of unarmed men who seem to be carrying tech stuff. They're trying to get over the ridge here and get away to the west. We got trouble outgunning them!"

"Okay, Warrior Leader, you call the strikes. Tac air code is Heavy Hedy One and he's on channel nine," Curt told her. He switched frequencies. "Heavy Hedy One, this is Grey Control. I'm switching your spotter to Warrior

Leader, who is on the ridge just south of town and above the railroad tracks and tailings pile. Listen to her. She has neat targets for you."

"Roger, Grey Control. Hello, Warrior Leader, Heavy Hedy One is here. How can we help you, ma'am?"

"You can blow the shorts of a company of men about five hundred meters west of the tallest communications tower on the ridge here, the one with the strobe obstruction light flashing," Joan Ward told the pilot.

"Roger, we got it, and we're rolling in on them! We'll give them a long-range burst, and you tell me if we've got the right target."

From that point, it was standard air-ground activity. Another squadron of tac strike aerodynes showed up, and Curt called down their strikes on the mass of men now frantically trying to retreat down the road from Bisbee toward them.

By sundown, it was all over. Hundreds of surviving intruders had surrendered. A few still tried to penetrate the swat flight's personnel to the east of the airport. Some of the uniformed men on the ridge next to the Warriors had survived the tac air strikes, made it down the other side, and hightailed it for the border. Bellamack let them get away. "Whoever planned this thing needs to know his irregulars got their assholes reamed," he said. "So I'm going to let a few escape to Mexico."

Tac Batt One began moving north toward Bisbee.

And they got a hot reception.

CHAPTER FIFTEEN

The intruders—those who were left—were surrendering in droves. They ran down the road in panic, their hands in the air. They were running from something behind them.

Colonel Bellamack ordered the three available Bravo platoons from the Companions, Warriors, and Ferrets to deploy the three dozen M60 Assault warbots on the road while maintaining the M44 Heavy Fire warbots and the LAMVs with the 75-millimeter Saucy Cans as a potential heavy fire base. Actually, the Hairy Foxes and Saucy Cans weren't really needed at this point; they carried the heavy weapons for support of the other warbots in the assault or provided heavy fire in the defense. This was neither. Sierra Charlies with their Mary Annes and jeeps were now needed to round up and detain the surrendering intruders.

"Greys all, this is Grey Head! Everyone on the road! Shoot if you're shot at! Accept the surrender! Disarm these men! Make them lie facedown in the ditch on both sides. Put a Mary Anne in charge of a couple of dozen at a time," Bellamack snapped.

It was getting dark quickly after sundown. The twilight faded fast. It was difficult to see anything but shadowy forms in the growing gloom, much less identify them as friend or foe.

And there was trouble to the north. The Mexican irregulars kept coming as if they wanted to get away from something behind them.

Suddenly, while he was getting irregulars to throw down

141

what weapons they carried, Curt heard the snap of rifle fire going over his head. The Sierra Charlies and their warbots on the road began taking fire from the north. Sometimes the shooting was high. But far too many rounds plowed into surrendering Mexicans, were absorbed by the body armor of the Sierra Charlies, or ricocheted off the armor of the Mary Annes.

"Incoming small arms fire!" Curt yelled, not bothering with the tacomm.

An amazing order came from Bellamack. "Don't return that fire! Get the prisoners out of the way! Put your Mary Annes across the road in a phalanx as a shield to take the incoming!"

It didn't take long for the Washington Greys to learn who was shooting at them.

"Americanos! Americanos de Bisbee!" was the panicky shout from most of the Mexicans.

"Grey Head, this is Tac Batt One Leader! Colonel, where the hell are you?" Curt called on his tacomm because he didn't know where his commanding officer was at the moment. The melee on the road was a typical firefight: pandemonium laced with confusion, the typical "haze of battle."

"Yeah, Tac Batt One Leader, this is Grey Head, I see you!" came Bellamack's voice. "I'm over on the left at the side of the road."

"Roger, Grey Head! Contact! Hey, if my Spanish is any good, these guys are being chased by someone from Bisbee who's apparently armed. That's probably why we're taking incoming! Do we have communications with anyone in Bisbee?"

"That's what I suspected and why I don't want you to shoot back. Stand by and we'll see if we can't talk to them! Grey Intel, this is Grey Head! Gibbon, can you get on any of the Bisbee freaks?"

"No, sir! That's straight AM or FM, and on different frequencies than we use. They can't hear us because they don't have frequency-hoppers . . . and even if they did

142

they don't have the freak-hop program."

"Don't you have a CB rig?"

"Negatory, sir! We've never had to operate in an area with CB radios."

"Grey Head, this is Marauder Leader!" It was the voice of Alexis Morgan. "I'm up ahead of you. I speak Spanish! I've talked to a couple of surrendered Herreronistas . . ."

"Herreronistas?" Bellamack asked.

"That's what they call themselves," Alexis explained. "They're running from the people of Bisbee! They say the Bisbee people are armed and took back their own town. Been a day-long fight in the streets. The reason we're getting so many surrenders here is because the Bisbeans aren't taking prisoners!"

"Jesus Christ, an armed citizen militia!" Curt breathed. The people of Bisbee weren't bound by the Hague, Geneva, and Manila conventions; they were repelling an armed assault on their homes by bandits, and they were giving no quarter. Curt guessed they were fighting mad and, at this point, extremely unreasonable. He was right about his first guess and utterly wrong about his second.

Bellamack came to the same conclusion at the same time. "All Greys, stand by with flares! I want flares! Lots of flares! On my command, light up the sky! Grey Intel, I want Sousa's 'The Stars and Stripes Forever' alternating with 'America, the Beautiful' coming from every available warbot audio transducer and vehicle loudspeaker. Throw in the 'Battle Hymn of the Republic' if you've got it! And lights! All Grey warbots and vehicles, lights on! All Grey personnel, helmet lights on! Dammit, I need a flag! Anyone got the national colors?"

Curt was on the east side of the road not fifty meters from the entrance to the Bisbee Municipal Airport. In a little rock-lined circle before the smoldering ruins of the little airport terminal was a wooden flagpole. Unnoticed during the entire day, the Stars and Stripes had flown from that pole. No Herreronista had noticed. No intruder had hauled it down. Being untrained irregulars, they

143

didn't think about it.

"National colors coming up!" Curt yelled, overloading his tacomm unit. With incoming fire from the north coming in all around him, he got to the pole and hauled the flag down. The flag had been a little singed by the fire, but it was still recognizable as Old Glory.

"Got it, Colonel!" he said in less excited tones once he had the cloth folded in his arms.

"I'm on the road!" Bellamack identified himself, waving his arms. "Give it to me!" He grunted and spun around as his body armor took a rifle bullet in his side.

Curt joined him. "What's up, Colonel?"

Breathing hard from the effects of the bullet impact on his body armor, Bellamack reached out and took a corner of the flag. He tried to hook the upper corner to the muzzle of his Novia. "We've got to identify ourselves as American troops! I'm going to walk up the road with this."

"Hell, give me the other corner of that! I'll go with you!" Curt told him. "No one will recognize it unless we stretch it between us."

Bellamack didn't say anything but shot a quick glance at Curt, then ordered over his tacomm, "Greys all, let's have the flares! And the music! Give me lights! Put spotlights on Major Carson and myself! And cease fire NOW!"

The sky lit up. The loud sound of John Philip Sousa's proud march filled the air, somewhat distorted because it was coming from so many warbots and vehicles. And bright lights illuminated two men walking slowly up the middle of the road with Old Glory stretched between them.

What a goddamned fucking dumb thing to do! Curt suddenly thought. *Here I am in the middle of a firefight standing with my balls bared to the world holding a flag and hoping I won't get shot by my own countrymen with something my body armor won't stop!* But there wasn't time to do more than just think about it.

The firing down the road from the north stopped.

144

In Curt's helmet tacomm, he heard the calm voice of Captain Joan Ward, "Grey Head and Tac Batt One Leader, this is Tac Batt Two Leader! We're down off the mountain. We're among the Bisbee people. And we passed the word for them to stop shooting at you! But, Colonel, I've got to say that what you're doing is outstanding! You, too, Curt! Goddam, what a pretty show of light and sound! Real patriotic, sir! Makes me proud to be an American!"

Knowing Captain Joan Ward, Curt wasn't really sure whether she was serious or gently pulling her new colonel's leg for laying on a little bit of everything.

It made no difference. The firing had stopped. Down the middle of the road came a big man with thatch of snowy white hair and carrying an M22 and enough caseless ammo packs to keep shooting for days. He was accompanied by an older woman with a Beretta Modello 44 submachine gun held at the ready and another man gracefully carrying a Remington bolt-action hunting rifle with a big scope on top.

"Goddammit, Colonel!" the big man with the M22 called out. "If you'd identified yourself sooner, we wouldn't have put fire into you!" He slung the M22 and thrust out his leathery hand as he drew up to them. "Paul Metzger, Lieutenant Colonel, United States Army, retired, formerly of the Ready Rifles."

The introductions were quick. Metzger was accompanied by Martha Wagram, retired out of Quartermaster Corps, and Skip Weller, retired Regimental Sergeant Major of the pre-warbot 28th Infantry Regiment, the Lions of Cantigny.

"What the hell did you do there in Bisbee?" Bellamack wanted to know.

"These bastards came in this morning, shot a bunch of people, and set fire to the police station before we could get organized," Metzger explained.

"Took us a little time to get the word out on the local telephone system," Martha Wagram went on. "Paul's next-door neighbor, Hilda Stellenbach, is ex-Signal Corps and made sure the phones kept working, although the Mexicans cut the landline and microwave links out of town. Hams and truckers got through."

"I know," Bellamack told her. "That's how we found out."

"So these Mexican bastards thought they were going to come into Bisbee and terrorize the place the way they did down at Norman's ranch," Weller went on. "Once we got organized by wireless phones and CB bricks, turned out we outnumbered them. They shot up the town a little bit, but they didn't expect what we gave them . . . which was an ass full of bullets. Glad you came along, Colonel; saved us a little time cleaning them out of town and let us capture more of them. Most of them would have hauled ass beyond the border otherwise."

"Well, Sergeant, we got here as quickly as we could," Curt told him.

"Where the hell did you come from, Colonel?" Metzger wanted to know. "And what the hell kind of warbot outfit are you? Never seen this kind of stuff, and never run into warbot brainies who fight in the field alongside their bots. . . ."

Bellamack grinned. "The Army in its infinite wisdom decided that there was a place for the human soldier on the battlefield after all . . . and I just learned a hell of a lot more about the truth of that today because I'm a warbot brainy who's had to convert to the new Special Combat doctrine."

"Well, it's about time the Army came to its senses!" Skip Weller muttered. "I took early retirement when they converted the Lions of Cantigny to robot infantry. But I want to know what Paul wanted to know: Where the hell did you come from? The nearest post is Fort Bliss . . ."

"The Washington Greys were ordered from Diamond Point to Fort Huachuca to protect the border," Bellamack explained. "We got in there yesterday afternoon. Had to put the post back together because the civilian contractor had let it go to hell. Got the word of the Battle of Bisbee at fourteen-hundred hours this afternoon and moved out at once."

"You moved a whole regiment here from Huachuca and put them in the field in less than six hours?" Metzger was having trouble believing what he heard. "Are you airborne troops?"

"Negatory, Colonel," Bellamack replied, giving the man the honor of addressing him by his former rank. "We haul ass and we came by road. But damn I'm glad it's over. My unit hasn't had any sleep in forty-eight hours."

"Well, we'll sure as hell take care of that, Colonel," Metzger said firmly. "The Washington Greys are invited to spend the night in Bisbee. We may be a little shot up, but we've got food and beds! Although we probably could have chased these bastards back across the border ourselves, we're damned glad you showed up to cut them off. So let's get these Mexican prisoners put away and under guard so your troops can back off; then the Washington Greys are invited into Bisbee."

"Thanks, but I think we'd all better keep our eyes on these clowns until my division commander tells me what to do with them or the Border Patrol moves in and does their job," Bellamack replied. He really didn't want to turn these irregulars over to civilians, especially since the intruders had shot up the town and killed people. The Washington 'Greys would handle the prisoners carefully, and Bellamack suspected that the Border Patrol would assume jurisdiction as soon as they could get their people into Bisbee. After all, this wasn't an official war, and the Mexicans weren't legally prisoners of war. It was a legal nightmare that Bellamack would just as soon be handled by someone other than the Army. But he wasn't about to let these civilians do it; they might overdo it.

"Okay, what can we do in the meantime?" Metzger wanted to know.

"Let's get the prisoners down and counted. My biotechs are on the way to treat the wounded," Bellamack explained. "I've got to assemble the regiment and see if we got anyone hurt, which I don't think we do or I'd heard of it. Major Carson, if you'll take charge of all this and work with Colonel Metzger here, I need to get on the horn to General Carlisle and get some fresh orders."

"Yes, sir," Curt snapped. "We going back to Huachuca tonight?"

"Hell, no! As quickly as we can get things organized, I think it would be an insult not to accept the hospitality of the people of Bisbee. After all, they fought their own battle. . . ." Bellamack started to go and then turned. "Major Carson . . . Curt . . . You were right and so was your first sergeant. There isn't anything like being shot at and shooting back. Colonel Metzger knows what I mean. . . ."

"I sure as hell do, Colonel Bellamack!"

"Welcome to the club, sir," Curt said.

Bellamack reached over, took the other corner of the flag from Curt, folded it gently, and handed it to Metzger. "By the way, here's the flag. Major Carson took it off the airport flagpole, so it belongs to the City of Bisbee, not the Washington Greys. You may want to put it in a place of honor in City Hall as a memorial to your dead and a reminder of what your people did in the Battle of Bisbee. . . ."

CHAPTER SIXTEEN

This time, it wasn't just the American ambassador to the United Mexican States that called on Sebastian Madera y Francisco, the Mexican foreign minister.

Lane Hay Lansing III was accompanied on this serious occasion by the Honorable Robert Homer Root, the secretary of state of the United States of America.

And Root had a thick folder of photographs in his attaché case.

Madera met Root and Lansing not in his spacious office but at the huge door leading to his anteroom where ambassadors and guests were usually kept waiting.

"*Señor* Root, my abject apologies for not meeting you at the airport when you arrived," Madera gushed in English, thrusting out his hand. "Your trip was made very suddenly without adequate advance notice. Otherwise, you would have been tendered the proper protocol when you debarked. . . ."

Root was new at this job. The new U.S. president's nominee had been confirmed by the Senate only a month before, following the precipitous resignation of the previous secretary of state. The departure of Root's predecessor ostensibly and publicly had nothing whatsoever to do with the Persian Gulf arms scandal . . . and that's exactly what the Administration wanted people to believe as long as possible. The new president discovered to his chagrin that the crony whom he'd put in as his first secretary of state *might* have been involved. No one knew, and the man wouldn't talk. So everyone played it safe.

Root had very little background in diplomacy. He'd

come to the cabinet position from a long business career culminating in the position of CEO of a major international petro-energy corporation who had arranged a substantial series of contributions to the new president's campaign coffers. Thus, Root knew how to deal with foreign politicians when it came to business deals. And he understood the problems of cultural differences. But he was a management-by-objective person to whom results counted. He furthermore was a man of his word and didn't deal with others whom he suspected might not be. Diplomacy was important to him only when it facilitated closing the deal or solving a problem with a deal already underway.

So he shook Madera's hand in a perfunctory manner and replied brusquely, "I would have talked with you by satellite, *Señor* Madera, but the Bisbee incident is far too serious for just a teleconference. Besides, I must talk with you in a frank manner . . . and I don't want the details of our conversation showing up on an audiotape at some future time. . . ."

It was obvious to Madera that Root was very upset. Lansing had warned him of this. The real reason why Madera hadn't been at the airport to greet Root wasn't the haste of Root's trip. That was a convenient excuse because the Americans had simply ignored the usual protocol. Madera's reason revolved around the furor created even in Ciudad Mexico by the Battle of Bisbee. Because of the post-battle media coverage—it had happened too swiftly and too far away from major telecommunications nodes for the media to get real-time coverage—the Mexicans had come off as the villains. The Mexican people didn't like that. They were enjoying the fruits of the recent open-border treaties and they liked the results of free trade with the United States and Canada. The Bisbee incident put all of this in jeopardy. The Mexican government appeared powerless to stop future incidents. This threatened the government of Mexican President Alvaro.

Which is exactly what Herrero and the *hermanistas* were

hoping for.

"Please come in, Mister Secretary," Madera offered, speaking strictly in English because of the severity of the matter and Mexico's shaky position at this moment. He led the two Americans through the huge doors into his office and asked them to be seated around a low table rather than before his elevated desk.

Root opened his attaché case to reveal not only papers and folders but a series of electronic units. He touched the stud on one of these. "Mister Minister," he told Madera, "if the high-frequency sound of this equipment bothers you, I'm sorry. Although I don't believe your office contains any hidden microphones, I'd rather not take the chance at this moment that it does. And I would appreciate it if you would draw the heavy drapes over those windows. This must be a totally confidential meeting. If any of what we say happens to leak, Mexico could be harmed as much as the United States of America."

Madera was insulted by this as well as being upset that his own hidden microphones would not get a record of the meeting. But there wasn't very much that he could do about it except to point out, "Mister Secretary, you have a witness here in the form of your ambassador to Mexico City. May I be offered the courtesy of having my deputy present?"

Root looked at him and simply said, "No."

Madera bristled. "Come now, Mister Secretary! I insist!"

Root's bland expression didn't change. "Then there shall be no conversations and I cannot guarantee what the United States Congress will do as a result of failed talks this afternoon. And I will then have to give a statement to the news media that will not be favorable to the government of Mexico."

"My government will not stand still for media blackmail!" Madera insisted.

"Then police your side of our common border, sir, as your government agreed to do in the Treaty of Nogales."

Madera looked glum and said nothing. There was nothing he could say. He'd already said it to Lansing: The Mexican army wasn't strong enough to hold the country's southern border and police the northern border, too. Not until the budget permitted it, and not until the increasing trade with the rest of North America improved enough to help the Mexican debt situation.

The *Securidad*, while not being as large, well funded, and proficient as the CIA, had passed along to Madera the gist of what Root had in mind. Although the details weren't clear, Madera had discussed various scenarios at length with President Alvaro, and Madera had been given a free hand by the Mexican cabinet to deal with this matter within the framework of solutions determined by discussing the scenarios.

"Very well, Mister Secretary, but this does not bode well for the future relationships between the United States of Mexico and the United States of America," Madera replied.

"We have nothing to apologize for, Mister Minister," Root reminded him. "Your citizens were the ones who committed acts of aggression and terrorism in Bisbee, Arizona, the day before yesterday." He reached into his attaché case and withdrew a large, blue-covered folder with gold borders; Madera recognized it immediately even without seeing the Great Seal of the President of the United States of America on its cover.

He handed it to Madera and got right to the point in his usual all-business manner. "I herewith transmit to you an official note of complaint from my president to President Alvaro," Root went on. "I request that you forward it to your president at once. Both the government and the people of the United States of America are incensed by the invasion of the United States by armed Mexican citizens and by the destruction caused by these irregular troops and our efforts to protect ourselves and eject them from our country. The United States of Mexico has violated the sovereignty of the United States of America. My government herewith demands a public apology, the payment of damages and reparations, and action on the part of your government to ensure the safety of our common border against future armed incursions and intrusions."

Madera made a show of examining the contents of the thick folder. It included written documentation in addition to photographs. He'd expected this. Lansing had delivered a similar document — albeit less imposing since the previous one had come only from Root himself, not the president of the United States.

Madera spoke slowly and earnestly. "My government was immediately aware of the Bisbee incident by virtue of our own reports as well as reception of news media accounts," he pointed out. "My government has assured me that it will make an apology to your government for the incident."

"That's an excellent first step in repairing the international damage caused by the Bisbee incident, Mister Minister," Root told him frankly.

Madera nodded and went on, "I sincerely hope so, Mister Secretary. And in the interests of maintaining good relations between our two countries — which have improved so much since the Treaty of Nogales — and while my government had no control or authority over the bandits who penetrated your borders and entered Bisbee, my government has already agreed to study the requests of your government for payment of reparations. While it is unlikely that my government will be capable of payment of all reparations because of our current monetary problems, we will agree to meet with representatives of your government to negotiate a reasonable monetary settlement of your reparations claims."

"That's encouraging," Root said. "We look forward to your reply regarding that matter."

"May I work with Ambassador Lansing on this?"

Root shook his head. "I ask that you work through Ambassador Lansing, but negotiations will be made with me."

"I see." Madera closed the folder and stood up. "I thank you for your high level of interest in this matter, Mister Secretary, and for your personal visit concerning the problem. Be assured that I will give it my utmost attention and the highest priority."

Lansing started to get to his feet as well, but Root put out his hand and motioned for the ambassador to keep his seat. It was obvious that the secretary of state wasn't through with his discussion and that he wasn't going to allow the Mexican foreign minister to cut off the conversation and meeting so bluntly. In Root's mind, other matters had to be brought forth.

"I am sure you will, Mister Minister," the secretary of state told him firmly. "However, you haven't mentioned the willingness of your government to take whatever steps are necessary to maintain security on your side of our common border."

Madera continued to stand because this put him above the secretary and the ambassador so that he looked down on them. "It is not possible for my government to garrison the border with troops at this time."

"We know that," Root revealed. "Stationing troops along the entire border would be a massive military operation requiring large numbers of soldiers. We recognize Mexico's overwhelming concern over the protection of its border with Guatemala. My government applauds and supports in principle that commitment to your defense. But your government still maintains militia troops in Sonora and Chihuahua."

Madera shook his head sadly. "I am told by our minister of defense that the numbers of those troops are insufficient to garrison the border effectively."

"We agree." Root surprised him with this answer. It was apparent to Madera that the American intelligence system with its agents and its high-tech spy satellites knew a great deal about the disposition of Mexican military forces. This was the impression that Root intended to present; military budget cuts of the new Congress had severely

154

affected military intelligence operations, but Root did not intend to reveal that fact. "However, we believe there are two solutions to the problem, Mister Minister. Would you care to sit down and listen to them?"

Madera knew his dismissal ploy hadn't worked. His attempt to turn it into a power play hadn't worked either. Without comment, he resumed his seat and said nothing.

"I want your assurances that this conversation shall go no further than your president and minister of defense, *Señor* Madera."

Madera merely nodded his head. If the microphones were still working in spite of Root's antibug device, they wouldn't pick up a verbal answer from the foreign minister.

"My government has strong reasons to believe, based on many sources of information — not the least of which were those bandits who were captured and interrogated by American authorities before they were returned to Mexico — that these border intrusions have been made by private armies of drug lords, dealers, and smugglers."

"We have taken the initial steps to bring these powerful people and their organizations under control," Madera explained. "We are not strong enough and we did not have enough information to be able to attack them directly. Therefore, my government decided to 'legitimize' them by offering them protection in return for a modest tax on their transactions. This would, of course, be the first step in eventually shutting down their operations. The information concerning each drug operation could be made available to the authorities in your government."

"That would be helpful and is a point for further discussion," Root agreed. He wondered what the cost would be. But this was no time to bring that matter up. He had an enraged Congress and an upset populace pushing him into doing something quickly. "Will your limited militia forces in Sonora and Chihuahua be able to put some pressure on the headquarters of these private armies?"

Madera shook his head. He might be able to get the

minister of defense to make a cursory show of force in this direction, but he knew that federal troops were already spread far too thinly in the northern states. "All that I can say is that we shall try."

"My government also intends to put pressure on these private armies," Root went on. "Please be advised that we shall make a military response to any future intrusions across our border by groups of armed Mexican citizens. Furthermore, my government will authorize its military units to engage in hot pursuit of these bands into Mexico to break them up in what has been a sanctuary for them."

This surprised Madera greatly. He hardly knew how to respond to an openly announced threat of invasion of sovereign Mexican territory by the United States. This was one scenario that had *not* been considered by Alvaro and his cabinet. "You cannot do that, Secretary Root! My government will immediately take the matter before the UN Security Council as well as the World Court in the Hague!"

Root didn't smile as he replied, "But we can indeed do it, Mister Minister. A treaty exists between the United States of America and the United States of Mexico that allows military units of either nation to engage in hot pursuit across the border in relatively unpopulated areas. . . ."

"What?"

"The treaty was signed in 1882 by our secretary of state at the time, Frederick Theodore Frelinghuysen, and your president at the time, Manuel Gonzales," Root explained. "The treaty was intended to stop the Apache Indian raids in both countries. The treaty was invoked in May 1882 when Major General George Crook pursued the Sioux chief, Chato, more than three hundred kilometers into Mexico. It was invoked again in 1885 and 1886 when Captain Henry Lawton pursued Geronimo more than three *thousand* kilometers deep into Mexico. When the Indian Wars ceased, the treaty was apparently forgotten. However, it is still on the books and still in force. My government hereby informs your government that we intend to operate in accordance with that treaty and order our troops to engage in hot pursuit of armed groups of insurgents, irregulars, or private mercenaries that enter the United States of America intent upon using physical force for whatever reason. We shall pursue them back into Mexico and break them up. Because your military forces in the region are weak and therefore unable to handle the situation, we are forced to undertake the task for our own security and protection. We shall endeavor not to cause damage to the property of your citizens and not to harm your citizens who do not resist. However, we shall engage any military forces of the Mexican government that attack our forces while our forces are in Mexico in hot pursuit."

Root rose to his feet. Madera was far too stunned by this announcement to react. It came as a complete surprise even to Lane Lansing. Root turned to Lansing, "Come along, Mister Ambassador. We have other work to do. Thank you, Mister Minister, for the privilege of having this audience with you. My government looks forward to further discussions with your government in this matter if such discussions are warranted. Good day, sir!"

CHAPTER SEVENTEEN

The traditional Club which the Washington Greys had established in one of the big buildings around the Fort Huachuca parade ground wasn't as plush and modern as the one at Diamond Point. But Major Fred Benteen of the Service Company and Lieutenant Harriet Dearborn, the regimental supply officer, had found enough money in the regimental fund to contract the operation to a nearby Sierra Vista restaurant. A week after they'd relocated to Huachuca, the Washington Grey again had a good bar and good food for Stand-tos and off-duty hours.

It was something well appreciated by both officers and NCOs alike. The Club, open to officers and NCOs, was a long-standing tradition in the Washington Greys. If officers and NCOs wanted to meet separately, that was their prerogative. The mixed Club had evolved when the Greys converted to a Robot Infantry unit over a decade ago. The distinction between officers and NCOs slowly disappeared as it had in the United States Air Force because the RI depended heavily on high technology as the USAF had for a hundred years. Officers were highly educated leaders and managers whereas the NCOs were highly trained technicians. Because of the esprit de corps of the Greys, that distinction was widely recognized by all just as the distinction between salaried and hourly employees is recognized within a nonmilitary corporation. No longer were the NCOs mere farm boys or recruits from city gangs, people with no education or training. NCOs weren't even assigned to an RI regiment like the Greys until they'd emerged successfully with specialist ratings from difficult Army training schools . . . even NCOs in the combat platoons. The United States Army, a purely volunteer force, had grown up and socially come at least as far as the late twentieth century.

The Club was also a morale booster, because the other facilities at Fort Huachuca were old and relatively primitive and the Greys suffered under the constant anticipation of another alert that might lead them into another Battle of Bisbee.

But nothing had happened now for over a week.

"One damned patrol after another!" Captain Alexis Morgan griped to Curt as they sat together in a corner of the Club one evening.

"Well, at least we're getting to know the terrain pretty well," Curt told her.

"Every goddamned rock on the hillsides and every goddamn pothole in every road," she complained savagely. This wasn't like Alexis. Curt sensed that the additional burden of company command was telling on her. "That doesn't bother me; it could be worse. What's tough to hack is the knowledge that those insurgents are going to strike again. I know it, Curt. I just know it! They've got to! That seems to be their strategy. That's what I got out of the interrogation of the prisoners before we hauled them back to the border."

Curt swirled the ice around the drink in his glass. "I don't think we have enough information yet. The men we interrogated didn't know very much, Allie," he remarked, using the familiar diminutive of her name that she permitted only Curt to use. He felt very close to Alexis. He'd been her company commander when she'd first joined the Greys out of West Point and Fort Benning, a raw, young second lieutenant who wanted to control the might and power of neuroelectronic warbots. But she'd been one of the first to adapt well to the personal dangers of Sierra Charlie officer.

She nodded. "That was to be expected. They were 'temporary mercenaries,' unemployed farmers and miners who were hired, given a little training, and promised their pick of the loot of Bisbee on top of their pay. Have you ever heard of their immediate commander, the man who recruited them, Pancho Garcia?"

"A lot of Panchos and a lot of Garcias in both Arizona and Mexico," Curt replied.

"Well, the man's first name isn't an ordinary Mexican given name, but it is an everyday nickname or *apodo*. And Garcia is as common a surname in Mexico as Smith is in the United States," Alexis said from her own experience as an army brat raised at Fort Bliss and therefore fluent on colloquial Spanish. "But why do they call themselves 'Herreronistas'? That doesn't make sense to me."

Curt shrugged. "If you don't know, no one in the Greys knows."

"We might have found out if we'd caught the unit on the ridge that was undoubtedly an elite outfit accompanied by a tech support bunch. They seemed to be elite personal troops of some sort," she recalled. Then she added savagely, "But they got away to the southwest!"

"Couldn't stop them all. Joan and her Warriors were outnumbered and outgunned up there on the ridge. If we hadn't been able to call in air support for her, we would have gone up there to get her . . . and that could have been expensive. Very expensive. An uphill fight all the way."

Alexis looked up from her drink and suddenly said, "I think I can make an educated guess at the Herreronista thing."

"Oh?"

"The word means 'the blacksmith's men.' *Herrero* means 'blacksmith.' But I can't figure out any significance to that," Alexis said puzzled.

Something clicked in Curt's memory. "I once knew a man called Gordo Herrero. Roommate and classmate at West Point. He was a Mexican national. Very sharp guy. Won an appointment by being an honor graduate of a military school over in New Mexico," Curt explained, trying to remember everything. "He went back to Mexico to serve in the army there. He said something about the fact

160

that his father wanted him to do it. He didn't have to. He had a hell of a lot of money, far too much for his own good. In four years, I never did figure out how he got so rich. He once told me his family was well-off in Mexico. I didn't probe because that was all he'd tell me. But he was an outstanding cadet, and he graduated ahead of me in the class." Curt sighed and recalled bitterly, "He also married the post beauty, a girl from Newburgh, real Nordic goddess named Fredrica Nordenskold."

Alexis sensed something in the way Curt said that, so she observed, "You'd fallen for her, too, hadn't you?"

"Did I say that? No, I didn't. But, yes, Freddie and I dated," Curt admitted. "It could have been the real thing, but Freddie had expensive tastes. She was too rich for my blood. When it came right down to a choice, she went for Gordo Herrero." He shrugged. "Ah, well, we've all got long-lost loves in our backgrounds, don't we?" Curt didn't need to refer to Len Spencer of the *New York Times* who'd romanced Alexis across Namibia in order to get a good story.

"Yes, we do, and there's no need to bring them into the conversation now," Alexis replied candidly with some sharpness in her voice that Curt hadn't expected. But she picked up the thread of Curt's conversation. "So this Mexican went home, taking your bird with him, eh?"

"Yup, and that's too bad in my estimation."

"Oh, really? I didn't think that losing a girlfriend would hit you that hard, especially not at the start of a career in the Robot Infantry."

"It did at the time, Al. But I was primarily referring to the fact that the United States Army lost a potentially outstanding officer. Gordo Herrero became a student of insurgent and guerrilla warfare . . . which is what we're involved in now."

"I see. You're right; he probably would have been a good Sierra Charlie . . . and we could sure use more outstanding Sierra Charlies."

Curt set his glass on the table and looked at her. "Incidentally, if I haven't told you before, you proved you're a good company commander at Bisbee. You did an outstanding job commanding the Marauders there."

"I had a good teacher, and you did tell me," she reminded him.

"I did?"

"Yes, that night after the episode in the Copper Queen Hotel bar when a lot of Bisbee people were plying you liberally with food and drink," Alexis said. "You were feeling no pain afterward, as I recall, even though you had one hell of a bruise on your left hip where your body armor had stopped a slug. But thanks again, anyway."

"How the hell did you find out about my hip bruise?"

"You don't remember much about that night, do you?"

Curt sighed. "I hadn't had much sleep in about forty-eight hours, Allie. None of us had. We'd charged down the hill from Diamond Point. We tried to put an old Army post back together. And we fought a major battle outnumbered ten to one. Those weren't three ordinary days. I don't remember very much, but, as I recall, you were pretty beat, too."

She nodded and smiled. "I was. We'd both been shot at. I wasn't as bushed as you were; but at least *I* was motivated enough to find where you were bunked in the Copper Queen Hotel that night. And I recall neither of us was worth much of a damn. But, oh my! That was a wonderful old brass bed! It certainly did its job. But tell me: Are we getting old, or was something wrong?"

"It improves with age like good wine, so we were probably both dead tired," Curt ventured to guess.

"I wonder how much action that old bed has seen?"

Curt doodled on a paper napkin. "Well, let's give it a hundred years or so. Round that off to make it about forty thousand nights. Figure roughly, oh, say, a fifty percent occupancy level and a fifty percent duty cycle. Ten thousand actions, I'd guess."

Alexis looked up at the ceiling thoughtfully. "Well, as I recall, this is the Wild West where men are men and women are damned glad of it. I think ten thousand might be a very conservative number."

Curt snorted and retorted. "But this is a place where the climate's fine for men and mules but hell on women and horses . . ."

"You will pay for that one," she promised him.

"No, I'm paying." Colonel Wild Bill Bellamack walked up to the table, pulled a wooden chair around, and sat down. "Next round, anyway. But if I'm interrupting anything, I'll bug out. Rule Ten is down right now."

"Colonel, you're not interrupting anything yet," Alexis explained. "Except perhaps a display of Major Carson's ego. Or my perfunctory and rapid deflation thereof. Incidentally, congratulations on the citation and award. The Silver Star is quite an honor, sir!"

"Your tactical battalion commander also deserves a compliment for the valor that led to his Bronze Star, don't you think?" Bellamack reminded her.

"At the time," Curt admitted, "I wasn't trying to be particularly brave. And I wasn't trying to be a hero. I was thinking it was a goddamned stupid thing for me to do, grabbing the corner of the flag and walking up the road with the colonel."

"Oh, you knew your body armor would stop the small arms stuff," Alexis told him.

"I didn't think about it," Curt admitted.

"Neither did I," Bellamack added. "That was the first time I'd really been shot at. It's a real sensation taking that first round in the body armor. I wondered what the hell happened until it dawned on me I'd been hit."

"I've never gotten over it," Alexis admitted. "I took one in the helmet in Trinidad, and *that* I never want to happen again!"

"She's right: she never quite got over it, poor girl," Curt kidded and told Bellamack, "I understand it shakes up the brains a little bit, Colonel."

Alexis started to retort, but said nothing. Instead, she just glared. Sometimes her sense of humor suddenly evaporated. This was one of those times. Curt could kid her in front of close friends, but she wasn't quite up to it in front of a new regimental commander whom she was getting to

163

know slowly. She was perhaps more reserved than Curt in accepting new colleagues and friends, probably a consequence of her upbringing as an Army brat coupled with her own career in a close outfit—which both Carson's Companions and the Washington Greys were. And, as Curt was noticing, Alexis Morgan was subtly changing.

But she did raise her glass to Bellamack. "Welcome to the club of them what has been shot at, Colonel."

"Let me get a drink, and then I can drink to that. And you did welcome me to that club. All of the Greys did. Don't you remember?" Bellamack asked.

"We did?"

"Yes, Captain, you did. At the bar in the Copper Queen Hotel."

"It was a little drunk out that night," she admitted.

"True." Bellamack gave his order to a civilian waiter who scurried over to the table at his wave. Not all citizens of Sierra Vista were as uninterested in the return of the United States Army as that civilian contractor's supervisor the night they arrived. The Greys and the forthcoming 17th Iron Fist Division meant business in a town that had reverted to a retirement and minor tourist center. Bellamack then turned back to Curt and said candidly, "That night, I discovered something very unusual about the Washington Greys."

"Oh? What might that be, sir?"

"I've served most of my career in one unit, as we all do," Bellamack explained to his two combat company commanders, "except for temporary assignments to various staff schools and the Army War College. I've even studied other units. But I must tell you that I've never known a regiment that's as . . . well, as *adult* as the Washington Greys."

"Adult, Colonel? I'm not sure I understand," Curt replied.

"Quite bluntly, Curt, this isn't a chicken-shit outfit," Bellamack remarked. "First of all, the regiment has a tradition and all personnel uphold it . . ."

"Goes back a long time, Colonel," Alexis reminded him.

"Our crest derives from George Washington's own coat of arms. Our colors have never been disgraced, and no one wants to be the first person to do that."

"Well, Colonel, there have been times," Curt reminded him. "Hettrick had us fly a black burgee until we reaffirmed ourselves at Ojomuise."

"And the people who caused that are no longer with the regiment, as I suspect you've noticed?" Alexis added.

"Naturally. They've gone elsewhere under conditions that didn't ruin their careers but ensured they'd never be in a position where they could make those same mistakes again," Curt added, thinking of the two company commanders who'd had trouble in Namibia, one as a wimp and the other with too much tiger juice.

"And that's the second factor," Bellamack explained. "Armies used to be mobs of kids . . . mostly teenagers who were impressed into service by conscription or misfits who couldn't find regular work elsewhere. This outfit is made up of adult, dedicated, knowledgeable people who have a decent respect for one another . . . and damned little internal politics over turf."

"You can thank Colonel Belinda Hettrick for that," Alexis told him.

"And generations of regimental commanders who handed her that legacy, Colonel," Curt pointed out, then added after a brief pause, "But Colonel, we do occasionally have disciplinary problems. The company commanders and platoon leaders sometimes see it, and they deal with it when it comes to their attention so that you don't get burdened. Mostly, it's handled by our first sergeants and platoon sergeants . . . who are goddamned good practical managers, by the way."

"Oh, I've watched them operate!" Bellamack exclaimed. "But this outfit still amazes me."

"Colonel," Alexis ventured to take the bit in her teeth, "I know that all outfits aren't like the Greys. I know you had the misfortune to come to the command of this regiment from one that ran into trouble. I think I can speak for the officers and even the NCOs: This is our profession, and the Greys are our home and our family. Each of us made the choice to be here . . . and it wasn't easy getting into the Greys. Gee-One knows that we screen pretty thoroughly and that if they send us a corker we'll see to it that the jerk voluntarily asks for a transfer out. It's happened, but not often. Also, we're the first personal combat regiment in the United States Army *ever* to have men and women fighting side by side in personal combat. And both the men and the women of the Washington Greys are very proud and jealous of that achievement."

Bellamack hitched his chair closer to the table and put his elbows on it. He'd tried to get to know Captain Alexis Morgan during his thus-far brief tenure as regimental commander. She wasn't as easy to get to know as Captain Joan Ward, who tended to be a bit more earthy. He also knew from observation that Alexis and Curt were a pair but also weren't overly possessive. In this quiet corner of the Club, accompanied by Curt, he suddenly discovered she was opening up to him a bit. "You intend to stay in the profession?" he asked.

"Where else could a woman find such interesting companions and such exciting work? Okay, some of the work gets dangerous, but not a lot of it. And the danger puts some teeth into it. Who the hell wants a job without knowing that you could lose the whole thing if you screwed up? Oh, some people, I guess, but not me!"

"I take it then, Alexis, that you don't intend to have a family?"

Alexis looked pensive for a moment, then told him, "I want very much to have a family. But not yet. Colonel, ask me again when I've got twenty years' service. Maybe I'll pack it in then if all other factors are right. Biotechnology is good enough right now that I'll still be able to have kids then. On the other hand, maybe I'll go for thirty-and-out, but I don't think the biotechnologists will be able to help me very much at that point. In any event, I don't have to make the decision yet. And Curt Carson taught me never to force a decision; if you don't have all the elements in hand, wait until you do . . . Except, of

166

course, in combat when you probably don't have that luxury and you've got to do something with what you've got."

Bellamack nodded. Alexis Morgan should certainly have no trouble finding a husband, he noted, and she certainly would have no problems bearing children. She was certainly not unattractive, and she was an extremely well fit and abundant but ample woman. He grinned and told her, "Well, I'm coming up on that twenty-and-out decision one of these days in the not-too-distant future myself. I'll have to decide on the fifty percent retirement pay, trying to find a new line of work, and having a family . . . or staying for thirty and counting."

"Do you have a fiancée?" Alexis asked.

Bellamack grinned impishly in a totally uncharacteristic fashion. "Let's excite Rumor Control Headquarters! Allow me to reply to that by saying 'several.' "

"Oh, my, that *will* be juicy, Colonel!" Alexis smiled.

"You may feel free to 'control' that rumor if you wish," the colonel added, then said, "I want to talk to some of the others here tonight. Something new has surfaced. I don't want to charge into the problem until we get some staff studies done and get some inputs from the combat companies. So I don't want to call an Oscar briefing yet, or even a planning session. But we need to start doing a little thinking and planning about the immediate future, not our far futures." He looked at both of them and said, "Call this one of Colonel Wild Bill Bellamack's strange new ways of doing things, but I just want to mention it to the two of you privately first. Start getting ready for the consequences of this: General Carlisle told me by telecomm a short while ago that the rules of engagement have been changed . . . all the way from the Oval Office. On the next Herreronista incursion into the United States, we will engage in hot pursuit into Mexico immediately to put a stop to this once and for all. No action required at this moment. Enjoy the evening."

CHAPTER EIGHTEEN

In the meantime, Curt had some other problems to occupy his attention.

Early one morning, he was preparing to conduct a training session with the Companions into the Huachuca Mountains. Curt felt they needed to have the experience of maneuvering, patrolling, and fighting in rugged terrain such as they might encounter in Mexico.

But before he got the Companions out in the rugged vastness of the mountains, he felt he should have a serious talk with his new platoon leader, Second Lieutenant Kathleen "Kitsy" Clinton.

He knew from the trek down from Diamond Point and the Battle of Bisbee that she was smart and on the bounce. But she had also shown herself to be somewhat headstrong, and a little bit resistant to things that were new and somewhat different from what she'd been taught. Curt was worried that she might be like many new young officers who were exceptionally proud of having made it through four tough years at West Point and then the very practical and nonacademic training of the Robot Infantry School at Fort Benning—which was another assignment that was certainly no bed of roses. He was concerned lest Kitsy Clinton come to the conclusion that her eduction was complete, that she could stop learning, and that she could put her brain in deep freeze and depend on what she'd already learned.

Curt wanted to head off that possibility right at the start. He'd seen it become the downfall of many officers, including some who'd served recently in the Washington

Greys. They'd been excellent warbot brainies but hadn't been able to become Sierra Charlies. They'd been unable to make the transition, either because they'd forgotten how to learn or because they discovered that getting shot at wasn't for them in spite of their public bravado.

It was one of his duties to bring new officers along so that they could someday command a company. If no one was available to take over, Curt couldn't be promoted up the line when the time came and the vacancy opened up. As in civilian industry where the advice was, "A good manager trains his own replacement," Curt wanted to make sure that Clinton's career wasn't stunted because he hadn't done his job properly as her company commander.

Kathleen Clinton's big problem was realizing that the M60 Mary Anne mobile assault warbots in Alpha Company weren't exactly like the neuroelectronic warbots she'd been trained to operate at Fort Benning.

So he called her to his ACV shortly before he mustered the Companions for the exercise.

"Good morning, Major!" she said brightly as she came in, whipped off her helmet, and snapped a salute.

He returned her salute and indicated the bench seat along the wall. "Good morning, Lieutenant. Please sit down. If I haven't told you before, I think you did well during the Battle of Bisbee."

"Thank you, sir!"

"In fact, your conduct was exemplary because it was your first time in combat and under fire," he added. "Many new officers get scared . . ."

"Sir, I didn't have time to get scared," she snapped.

He shook his head. "Oh, yes, you did, and you know it. I'll get to that in a minute. But first of all, Kitsy, you've got to learn that our Sierra Charlie voice-commanded warbots are a hell of a lot different from the NE warbots, where you became part of them through linkage. These machines of ours are *not* part of us. They're separate machines that must be given orders and then

169

monitored to ensure that they don't get into a situation the orders can't handle. Our Sierra Charlie warbots are akin to the old infantry grunt. Although they've got Mark Five AI, they're even more stupid than many of the conscripted infantrymen of five hundred years ago. Sure, they're smart enough but they're *not* the same as the infantry soldiers of the American Army in the last hundred years. You'll never have disciplinary problems with them, but they're about as bright as a three-year-old child. You've got to treat them as being somewhere half-way between a real bright computer and an NE warbot that's an extension of your own mind. You must remember that they can do a little thinking for themselves but they *must* have continual supervision."

"So please tell me exactly what I'm doing wrong, sir," Clinton wanted to know.

"Your squad leaders Koslowski and Elliott must stay with the three Mary Annes they're each responsible for commanding," Curt explained. "Let Nick Gerard handle the minute-by-minute running of your platoon so you can do your job as the platoon leader."

"I thought that's what I was doing, sir," Clinton remarked, puzzled.

"No, you're keeping your sergeants grouped near you. You're splitting your platoon into two action elements: humans and warbots. You keep your sergeants as part of your fire base and you assign the dangerous part of the mission to your warbots."

"Isn't that what warbots are for?" she wanted to know, recalling her training at Fort Benning with neuroelectronic warbots where the bots did all the dangerous grunt work while the troopers ran the operation from the protected safety of the armed linkage vans.

Curt shook his head. "No, a Sierra Charlie warbot is more than a substitute for a human soldier, Kitsy. It's a cross between a miniaturized special-purpose tank and a very strong but not-so-smart infantry private. You're not

170

letting your sergeants run the platoon that way."

"I was under the impression that we did reasonably well during the Battle of Bisbee," she recalled. "In fact, Major, you just commended me for it."

"I was commending your action under fire," Curt reminded her. "That was your first combat action, wasn't it?"

"Yes, sir."

"How do you feel?"

Kitsy Clinton hesitated, then replied with some hesitation, "Different. Strange. But I'm okay now, Major!"

"Don't be so sure about that. I did indeed commend you; you proved you're a fighter. But you didn't prove that you're a leader. If I know Nick Gerard—and I do—he covered your ass for you and kept you from making deadly mistakes," Curt pointed out. "From what I saw, Gerard ran your show but let you take the credit as the platoon leader. You were new and green, and Sergeant Gerard didn't want you to be embarrassed or to usurp your command authority."

"Major, I don't want my record to be blemished by a negative operational or evaluation report . . ." she began.

"Kitsy, who said anything about anything going in your evaluation report?" Curt interrupted her. "You're an officer now and you must not act like you're being graded on every move you make. I must fill out your evaluation form annually, so it isn't your isolated daily actions that count but your overall performance during the year. Part of the evaluation is my impression of your ability to seek self-improvement, your adaptability to new situations, your potential, and your ability to accept this sort of constructive criticism. You're still in training and you will be for a long time." He paused for a moment, then added easily, "Hell, Kitsy, we're all still in training, because we're doing something new and writing the book as we go along. Let me say one more thing: Some people might think that your propensity for surrounding yourself with your sergeants indicates a latent fear of being exposed to incoming fire."

Kathleen Clinton bristled. "Major, I'm not afraid of combat or I wouldn't have opted for the RI and would not have applied for assignment to the Greys!"

"I'm sure that's so. But when you try to tell me you weren't scared before the shooting started near Bisbee, I know you're covering up. Why? Because combat is one of the most frightening things a human being can face — the fear of immediate death in an unknown and unsuspected manner or, even worse, the fear of being mutilated, which is even stronger in women than men. We *all* face that sort of fear, every one of us, every time we go into an engagement. You may or may not feel safer with your sergeants around you. But, believe me, if you let your sergeants get out there and deploy their warbots properly, the warbots will take the incoming so that you and your sergeants can handle the human side of the situation: Doing what no warbot can ever be built or preprogrammed to do, which is tackling the unsuspected."

Kathleen Clinton was chagrined. She suddenly looked very vulnerable. "I'm sorry if I failed you and you think I'm a coward, sir."

"I didn't say that, Kitsy. You're no more of a coward than any of us. We all get scared," Curt admitted. "Now on this upcoming exercise, I want you to work with Platoon Sergeant Nick Gerard and let him work in turn with Koslowski and Elliott, who are, by the way, two very sharp fighters."

"Yes, sir. I know they must be. They were both promoted to sergeant as a result of Namibia," Clinton remarked. "I'll do my best, Major."

"I know you will," Curt said gently.

The ACV's tacomm chimed, and Curt called out, "Companion Leader here!"

"Curt, this is Grey Person," came the voice of Major Pappy Gratton, the regimental adjutant. "I hate to do this to you, but I've sent a video crew over to see you."

"News media people? Oh, great!" Curt replied. "I'm about to depart on a training exercise, Grey Person. Can I sluff them off on someone else?"

"Negatory, Companion Leader," came the reply. "They're a documentary unit. They'll be with us for several weeks at least. Grey Head suggested that this crew start out with you since you're the oldest and most experienced Sierra Charlie unit in the regiment."

"Thanks a lot, Grey Person!"

"Don't blame me!" Gratton's voice came back. "The orders came all the way down the line from PAO in the Pentagon. According to Major Hampton, you did such a fine job with that reporter in Namibia that you've got this one."

"Tell Wade he just used up about a dozen favors," Curt snapped back. "Roger, Grey Person. Where are they?"

"Should be pulling up near the ACV within the next few minutes."

"I'll go watch for them. Companion Leader out!" Curt sighed and told Kitsy Clinton, "Head-to-head session over. Let's go find out who these people are, what they want, and how fast we can shuck them off onto another company. As a matter of fact, I may assign you to shepherd them."

"Me? Why me?" she asked in surprise.

"Because you'll have to explain everything to them," Curt told her, "and you'll learn a lot about the Sierra Charlies in the process. . . ."

The two of them went out the rear ramp of the ACV in time to see a bright international orange four-wheel-drive pickup truck with a camper shell drive into the Greys' bivouac. It was abundantly obvious where it was from and what its purpose was. Emblazoned across its sides were the bright, electric blue words, "KFCB-TV Phoenix." Below that in smaller (but not much smaller) letters was "Around Arizona with Ed Levitt."

A tall young man opened the cab door and climbed out. He had a shock of yellow hair that fell over his eyes the a face of a typical all-American boy. This surprised Curt, because television personalities were usually slicked-up, urbane, air-sprayed, blow-dried, super-pretty people. This one looked like the guy next door. He was dressed in well-used jeans and a khaki shirt with sleeves rolled up. The cowboy boots he wore were splattered with mud and covered with dust.

He walked up to Curt, extended his hand, and said in a boyish voice, "Howdy, I'm Ed Levitt, KFCB in Phoenix!"

Curt shook hands with him and introduced himself and Lieutenant Clinton.

Levitt was accompanied by a young woman with long, dark hair, a lean and aesthetic face with a large mouth, and a powerful body that was far from feminine although she wore rather tight jeans and a plaid cotton shirt along with large, very dark sunglasses over her big eyes. "This is Marjorie Bogen," Levitt introduced her.

She just waved at the two of them. "Hi!" she said in a surly, disinterested manner without much enthusiasm.

"Marge is my camera operator," Levitt explained. "She wrestles the camera and other gear while I wrestle the script and commentary."

"Welcome to Carson's Companions," Curt told both of them. "What can I do for you?"

"Nothing," Levitt replied pleasantly. "I'm here because this is part of my job. Marge and I travel Arizona looking for the sort of interesting human angle stories that the other crews don't find in the big cities of Phoenix, Tucson, and Flagstaff. Sort of down-home, old West stuff."

"Well, Mister Levitt, we're certainly a long way from the old Wild West here," Curt tried to point out.

Levitt grinned. It was an infectious grin. "No, if you guys do what I expect you're going to do and follow the

174

orders you've been given, this is going to be just like General Crook or Captain Lawton chasing Geronimo into Mexico back in the nineteenth century! And *that's* going to be a damned good story, Major! So that's what Marge and I are going to do: stick with you like glue into Mexico!"

"You seem pretty damned sure we're going to do that," Kitsy Clinton observed.

"Yes, ma'am," Levitt told her. "That's what came over the AP wire from Washington last night, which is why we're here today."

"We've been sort of isolated from the news reports down here, Mister Levitt . . ." Curt began.

"Call me Ed, please. Here's the hard copy off the wire last night." The television personality handed Curt a rumpled sheet of paper.

Curt didn't exactly like what he read:

WASHINGTON (AP)—Spokesmen for the State Department and the Pentagon announced this afternoon that American Army units have been repositioned along the border in readiness to repel any further invasions of the United States by bandits from Mexico which have twice caused death and destruction in southern Arizona. However, now American robot infantry units will be able to engage in hot pursuit of bandit gangs into Mexico, where they will attempt to locate and isolate the headquarters of these terrorist units.

Invoking a little-known and long-forgotten treaty signed in 1882, American warbot units will be allowed to penetrate as far into Mexico as necessary.

Mexican President Alvaro commented that the Mexican army could not spare troops from the Guatemalan front at this time and welcomed the assistance of the United States in putting down these terrorist bands in the Mexican states of

175

Sonora and Chihuahua provided that American forces acted within the provisions of the treaty and did not destroy the property of innocent Mexicans or otherwise harm noncombatants. Alvaro pledged the cooperation of Mexican authorities in Sonora and Chihuahua.

Senator Blackmore (D., Minn.) immediately introduced a bill in the Senate late today that would revoke the old treaty and withhold funds from the Department of Defense for this activity. However, Senator Ashurst (R., Ariz.) quickly pointed out that the Senate can only confirm an international treaty and cannot revoke it. Revocation can be made only by executive order of the President according to the verdict of the federal courts when former Senator Barry M. Goldwater of Arizona sued the federal government over President Jimmy Carter's revocation of the Panama Canal treaties and turned control of that waterway over to the Panamanians.

There was more, but Curt didn't read it. Again, the Washington Greys were going to be the focus of media attention as they'd been in the Namibian operation. It didn't make him very happy. The newshawk on *that* mission had caused him all sorts of grief.

Ed Levitt was a handsome young man with a boyish appearance that could cause women of all ages to want to mother him. In fact, that was part of his appeal on the tube.

Now Curt had no direct command over Captain Alexis Morgan as a subordinate . . . and Alexis was an incurable romantic beneath her soldierly exterior manner. Curt had a new young lieutenant to take her place in the Companions, and he was frankly concerned that he'd run into a repeat of Namibia.

So he handed the AP hard copy back to Levitt and told him, "Very well, Mister Levitt . . ."

"Ed."

"Very well, Ed, stick with us if that's what you want. I'll be available to answer your questions. I ask that you see me before talking with other members of Carson's Companions."

"May I ask why, Major?"

"Curt."

"May I ask why, Curt?"

"Yes, and I'll give you a straight answer, Ed," Curt told him bluntly. "We are *not* ordinary warbot brainies who let the warbots do all the fighting while we lie on our asses in the linkage van."

"Yes, I've read up about you. I try to do my homework."

"Good. Then you know that we get shot at. A lot. We got shot at in Bisbee. Some of us took rounds in our body armor. If you stick with us in combat when things turn to slime, you and your camera operator are going to be shot at, too. So I'm going to insist that both of you check out a set of body armor from Supply and *wear it* when we do. I don't want Doctor Gydesen to have to spend time patching either of you up when you get hit."

"Good idea. I'll take you up on that body armor," Levitt told him easily. "Now, about interviewing without your permission . . ."

"At the moment, we're not fighting, but we're training for the day when we'll have to fight again . . . and we will have to fight again," Curt replied. "I don't want you in the way. I don't want you distracting my people when they've got a job to do. It could mean their lives in combat. When and if we do roll into Mexico, my troopers will be busy. I'll want you to stay out of their way . . . or I'll take you out of their way, if I have to. And, quite frankly, Mister Levitt, it gets sort of lonely out in the boondocks, as we found in Namibia. So I don't want you romancing my ladies, even in off-duty situations. . . ."

177

Levitt laughed loudly. "Curt, I'm happily married!"

"How often do you see your wife in the sort of job you do?"

"Often enough! Rest assured I have absolutely no intention of cheating on my wife, Anne!"

Marge Bogen spoke up for the first time. "He means it" was all that she said.

CHAPTER NINETEEN

It happened on Captain Joan Ward's watch while she was commanding Tac Batt Two with her Warriors patrolling between Coronado National Monument and Bisbee Junction with Frazier's Ferrets east of there to the vicinity of Douglas.

And it happened just while the Cottonbalers were beginning their relocation move out of Diamond Point to Ajo.

Further compounding confusion with commotion, the command and staff of the 17th Iron Fist Division was moving to Fort Huachuca. This confused communications to some degree and made them somewhat less than desirable.

And when it happened, the Cottonbalers had to change plans and head for Sierra Vista.

It was late afternoon. Carson's companions had spent the day resting up from the previous day's patrol activities, engaging in more training, and continuing to help prepare the post for the arrival of the Iron Fist Division.

"Like I was back in basic training again," Sergeant Edie Sampson complained. "Except these latrines are *old* and I can't get the hard-water stains off them! My mother didn't raise me to clean latrines forever!"

"You think you got troubles?" Nick Gerard retorted. "I've spent days being a goddamned plumber! Do you know how long a simple rubber or plastic cone seal lasts in a valve with this water? Less than ten years! And guess how long this post has been here and how old some of the plumbing is? Jeez, they've got some *lead* pipe

179

in these old buildings! Wonder how many soldiers died of lead poisoning?"

"That ain't nothing!" was Sergeant Tracy Dillon's gripe. "The place is a damned museum! Have you ever seen — actually *seen* — knob-and-tube electrical wiring with gutta-percha and tar insulation on the wire? And your damned rubber seals are nothing, Nick! Plastic insulation on electrical cable loses its plasticizer in this sort of heat; so you just touch it and it cracks or breaks! How long since you been bit by hundred-and-twenty-volt stuff wiring up a house?"

Sergeant Henry Kester was philosophical about it. "Aw, quit gripin'! You're learning a trade . . ."

"With old electrical wiring or lead pipes?" Edie Sampson asked.

"Yeah, when you retire, you can always get a civil service job as a museum curator with the Smithsonian," Kester advised her.

Naturally, Carson's Companions preferred to do maintenance and repair on their own warbot equipment, vehicles, and small arms. That was modern technology, and they understood it better.

Curt kept busy studying maps of northern Sonora and Chihuahua with Lieutenants Jerry Allen and Kitsy Clinton. He was trying to get a feel for the sort of country they might have to operate in if they engaged in hot pursuit, which he didn't think was such a great idea anyway.

Curt didn't like what he saw on the charts any more than he liked the idea of hot pursuit of guerrilla troops into a foreign country.

In the first place, it was a replay of Namibia: No two maps matched, and there was little indication which one was the most accurate and up-to-date. Two different sets of road maps published by the same company in Mexico City showed widely different road data although both bore the same copyright date. The Defense Mapping

Agency hadn't paid too much attention to Mexico for the same reason it had ignored Namibia: No troops were expected to have to operate there. It had been well over a hundred years since an American army had entered Mexico. The most detailed maps turned out to be World Aeronautical Charts published by the Commerce Department's National Ocean Survey. So again it was a situation where the maps didn't match each other and the high-resolution satellite images matched none of the maps.

Secondly, Curt didn't like the terrain. It was rugged mountain country with few good roads. The Sierra Madre Occidental range was one of the most rugged and uninhabited parts of the continuous cordillera of mountains that ran from Alaska to the tip of Tierra del Fuego. His two young officers agreed with him: It was going to be pure hell trying to chase guerillas, insurgents, or bandits through that sort of country.

The Zulu Alert klaxon went off at 1437 on a muggy Arizona monsoon afternoon. It was echoed by its brothers in every ACV in the bivouac compound. "Greys all, Greys all, this is Grey Ops," came the voice of Captain Hensley Atkinson over every tacomm unit. "Tac Batt One, report for Oscar briefing. Tac Batt Two, assemble covertly at Cochise College Airport and stand by to participate in teleconferenced Oscar briefing. Tac Batt One, be prepared to move out following Oscar briefing. Tac Batt Two, be prepared to go into action at any time."

"Holy shit, here we go!" Jerry Allen exploded.

"Don't be so sure," Kitsy Clinton told him. "It was a false alarm two days ago."

"Let's not try to outguess the colonel," Curt warned them. "He's got communications networks we aren't privy to. Drop your beer and grab your gear! Sergeant Kester?"

"Right here, Major!"

"Muster the company! Round up the Companions and

181

let's find out what's going on!"

"Yes, sir! I heard. They're already on their way."

Together, the Companions marched over to the regimental OCV. Although most of the post buildings had been cleaned up and made ready, the divisional equipment hadn't been moved in yet. So the Washington Greys were still working with the mobile command equipment brought down from Diamond Point. Therefore, no snake pit existed in which to hold Oscar briefings. As before, it was held on the ground alongside Bellamack's big Operational Command Vehicle.

Again, the big map of southeastern Arizona was projected on the OCV's side. This time, however, the regimental staff had memory modules preprogrammed for each combat company commander as well as for the units of the Headquarters and Services companies.

Curt plugged the nanochip into his portable tacomm and watched while the graphics display came up.

Ed Levitt and Marge Bogen were there, getting it on videotape. Levitt agreed easily to Bellamack's request that no real-time programming be released for broadcast showing briefings or other critical activities where the coverage could provide valuable information to the bandits in Mexico. After all, a TV set in Nogales could easily pick up the Tucson stations.

Colonel Bellamack descended from the OCV at that point, whereupon all the officers and NCOs present rose to their feet.

"As you were," Bellamack told them. "Sit down and get the load off your feet. We're probably going to have plenty of walking ahead of us. Tac Batt Two, this is Grey Head. Are you on the net?"

"Roger, Grey Head, this is Tac Batt Two," Joan Ward's voice came back. "We have both audio and visual."

"Very well, listen up because here's the situation," Bellamack briefed them. "The pride and joy of the Space Force, Reconsat Poker Hand Eleven, picked up a convoy

182

of trucks in Mexico heading north toward Agua Prieta. The data has just been double-checked by a Space Force RS-17 Hot Bird flying north of the border. Border Patrol and DEA monitoring posts also confirm. This is not—repeat, not—the usual Mexican truck traffic, although the convoy tried to disperse to make it appear to be nothing more than a lot of trucks converging on Agua Prieta for the weekend. No question about it: they're Herreronistas—which is what we were told they were called, God knows why, and so we'll call them that. How do we know the trucks are full of Herreronistas? Easy! The dumb bastards didn't even bother to put the canvas 'paulins over the truck beds to cover up the men and rifles! They're covered now; they're within ten klicks of the border and it's starting to rain around Douglas."

"Sure as hell is, Colonel," Captain Joan Ward's voice came back. "Another monsoon thunderstorm here. But we can *see* the convoy spread out along Mexican Highway Two down there! Do they think we're not looking?"

"I don't know what they think," Bellamack replied. "I do know what our orders are. Our estimate is that they have about a thousand men and that they will cross the border this evening and circle around the west side of Douglas in order to prevent the sort of armed opposition from citizens that they encountered in Bisbee. That took them by surprise, and they didn't like American peasants shooting at them with better small arms than they had! We estimate border penetration between Cochise College Airport and Pirtleville. Initial units will be the technical one we saw in Bisbee protected by the elite Herreronista guards. We anticipate their job will be to cut off telecommunications north of Douglas. The main body will then cross the border. We anticipate that their objective will be the Arizona state prison at the Bisbee-Douglas Municipal Airport, where they may attempt to release prisoners. We will stop them, attempt to prevent their retreat into Mexico, and engage in hot pursuit of those units that do manage to get back across the border. Code name is Operation Black Jack. Here are individual company assignments:

"Ward's Warriors and Frazier's Ferrets will stand by in defilade ready to move eastward along Highway Eighty to cut off the retreat of the main body after it crosses northward. This time, Captain Ward, make sure that you cover your rear; the Herreronistas may be holding five hundred or so men in reserve to catch you between two units."

"Yes, sir! Can I expect reinforcements from the rest of the regiment, and, if so, when?"

"Tac Batt One under my command will depart Fort Huachuca in no more than thirty minutes to proceed at top cross-country speed along Highway Ninety and Highway Eighty to Cochise College Airport," Bellamack explained. "Our ETA at the airport is two hours from now. That will work out just about right. We want to let the Herreronistas get across the border, then confront them and chase them back. It may be a night fight. We may have tac air, and we may not."

Captain Alexis Morgan raised her hand. "Colonel, do I understand that this will be a hot pursuit mission?"

"Yes, Captain, Operation Black Jack is a hot pursuit mission. We will pursue the Herreronistas back across the border and maintain contact. This will be the primary job of Tac Batt One. The Warriors will join Tac Batt One in the pursuit. Once any prisoners have been secured—the Arizona Department of Public Safety and the Border Patrol have both agreed to handle prisoners this time—Frazier's Ferrets will join the Greys.

"All companies will carry full mobile combat logistical supplies. Captains Ward and Frazier are responsible for informing Lieutenant Dearborn or her assistant of their shortfalls so that Supply can bring these along. Do this in the next thirty minutes.

"The rules of engagement for Operation Black Jack

184

have been changed. We are allowed to engage in hot pursuit under direct orders from the White House under the terms of the Treaty of 1882," Bellamack explained. "You may return fire if fired upon. You are urged not to engage in wanton or unjustified destruction of nonmilitary equipment or facilities. But if a house is being used as a fire base, you are authorized to take it out. We are not authorized to appropriate civilian equipment or food for our use.

"We will be supported by the Cottonbalers now on their way down from Diamond Point; they will follow us into Mexico. The Can-Do is being airlifted out of Charlotte Amalie in the Vee-Eye tonight; they are not going to El Centro but direct to Libby Army Air Field at Fort Huachuca; the Can-Do will serve as a reserve force.

"We will not—repeat, not—have tac air support for Operation Black Jack in Mexico."

This last announcement of Colonel Bellamack's was greeted by a muffled muttering. Air support was considered to be vital for missions into moutainous terrain; that was a lesson that had been learned the hard way in Namibia.

"Nor can we expect to be resupplied by air-drop," Bellamack went on. "The reason is ridiculous. The Treaty of 1882 permits hot pursuit on the ground but makes no mention of the use of the skies for tactical or logistical support purposes. That treaty was signed twenty-one years before the Wright brothers flew! Mexico has firmly stated that it will follow ICAO and other international rules of the air, will not allow its airspace to be violated, and will not permit air support of American ground forces operating in the country."

He paused and looked around. "Very well, you have the rest of the Operation Black Jack details in the nanochip modules given to you for your battle computers. Any questions before we break this up?"

"Colonel," Captain Alexis Morgan piped up, "the Mexicans have border outposts and highway checkpoints. Couple of them are on the routes we may take. How do we handle them? If we get separated, how much do we give them?" Morgan, born and raised in El Paso, Texas, had experience with the Mexicans and spoke the language as well.

"Pardon me, Captain? I don't understand?"

"*La mordida.* The bite. What's the maximum we're going to pay them and be reimbursed for?"

Bellamack didn't think it was funny, although a ripple of laughter ran around the group gathered before Bellamack's OCV. "Captain, I assure you that all you have to do is to point one of your Saucy Cans at the *transito.* Even the stupidest one will understand that you have a far bigger gun than he does. Be polite, say *gracias, no comprende,* button down, and move right along."

"Colonel, we're going to end up shooting some Mexicans. That procedure challenges their *machismo,*" Alexis warned.

It was apparent that the colonel didn't think so. "Thank you, Captain," Bellamack said and looked around. "Any other questions?"

"Colonel," Curt said, standing up, "what is the objective of Operation Black Jack?"

"Objective? Hot pursuit of the Herreronistas into Mexico to find and destroy their headquarters, Major."

"Do we know where their headquarters is located, sir?"

"No, that's one thing we're going to find out. When we find it, we'll destroy it."

This bothered Curt. It was contrary to good military principles. "In other words, Colonel, we have no objective?"

"That's right, Major. Operation Black Jack is a reconnaissance in force."

Curt didn't like that idea. He recalled what Ed Levitt had said about the United States Army chasing Apaches into Mexico. One of those expeditions had penetrated more that 3,200 kilometers into Mexico and returned empty-handed, being harassed all the way by Mexican troops.

"Any other questions?" Bellamack asked. Again, he looked around. No one had any questions. Curt knew they would later on.

"Very well, move out!" Bellamack snapped the order. "You've got thirty minutes! We'll join Tac Batt Two in two hours. I don't think the Herreronistas will cross the border before it gets dark. But let's assume that they can see us because we can see them. Assume they know we're in the area, so make sure and check minus-x *constantly*. Cover your asses because the Herreronistas might have this set up as a trap to surround us. I think they're going to get the surprise of their sweet lives when they find out we're chasing them back into Mexico!"

CHAPTER TWENTY

Combat rarely takes place as planned. Military operations can be run by the book if the book is carefully written and if large numbers of troops are involved. Operation Overlord, the D-Day invasion of Normandy in 1944, still stands as the largest and most complex military operation ever carried out. But when, where, and under what conditions actual small unit combat occurs is affected by many different factors. Even Operation Overlord had its glitches and mistakes when it came to small units of regimental size or less.

But it looked like Operation Black Jack wasn't going to involve any combat at all. It had been a hurry-up-and-wait affair. Tac Batt One and the regimental headquarters and support units had busted their buns to get from Fort Huachuca to their positions west of Douglas in two hours. And when they got there, they went powered down to wait.

"Nothing. Absolutely nothing," Curt observed from the hidden position in the dry bed of Whitewater Draw 6,500 meters west of the Douglas-Bisbee airport and its on-site state prison. In spite of the afternoon thunderstorm, the air was perfectly clear. Curt could easily see the tall stacks of the long-abandoned Copper Queen smelter on the northwest side of the town of Douglas.

The big vehicles of the Washington Greys were all tucked away in the dry creek bed of Whitewater Draw on the left flank and scattered among the scrubs and trees through the center and down to the right flank anchored by Ward's Warriors a kilometer north of Highway 80 and the Southern Pacific Railroad tracks running almost parallel to the Mexican border.

Taking cover in a dry wash wasn't considered a super-safe activity during the Arizona monsoon season when a distant thunderstorm could cause a sudden flash flood. But no thunderstorms in the area were in locations that could feed this particular dry wash.

Curt had allowed his troops to stay inside the air-conditioned comfort of their vehicles because the temperature was still over 100 degrees Fahrenheit and the relative humidity was more than 50%. The heat stress index made it feel as if it were more than 125 degrees F. The commonly held idea that Arizona is a hot, dry desert is only half correct. It's hot, but during the late summer when the southwest winds bring moisture up from the Sea of Cortez and the Pacific Ocean, relative humidities can soar above 70%.

"Companions all, this is Companion Leader," Curt advised his troops via tacomm. "If you have binoculars, IR vision scopes, and or any other piece of equipment that uses lenses, I want you to place them outside your air-conditioned vehicles. Put them up on the lip of the turret hatch. Or put them outside the rear ramps. If you keep them inside and let them cool down, they'll fog up immediately when you take them outside. Get them outside and let them come up to ambient temperature. And be careful of your sun visors and other face shields. Put them outside, too, because they'll fog up the instant you debouch from your vehicles."

"Roger, Companion Leader. This is Companion Alpha," came Kitsy Clinton's voice. "I just poked my head up through the turret hatch for a real-world view and discovered that. Thank you for the advice."

Curt turned to his first sergeant. "Henry, the sensors report anything?"

Master Sergeant First Class Henry Kester shook his head. "Negatory, Major. Nothing on IR. Wind's out of the west, so no chance of picking up anything on the olfactory sensors. In short, no stink of troops. And no communications traffic other than normal commercial stuff."

"How about the magnetic anomaly detector!" Any vehicle such as a truck created a miniscule disturbance in the Earth's magnetic field around it, and suitably sensitive sensors could detect this change as far as 10 kilometers away.

Kester shook his head again. "A few vehicles moving on Highway Six-sixty-six, but that damned high-voltage power line out there tends to mask anything to the east of the highway." The old soldier turned to his company commander and remarked, "Major, I don't think the Herreronistas will do anything until after sundown when it cools off a bit."

"What leds you to say that, Henry?"

"Hell, Major, even Mexican farmers who spend most of their lives outdoors don't do much of anything on a muggy day like this. Carrying off an offensive operation in this stinkin' weather sucks the piss and vinegar out of even the best-trained troops. Highly motivated assault or special forces combat teams can hack it to limited objectives on foot to maintain IR, radar, and MAD stealth, but . . ."

"Henry," Curt interrupted him as a sudden thought crossed his mind because of Kester's offhand remark, "what's happening east of the airport?"

"Nothing that I can see, and I can see plenty on the sensors. Pretty damned flat out there this side of Leslie Canyon Road. Then the ground is a little broke up . . ."

"Remember that special unit Captain Ward ran into on the ridge above Bisbee?" Curt recalled. "The tech outfit and its special commando-style defense force that cut the communications links? Could they be working their way northward on the east side of Douglas?"

"Not in vehicles or we'd spot them. On foot, maybe, but it's probably an all-day hike."

190

"And if you were going to penetrate this border now after two terrorist raids had alerted everyone, would you do it in vehicles?"

"Hell, no! I'd do it on foot and try to act like the usual Mexican foot traffic back and forth across the border!"

"And maybe that's exactly what's been happening, and maybe these tech commando troops have been at it all day," Curt said. He punched up Bellamack's frequency. "Grey Head, this is Companion Leader."

"Grey Head here. Go ahead, Companion Leader."

"Grey Head, do we have any data from Grey Eyes covering the east side of the action area?" Curt asked, wondering if Captain John Gibbon had put any aerial recon bots aloft to check out the region Curt was concerned about.

"Negatory. Do you suspect something?"

"Affirmative! The area to the east of town is far more open and uninhabited than it is here," Curt observed. "If this guerrilla operation follows the same general plan as the one in Bisbee, special tech and support forces will move in ahead to cut communications. I suspect they'll be coming up the east side of Douglas. At least, if I were doing it, that's what I'd do."

"Grey Eyes reports that the weather is still too turbulent and gusty behind that thunderstorm to the east," Bellamack replied. "He couldn't keep birdbots aloft in the rough air. But why do you suspect this?"

"Colonel, do we have any recon of that area?"

"No, but the latest high-resolution surveillance satellite images show nothing, although they're two hours old by now."

Curt knew the tactical infrared and radar sensors really didn't have the range to see troops on foot out where he thought they might be: coming through the hills about 26 kilometers east of his present position.

He wanted to go take a look.

"We don't know what's going on over there, Grey Head," Curt pointed out. "Request permission to take Companion Alpha and conduct a brief surface recon patrol out as far as Leslie Canyon Road."

"Negatory. Permission denied. I don't want to split my forces," Bellamack told him.

"Grey Head, Companion Leader and Alpha will be gone no longer than two hours."

There was silence while Bellamack checked the disposition of forces. He saw what Curt saw on the tactical displays: The 7th Infantry Regiment (Special Combat), the Cottonbalers, was already in Bisbee. Although they were a green Sierra Charlie outfit just transitioning from a warbot brainy unit, they were available as backup reserve only 20 kilometers to the west. The Cottonbalers didn't yet have the mobility experience of the Greys, but they could be on the line in a little over 30 minutes if necessary. Bellamack, with his recent experience as a warbot brainy, evaluated all this and finally replied to Curt, "Companion Leader, I repeat: I do not wish to separate my forces. We'll wait until we can get birdbots aloft for recon or can pull down another high-res satellite image. If this raid is being carried out on foot like it was at Bisbee, the bastards will be dispersed and hard to hit. I don't want to stretch our capabilities at Luck Management right now. Maintain your position."

"Roger, Grey Head. Companion Leader will comply." Curt was pissed, but he didn't really understand the reason for it. He told himself that his regimental commander, being new at the job and new to the Sierra Charlies, didn't really understand the situation. Curt wanted to go look for the enemy. Had Belinda Hettrick still been in command, Curt believed she would have allowed him to make a modest recon; he believed she'd always understood his urge to move and move fast, to be a hunter who beat the bushes rather than one who waited in a blind for the quarry to come to him.

What he didn't understand and should have if he hadn't been indulged by the former regimental commander, was that Colonel Bellamack was playing it cool and safe with heavy security to hide the regiment from the enemy, waiting for the enemy to make its presence known, and ready to utilize surprise, movement, and mass when he did find out. Bellamack had a different way of fighting, and Curt hadn't learned it yet. The war gaming and field exercises around Diamond Point hadn't really revealed Bellamack's approach and policies in combat, and the Battle of Bisbee had been so straightforward that it had basically served to give Bellamack a chance to get his feet wet in a Sierra Charlie combat situation.

But Curt did indeed know that the colonel had to call the shots and it wasn't up to Curt at this point to make waves. After all, he and Bellamack had a contract. Curt wasn't about to break it. He'd support Bellamack. And he'd done his job by bringing a potentially dangerous situation to the colonel's attention.

So he was surprised when Bellamack called him on a scrambled command frequency thirty seconds later and remarked, "Major, a commanding officer doesn't have to explain his orders or why he gave them, but if I have the time to do it, I will. If the raiders come up the west side of Douglas, we'll catch them on their left flank along their entire column. If they come up the east side as you think they might, we'll see them far enough in advance to move to a new defensive line around the airport. In either case, I want to use the von Moltke strategy."

Helmut von Moltke of the Prussian general staff during the nineteenth century developed the principle of defensive offense. This was tricky to carry out successfully but very effective when engaging a force with more strength or even unknown strength. One deploys into a strong defensive position and allows the enemy to assault it. Even Clausewitz taught that defensive tactics were stronger than offensive ones. The objective is to allow the enemy to expend personnel and materiel against the defensive position until his strength is sapped. Then the defending force assumes the offensive and counterattacks from its stronger position.

Curt had a better appreciation for the colonel. The man hadn't forgotten what both of them had learned in military history classes at West Point. During the Battle of Metz, which concluded the Franco-Prussian War of 1870, Moltke put eight corps across the line of French retreat out of Metz. Marshal Bazaine couldn't fight his way out of Metz to join the rest of the French army and went down in defeat. A similar situation occurred a few days later around Sedan, where Moltke also trapped Louis Napoleon and the rest of the French Army under Marshal MacMahon. The Second French Empire collapsed as a result.

"Colonel, I hope they come up the west side. It'll be easier to engage them on the flank," Curt observed. "We have a much better chance of wiping them out there than if we have to engage them with a frontal attack in the east."

"Major, perhaps my ultimate objective isn't clear," Bellamack replied. "My orders are not to destroy the raiding force."

"Sir?"

"My orders are to pursue it back into Mexico, locate its base, and destroy it," the colonel explained carefully. "If we wipe it out here, there will be other raids once more men are recruited and armed in Mexico. If we're going to stop this sort of shit on our border, and if the Mexican army can't, then we've got to get to the source and make sure that no further raiding forces can be put together by whoever the hell is responsible."

Curt silently admonished himself. He was beginning to think in the same terms as his old nemesis, Marty "Killer" Kelly, whose philosophy was simple: "Kill 'em all! Let God sort 'em out!" The operations in Trinidad and

194

Namibia had served to reinforce his American "unconditional surrender" outlook, even though the Army had pulled out of both Trinidad and Naimibia once its objectives had been reached and the mission accomplished.

Bellamack went on, "Curt, I want us to make these bastards start running. I want us to stay on their ass and keep them running. I want them to lead us right back to their base in Mexico. I don't want us to kill Mexicans; I want us to get the sonofabitch who's behind all of this. Period. That's what my orders say and what General Carlisle expects the Greys and the Cottonbalers to do. And that's why I've got to keep the regiment together. If we get spread out all over Hell's half-acre, we could get clobbered when we chase the bastards back across the border into *their* turf. If we have to split forces, we've got the Cottonbalers along with us, and the two regiments can operate separately if necessary."

"I understand, sir."

"Good! Because, as I told you earlier, if things go to slime and I get creamed, you are *de facto* second in command . . . and Wade Hampton knows this, by the way."

"Incidentally, Colonel, who's in overall command of the two regiments?"

"General Carlisle, of course!"

"Good. I wouldn't want another Victor Knox going for glory in this operation."

"Knox? Oh, Zahedan! Don't worry."

"I won't, Colonel. General Carlisle ran the Namibian operation when the French field marshal decided to be a hero and got trapped."

"Yeah, I know. Have your Companions break for dinner now. I'm asking the companies to chow down in sequence . . . and I just hope no one has their dinner interrupted . . ."

Naturally, things never work out quite that way. . . .

CHAPTER TWENTY-ONE

The bird robot—the birdbot—was shaped to look like a red-tailed hawk, a big one. It soared and wheeled 1,000 meters over the darkening high desert landscape, but it wasn't looking for food. Its optical sensors were searching for people.

The birdbot was being run by Sergeant Christine Burgess, who was lying on her back on a linkage couch in the regiment's only remaining Operational Command Vehicle configured for neuroelectronic warbot operation. Sensors in the couch and the tight-fitting helmet over her head picked up her electrical brain waves. A computer recognized the patterns of these neural signals and encoded them for transmission to the birdbot as commands. The birdbot's "eyes" were sensors that could be commanded to respond to visual, infrared, or ultraviolet portions of the spectrum. The signals from these were transmitted back to the OCV where the computer translated them into electronic impulses sent to downlink electrodes in contact with the sergeant's back and head as she lay on the couch.

Thus, Sergeant Christine Burgess saw what the birdbot saw. Although she could control it and make it go where she wanted because it was an extension of her, most of her work of keeping the birdbot in the air was done by the computer serving as an autopilot. The act of flying by wing-beating is such a complex activity that it would have required most of the sergeant's attention without the automatic pilot.

It was as though Burgess was actually in the birdbot. She was one of two birdbot operators aloft for the Washington Greys. Sergeant Bill Hull was in linkage with another birdbot. He was searching a different area than Burgess.

Burgess suddenly thought she saw something through her birdbot.

She let the bot swing another two circles in the sky while she double-checked.

She was viewing the desert below by infrared because it was after sunset without enough light for the visual sensors to operate.

Grey Eyes Two, this is Grey Eyes One, she thought to Sergeant Hull. *I believe I've found something. Can you swing over here and have a look to confirm my IR readings?*

Grey Eyes One, Grey Eyes Two has you in sight and I'm locking on your scan area, Bull's thought told her as it was transmitted from his linkage hardness to hers through the computer. *Okay, I see something. Maybe a large herd of cows . . .*

That could be a possibility. The IR image is smeary. Cover me while I go lower to get better resolution.

Burgess descended in wide circles to 300 meters.

Grey Eyes, this is Grey Eyes One! Tally ho! I have targets! Burgess reported through the computer to Captain John Gibbon, the regimental communications and intelligence officer. *Get them up on the displays! About one thousand men in two ragged columns coming up the old pipeline alignment toward the airport from the southeast, distance about ten kilometers from the airport!*

"Roger, Grey Eyes One! Got 'em!" Gibbon wasn't linked to the computer and its intelligence amplifier. He replied to both of his recon birdbot operators vocally; the computer translated the sound waves into neuroelectronic signals that went in through their linkage harnesses and were perceived as sound in their brains. "And I've pinpointed them on long-range monopulse radar as well! Good job! Keep track of them!"

He switched frequencies on his tacomm while he keyed in the commands to display Grey Eyes One's information on the regimental tactical displays. "Grey Head, this is Grey Eyes! We have contact! Data on the tac display bus now!"

Colonel Bellamack saw the information. So did all his company commanders. It was also relayed back to the Cottonbalers and General Carlisle's divisional CP near Bisbee.

"Greys all, this is Grey Head!" Bellamack snapped the command. Thanks to Curt's inputs, he was prepared for this change in plan. The raid was indeed coming up the east side of Douglas toward the airport. This meant a head-on confrontation rather than a flanking contact. "All units, move forward in line of skirmishers at fifty klicks if possible. If not possible, notify Grey Head ASAP, and we'll slow down to allow you to maintain the line. Cross Highway Six-six-six and be prepared to meet the intruders after crossing. Stay in vehicles until contact is established, then deploy warbots, Mary Annes on the point with Hairy Foxes providing backup fire support. Looks like we'll catch them on their left front quarter, although we may actually be on the left flank of the rear of their column. Warriors and Ferrets, be prepared to speed up your cross-country if it looks like we can hit them along the entire column length simultaneously. Our objective is to stop them with superior firepower, take prisoners if possible, and get the rest of them to turn around and run. When they run, we're going to chase them! Remember our mission: We are not to destroy the raiding party; we are get them to retreat into Mexico so that we can follow."

Curt had come alive at the first words from Bellamack. So had Henry Kester, who had immediately instructed their Armored Command Vehicle to start up. "Drive by infrared, Henry," Curt instructed him as he turned down the intensity of the deep-red night lightning inside the ACV.

"I sure as hell ain't gonna show lights, Major!" the old sergeant snapped back as he gave movement instructions to the ACV's robotic computer.

"Companions all, this is Companion Leader! Move out and formate on me. Passive sensors only, maximum range, maximum sensitivity. Maintain line of skirmishers with a hundred meters max between vehicles. Don't crowd the Marauders on the left flank or the Ferrets on the right. This is standard open country maneuvering, so keep the tac display eyeballed and stick your heads out of your turrets occasionally, even if it's muggy out there. Put any contact data on the display bus as soon as your systems can discriminate it. Move out!"

Amid the positive responses from his two platoon officers, Curt moved to clamber into the turret and open the hatch. A wave of muggy, hot, and humid air greeted him. He was glad he'd left his optical gear outside. He slipped into his helmet and keyed up the tac display on the visor.

The only problem that the Greys had when moving in their vehicles was the muted thunder of their vehicle engine exhausts accompanied by the muffled high-pitched whine of the turbines. The engine exhausts were suitably stealthed by exhausting them to the rear of each vehicle through "black hole" IR heat suppression baffles.

The ACV lurched out of the dry wash and plunged through an ancient fence that surrounded an abandoned agricultural field once kept green by circular irrigation. The land ahead of them was much the same, old agricultural land that had been allowed to go fallow while the rains leached the irrigation minerals out and rejuvenated it.

"Marauder Leader, this is Companion Leader," Curt called to Alexis. "Radio check."

"Read you loud and clear, Companion Leader. We're copacetic here," Alexis's voice came back.

"Just checking," Curt told her.

"Appreciate it. How you?"

"Orgasmic."

"Good. Write when you get work," Alexis kidded him, letting him know diplomatically that she was running her own show now but would appreciate Curt's help if things went to slime in a fur ball.

The skirmish line crossed Highway 666, then the railroad track leading into the airport, originally a World War II army air base as was evident from its basic runway layout.

"Sonofabitch!" came the tacomm cry from Jerry Allen. "The bastards don't even have point elements out! They're marching in two ragged columns, no order or discipline, just walking right up on the airport!"

The infrared images on Curt's visor display were now strong and sharp. When he ducked his head to look at the better display below the hatch coaming, he could almost make out arms and legs on the individual IR returns.

"Range four-five-zero-zero!" Kester called out.

"Greys all, this is Grey Head! Hold your fire unless fired upon. If you're not fired upon by the time the range closes to five-zero-zero meters, then open fire with air bursts from the Saucy Cans and Hairy Foxes. If range closes to three-zero-zero meters, you may order Mary Annes to open fire with antipersonnel scatter rounds and you may open fire with machine guns and rifles. Bravo units, stand by to fire either yellow flares or ultraviolet laser designator para shells. Green indicator

200

signifies message received and understood."

Curt toggled the green.

Morgan's Marauders were the first to make contact.

All hell broke loose on Curt's left flank as Alexis's troops went into action. Second Lieutenant Ev Taylor commanding Marauder Alpha called the open-fire and deployed his Mary Annes while Ellie Aarts brought Marauder Bravo's Hairy Foxes into action.

"Grey Head, Marauder Leader! We've caught the front of both columns!" Alexis reported. "We're going to cross the head of the columns and keep them from advancing any further."

About that time, the Companion Alpha Robot Transport Vehicle commanded by Sergeant Jim Elliott on Curt's left halted while its turret-mounted 15-millimeter gun opened up with burst fire and its aft ramp came down to disgorge its six Mary Annes. Elliott was with them. On the right, Sergeant Charlie Koslowski did the same with his RTV.

"Grey Head, Companions are engaged!" Curt reported, then ducked into the ACV. "Shake it, Henry! Let's get out with our jeep!"

"Major," Kester reported from where he was watching the high-resolution tactical display, "the intruders ain't returning the Marauders' fire. Or the fire from our own RTVs."

Curt stopped midway to the rear exist, his Novia already slung over his shoulder and his helmet strap buckled under his chin. "Say what?"

"They ain't firing back!" Kester pointed out. "They ain't putting up any fight at all! They're retreating! Hell, Major, they ain't even shooting back! It looks like a rout!"

"Damned if doesn't look that way! Sonofabitch! Henry, I'm going to mount up the troops, let them radio-command the warbots, and go into high mobility chase

201

mode. If Morgan will do the same, maybe we can turn the whole front end of the column!" Curt suddenly decided.

"Yes, sir! No damned sense in having our people get shot at in the open if the warbots can do the job without close supervision. Going high mobile beats the hell out of riding an ATV!"

"Companions all, Companion Leader!" Curt called in tacomm. "Personnel, remount your vehicles, go to radio voice command of warbots, convert into high mobile mode!" He switched channels and went on, "Marauder Leader, Companion leader!"

"Go!" It was Alexis Morgan comm shorthand that Curt was well acquainted with.

"Suggest we go high mobile and chase. I've ordered my personnel back to vehicles, warbots into radio voice command."

"Sounds like a winner. Got a plan?"

"Yeah, we turn the forward elements of this column back on itself. Force the whole outfit to run back for the border."

"I'm with you! I'll swing to the east, you hold down the west. We'll pick up the Ferrets and the Warriors as we roll up past them."

"Companion Leader, Grey Head. What's the story?" Bellamack wanted to know.

"Sorry, Grey Head, thought you might be following if you were monitoring," Curt replied. "We've made contact, opened fire, and received no return fire. The intruders are retreating. The Companions and the Marauders have gone high mobile and will turn the column back on itself. Ferrets and Warriors can join us when we roll the column back past them. Then we can chase them to the border as planned."

"Roger, Companion Leader, proceed. Grey Head, Grey Staff, and Grey Support will swing in behind you,"

Bellamack told him. "Don't lose contact."

"We won't," Curt promised. "In high mobile mode, our warbots and vehicles can roll faster than the insurgents can run . . . and for a lot longer time. They're on foot. Must have left their trucks on the other side of the border. We'll just keep steady pressure on them."

"I'll get a birdbot down there to have a look at where they've parked their vehicles," Bellamack added. "I want to spot those trucks and put coded beacons on them if I can. Lot easier to follow these bastards if they're in trucks anyway. Our recon sats can see them. And our MAD sensors can follow them if all else fails." Bellamack would put his Headquarters support units to work, get a couple more birdbots in the air, and have them emplace microchip radar beacons on the cab roof of every truck the Mexicans had used to bring the troops up to the border.

Curt was surprised by the totally unsophisticated tactics of these insurgents. They had no recon. They had no light artillery support. They apparently had no large-caliber recoilless pieces. They appeared to be a mob of untrained, undisciplined peasants armed with rifles and submachine guns. How the hell did they expect to stand up against a twenty-first century warbot regiment with body-armored soldiers carrying advanced assault rifles and supported by advanced aerial recon warbots, armored mobile assault warbots, heavy fire warbots, and 75-millimeter general-purpose light artillery . . . plus all the sensors and communications necessary to keep such a regiment fighting and vehicles that would allow them to move fast on the battlefield under fire?

Two answers occurred to Curt as they began to roll southeasterly at about five klicks, keeping contact with the retreating insurgent force.

First of all, maybe the insurgent leaders, the commanders of the Herreronistas, didn't think the United

States would call out its sophisticated warbot units, which were committed either to training or to trouble spots elsewhere in the world. Maybe they thought that the United States would be forced to counter the raids with regular Border Patrol and DEA personnel and equipment. This sort of massed mob tactics might work against the BP and DEA, neither of which were very strong.

Or perhaps the raids were feints of some sort designed to lure American troops into hot pursuit into Mexico. But why? Who would gain by doing that? He recalled that the Mexican army was fully engaged along the border with Guatemala, therefore leaving the northern sections of Mexico stripped of regular troops capable of putting down bandits. Was the political opposition attempting to discredit President Alvaro's regime by enticing American armed forces into northern Mexico? Apparently Alvaro was going to let American troops into the country because he couldn't do anything about it . . . yet. Curt was disturbed over the fact that Operation Black Jack would not have air support in the form of tactical strike aerodynes or resupply air drops. *That* would really put a crimp in Operation Black Jack, especially if these guerrillas had any sort of air capability south of the border.

It seemed to Curt that the Greys and the Cottonbalers would both be exposed to not only potential counterattacks by the Herreronistas in their own territory but also to possible harassment by Mexican government units.

Well, he wasn't calling the shots on this one. The Greys had orders to engage in hot pursuit. He'd follow orders. But he'd also watch minus-x while he was doing it.

In the meantime, the pursuit was a rat chase. The insurgents didn't fight back even when they had the opportunity to use a line of defense such as Highway 80

204

and the abandoned Southern Pacific right-of-way. Nor did the raiders attempt to take the 1,800-meter hill some 14 kilometers east of Douglas; they could have maintained a fire base up there that would have caused the Greys considerable harassment. But they went straight for the border, picking up their wounded as they went but leaving their dead.

Since this wasn't a shoot-to-kill chase, the Greys economized their ammo expenditure, firing only an occasional flare burst round over the retreating column or putting small-arms fire into the column when it showed a tendency to slow up. Curt spotted only eight dead raiders. The Herreronista losses had to be slight; they weren't making a stand that would increase their casualty potential.

"This is a turkey shoot," Master Sergeant Henry Kester quipped.

"Yeah, it's too easy," Curt agreed. "Think they'll make a stand when they get across the border?"

Kester shrugged. "Maybe they will. Maybe they won't."

"What would you bet on?"

"Ten says they won't make a stand. Major, these are raw, undisciplined, untrained irregulars," Kester pointed out. "They're not even putting up the sort of fight we got out of them at Bisbee. I think we hurt them real bad in Bisbee and we're dealing now with second-line raiders who were maybe promised the loot from sacking the airport and the prison . . . and who turned tail when they discovered they were stacked up against the United States Army."

"You're probably right," Curt muttered.

"Take the bet?"

"Negatory! I haven't won a bet with you in years! Of the many things you've taught me, one of them is not to bet with you, Henry!"

"Lost your sporting blood, Major?"

"Hell, no! Just to prove it, we're about to cross the border, and I'm going to do without getting a reconfirmation from the colonel," Curt told him, pointing out the position of the line on the tac display.

At twenty-four minutes past midnight, the Washington Greys Regiment of the United States Army crossed the border from Arizona into Mexico.

CHAPTER TWENTY-TWO

The Arizona-Sonora border east of Douglas was marked by the remains of a cyclone fence erected decades ago. The United States government hadn't bothered to tear it down when the Treaty of Nogales made it unnecessary. Of course, even by that time the fence had so many holes and gaps that it was merely symbolic. Over the years since, both Mexicans and Americans had pilfered bits and pieces of it for their own use. Few of the steel posts that had supported it and none of the barbed wire that once topped it were left.

Curt didn't remember which of the Greys' vehicles crossed the border first, thus precipitating the first armed invasion of Mexico by the United States in more than a century.

But when it occurred, nothing happened.

The Greys weren't set upon by fresh hordes of Mexican guerrillas.

Their vehicles and warbots weren't attacked by troops of the Mexican army.

And the night image of the landscape on the infrared sensors didn't change.

Nor was there any natural reason for the terrain to change. The boundary line was a man-made one which had been delineated by the Gadsen Purchase of 1854.

When Curt's ACV crossed Mexican Highway 2, he halted his company temporarily and called Bellamack on the regimental tacomm frequency because he'd encountered the unexpected. Either S-2 had fucked up again or something had changed in the heat of the Douglas Pursuit. "Colonel, we don't see any trucks or other vehicles on this highway where they were reported several hours ago. Did some of the raiders load them up and leave the rest of the band without transportation?"

"Negatory," Bellamack replied on the command net. "I don't know yet. I was busy with the details of the advance and contact, so I must admit I didn't pay any attention to the trucks. I became engrossed in our own movements after we moved out of position in Whitewater Draw. Those vehicles must have either moved out of the area after deploying the troops late this afternoon or dispersed along Highway Two and down toward Nacozari. Stand by; in about five minutes when we can get a high bit rate channel clear for Georgie, my tac display will have a taped replay of the overall movement situation that took place while we were advancing eastward to make contact."

"I'd appreciate it if you'd put it up on my display, Colonel," Curt asked him. "Honest to God, I'm antsy as hell about where those humpers went . . . and why. In the meantime, what are my orders, sir?"

"Retain contact. Engage in hot pursuit."

"All night long?"

"As long as required, Major. We've got 'em on the run, and we're going to chase their asses to Guatemala if we have to!"

Not without being resupplied! Curt thought. The Greys could operate for another three and a half days without logistical support. After that, they'd need fuel, water, and food. These supplies would have to come in by land behind them unless the United States changed its rules of engagement and opted to attempt air resupply either by drops or landings. The Greys could go short-rations on water and food, but the vehicles would burn up fuel during the chase. Curt knew that no one in the Greys would trust local fuel, water, or food except in an emergency. All those items would probably be contaminated or polluted. Bad fuel could chew up the turbines in the vehicles and maybe even damage the heavy turbine-powered warbots. The water and food would undoubtedly do their classical intestinal clean-out jobs on the Sierra Charlies in an unintentional form of biological warfare.

"If I'm going to run chase mode all night, Colonel, I need to halt for a few minutes and get out of high-mobile combat mode. My people need to round up their warbots and remount them for transport in their RTVs. That's the only way we can conserve warbot power for when we really need it," Curt advised his regimental commander. "If we leave the warbots out and running on the ground, we'll cut into our fuel reserves . . . and we don't know how long we're going to be running this chase and when we'll be refueled."

"Good idea. Halt and pick up your warbots. Go to cross-country chase mode. I'll pass the word to the other Greys. Once you've done that, get rolling and stay in hot pursuit."

Curt stopped the Companions on Mexican Highway 2 and allowed them to round up their warbots and trundle them back into the Robot Transport Vehicles. While this was going on, Curt's attention was called to the tactical display screen by Master Sergeant Henry Kester.

"Major, I'm glad you didn't take the bet. I might be losing my ass right now. Look here: When the Greys stopped to pick up the bots just now, the raiders quit running as they got to them hills to the southeast," the old soldier pointed out.

Kester was right. The infrared sensors had kept their lock on the warm human bodies of the guerrillas and the tactical computer had processed that location information onto the tactical display screen inside the ACV.

"What the hell are they doing? Regrouping?" was Curt's anxious question. "Does it look like they're preparing for a a counterattack now that they've got us on Mexican soil?"

Kester shook his head. "No, sir. They just plain stopped running away from us. Bingo. Halted. No regrouping. No movements that look like they might be preparing for a counterattack. Matter of fact, now that they've occupied those hills about three thousands meters south of us, they've got the high ground. Maybe they're just going to sit out there on those hills and invite us to attack them."

"Orgasmic! And it looks like the main body is going over the ridge so we can't get IR track on them. Only a small contingent seems to be waiting just this side of the ridge line," Curt muttered and called Bellamack about it.

"Roger, Companion Leader. I see it, too," the colonel's voice came back. "Do you have any idea why they stopped?"

Curt thought a moment, then said, "Yes, sir. They've marched thirty kilometers since sundown. The last fifteen of those have been under fire from us."

"So? We came all the way from Fort Huachuca in the last twelve hours!"

"Yes, Colonel, but they didn't ride vehicles. They walked. I think they're exhausted."

"Hell, thirty klicks are nothing! Don't tell me that you didn't take any fifty kilometer hikes when you were at West Point!"

"I did, Colonel, just like everyone else. But that was damned near ten years ago when I was a lot younger and accustomed to doing a lot of walking, especially marching. But damned few of us in this converted warbot outfit have walked fifty klicks in years," Curt admitted grimly. "Furthermore, when you and I took those fifty-klick strolls through Bear Mountain State Park, we'd been fed pretty damned well—lots of high-energy foods—and our mess along the way was pretty good, too. These guys up on

210

those hills were probably stuffed with tortillas and beans before they shoved off yesterday afternoon. How far could you walk under those conditions, sir?"

"I suspect they've run into another problem," came Alexis Morgan's voice. This was the regimental command net, and even Curt had overlooked the fact that the other company commanders were listening to all this. "I think they've discovered they've been given the knobby purple shaft."

"What do you mean?" Bellamack wanted to know. "Specify!"

"They probably expected to find their vehicles waiting for them on the highway," Alexis observed. "They got there and discovered the trucks had gone somewhere else. Hell, under those circumstances I'd find a place I could defend, and I'd stop, too. I'd be in my own territory. I'd guess that the *gringo* warbot outfit wouldn't go much deeper into Mexico. So I'd circle the wagons, get some rest, and hope that the vehicles came back, wherever they might have gone. Probably didn't upset them very much, Colonel. You've got to remember that they don't pay attention to the clock the way we do."

"Okay," Bellamack snapped, "but I don't want to let them just sit there. We're supposed to engage in hot pursuit. That means we're going to push them. Once all companies have warbots aboard, continue to move southward. Let's see if we can draw fire from them as we approach."

"I think we might want to be ready to deploy the warbots again," Curt ventured.

"If you have to, do so."

"Comment, sir." It was Captain Joan Ward. "The only reason we kept ourselves out of deep slime in Namibia, especially around Strijdom Airport, was the outstanding reconnaissance we had. We knew where every military unit was located."

"Furthermore, Colonel," Alexis added, "a night approach

211

march and assault against an enemy that's had the opportunity to take high ground *and* circle the wagons could be expensive . . . and leaves us wide open to a possible counterattack at first light if we fail."

"And we really don't know the lay of the land out there. We did indeed get into trouble in Namibia when we tried to move at night through badly charted territory. Hell, we don't know where we're going right now any more than we knew it trekking into the Namib hills. Our maps of the area south of Agua Prieta aren't very good," Joan Ward went on. "The maps don't match the latest satellite data. Even Georgie's data base is skimpy. No one ever thought we'd have to fight down here."

"Come to think of it," Alexis Morgan said suddenly, "I believe I can rectify that tomorrow morning."

"One more thing, Colonel," Curt put in. "We've had to rebuild our teams while we brought the regiment back up to strength. So we haven't had time to do night assault training."

"Any warbot unit must be able to move and fight at night!" Bellamack asserted.

"Yes, sir," Curt put in, "but we're not a regular warbot outfit and we're up to only Class Two combat readiness as Sierra Charlies because of our Namibian losses."

Silence ruled the tacomm net for a full ten seconds before Bellamack replied, "Considering our mission objective, I want the regiment to deploy tonight to within a thousand meters of those hills and to be ready to move forward again at daylight. I can't put recon birdbots up right now; our operators have been in linkage with them for almost twelve hours, and they're exhausted. I'll have Gibbon get recon birdbots aloft again as soon as he has an available warbot brainy to do it. I anticipate having fresh birdbot recon and a hi-res reconsat image by dawn. In the meantime, be prepared for the enemy to hold his position and defend himself during what's left of this night. If he doesn't move by dawn, we'll lay a saturation barrage on his positions and make him run again."

Captain Russ Frazier, newly promoted and taking over the company that had now become Frazier's Ferrets, spoke up tentatively for the first time. "Colonel, if we're going deep in hot pursuit without air resupply, do you really want us to plaster that hill? Shouldn't we be conserving ammo? We don't have a lot of it to throw away if we've got to depend on ground resupply for this deep pursuit mission."

"Don't worry about supplies," Bellamack assured them all. "We'll use the four hours we've got until dawn for getting all of you juiced up again. Logistics isn't your worry on the firing line. Major Benteen and Lieutenant Dearborn are doing the worrying about that. Rest assured: The Greys and the Cottonbalers can be supplied by ground well into Mexico if required. So stand by to take on stores and be ready to move if the enemy moves. If he wants to fight here, we'll fight and get him to run again. But I don't think he'll fight. I think he's going to run as soon as he gets rested and figures he's got the opportunity to sneak away without having us riding up his back."

There was another pause, and he added, "If he doesn't move by daylight tomorrow and elects to stand his ground, we'll move on him vigorously once we get recon and know where he is. However, if our sensors indicate he's moving out southward, we will maintain contact. The objective of the mission remains the same. We'll dog his tail down into the mountains if we have to. Sooner or later, we'll get the chance to bust him up at his headquarters so he won't be able to harass our border again."

Curt decided that Bellamack certainly did have a different way of commanding. The colonel was opportunistic; he changed his mind a lot. This wasn't a bad trait; Bellamack wouldn't lead the regiment into a Balaclava situation just because his orders or his operational plans were at stake.

213

He wasn't gung-ho enough to ram his troops into a knife fight. But he wasn't yet aggressive enough for a Sierra Charlie. He hadn't yet learned the trick that Belinda Hettrick had taught them all: Hold them by the nose with fire and use movement to get around behind and kick them in the ass. Curt could certainly see Bellamack's old warbot brainy training and experience behind most of Bellamack's tactical decisions thus far, and he believed the colonel was going to learn fast in Operation Black Jack.

"Orders," Bellamack went on. "The regiment to deploy in an east-west line. Warriors on the west. Then the Ferrets. Then the Companions. And the Marauders covering the left flank. Maintain surveillance of the enemy. Prepare to take on stores. Maintain readiness to move on fifteen minutes' notice. Other than that, you might try to let your troops grab an hour or so of sack time. As company commanders, you'll be lucky to get any rest at all. Goes with the territory, warbot brainy or Sierra Charlie."

"Still more tired commanders than tired troopers," was Curt's comment.

"Amen, Major! So move into line. Don't worry about the rear. The Cottonbalers under Colonel Calhoun are covering our asses north of the highway astride the border. They're going to follow us and learn how to become Sierra Charlies the same way you did: By doing it. Now get cracking! Tomorrow we're either going to fight these bastards to get 'em to run, or we're going to start right off chasing their asses further into Mexico. And that's where we are now. When the sun comes up, the good people of Mexico are going to find American troops on their soil for the first time in a long time . . . and some of them are not going to like it one little bit. So everyone be ready to handle some damned upset Mexicans. . . .

CHAPTER TWENTY-THREE

Carl von Clausewitz called it "friction in war." Colonel Trevor N. Dupuy noted that "combat activities are slower, less productive, and less efficient than anticipated."

That was the case when Lieutenant Harriet Dearborn's Supply Company attempted to refuel and reprovision the Washington Greys in four hours. It was dark. The troops were tired.

And everyone was skittish about the possibility that they could come under fire from the raiders' positions only 1,200 meters southeast of them. While a 7.62-millimeter round wouldn't penetrate body armor at that distance, no one wanted the discomfort of having to refuel and replenish while wearing body armor.

No one was sure whether or not the raiders had any 15-millimeter high-velocity sniping rifles. The Mexicans had developed one, the M4, which used American M26 caseless ammo. But the gun had quickly acquired the sobriquet of Manojo or "handful" because it could throw its heavy slug at more than 1,000 meters per second. The Mexican army liked it, but its soldiers didn't. Even with a sophisticated antirecoil muzzle brake, it was more than just uncomfortable to fire it. Since the Mexican Army had no warbots capable of handling such a heavy rifle, the guns were pilfered, stolen, and otherwise removed from caserns because no one gave a damn about them. So no one knew how many had found their way into non-army hands in the past five years.

As a result of the delay, the sun was high in the sky and it was 0815 before Dearborn gave an exhausted report to Bellamack that the regimental replenishment had been completed.

Curt was in the regimental OCV with the other combat company commanders when it happened. He saw a quick flush of anger on Bellamack's face, but the colonel quickly suppressed it. Dearborn and her supply troops had worked as quickly as they could under the circumstances.

What was really bothering Bellamack was the recon information coming in from birdbots.

"God damn it!" Bellamack exploded. "We've lost them! The Herreronista guards on this side of the ridge stayed put, but the main body that moved into défilade behind the hills last night took off shortly before dawn! They're heading cross-country down the Rio Bate Pito! And they've got fifteen kilometers on us now!" Bellamack was now referring to the irregular Mexican units by the name revealed by one of the Bisbee prisoners: Herreronistas. There was no more talk of "raiders" or "intruders." The Greys were the intruders now.

"Colonel," Curt told him, "we can make that up in a couple of hours. We'll have to shag ass, but we can do it."

"We trekked a couple of hundred klicks across Namibia without any roads at all. We can sure as hell do better here, even with a dirt road," Captain Russ Frazier pointed out.

"But what the hell are we getting into? The maps aren't worth a shit," Bellamack swore. "That looks like open country down there."

"Well, Colonel, looks like we'll just have to work the hell out of the birdbot operators to get us the recon we need," Joan Ward suggested. "Some of us old warbot brainies can fill in on the couch when John Gibbons's people get tired. We ought to be able to keep three or four birdbots aloft for

216

recon."

Bellamack looked around at his company commanders. Captain Alexis Morgan was prominently absent. "Where the hell is Morgan?"

"She went off in the direction of Douglas about an hour ago with Ed Levitt in his television van," Russ Frazier reported.

"What the hell is she doing in Douglas? And with Levitt?" Bellamack asked rhetorically.

As if anticipating his question, Captain Alexis Morgan came through the door in the aft hatch. Ed Levitt was with her, and he was followed by Marge Bogen with her videocam on her shoulder. Morgan had rolls of paper under her arms. Quickly laying them on the tac display so she wouldn't drop them on the floor she saluted and grinned. "Sorry I'm late, Colonel. Had to run a little errand."

"Oh? Where the hell did you go and why?" Bellamack was set to chew her out. He never got the chance.

"I went into Douglas with Ed," Alexis started to explain.

Ed Levitt broke in and said, "I know a guy who runs a store that caters to people going into Sonora on hiking vacations. I got him out of bed, bought him breakfast, and convinced him to open the shop for us."

"And I bought every chart of Sonora and Chihuahua I could find," Alexis explained with enthusiasm.

"We already have charts and maps," Bellamack told her.

"Sir, all of us know our data base isn't worth a damn," Alexis reminded him and began to unroll the huge sheets of paper. "Look at these!"

Curt got a quick glimpse and began to grin, too. They were 1:250,000 topographical maps similar to U.S. Geological Survey topo charts available in the United States. But these bore the words *Carta Topográfica*.

"There isn't a tourist supply store in any of the border towns that doesn't carry a complete set of Mexican topo maps prepared by the *Instituto Nacional de Estadística Geográ-*

fica Informática, their equivalent of our Geological Survey. Sometimes you can't get these maps even as far from the border as Tucson, but they're nearly always available in the border towns," Levitt explained.

"I bought two copies of everything, Colonel," Alexis pointed out. "Six-fifty a sheet. Damned good thing I had my mad money along. Also cost me ten bucks for *mordida* to get across the border both times, even though the *jefe* was a reasonable man. He was sort of confused because of all the military activity going on, and he didn't like the idea of a woman army officer toting a gun back and forth across the border. But I spoke his language and acted with authority and let him maintain his *machismo.* So . . ." She shrugged.

"I knew the chief at the Mexican border crossing," Levitt added. "He sees me come through a couple of times a year with our video gear. I've already paid my *mordida.* I bring him the surplus video sets from the main studio in Phoenix. . . ."

"Morgan, I'll arrange to have you reimbursed . . . out of the regimental general fund if I have to," Bellamack told her, gaining a new respect for this competent woman officer. The colonel was obviously delighted. "Morgan, how the hell did you know about the availability of these Mexican maps?"

"Sir, I'm an Army brat who was raised at Fort Bliss in El Paso," Morgan explained. "We used to buy the *carta topográfica* when we went four-wheeling into Chihuahua on vacation."

"And I knew where the store was in Douglas and also knew the proprietor," Levitt added.

Bellamack had read Morgan's 101 File, but this personal item in her background had slipped his mind because it hadn't seemed important until now. He recalled some other items now. "You speak Spanish, don't you?"

"Sí, Coronel! Me falta práctica."

218

"Yo hablo español también," Ed Levitt added with the words rolling out in the manner of someone who was quite at home in the language.

"I'm glad to know that," Bellamack observed. "Both of you will probably get lots of practice." He looked down at the topo charts, noted that their pub date was only two years old, then quickly handed them to Captain John Gibbon. "John, put these on your fax translator and get them into our computer data base."

"Sir, we haven't got one," the intelligence and communications officer replied. "A fax translator isn't part of our authorized equipment list."

"How the hell am I going to get copies of these into Calhoun's hands?"

"Have him go into Douglas and buy them, Colonel," Gibbon suggested.

Alexis Morgan shook her head. "Lots of tourist hikers down in Sonora this summer. The shop had only two copies left. I cleaned him out."

"I can tackle that problem," Ed Levitt offered. "We transmit scripts and other written data back and forth to Phoenix via satellite using video-frame data-burst equipment. We can upload these maps via satellite data burst to Phoenix and arrange for them to be modemed to your master computer at Diamond Point. Your master computer can certainly download the charts into your mobile data bases, can't it?"

"Damned right it can! And into the Cottonbalers' equipment, too! That's great! Sometimes I'd be damned glad to have commercial gear like that available, Levitt! It would take us a year of work to get the stuff added to our authorized regimental equipment lists. Here, take a set of charts and get busy," Bellamack said. "In the meantime, we'll keep the other set here. Right now, we've got to move. The Herreronistas are getting five kilometers ahead of us every hour."

Bellamack noted the tac display board. "About a hundred men still holding the hills southeast of us. General Carlisle says we're not to bother with them. He's sending Colonel Calhoun and the Cottonbalers up against them. The Cottonbalers need some combat experience. This is their first action as Sierra Charlies. The General figured this would be a good place to let them take on someone who's shooting back at them. So when the Cottonbalers attack, we'll go around those hills buttoned down and rolling."

Looking around at his company commanders, he went on, "When the Cottonbalers finish up in the Agua Prieta hills, they'll proceed south parallel to our route but they'll go down the road and railroad to Nacozari. They'll be a mobile force on our right flank. We're the main chase unit. We're going after the main body moving generally south by southeast along the Rio Batepito. Our objective today is to regain contact with the Herreronistas and let them know we're hot on their ass. So we'll stay on the road. We ought to be able to regain contact fairly quickly. But, as I said, we've got to hustle. So I'm putting us into hustle mode."

He keyed up a force column pictorial and overlaid it on a shaped topo chart which appeared on the tac display. "From a study of the combat history of this outfit, I've decided to stick with the familiar, with what you people know best. So I'm putting Carson's Companions out on point as usual. Curt, that's what happens when you do an outstanding job! Levitt, since you speak the language, will you accompany the point company?"

"Be glad to, Colonel. Best place for Marge and me to get video coverage," Levitt pointed out.

"Sir," Alexis broke in, "I also speak the language. I'd like the opportunity to have the Marauders on point for a change."

Bellamack shook his head. "I want my most experienced

220

combat commander there, Morgan. So the Marauders will follow the Companions and be relief point unit. The Warriors will be in the third slot, then the regimental headquarters and supply convoy. Frazier's Ferrets will be rear guard. Normal route march, high mobile noncombat mode. Although I don't anticipate the Herreronistas to stop and fight, be prepared to send out flank guards and move into skirmish line, Marauders right and Warriors left with Ferrets as mobile reserve. Russ, I may have to ask you to do the end run if necessary. It's about sixty kilometers to the first decision point at a wide place in the road called Batepito. That's where the Herreronistas will either go right or left."

"Unless they disperse into the hills as they go," Joan Ward pointed out.

Bellamack shook his head. He was getting used to the free flow of comments and suggestions that characterized an Oscar briefing of the Washington Greys. "I seriously doubt that. They'll stick to creeks and rivers where water is available. They may be able to carry enough food to keep them going, but out in this country no one can possibly carry enough water to keep going for days on foot. We're lucky; we have more than five thousand liters of potable water. Which also means, by the way, that we'd better not waste it until we find a water source where Supply can snuggle up their pumps and filtration units in order to top our tanks. Incidentally, same goes for ammo; don't shoot just to be shooting. If someone takes a shot at you and you can target him, shoot back. Otherwise, maintain contact."

"If the Herreronistas stop, do we attack them?" Alexis wanted to know.

"If they stop, we stop. If they attack, we shoot back. If they don't move and don't attack, we'll probably push on them a little. Depends on what they do and where they do it," Bellamack clarified.

"And if we run into *federales?*"

"If they shoot, shoot back. Otherwise, I'll expect Captain Morgan or Ed Levitt to be on hand to translate for me because I don't want to tangle with Mexican army troops if I can help it. They aren't the enemy. The Herreronistas are." Bellamack checked the clock on the wall. "Time's a-wastin'! The Cottonbalers are scheduled to attack the Agua Prieta hills in thirty-two minutes. They'll open up with a barrage, then move forward. Let them leapfrog through us. Then we'll move left and go around the east side of the hills. We may meet some of the Herreronistas retreating from the hills; if so, we'll pursue them. I'm not going to issue orders any more explicit than that. This is a fluid situation, so monitor the tacomm. Any further questions? No? Very well, dismissed!"

As they left the regimental OCV, Curt touched Alexis's shoulder and told her, "Allie, let me know when the Marauders want to take the point. I can arrange for the Companions to get fatigued. . . ."

"I'll do that," she told him crisply.

"Hey, I didn't ask for the point. Bellamack gave an order," he reminded her.

"So what the hell do I have to do to prove that the Marauders are good at that sort of thing? After all, I was a Companion platoon leader and you taught me . . ."

"As I told you, let me know when you want to take the point," Curt said.

"I don't need your charity, Major!" Alexis was getting feisty under pressure.

Curt stopped and grabbed her arm this time, stopping her as well. "Goddammit, Captain Morgan, what the hell's gotten into you?"

She whirled and faced him. "I bust my ass to go into Douglas this morning for the Mexican topos, and I never get so much as a 'thank you' from the colonel! Not even a 'well done.' And you're probably thinking that I must have enjoyed going with Levitt . . ."

"Well, he is a handsome guy, Alexis . . ."

"And he's married! I, too, learned duty, honor, country. It would be conduct unbecoming an officer if I put the chase on a married man!" Alexis snapped. "I may have gone soft in the head with Len Spencer in Namibia, but that doesn't mean I go after anything with balls! After what you did with that pretty Hindu fluff in Trinidad, I think we're even on that score anyway. And I never got to know that Eurasian bitch-doctor in Zahedan! So bug off, Major! I'll be standing by to relieve you on point when you can't hack it . . . sir!"

Curt released her arm. He knew her well enough to realize she was dog-tired and feeling the stress that comes with the first year of commanding a company and having to worry about more than twice as many people and lots more administrative detail. The two of them had had a long-standing contract. Curt realized that it would have to be modified slowly and carefully now that Alexis had her own company.

He also was worried that company command might change her. It was already showing signs of doing so. That alone had changed the relationship between them from superior-subordinate to equal status as company commanders, although Curt still outranked her. At their level, the difference in rank was minimal insofar as the RHIP factor went; the big jump was the next one from Major to Lieutenant Colonel, the one Bellamack was having his own difficulties assimilating.

"Captain," he told her levelly, looking her straight in the eyes, "we may run into the Herreronistas retreating from the Agua Prieta hills. If either of us runs into them first and needs help, I suggest that we immediately go to tactical battalion procedures. If they've still got a hundred men there, they'll probably fight like hell when they find themselves surrounded and their retreat cut off. And we'll be outnumbered, so we'll need every bot and Sierra Charlie

223

we have between us. I know I can count on you, and you'd better understand that you can count on me . . . as always. In the meantime, lighten up. We've got no time right now for any more confrontational discussion."

And with that, he turned and strode to where the vehicles of Carson's Companions were parked, waiting.

CHAPTER TWENTY-FOUR

It had been a lonely night. Furthermore, even in August, it had been nippy on top of Cerro Caliente at 2,000 meters' elevation. The mountain had not been named because of the weather along its ridge but because of the geothermal activity within it that produced not only hot springs but actual steam vents. The Herrero family had harnessed these to provide an independent source of electrical power for Ghost House.

So Fredrica Herrero had spent a night that was not only a little cold but also lonely. She enjoyed the warmth of her husband alongside her in the huge bed. She became frustrated and impatient when he wasn't there . . . which was more often recently. She didn't like that. Gordo Herrero was the one person she could cling to in a dangerous and vicious world. And she didn't like what he was doing now.

Dealing drugs was one thing. Waging warfare was something else.

And Gordo was out running his private little war up near Douglas.

That was something Fredrica Nordenskold Herrero decidedly did *not* like or approve of.

She was no mere beautiful, sensual mannequin. Although her *macho* husband didn't know it and would not have approved of it had he known, Fredrica kept abreast of the family "business." Furthermore, she knew precisely what was going on, and she also knew and understood

Americans because she was one.

Thus she lay there with the morning sun streaming through the windows and gleaming off the satin sheets and her long, golden hair . . . and she fretted.

It was becoming more and more difficult for her to get a good night's sleep. She awoke every night at about 3:00 A.M. with racking attacks of anxiety syndrome, frightened of things she could not identify, and shaking in fear and terror. When Gordo Herrero was there, he could calm her with his presence and his warmth and his tenderness. And he could satisfy her sexually in a way that took her mind from her unknown fears.

But she didn't fret long that morning. The annunciator alongside the bed chimed.

It wasn't an alarm; Fredrica Herrero had not used an alarm clock since her husband had retired from the Mexican army and they'd moved to Ghost House. She always got up when she felt like it.

Fredrica rolled over to get the sun out of her eyes. A glance at the clock told her it was almost 11:00 A.M. She'd slept late again. So she called out in a sleepy voice, *"¡Hola! ¿Quién habla?"*

It was her *mujer* Renya. The housekeeper informed her deferentially, *"Señora,* your husband wants to speak with you on the radio telephone."

The satin sheets swept back in a flurry as Fredrica threw them out of her way and rolled off the bed to her feet. Although she usually slept nude, the chill of the night had caused her to put on a warm nylon negligee. Nevertheless, it was still cold enough in the bedroom that she grabbed a peignoir as she rushed toward the door. "Renya, quickly! Have Miguel connect to the telephone in my dressing room!"

It definitely wasn't normal for Gordo to call her at this hour of the day, even when he was on a business trip. Fredrica knew something had gone wrong. She was fright-

226

ened.

The dressing room was warmer, but the telephone handset was cool in her hand as she picked it up. "Gordo? *Amorcito!* Are you all right? Where are you?" she said breathlessly into the phone.

The brief delay told her that Herrero was communicating via satellite link. "Freddie, I'm okay," his voice came back. "I want you to pack and be ready to leave Ghost House in two hours! I've spoken with Carlos Mota, and he will have an aerodyne there to pick you up and take you to Puerto Vallarta at once!"

"Puerto Vallarta? At this time of year? Gordo, you must be joking! It's like a Swedish sauna there right now!" she objected.

"Don't argue with me, woman! I said Puerto Vallarta. *Tío* Mota has arranged suitable lodgings there for you. And Puerto Vallarta is a place where the *hermanistas* are capable of providing adequate protection for you."

"What's wrong, Gordo? Where are you? What's happened to make Ghost House so dangerous that you want me out of here?" she wanted to know. "Why do I have to abandon my home?"

She heard a sigh on the other end. Herrero put down his Iberian *machismo* because he knew it wouldn't work on this headstrong American woman. He'd made a conscious choice when he'd married her—or so he'd convinced himself at the time, not willing to admit to himself that Fredrica Nordenskold had become an obsession to him—that he'd somehow either force the American beauty to become a proper Mexican wife or that he'd manage to live with her fierce independence. The former hadn't worked, of course. And he was never sure whether or not he could manage to live with such an independent woman in spite of his love for her. Sometimes he felt that it was tearing him apart.

"Freddie, the American army crossed the border into

Mexico last night after we mounted our raid on the Douglas airport."

"I thought they might when you attacked Bisbee. You underestimated them, Gordo, just like you did in Bisbee. How many of our people were killed last night?"

"Only about seventy killed or captured when the Americans attacked my rear guard this morning."

"In Mexico?"

"Yes, southeast of Agua Prieta."

"Gordo, stop it! Stop what you're doing! Stop it right now! You're killing people and you're going to kill more! Didn't you anticipate the Americans would invade Mexico if provoked? They've done it before!"

"Don't lecture me, Freddie! That's exactly what I wanted the Americans to do!"

"You *wanted* the United States to invade Mexico?" Fredrica was having trouble believing what she heard.

"Of course! Can you think of anything that will bring down the Alvaro government faster?"

"I didn't think you were going to start a full-scale war to do it!"

"I'm not, Freddie. I don't intend to fight the Americans. I'm going to let them chase me into Sonora, into the Sierra Madres. The deeper into Mexico the Americans go, the quicker Alvaro's government falls. Especially if he makes no attempt to defend the country, which he can't because his troops are pinned down on the southern borders."

"And how many people are going to be killed trying to fight off the Americans?" Fredrica wanted to know.

"Only the stupid ones, Freddie," he told her, knowing of her own beliefs regarding the stupid and the dead.

"Gordo, get out of there!" Fredrica told him. "Let your peasant army disperse into the hills and get out of there! The Americans may stop when they discover your Herreronistas have disappeared."

228

"No, that's not what I have to do, Freddie," Herrero told his wife. "I'm going to continue to withdraw until the American supply lines are stretched out. I'm going to lead them into the Sierra Madres where we can cut them up with short raids. But I'm not going to discuss my tactics with you, Freddie. There's a chance that the Americans may penetrate as far south as Ghost House, and I don't want you to be there if they do. So I want you to leave for Puerto Vallarta when Mota's aerodyne shows up."

"No, Gordo," Fredrica said firmly.

"Don't you disobey me, Freddie!"

"I'm not going to Puerto Vallarta! If you're in danger, I want to be with you! Where are you?"

"I'll be south of Morelos tonight. That's about as far as I can push my soldiers on foot."

"I'm coming to you!"

"Absolutely not! This is a difficult and dangerous life, very primitive, very rugged. I don't want you here!" he told her just as firmly.

"Dangerous? You know the Americans and their warbot army, Gordo!" Fredrica reminded him. "Their warbots won't shoot at unarmed civilians such as myself!"

"The Americans didn't send their Robot Infantry against me," Herrero suddenly explained. "These are new Special Combat regiments, the ones they used in Trinidad and Namibia. The Seventeenth Division, General Jacob Carlisle's outfit from Diamond Point, Arizona. Matter of fact, Freddie, one of the reasons I want you somewhere else is that I've gone over the order of battle of the Seventeenth Division. One regiment, the one leading the chase into Mexico at the moment, is the Washington Greys. You and I both know several officers in that regiment, including Curt Carson."

"Curt? Curt Carson's commanding one of the units invading Mexico?" Fredrica remembered Curt fondly. If it had been an even toss-up between Gordo Herrero and

Curt Carson and the personal wealth factor eliminated, Curt would have been her choice. Now, knowing what she did of Gordo Herrero's "family" and its source of wealth, and all the problems that it caused, she thought she might have made a different choice. Especially since her husband was instigating a de facto war in which innocent people were being killed.

"He's only a major, and he's still commanding only a company in the Washington Greys," Herrero informed her, proudly inferring that he had risen to the rank of full *coronel* or colonel in the Mexican army and was at this time commanding a far larger paramilitary unit than Curt Carson. "So I want you out of Ghost House and in a safe place further south. I don't want a situation where you might be captured by the Greys and used as a hostage against me. . . ."

"Americans don't take hostages, Gordo!" she informed him.

"Just as they invaded Mexico, they've done it before and they'll do it again," he predicted.

"Gordo, when will I see you again?"

"I don't know," Herrero told her. "It may not be until this is all over, when the Alvaro government has fallen, when the Americans have retreated back to their country. How long that will take, I do not know. Freddie, you are going to have to be a good military wife. You are going to have to be where you are safe. And you will just have to wait until the campaign is over."

Fredrica Herrero suddenly knew what she was going to have to do. The plan was not complete in her mind yet. In fact, it was never completed, never thought through, never analyzed. And she certainly didn't consider all the consequences of what she wanted to do. But an impulse drove her. She would do what she wanted to do because it was the only way she could have some effect on events. It was the only way she could see to bring this crazy, bizarre killing to an end and her husband back to her.

But she dared not tell her husband.

So she suddenly went meek, mild, submissive. "Very well, Gordo, my love, I will do what you wish. I will be packed and ready when *Tío* Mota's aerodyne arrives."

If Fredrica's surrender to his wishes was sudden, Herrero didn't suspect anything. Instead, he told himself that it was about time Fredrica started acting like a wife *should* act. Perhaps it had taken the element of danger to bring her to her senses. "Good. I'll call you again when I have time, my love. I must go now! *¡Mi hijita, se buena!*"

Herrero cut the connection from his end without waiting for a farewell from his wife.

That made Fredrica angry. It further reinforced her resolve to do what she'd just determined she must do.

"Renya!" she called out to the voice-actuated intercom on the wall. "I want you! Come!"

Her housekeeper was in the dressing room almost immediately. "*¿Sí, Señora Herrero?*"

"Renya, I want you to pack a bag for me at once," Fredrica told her. "I want as many changes of lingerie as possible, and I will choose several outfits to wear." She rapidly pushed her way through clothing hanging in one of the closets, pulling out one outfit after another and almost throwing them at her housekeeper. She knew that she'd need rugged outdoor clothing, but she also wanted it to be provocative if possible. She selected several very feminine articles as well.

When she appeared on the patio for breakfast, she wore khaki slacks and shirt and carried a broad-brimmed felt hat and a leather jacket. Renya followed her with a large travel case. As Fredrica sat down for what was really a brunch, she indicated for her housekeeper to sit as well. "Renya," she told her as she began to eat, "I will be leaving when I finish eating. Another aerodyne will arrive in about an hour and the pilot will ask for me. Do not lie to

231

him, but tell him that I left earlier in one of our personal aerodynes and you do not know where I went. I anticipate returning to Ghost House with Colonel Herrero when he comes back. Is that understood?"

Renya said it was but thought it was unnecessary for her lady to warn her about lying. The housekeeper had been with the Herrero family for years, and she knew what happened to people who were caught lying. So Renya didn't question her *señora* further. The Herreros always had good reasons why they did something, and it wasn't healthy for the hired help to pry too deeply into these affairs.

Fredrica asked Renya to send up the *teniente*, Emilio Orozco, who appeared on the patio and nodded his head deferentially. Actually, he had no need to do that, because he knew Fredrica Herrero very well—intimately, in fact. Colonel Herrero was often absent on business for long periods of time. Fredrica and Emilio shared the secret; if either spoke about it, one would be quickly dead and the other wishing for death. Thus, either one could ask the other for a favor without recrimination. Fortunately, Fredrica had chosen well; Emilio's requests were always modest in nature, although he could have asked for anything.

He sat with his *señora* as she finished brunch. "Emilio, the *coronel* spoke with me this morning and wishes me to undertake a very dangerous secret operation for him. I need you to fly the aerodyne. We must go into northern Sonora. I will give you more information about our destination once we are airborne. Will you fly for me?"

"*Señora*, as you know, for you I will do anything as long as it is not contrary to the orders of the *coronel*," Emilio replied easily, then smiled. "Fortunately, the *coronel* cannot give orders concerning everything, eh?"

"Fortunately," Fredrica echoed. "Is the AeroBianchi fueled and ready, and do you have your overnight kit aboard as usual?"

232

Emilio looked surprised. "You would make me fly a mule when you have a luxurious Rolls Apollo?"

"I want the most reliable, economical, and rugged aerodyne we have, Emilio," she told him. "Where are we going, we may not be able to have it fixed if something goes wrong."

"I can fix the AeroBianchi with scraps of wire and strips of cloth!" Emilio told her proudly with a grin.

"I know you can, which is why we're taking it." She put down her napkin and rose to her feet. "We are leaving now."

"Now?" Emilio was surprised.

"Now. 'But I have promises to keep, and miles to go before I sleep.' Never mind. It was once said by an American poet. *Estoy lista. Venga.*"

CHAPTER TWENTY-FIVE

"Grey Head, this is Marauder Leader. The Herreronistas have halted their retreat. Furthermore, they've done so in an excellent defensive position," the voice of Captain Alexis Morgan came over the regimental tacomm frequency.

It was now about a half hour after sunset. It had been a slow chase. The Greys could move much faster than the Herreronistas, who were on foot, so it was slow going because the orders were explicit: Maintain contact but do not attack. This made it tough for the point company, and Carson's Companions were exhausted from the continual adjustment of speed required to maintain contact without assault. In more ways than one, Curt was glad that Bellamack had decided to allow Morgan's Marauders to alternate on point with the Companions. At the moment, the Marauders were on point and had been for the past three hours, with the Companions trailing them in the long column formation of the regiment that stretched northward.

Curt directed his attention to the tac display in his ACV. Ed Levitt had done what he said he would; the data base now included the information read from the Mexican topo charts. (Someone in G-2 at higher levels was going to get a royal ass-chewing about that fuck-up, Curt decided.) The electro-optical sensors—infrared, visual, and ultraviolet, plus the more detailed resolution from passive UV laser—showed the Rio Batepito at Morelos joining the Rio Bavispe flowing in from the east through a very steep canyon. The road swung to the north of the 1,300-meter Cerro Prieto. The Herreronistas had occupied this high ground and apparently stopped for the night with their main body behind the hill. Morgan's Marauders were at that moment about 1,500 meters north of the Herreronista position. This put Morgan's Marauders right out at the limits of 7.62-millimeter lethal range.

"Marauder Leader, this is Grey Head," came the call from Bellamack. "I want you to withdraw to the regimental headquarters position. You've been on point for three hours. I'm moving Frazier's Ferrets up to picket duty tonight; they haven't been shot at today."

Morgan's voice came back, "Roger, Grey Head. Thanks for giving us the night off. It wasn't easy maintaining point today. We're used to maneuvering rapidly to attack, then attacking . . . not this chase stuff."

Bellamack then ordered, "Regiment halt! Ferrets relieve Marauders on point as pickets. Marauders and Warriors deploy east and west of the regimental convoy. Companions withdraw to serve as rear picket tonight. Grey Eyes, I want recon birdbots out as long as you can keep them aloft; if the Herreronistas move out tonight, I want to move, too."

"Colonel," Curt broke in, "we don't think they're going to move out tonight. They must be pretty damned exhausted after marching fifty kilometers on foot."

"That may be the case, Major, but I don't want to bet my silver oak leaves on it," Bellamack replied. "Some of these native irregulars have a lot more stamina than we think."

If they're motivated by religious zeal, perhaps, Curt told himself, drawing on his own combat experience. At the moment, Curt didn't see that the Herreronistas were anything more than a loosely organized group of peasant guerrillas, and there was no religious zeal driving them. Fear, perhaps. The elite force encountered in Bisbee hadn't been located yet among these Herreronistas, and perhaps the disciplined and well-equipped elite troops were serving in the role of the fabled "KGB Reserves," utterly loyal and strongly disciplined units that followed Soviet "teeth" units into battle and simply shot anyone who broke or retreated.

"If the main body takes a short rest and continues to move southward under cover of darkness, then we've got to go after them," Bellamack pointed out. "We may have to carry out a night assault on Cerro Prieto if they try to withdraw their main body under the natural defensive positions on that hill. Captain Frazier, please send a stealthed squad out on patrol to the east of Cerro Prieto to probe the Herreronista defenses there; Gibbon, back him up with a birdbot."

"I remember," Master Sergeant Henry Kester grumbled, "an old cartoon that said something like, *When they run, we try to ketch 'em. When we ketch 'em, we try to make 'em run.* Jeez, what a drag! Fifty kilometers, and they stop for the night in a place they can defend until hell freezes over, which ain't gonna happen here in the next few years."

"Well, at least we know where the hell they are, Henry," Curt replied as he studied the tac display. "And they walked the whole damned fifty klicks, which means they're more tired than we are."

"Maybe. Maybe not. But I'll be glad when we've got enough darkness that I can go outside and take a leak without getting shot at."

"Yeah, you're right. We haven't spotted that elite outfit of theirs yet, and they may have IR night scopes on sniping rifles," Curt pointed out.

"Well, I ain't had that part of me shot up yet. And don't tell me it's too small to hit, Major. Ten thousand women think otherwise."

"Ten thousand?" Curt jested with his old Master Sergeant. "Did you keep a diary?"

Kester tapped his head. "No, sir, it's all up here in ROM now."

"Okay, Henry, go outside and take a leak," Curt told him. "If there's a convenient place to do it around here before we withdraw to the regimental convoy, please dump the holding tank."

"Yeah, we've been filling it up all day, haven't we?"

While his Master Sergeant was outside and while he was waiting for the opportunity to move out of column and back to the flank of the regimental portion of the column, Curt studied the lay of the land ahead of them. He was still doing that when Kester came back. The Master Sergeant looked over Curt's shoulder and remarked, "Hell, Major, if we have to make a night assault on Cerro Prieto, that shouldn't be any big deal if all the Herreronistas has is small arms stuff. That hill ain't more than four hundred meters high. I'll bet we could take it with Mary Annes provided they had Hairy Foxes for fire support."

"Probably, probably," Curt muttered. "But that's not our objective."

Kester nodded. "Yes, sir. You don't need to remind me of that. Our objective: Chase their asses as far into Mexico as we can and break up their base of operations, if we can find it . . . or if they'll lead us to it, which I don't think they will."

"How's the weather outside?"

"Still hot and humid. No thunderboomer in the area, but I could see lots of anvil tops all around us."

"Okay, let's re-deploy the company in accordance with the colonel's orders."

They passed through Frazier's Ferrets on their way to establish rear guard over the night's bivouac, swung around the cluster of regimental OCVs, CTVs, and BSVs, and located the Companion vehicles in an arc around the rear of the column. By the time they'd done this and broken out the evening's rations, it had cooled down enough to eat outside. This was a boon because they'd been in their vehicles all day, albeit in the comfort of an air-conditioned environment. Curt didn't want his Sierra Charlies to get soft doing that sort of thing; they had to be ready to dismount and fight in whatever weather was occurring outside at the moment. Weather rarely co-operates with combat. In fact, weather has often had a major impact on the outcome of battles.

Field rations weren't sumptuous, but they were tasty, hot, and satisfying. Army food had come a long way, pri-marily because of progress in commercial food packaging, preservation, and rapid preparation. When things really got tight and the troops had to eat under fire, the food couldn't be quite as good. But it was far better than bully beef and biscuits, K rations, shit on a shingle, or even mystery stew that had been the lot of field soldiers during the twentieth century. Before that time, with the occasional exception of the Napoleonic armies, soldiers had to live off the land. According to modern nutritionists, it was a won-der any of those old-time soldiers had enough energy to fight, judging by what they had available to eat.

After seeing to it that the Companions were fed and the situation under control so they could get a good night's sleep as the rear guard of the column, Curt walked the few hundred meters over to Captain Alexis Morgan's ACV.

"Evenin', ma'am!" Curt hailed Alexis as he walked up and touched the visor of his helmet.

"Good evening, Major," she replied, a note of exhausted testiness in her voice.

"Yeah, I agree. Rough day," he said, sitting down beside her and leaning back against the running gear of her ACV.

"Goddamned supply outfit!" Alexis growled. "Loaded us up with creamed chipped beef dinners! Looks like that's all the Marauders are going to eat for the next couple of days!"

"Trade you for some franks and beans," Curt told her. "We've got a surplus of those."

"Deal. I'll have Carol Head check with Henry Kester."

"You working in okay with Sergeant Head?"

She nodded. Being in a rear position, she'd removed her helmet, and her short curls bobbed as she moved her head. Somehow, although Army regulations and the regimental TO&E listed no requirements for S-4 to supply cosmetics or even hair-care products for the women of a Sierra Charlie outfit, where it was a mark of distinction to allow your hair to grow, Alexis always managed to look quite feminine in spite of unisex combat clothing. "Carol's a good man. I depend on him even more than Nick Gerard. Different person. Lots more experience. Gerard was an excellent platoon sergeant, and he'll make a good first sergeant some day soon. But with my first company command, I needed an experienced first sergeant. And Carol knows how to run the Marauders. Believe me, he shares none of the problems the former company commander had about converting to the Sierra Charlie doctrine. He'd never say anything about a former company commander, but it's obvious enough that he'd had some trouble with him."

"Some people aren't cut out for the Sierra Charlies, Allie," Curt reminded her.

"Then they should have some way to ease them over into full warbot outfits as warbot brainies."

"They will. Army learns slowly."

"Sure as hell does," she admitted bluntly. "And it's us troops in the field that have to put up with the problems."

"Well, we're the first Sierra Charlie outfit. We get to make all the mistakes. Thank God we don't make them all at once! Better that the Army learn from field experience than from some tech-weenie doing battle sims and playing war games with a computer."

239

"Air intruder alert! Air intruder alert!" came the computer voice from the Marauder ACV. "Unidentified aerodyne approaching, bearing zero-one-zero, speed one hundred knots, range twenty-four kilometers, radar transponder beacon squawking civilian ID code. No stealth, no countermeasures. Radar signature indicates it is a civilian AeroBianchi light cargo vehicle. Estimated time of arrival at regimental center is ten minutes."

"What the hell?" Alexis asked rhetorically.

"Civilian? Coming in from the north? And an Aero-Bianchi? Hell, no one flies those iron frisbees in the States." It didn't sound right to Curt.

"Mexican," Alexis guessed, correctly as it turned out. "The AeroBianchi is a favorite among ranchers. Iron frisbee, like you said."

Curt was on his feet and running back toward his ACV. "We'll come to full air assault alert for this one!" he yelled.

He anticipated the regimental commander. "Greys all, this is Grey Head! Unidentified aerodyne approaching! All units to Zulu Alert to counter possible air attack. Button down and power up! Companies debouch your Mary Annes and Hairy Foxes and be prepared to shoot." It was Major Wade Hampton's voice, the second in command. "But hold your fire until we see who it is and what they want. Could be some rancher who got lost or just happened to blunder into us. We're scanning for additional aerodynes, but negative on additionals at this time."

Curt clambered up the glacis of his ACV and dropped through the hatch. He saw the RTVs of Alpha and Bravo companies deploying their Mary Annes and Hairy Foxes.

Henry Kester had the ACV in air defense mode already. "Companions in air defense deployment, Major," he reported. "All vehicles tracking and ready to fire. We'll have the Mary Annes in position in two minutes, the Hairy Foxes in three."

Curt checked the tac display. "It's coming right straight

240

at us."

"Yes, sir. No jinks or zangs. If it's in attack mode, it's a sitting duck," Kester observed.

Curt grabbed his night vision scope and stuck his head out of the turret hatch with the idea of getting a visual on the incoming aircraft. But he didn't need to use the IR aid. The incoming aircraft was plainly visible to the north, its strobes flashing and its landing lights making it a very bright star against an incredibly starry sky.

No one in his right mind would approach a military formation under those conditions . . . unless it was a signal not to shoot.

Curt was plugged into the regimental tacomm net, and he heard the voice of Staff Sergeant Emma Crawford of Gibbon's comm-intel unit calling on the Mexican aeronautical or "unicom" frequency, 131.0 megaHertz: "Unidentified AeroBianchi aerodyne proceeding from the north toward Batepito and Morelos, this is the United States Army Third Robot Infantry Regiment at Batepito. Our call sign is Grey Air. Identify yourself or be fired upon. I repeat: Identify yourself or be fired upon. Over!"

The reply was instantaneous, but it startled Curt. A male voice speaking reasonably good aviation English said, "Grey Air, this is AeroBianchi Xray-Charlie-Mike-Papa-Alpha. Do not shoot! We are an unarmed civilian aircraft. We wish to land near you. I have a passenger who wishes to speak with one of your officers, Curt Carson."

"AeroBianchi Xray-Charlie-Mike-Papa-Alpha, this is Grey Air," Emma Crawford snapped back. "Please identify yourself and the passenger who wishes to speak with one of our officers."

"Grey Air, Mike-Papa-Alpha, my name is Emilio Orozco. My passenger is *Señora* Fredrica Nordenskold Herrero."

Oh, my God! Curt thought. *Freddie, you beautiful animal, you! My wild-ass hunch was right! Gordo Herrero's behind all of this! But why?* He wanted to find out. And now for some strange reason they might be able to. It could cut short this wild chase into the wilderness of the Sierra Madres Occidental. This was probably the Big Breakthrough. Unless Freddie Herrero was playing some sort of a game. But he wouldn't know until he talked with her. So he keyed his tacomm and called, "Grey Head, this is Companion Leader. I know the lady! Let the aerodyne land!"

CHAPTER TWENTY-SIX

"AeroBianchi Mike-Papa-Alpha, come to hover at your present position," Staff Sergeant Emma Crawford's voice on the tacomm instructed the incoming aerodyne.

"Companion Leader, this is Grey Head!" It was Bellamack this time, not Hampton. "What's the situation? Do you know this woman he named?"

"Yes, Colonel, I do," Curt replied. "She's from Newburgh, and I used to date her at West Point. She married a classmate, Luis Sebastian Herrero, a Mexican honor legacy."

"Do you think this could be a trick?"

"Hell, Colonel, I don't know!" Curt replied in exasperation. "Freddie might be bearing a message from Herrero himself. I suspect he's the leader of these renegades who call themselves Herreronistas."

"Why didn't you tell me about Herrero?"

"Colonel," Curt admitted, "when we found out that this outfit called itself the Herreronistas, I had a wild idea that Herrero might be behind these raids, but there was no data to back it up. It might have been just a coincidence. Last I heard, Gordo Herrero was a full colonel in the Mexican army. And I haven't got the foggiest notion what the hell is going on or why his wife came here. But if we allow only one unarmed civilian aerodyne to land and if we can talk with Fredrica Herrero, we're sure as hell going to learn *something!*"

"That aerodyne could be a bomb," Bellamack mused, his Mid-East warbot brainy experience showing. "Could be loaded with explosives."

"Not if Fredrica Herrero is in it," Curt observed. "I can vouch for the fact that she thinks very highly of her own skin."

"Colonel," Alexis Morgan put in. "Fanatical, suicidal zeal isn't part of the Mexican culture. The Muslims go to paradise if they buy it on a suicide mission. The Mexicans don't."

"Let the aerodyne land," Bellamack decided. "Carson, she wants to see you. Get your jeep out to a favorable landing location with a couple of flares and bring that aerodyne in north of the bivouac, *not* in the middle. Meet it when it lands and escort the occupants to my OCV. Morgan, cover him with the Marauders."

"You bet I will!" came Alexis's quick reply.

Oh, shit! Allie's letting her brass get green again! he thought quickly in the West Point cadet slang for jealousy. He and Alexis had their own special contract that went a little further than most. But he didn't dwell on it. He didn't have time. "Companion Alpha and Companion Bravo, this is Companion Leader," he called his platoon officers. "Alpha, I want you with me; have one of your Mary Annes cover. Bravo, deploy a Hairy Fox in case we need to waste the aerodyne quickly. Henry, get Companion Leader jeep deployed and out to a suitable area."

While he was doing this, Emma Crawford was giving landing instructions to Emilio Orozco in the aerodyne.

The AeroBianchi was indeed a heavy hauler designed to operate in dusty climes. It featured deeply ducted and screened intakes and a deployable deflector lip around its edge to reduce ground billow when it landed or took off. It made a gentle and graceful landing without a bounce about 50 meters north of Curt's ACV. Curt was there. So was Kitsy Clinton with her Mary Anne. And standing not

244

very far away was Captain Alexis Morgan with her jeep and a Mary Anne. As the turbines powered down and the maelstrom of air subsided, floodlights flicked on under the 'dyne's belly.

It was a truck, not a limo, so it didn't deploy a walk-down ramp but a simple ladder.

Fredrica Herrero knew how to make an entrance. She stepped down the ladder backward, being very careful to get each of her high-heeled strapped sandals correctly placed on every rung. Her attire may have been uncolorful and somewhat plain, but there was no question whatsoever that this woman was extremely wealthy, because she was dressed in the obviously flamboyant and expensive style of those who can easily afford high fashion. Her khaki slacks tapered down her long legs and were very tight across her hips. Above the wide military belt that cinched her narrow waist, the butterfly sleeves of her otherwise tautly tailored khaki shirt allowed her long arms to reach the rungs of the ladder. She'd left her broad-brimmed felt hat inside, and her hip-length blond hair swung freely behind her as she descended.

When she reached the bottom and turned, she had aroused every man in the Washington Greys who was watching — and suddenly most of them within visual range were indeed watching — and made every woman either intensely jealous or envious.

Watching her, Curt had to admit that the years since he'd seen her last during her West Point wedding to Herrero had done nothing to diminish her stunning Nordic beauty. In fact, if anything they had enhanced her already incredible sensuality. Curt had known that Gordo Herrero's family had wealth beyond imagining, and Fredrica had used that wealth artfully to enhance her appearance. In spite of the bitter memories she'd left with him by marrying Herrero, Curt again felt a twinge of lust for her.

But if she was indeed the wife of the man whose mercenaries had raided and killed in the United States, he knew that now she had to be treated with extreme care as a potential enemy. Or at least as a messenger from an enemy. On sudden reflection, however, he couldn't fathom why Herrero would have sent her or why she would accede to such a request from her husband. Freddie was a strong-willed woman and always had been. His curiosity about her mission was stronger than his lust, and he knew he had to keep both under tight control in this situation.

So he stepped forward into the ramp floodlights of the aerodyne and removed his helmet so she could see him.

"Hello, Freddie, what are you doing here under these circumstances?" he said to her.

"Curt!" She exploded into action by throwing her arms around him and hugging him.

Curt took her arms from around his neck. "I understand you wanted to see me," he managed to say.

"Oh, yes, yes!" she breathed, stepping back. "I want to end all this senseless killing and destruction."

"Well, that's a pretty big order. How do your propose to help?"

She simply stood back and looked him over. "My, army life has indeed been good to you! In fact, I think you've grown more handsome! And a major now!"

"As usual, you look outstanding, too," Curt returned the compliment, then tried to get down to the business at hand. "How's Gordo? Where is he? And how come you flew out here in the middle of nowhere? What's up?"

"I haven't seen Gordo in weeks," she admitted. "And, yes, I do want to talk to you about all of this, which is why I'm here."

"I think," Curt ventured, "that we'd better get these lights out and go over to the regimental commander's vehicle. The Herreronistas may have sniping rifles that could reach this far; if so, we're sitting ducks right now. . . ."

"Oh, they don't have any M-Fours," she advised him.

"Did you fly this AeroBianchi yourself, or is there a pilot aboard?" Curt asked, looking up at the hulking ship. "And how many others did you bring? Better have them come out right now. Back there in the dark are some itchy trigger fingers, and I wouldn't want our troops to accidentally put a lot of holes in your aircraft. Or you."

"I have only one person with me," Fredrica admitted. She turned and called up into the open belly hatch, *"¡Emilio, venga aquí pronto!"* Then she added to Curt, "Emilio Orozco is my pilot. He's my husband's *teniente.*"

Captain Alexis Morgan stepped into the circle of light and remarked, *"Señora, en ingles teniente es* lieutenant. *¿Es su esposo el soldado?"*

"I speak English quite well, Captain," Fredrica replied coolly, addressing Alexis by her rank to indicate that she recognized American military insigne. "And so does Emilio. And please lower that Novia rifle; I'm unarmed and so is Emilio."

Alexis was trim and in excellent physical condition. Furthermore, she wouldn't stand down to any woman when it came to her figure. But she greatly envied this woman's sensual body and the way she was able to display it in her fashionable clothing. And because Fredrica knew Curt— apparently quite well—from earlier times at West Point, Alexis was unabashedly jealous of the woman. In fact, she hated Fredrica Herrero in the unique way women hate other women for reasons unfathomable to men.

Lieutenant Kitsy Clinton, on the other hand, was petite and very slender. As she stood there slightly behind and to the left of Curt looking at the glamorous blonde, she was also envious but in a quite different way. Fredrica Herrero made Kitsy feel ugly, unattractive, and less of a woman. In Kitsy's case, this didn't exhibit itself as hatred but as curiosity. She wanted to know how Fredrica did it. Kitsy knew that money could often buy anything when it came to twenty-first-century biocosmetics, but she was fairly cer-

247

tain that this Nordic goddess possessed natural beauty, something that didn't come from cosmetic surgery or bio-chemical treatments.

In any event, Fredrica Herrero didn't exactly engender friendly attitudes among the women of the Washington Greys right from the very first.

Emilio Orozco, on the other hand, was a darkly hand-some man with the typical Mexican mustache and a broad face. He wore a broad-brimmed straw hat, quite atypical of an aerodyne pilot, and carried what appeared to be Fredrica's large handbag. As he reached the ground, Kitsy Clinton stepped up to him and told him, "Please let me see what's in the bag."

"It's only my handbag, Lieutenant," Fredrica explained.

Kitsy looked straight at her and said bluntly, "And it's large enough to carry a Mendoza submachine gun, too. Sorry about that, but at this point we'd feel a lot better if we had a quick look."

Emilio shrugged and opened the bag for Kitsy. Fredrica said nothing.

It contained no weapons, only the usual woman things plus a wallet stuffed with both American dollars and Mexi-can pesos, plus Fredrica's United States passport. Kitsy indicated that Emilio could hand it to the woman.

"Satisfied, Lieutenant, now that you've inspected my personal belongings?" Fredrica's voice was also cool.

"Yes, ma'am, thank you," Kitsy replied with equal cool-ness but considerably more couth. "Mrs. Herrero, your husband's troops have been shooting at us, and we're just a tad skittish about things at the moment."

"I can well understand that," Fredrica suddenly said, the ice gone from her voice. "Well, Curt, I want to set things right again. Where can we talk?"

"As I said, my regimental commander wants to talk with you," Curt told her. "Let's go over to his command vehicle. Emilio, please come with us."

During the short walk, Fredrica tried to make small talk. "Where have you been all these years, Curt?"

"Around," Curt replied brusquely. "I've been with the Washington Greys since I graduated, and we've been in a lot of places — Munsterlagen, Persian Gulf, Zahedan, Trinidad, Namibia."

"Oh, yes, I read about that. You were there?"

Curt nodded. "And you, Freddie? What have you been doing?"

"Being a wife to Gordo Herrero," she said simply.

"Are you happy?"

"Once. Not very much now."

"Oh? Why?"

"I don't approve of what my husband is doing now," Fredrica snapped. "Killing people and destroying their property is wrong, even if it does protect the family interests. . . ."

"What are the Herrero family interests, Freddie?"

"Habit-forming chemical substances for the weak-willed people of the world who should be allowed to poison themselves anyway. It gets them out of the way of those of us who are stronger . . ."

"Gordo Herrero is a drug dealer?" Curt asked in disbelief.

She shook her head. "No, not just a dealer. Gordo would never sell directly to people on the street. Back in the twentieth century, the Herrero family saw a market need and started a business to satisfy the market. It's strictly a business. In your terms, Gordo might be considered a wholesaler, a shipper, a warehouser."

In spite of his surprise, a lot of things suddenly began to make sense to Curt. Questions a decade old were answered by Fredrica's simple statement.

Gordo Herrero had been one of Curt's best friends at West Point. Now Curt realized that all of Herrero's affluence had come from the dirty business of providing drugs to Americans. That wealth had allowed Herrero to get this woman as well. A quiet anger welled up in Curt.

But, he told himself, perhaps it was poetic justice. Married, Curt could never have become a warbot brainy or a Sierra Charlie. He probably would have been slipped into some noncombat specialty, never to lead troops in battle. Although Curt was no war-lover, he had experienced combat and knew what General George S. Patton meant when he'd said, "Compared to war, all other forms of human endeavor shrink to insignificance."

But a West Point graduate becoming a Mexican drug lord? That made Curt very angry because, in his mind, it sullied the proud reputation of his school.

Now this sensual woman from his past had reentered his life at a most inopportune and critical point in time. Was she deserting her husband? Why?

Curt didn't want to say much more until there were others present, namely his commanding officer. He was in a difficult position both professionally and emotionally. He didn't like that. Not one damned bit.

CHAPTER TWENTY-SEVEN

Major Curt Carson said nothing more as he led Fredrica Herrero and Emilio Orozco to Colonel Bellamack's OCV.

Wild Bill Bellamack was appropriately gallant to Fredrica, although Curt detected suspicion lying beneath the man's polite demeanor.

But it was Fredrica who opened the discussion. "I'm here in an attempt to bring this military operation to a halt," she said firmly. "But before we discuss matters further, I want an agreement between us."

"I'm not sure I can enter into an agreement with you, *Señora* Herrero," Bellamack told her bluntly. "In fact, I'm not exactly certain what your status is at the moment."

"I'm an American citizen," Fredrica said proudly, producing her United States passport. "I may be married to a Mexican citizen, but I've never renounced my American citizenship."

"What is your status with the Mexican government?"

"The same as it is with other Americans who marry Mexican citizens or Mexicans who marry American citizens," she replied diffidently. "Under the Treaty of Nogales, we may live in either country and retain the citizenship of our choice."

"I wasn't really concerned about your citizenship, *Señora*. I'm more concerned about your loyalties," Bellamack told her frankly.

251

This caused her to bristle. "I'm trying not to take sides in this unofficial war. I dislike war! I've told my husband to disband his personal army and stop killing innocent people He didn't, and it's tearing me to pieces."

"Very well, what are your terms? What do you want, and what do we get for granting it?" Bellamack knew he couldn't agree to anything, but he needed to find out whether or not what Fredrica Herrero had to offer was worth getting in touch with divisional headquarters and bringing General Carlisle into the meeting via two-way interactive telecommunications.

"I want the full protection of the United States government for me and my husband, if he'll come with me," Fredrica stated. "I want immunity for the two of us against any crimes the United States may believe we've committed under federal law. I want guarded domicile for us in the United States. And I want full protection for and access to our various overseas bank accounts."

"I can't give you what you want," Bellamack admitted frankly, then added, "But I'll try to bring the necessary American agencies into the discussions. What do you offer in return?"

"Information."

"What sort of information?"

"You must know by now that you're not fighting the Mexican army . . . yet. I'll give you the full background on the Herreronistas and reveal my husband's strategy. I'll tell you why he's doing what he's doing. Furthermore, I'll lead you directly to Casa Fantasma, our home. It's the headquarters of the Herreronistas. And more. But I won't tell you anything else now without your agreement to my terms. And you'll never find Casa Fantasma otherwise. Without my help in bringing this nightmare to a halt, you'll only chase the Herreronistas deeper and deeper into Mexico. The Herreronistas will harass you from all sides as your lines of communications and supply grow longer.

252

Eventually, the Mexican government will change its current policy and send its troops to drive you back across the border. There will be more killing. More innocent people will be hurt. More property will be destroyed. But I can bring all of this to an end within a few days."

"We could certainly wind this up quite rapidly if your husband knew you were here," Bellamack ventured.

Fredrica looked haughtily at him and told him bluntly, "How? By holding me as a hostage? I'm an American citizen. How can you hold me prisoner at all? Imprison me, and I guarantee that when this is all over, I'll have you in court *and* a court martial as well!"

Bellamack looked at her in silence for long seconds. She was right. He couldn't hold her under any pretenses. He had absolutely no authority over her whatsoever. If he'd been an international lawyer rather than a military field commander, he might have sought a loophole in a law somewhere. But he was unwilling to take the chance right then. Finally, he told her, *"Señora,* you've made a tempting offer. As I told you, I'm in no position of authority where I can give you the assurance you ask for. Please let me talk with my superior officer. He's going to have to discuss this with other American officials. Please accept our hospitality for the night and allow me to speak privately with General Carlisle."

"I must have an answer before dawn," Fredrica put in. "My husband doesn't know I'm here. At first light, the Herreronistas will see the AeroBianchi and its presence will be reported to him." She didn't mention that Herrero already didn't know where she was, that the *hermanista* aerodyne scheduled to meet her at Casa Fantasma had discovered her gone, that the pilot and Carlos Mota had probably already reported her disappearance to Herrero, and that her only remaining course of action was to lift off before dawn and get as far into the United States as possible. In any event, Herrero might be distracted from his current war operations and come looking for her. It might break up the Herreronistas. But if she didn't get the protection of the United States, she knew she'd be a hunted woman for the rest of her life.

It had been a very complex act. Fredrica Herrero had a devious and covetous mind, but she wasn't brilliant. She'd never had to be. And she was incapable of considering all the aspects of what she'd done and following them through to logical conclusions. She had one trump card to play: gaining the protection of the United States government in return for her information. If they didn't rise to the opportunity, she only knew she'd have to go on the run and live opportunistically in the United States for as long as she could.

And that might not be for very long. She was certain to be spotted, and the power of the drug lords was ruthless.

"Captain Morgan and Lieutenant Clinton will see to your comfort, *señora*," Bellamack told her. "Please accompany them. Captain Morgan, you have the responsibility for *señora* Herrero. Major Carson, I want to speak with you."

When the ladies had left, the colonel turned to Curt and simply asked, "Well?"

Bellamack was seeking Curt's intuitive inputs gained from that amazing conference. So Curt told his regimental commander, "Sir, that was classic Freddie, all of it. She's a beautiful woman . . ."

"That she is."

"But sometimes she isn't very bright," Curt went on. "She went for money, power and the good life when she married Herrero. Whatever's happened, Herrero and his drug ring are probably in some sort of trouble. Otherwise, he wouldn't be pulling this private military crap. Could be that the Mexican government is on his ass. I don't know. I don't follow that sort of thing. I've got my hands full with my military responsibilities."

254

"Do you think it's worth following up on her offer?" Bellamack wanted to know.

"Hell, Colonel, it wouldn't hurt. What have we got to lose?" Curt pointed out. "The protection issue is out of our hands, but I'd certainly forward her requests to General Carlisle. The United States government has offered this sort of protection to others in the past."

"Can we trust her?" That was the crucial question in Bellamack's mind.

"I think so."

"Why?"

"She talks like Fredrica Nordenskold has always talked," Curt observed. "Being brought up in Newburgh in the shadow of West Point, she couldn't avoid the military. A lot of the local girls find the uniforms and the glamor hard to resist. And admit it, Colonel, we male cadets always were handsome and desirable dates, right?"

"Yeah, but speak for yourself, Carson! I did all right, thank you, and this is not the time to discuss that. Why is she so opposed to her husband's military operations with the Herreronistas?" Bellamack wanted to know.

"The Swedes in Europe have been neutral for over a century," Curt pointed out.

"So?"

"So why do they have an army? And an air force? And a military-industrial complex that sells only their out-moded weapons systems to other countries? Why? Because they're neutral. But they have the only honest-to-God *defensive* military organization in the world."

"What the hell has that got to do with this?"

"Fredrica is only second-generation Swedish-American," Curt pointed out. "Her father is a retired *Flygvapnet* pilot who got a good job with a transatlantic cargo carrier operating out of Stewart International Airport in Newburgh," Curt explained. "Her view of the military is the one she got from her father. She accepts the military in a defensive

255

role, but not in the offensive mode. The Mexican army has been a defensive army since 1848. She had no trouble marrying a man who would become a Mexican army officer. But when he became an aggressor on his own, she couldn't take it. So, yes, I think she's serious. And if the United States won't protect her and her husband at this point, she's a dead woman. She may be a dead woman anyway if her husband ever gets his hands on her again."

Lieutenant Colonel William Bellamack would never admit it, but Fredrica Herrero's beauty did affect his decision. Curt knew it at once because he'd been affected the same way. All military decisions are not made by cold logic according to doctrine. In fact, most of them are made under quite emotional circumstances. Granted, the emotions are somewhat different from those created by a beautiful woman.

Bellamack turned and keyed his comm gear. Within a minute, he had Major General Jacob Carlisle on two-way interactive satellite video from the division headquarters in Douglas.

The colonel explained the situation to the general.

"Dammit, Bill, Curt Carson must have been teaching you how to hand me real dirty, messy, difficult little problems," Carlisle replied without rancor. "I don't know whether this will fly or not. I'll have to take it up the line and hope to hell someone at the Pentagon is still awake. The guys at State never sleep, of course, but that's part of their job. Dawn, you say?"

"No later than oh-four-thirty on the decision, General. Otherwise, she'll be out of here."

"Can you keep that aerodyne on the ground?"

"No, sir, I wouldn't do that," Bellamack replied. Then, lest his response be considered only gallantry in action, he justified it: "Come first light, the Herreronistas will spot it and report it to their commander. Fredrica Herrero is already in trouble, but they don't know where she is. This

256

will locate her. The Herreronistas may attack in an attempt to destroy the aerodyne and kill her before she spills too much to us."

"Okay, I've got nine hours," Carlisle replied with finality. "Let me see if I can perform a miracle."

"General, Colonel, we've got more time than that," Curt put in.

"Say what?" Bellamack replied.

"*Someone* in the Greys knows how to fly that AeroBianchi," Curt pointed out. "The Herreronistas don't have recon; they won't see it leave if it doesn't show lights. Fly it out of here and up to Douglas tonight. Hell, maybe we can even get Emilio Orozco to do it in order to protect Freddie."

Wild Bill Bellamack shook his head. "No, I don't want Orozco free with an aerodyne, even if we did put a guard with him. Things could happen. He could easily fly it right over the mountain to Herrero. But you're right. Probably someone in the maintenance unit can fly that humper."

"We can get it back later and use it for our own air purposes," Curt pointed out. "The Mexicans wouldn't let us bring our own aerodynes in here for air support, but that AeroBianchi carries Mexican registration . . ."

"Good idea! Do it! I'll tell my staff we're expecting it," Carlisle said. "In the meantime, I'll try to work out this deal for Herrero's wife. Maybe I can do something if I have a little more time to work on it."

Bellamack looked at his de facto second-in-command. "Major, get with Captain Otis and have one of his maintenance specialists fly it back to Douglas. Do it now."

"Yes, sir! We move out again in the morning?" Curt wanted to know.

"You bet! When our recon shows the Herreronistas starting to move, we move with them," Bellamack stated firmly, then exhibited a decidedly devilish grin.

257

And Major General Jacob Carlisle added, "If they won't move, kick their ass. A little artillery on Cerro Prieta might convince them to get the hell out. As I recall, the last time something like this happened in this country, someone named Zachary Taylor told his artillery commander, 'Double-shot your guns, Bragg, and give 'em hell!' Bill, do just that if you have to."

Curt grinned, saluted, and left to carry out the order.

Captain Elwood Otis was most helpful. "Hell, yes, Curt! Sergeant Nancy Roberts is our aerodyne expert. She can fly any 'dyne, especially the civilian ones like the Aero-Bianchi. I'll have her ferry it to Douglas."

"If you don't need here here, have her stay with it," Curt suggested. "We might want it back pretty damned quick. So have her top off the tanks. We'll probably need every klick of range we can get out of that humper."

That done, he tried to find Fredrica. His first guess was right. Alexis Morgan had sequestered her in the Marauder ACV. And Freddie didn't look very happy about it. She preferred to be with men, and she felt totally out of place with these alien women warriors.

"Oh, Curt, am I glad to see you!" Fredrica exclaimed as Curt entered the ACV.

"Captain Morgan seeing to your comfort?" Curt asked.

"No! Your Captain Morgan over there is treating me like a prisoner!" Fredrica complained. "I'm an American! I don't like being kept inside this armored vehicle like a prisoner."

"I don't really care what your status is, honey," Alexis told her coolly. "I was given responsibility for you. I wouldn't want you to go outside and get lost or shot. After all, we *are* within lethal range of anyone with a sniper's rifle on Cerro Prieta, especially since you're not wearing body armor."

"Colonel Herrero's troops have no sniping rifles," Fredrica pointed out. "Except for his *caballeros,* the Herreronistas are stupid peasants, farmers, and miners."

"Freddie, do you have any belongings in the AeroBianchi?" Curt asked her.

"Yes. My overnight bag."

"Let's go get it," Curt told her. "I'll accompany you. The colonel doesn't know how long it will take to work out the details of your agreement with American government officials, so we're ferrying your aerodyne out of here as soon as possible and taking it back to Douglas."

"No!" Fredrica exploded. "That's my aerodyne! You can't take it! If you can't meet my terms by dawn, I'm leaving!"

Curt shook his head. "Sorry! We want your information, Freddie, but it may be impossible to get all the government actions taken care of overnight. You'll be safe with us, and you'll get your aerodyne back."

"I'm an American citizen! You can't take my property!"

"It's a target where it is, and it may get clobbered. And we're responsible for your safety since you came to us. So we can't let you bug out of here now; you'll be killed. You got yourself into this, Freddie, and the consequences are that you're going to have to stay with us until we can get you safely out, whether or not we make the arrangements you demand."

Fredrica didn't answer but sat and pouted.

"You want your bag?" Curt asked.

"Yes."

"Come along then."

"If you don't mind, Major, I'll tag along," Alexis said, getting to her feet and putting on her helmet. She picked up her Novia. "After all, Colonel Bellamack did order me to be responsible for her."

Curt knew damned good and well that Alexis wasn't about to let Fredrica out of the ACV with him all alone. Alexis didn't trust this woman. Not one damned bit.

The three of them walked over to the AeroBianchi. Curt

went up the ladder first, followed by Fredrica. As Fredrica cleared the top rung, she hit the access ladder retract switch and the ladder quickly retracted into the aerodyne before Alexis could reach out and grab it.

"Why the hell did you do that?" Curt yelled.

Fredrica turned, grabbed him, and kissed him hard.

He pushed her back, although he really didn't want to. It had been years since he'd kissed Freddie. It was always an occasion. "Knock it off, Freddie! We . . ." he started to say.

"Curt! I can fly this AeroBianchi! Let's go! We can fly to the States, and I've got all the passbooks to the overseas bank accounts and . . ." Fredrica tried to tell him.

"You're asking me to desert," Curt snapped, "and I won't do that for anyone, even you!" He hit the access ladder button and watched as it dropped. "Now, where's your goddamned bag, Freddie!"

She was crying, but she defiantly reached into a storage locker and got it out. She was in over her head now, and she knew it.

Curt felt he was getting that way, too. And he didn't like the idea.

As soon as the ladder was fully deployed, Alexis came up it in a rush. "What the hell's going on?" she wanted to know.

"Freddie hit the retract button by accident," Curt told her.

"Sure she did, Major! Okay, *Señora* Herrero," Alexis said and then continued, speaking in rapid Spanish. Curt didn't follow what she said, but he got the gist of it from the tone of Alexis's voice.

Fredrica Herrero was still defiant as she proudly descended the ladder. Alexis nodded her head toward the ACV. "Major, we'll be in my ACV. See you in the morning."

CHAPTER TWENTY-EIGHT

"The Herreronistas are withdrawing from Cerro Prieta and the main body has started to move southward out of its overnight position between Azogues and Oxaca. They seem to be maintaining their organization. No one appears to have broken off and disappeared into the hills," came the intelligence report from Captain John Gibbon summarizing the findings of the predawn flight of his comm-intel unit's birdbots.

"Orgasmic!" was the reply from Colonel Wild Bill Bellamack, who was beginning to use the Grey's slang with greater ease. "Greys all, this is Grey Head. Pick it up and move it out! Companions on point, Marauders on backup, then the Warriors, Headquarters, and Ferrets on rear guard! Marauder Leader, how's our guest?"

"Madder than hell," Alexis Morgan reported.

"Tango Sierra! Tell her General Carlisle hasn't been able to get a decision out of Washington yet. Maybe later today," Bellamack advised. "In the meantime, she's along for the ride. And don't let Levitt get to her."

"Yes, sir!"

Curt didn't have time to worry about that. He was going to have his hands full getting the Companions up and moving out to maintain contact with the Herreronistas.

He wasn't positive that the Herreronistas had totally evacuated Cerro Prieta, so he had the Companions keep their sensors out and searching. They were beginning to

261

enter the western foothills of the Sierra Madre Occidental, and they were now proceeding up a river valley with high ridges on both sides. This he didn't like, especially because the Greys were in hostile territory. Doctrine really required that they put units on both ridges and move along with the main body, but those hills were far too rugged. Curt hoped to God that the Herreronistas were really nothing more than an irregular group of guerrilla infantry armed with rifles.

The road was lousy. It didn't follow the river bottom. It looked like it had been simply bulldozed over the old trail shown on the earlier maps. They passed through Oxaca, a wide place in the road with a few Mexican hovels and perhaps a dozen women and children who watched them sullenly from the side of the road. No one seemed happy to see Americans. The Greys were soldiers, and these people knew too much about *soldados*.

The place stunk of wood smoke and privvies. In a day's march, the Washington Greys had gone from the civilized world back to the Stone Age. To Curt, this was worse than Namibia and reminded him of Zahedan and other places in the Mid-East; people had lived here for millennia and hadn't tried to improve their lot. They lived as countless generations before them had lived in a world of Again and Again with nothing to look forward to but another day that was just like the one before. Curt came from a different culture, and he couldn't visualize living in a place like Oxaca.

Ed Levitt seemed to be right at home, stopping to chat with the inhabitants, then speeding up to regain his slot in the convoy behind Curt's ACV.

About seven kilometers south of Oxaca, the road was merely a graded path up the mountainside with many blind turns, lots of ruts, many potholes, and some mud holes from the monsoon rains. Out on point, Kitsy Clinton's ACV went around a blind corner. Curt was sitting in the turret hatch and heard the sound of a blaring horn followed by the unmistakable thump of metal meeting metal.

"Companion Leader, this is Companion Alpha!" came Kitsy Clinton's voice on the tacomm. "Some sonofabitch in a truck just rammed my ACV head-on!"

"Anybody hurt?" Curt asked anxiously.

"Negatory! Just shook up!"

"Is it a Mexican military truck?" Curt wanted to know next.

"Negatory! A crazy Mexican civilian!"

Curt noticed that Ed and Marge had piled out of their four-wheel-drive camper carrying camera gear and were running past his ACV. "Come on, Major!" Ed called. "It's a *troquero,* a trucker. They drive like crazy on these mountain roads!"

"Companion Leader to Grey Head! Column halt!" Curt yelled into the tacomm, then grabbed his Novia. "Henry, hold down the fort. I'm going to see what the hell happened!" He clambered out the hatch and slid down the glacis plate to the ground.

Around the blind corner, Curt saw that it was indeed a confrontation.

But ordinary commercial vehicles don't ram an ACV with impunity. The Mexican truck had obviously come off the loser.

And it was the damnedest truck Curt had ever seen.

An incredibly ancient twentieth-century "deuce-and-a-half" Army 6 × 6 with its bed removed and loaded with an enormous pile of baled hay, it was painted in gaudy stripes, with doors, fenders, roof, and hood all different colors as if it had been put together from parts of different-colored trucks. It had white wheels, and save for a coat of recent road dust, it was clean and polished. Fringed curtains with dangling dingle balls were strung across the windshield, and numerous crosses, medallions, and other objects of religious art dangled from the mount for the rearview mirror (gone) and the sun visors (also gone). Over the windshield was painted the legend, *"Planchada de peatrones."* On the driver's door was the motto, *"Pa' el Vino y las mujeres nacieron los choferes."*

The driver was on the ground in front of his truck surveying the damage, and he obviously wasn't happy about it. Clinton's ACV glacis plate had neatly contacted the radiator and put a firm horizontal fold in it. Hot coolant was streaming all over the dirt road, making a huge puddle. The hood was bent upward. Steam and the smell of hot oil were everywhere.

"You hurt, Lieutenant?" Curt asked a somewhat shaken Kitsy Clinton.

"No, sir," she replied, but Curt could see she was upset about this. "But I don't know where he came from! I came around the corner and there he was! He was going like hell and he didn't even *try* to stop! And I couldn't stop in time!"

Ed Levitt was engaged in animated conversation with the *troquero*. Curt joined the two.

"What's the story?" Curt asked.

"Oh, he's just mad," Ed reported easily with a smile. "Wants to know what the hell we're doing on this road. Claims he had the right of way because he sounded his horn first."

"Well, that's just too goddamned fucking bad. This is holding up the whole regiment. We've got to get his heap out of the way." Curt looked around. There was a spot alongside the road where the truck could be parked. "Kitsy, get back in your ACV and push this pile of junk over into that wide spot alongside the road. Ed, tell him I'll ask the colonel if a couple of our maintenance techs will help him get it fixed." He looked at the steaming truck again, then added, "Except that truck is strictly Stone Age! I don't know how the hell we'd ever fix an old liquid-cooled internal-combustion engine's heat exchanger like that! Probably never even find a new part for it!"

Ed exchanged some more rapid-fire Spanish with the trucker. Finally, he explained to Curt, "He says 'hell no' on the help. He told me in no uncertain terms that he can fix it himself, and what kind of a man do we think he is? But he says it's our fault, so if we'll give him five thousand pesos he can pull the radiator, walk it back to Bacerac, and get it soldered up."

"Five thousand pesos?" Curt yelped.

"That's about twenty dollars," Ed advised. "You got twenty bucks on you?"

"Hell, I never carry money going into combat," Curt told him.

Ed pulled out his wallet and extracted a twenty-dollar bill. "The Greys can owe me for this one," he said, handed the bill to the *troquero,* and lapsed back into rapid Spanish with him. When it stopped, Ed told Curt, "He wants a ride into Bacerac after he pulls the radiator."

"No deal unless he can get it off by the time Russ Frazier's rear guard passes here."

More Spanish between Ed and the *troquero.* "No problem," Ed reported.

"Hell, I wish I could stay and watch it," Curt remarked. "Looks like it could take him all day. How the hell can he do it in an hour or so?"

"You've got to understand, Curt," Ed explained to him, "that these Mexican truckers are born mechanics. This guy can probably keep this heap of his running with stuff you wouldn't believe could work. And it runs damned good, too!"

"Well, yeah, I can understand that. Except for accidents like this, which can't be anticipated, I guess he's got to keep this truck running come hell or high water. Otherwise, he could get stranded out here for days."

"Yup! Be fun to watch him work on it. I'll bet he has a

265

small fortune in tools stashed away in that cab. In fact, I think I will. It's bound to be good tape. I'll catch up with you."

Curt reported back to Bellamack, and Kitsy maneuvered her ACV to push the truck clear of the road. While she was doing that, Curt asked Ed, "What the hell do all those mottoes mean?"

"Well, they sort of express the personal philosophy of the driver," Ed said.

"What do they say?"

"The one over the windshield translates loosely as: 'The pedestrian flattener.'"

"And the one on the door?"

"You'll like that one. It says, 'For wine and women, drivers were born.'"

"Yeah, I do like it," Curt admitted. "Too bad the regs are pretty tough about letting us name our own vehicles."

"Peacetime," Ed pointed out. "Get in a war, and no one cares because then it's a matter of winning, not taking care of the taxpayers' equipment. . . ."

"Amen, brother . . ."

Ed touched Curt on the sleeve and motioned him to one side. "Did you notice what I noticed when we went through Oxaca?"

"Looked like a Stone Age village to me," Curt admitted.

"No young men," Ed said.

"Huh?"

"No one there but women, kids, and a few old men. Furthermore, it didn't look like an army of about a thousand men had just gone through it. It wasn't looted," Ed pointed out.

"You're right, of course. I didn't notice," Curt admitted. "Did the women want to talk about the Herreronistas?"

Ed shook his head. "Nope. Not a word. They just went silent on me when I brought up the subject."

"You think the men joined up with Herrero?"

266

Ed nodded. "But not like you might think. You have to know these people to understand what might have happened. I'll bet I can restructure the scenario. Someone came into Oxaca in a big car or an aerodyne. They had a lot of money. And a lot of promises of looting American border towns. All of the men in the village who were fit to fight at all went along. Maybe twenty of them at the most."

"Why? These people don't seem like fighters to me."

"They're really not. But I'll bet it was cash in advance. Furthermore, if a man didn't go, he wasn't *macho*. There was ample opportunity for Herreronistas from Oxaca to desert when they came back through the village; they didn't."

"So?"

"So the deeper we go into Mexico, the more villages we'll go through," Ed Levitt told him bluntly. "And that's going to give Herrero and his officers more opportunities to fabricate tall tales about how the *gringo soldados* looted homes and raped women. It isn't going to be very long before the Herreronistas are going to be mad enough to jump us."

"Shit!" Curt blurted out. "Okay, Ed, thanks for the inputs. I'll pass them along to Bellamack. Getting all the tape you want?"

"No." Levitt was upset at that question. "I can't get near Fredrica Herrero. She's the big story. But Bellamack asked me to keep a lid on it."

"Do that," Curt advised him. "If you break a big story about her before the government arranges protection for her, she's a dead woman."

"Yeah, but . . ." Ed started to say, then stopped.

"But what?"

"I can prevent that," the television man explained. "She's got a fascinating story, something almost right out of a soap opera. And she's a beautiful woman. She's going to look great on the tube. I'll splash her all over every video screen in every home in North America. She'll be too damned well known for someone to kill her . . ."

"Ed, I think you overrate the power of the media," Curt replied seriously. "The druggers will get her no matter what you might do to make her a celebrity."

"Well, maybe, but I'll honor the colonel's request and sit on the story until Washington makes up its mind what it's going to do."

"Thanks, Ed. I appreciate that."

"You used to know her when you were at West Point, didn't you?"

"How did you find that out?" Curt asked.

"I've got my antenna tuned to Rumor Control, too."

"I'll tell you more about it when I've got more time," Curt promised, seeing that Kitsy had pushed the damaged truck off the road. "You get your tape, and I'll see you later."

Shortly after noon, the head of the column reached Bacerac some 60 kilometers farther south. It had been rough going all morning. Curt was glad to pull over to the side of the road through the town—it was a town, not a village, with about two thousand people living in it—and let Morgan's Marauders slip past into point position.

Curt called on the tacomm to Alexis as her ACV went by, "Are you going on point with Freddie aboard?"

"Negatory, Curt," Alexis replied. "I shipped her back to Bellamack's OCV under Edie Sampson's care. She's riding with the boss. Sorry about that. Didn't mean to destroy your afternoon."

"What do you mean?"

"Don't tell me you weren't looking forward to having Freddie transferred to your ACV while I took the point?"

"Well, it might have been nice, but I'm not going to have time to pay her much attention."

"Like hell!" Alexis told him. "Only a eunuch would ignore that woman! On the other hand, I guess I shouldn't complain that the men in this outfit started swinging from the chandeliers and beating their chests when they saw her."

"Marauder Leader," Curt advised her in formal radio protocol, warning her that he'd switched from familiarity to formality, "this valley appears to be getting steeper ahead. Looks like we'll have to cross a saddle rise about thirty klicks down the road. And the data indicates we may get into some heavily forested areas doing so. I suggest you utilize extreme caution in the high country ahead."

"Roger, Companion Leader, I read you," Alexis came back with equal formality.

"Suggest you put a couple of Mary Annes out in front of you."

"That will slow us down," Alexis reminded him. "And I'll have to put a Sierra Charlie out there on an ATV with them. I think I'd just as soon let my troops ride behind armor."

"Roger, Marauder Leader. It's your show," Curt told her, but he didn't feel good about it. Utilizing open-country pursuit tactics in chase mode while plunging through mountainous areas covered with heavy timber wasn't the way he'd do it. But he wasn't Morgan's CO any longer. She was on point now and would have to run the show her way . . . unless Bellamack gave orders to the contrary, which he didn't do.

Bellamack was busy on the satellite net with Carlisle. Wade Hampton told Curt something was cooking on the Fredrica agreement. The Headquarters Company commander said he'd bring the matter up with the colonel as soon as possible but otherwise continue as before.

So Curt concentrated on closing the gap behind the Marauders as much as he dared without running up the tailgates.

They were working their way up the steepening grades of the road along the headwaters of the Rio Babidanchic and had entered heavily wooded terrain south of Huachinera when another truck incident took place.

"Grey Head, Marauder Leader," came Alexis's call to Bellamack. "Column halt! I've got an overturned Mexican *camión* up ahead and what looks like a road repair crew trying to heave it upright again."

That wasn't what it was at all.

A 7.62-millimeter slug ricocheted off the turret armor just below the access hatch where Curt was watching the road.

CHAPTER TWENTY-NINE

"Greys all, this is Marauder Leader! We've been ambushed!" came the communication from Alexis Morgan. "Heavy small arms fire from the left flank up the hill along the whole column!"

Curt ducked his head down until only his helmet and eyes appeared over the lip of the turret hatch. Small arms fire was peppering his ACV now. "Grey Head, this is Companion Leader! We're also taking fire! Marauder Leader, let 'em shoot! It's only five- and seven-millimeter stuff!" He yelled down to Kester, "Henry, get the millimeter radar on the incoming! Give me some fire source data!"

"Too much of it!" was Master Sergeant Henry Kester's quick reply. "The system is overloaded!"

"Greys all, this is Grey Head! The whole column is under attack!" came the call from Bellamack.

Curt caught a glimpse of things arcing through the air with trails of flame behind them. Not all of them were thrown accurately. When they hit the ground or a vehicle, orange flame sprayed everywhere.

"They're throwing Molotov cocktails!" Jerry Allen yelled.

Curt recognized the bottle shapes flying through the air. "Companions, active halogen flame suppression!" He knew the outcome would be determined by who had the greatest supply of bottles/gasoline or halogen fire suppression material.

His ACV autopilot was reacting according to prepro-gramming, and Kester didn't override it. The ACV turned into the assault to provide a smaller target and protect the running gear.

At the same time, other sorts of things were being thrown out of the woods. They looked like tin cans trailing rippling cloth streamers.

Because of his experience in Munsterlagen during the German Reunification affair and against terrorist attacks in the Mid-East oil patch, Curt immediately knew what they were:

The cannister objects were homemade versions of the old Soviet RKG-3M antitank hand grenades—except these were "tinnie bombs" fabricated from empty tin cans filled with plasticex which had been carefully and dangerously melted into liquid form over a fire, then poured into each can to form a shaped charge. A simple impact fuse made from a decapitated old center-fire brass rifle or pistol car-tridge completed the weapon. A 25-centimeter strip of cloth taped to the back of the can served to stabilize it in flight so that it would have a better chance of landing with the shaped-charge forward end against a vehicle. Tinnies were dangerous as hell to make, and the guerrillas had probably lost a few dozen men manufacturing them. Tin-nies were unreliable and pretty useless against Chobham or Exman armor. But even if only a few of them hit a vehicle and went off correctly, they could puncture only about 100 millimeters of hard armor plate, not high-tech armor. And they made good-sized potholes in the already rutted dirt road if they didn't hit a vehicle.

Fortunately, the Sierra Charlie vehicles used lightweight high-tech armor that was immune to anything up to 75- to 100-millimeter HEAT or Armor-Piercing Discarding-Sabot Kinetic-Kill rounds . . . especially atop each vehicle. For decades, the Army had anticipated fighting the Big Red Tide in central Europe, and protection against Soviet overhead anti-armor grenades and air-launched kinetic-kill projectives—flying high-velocity tungsten or depleted uranium "pool cues"—had been built into vehicles almost as a matter of tradition.

But all of this was prelude to what then occurred.

And Curt was waiting for it.

Human forms began dashing toward the column of vehicles from the woods. They were running under a heavy cover of small arms fire which was intended to make the Sierra Charlies keep their heads down and not shoot back.

It didn't work exactly that way, of course.

Under command of the robotic vehicle autopilots, the 15-millimeter automatics on the ACVs and RTVs traversed and opened fire.

Curt had to put his Novia over the lip of the turret hatch and fire directly at them, adding the 7.62 millimeter high-velocity rounds to the hail of 15-millimeter slugs being sprayed by the ACV's gun.

But they weren't quite fast enough.

Some of the attackers got through to the vehicles. They were carrying tinnie bombs made from two-liter tin cans simply filled with melted plasticex with no shaped charge. They rolled these under the vehicles or perched them atop the aft decks or fenders.

One was left on the rear deck of Curt's ACV. He could see the simple fuse sputtering.

Curt yelled, "Companion One, hard left turn now!"

The ACV responded, and the can toppled off the back deck. It exploded on the ground behind, causing the ACV to buck.

Other tinnie bombs were going off on the ground and on vehicles. Curt saw Kitsy Clinton's platoon ACV disappear in a blast that went off underneath it. One of Jerry Allen's RTVs had a tinnie bomb go off on its aft deck.

At this point, with the initial assault completed, it was time to counterattack quickly. At this point, he was glad he'd insisted—in spite of some grumbling among the Companions—that everyone wear body armor even while in high-mobile chase mode where such protection wasn't normally required and the body armor usually not worn. It wasn't its weight that bothered people; it was its tightness and lack of open weave, factors which combined to keep a person wet with sweat all the time and therefore very uncomfortable. The only saving grace was that the Companions could ride inside their air-conditioned vehicles and thus maintain a reasonable level of comfort, although nothing could eliminate the chafing that often accompanied wearing body armor for protracted periods of time.

"Companions all," Curt snapped into his helmet tacomm, not wishing to trust the possibility that his ACV tacomm had been damaged by the blast, "dismount warbots! Fight on foot! Alpha, engage in warbots-leading mode, marching fire! Bravo, dismount and disperse Hairy Foxes, overhead fire up the hill, rolling barrage!"

"Companion Bravo Four is out of action," Jerry Allen reported. "A tinnie bomb apparently destroyed the ramp deployment mechanisms. Half my Hairy Foxes are bottled up inside."

There was no response from Kitsy Clinton. "Companion Alpha?" Curt called.

Out of the cloud of dust that enveloped Clinton's ACV, Kitsy appeared with Nick Gerard, dismounted, and moving. The ramps on her two RTVs were down, and her Mary Annes were moving out. "Companion Alpha here!" was her rushed reply. "We're deploying ASAP!"

"You okay?" Curt asked his new platoon leader.

"Shook, but functional! Jeez, that was a blast!"

"Major, our rear ramp is disabled!" Henry Kester reported.

"Out the top and fight on foot! Leave the jeep here!" Curt snapped and bailed out of the hatch, rolling and sliding down the front of the ACV to the ground while bullets smacked the armor around him. "Companions all! Marching fire! As skirmishers! Move it! Move it!" He wanted to get moving and shooting as quickly as possible.

It was another battle similar to Rio Claro on Trinidad when the Greys had been attacked on the left flank by disciplined crack troops. However, here the guerrillas had the advantage of the slope; they were uphill in dense woodland. They had the advantage of surprise and probably mass. But Curt knew he had firepower superiority, maneuverability, and the shock of an immediate counterattack on his side. He also had disciplined, trained troops.

Kitsy Clinton was on his immediate right, advancing in the open between two of her Mary Annes, her Novia on her hip burping three-round bursts in the general direction of the enemy. Nick Gerard, Charlie Koslowski, and Jim Elliott were right with her, dodging and weaving, shooting from the hip, using the Mary Annes as occasional cover, and ripping off bursts of Novia fire in the general direction the Mary Annes were shooting their 25-millimeters under control of their gun director sensors and systems.

Overhead Curt heard and felt the 50-millimeter rounds from the six Hairy Foxes Jerry Allen had managed to get out of his second RTV.

It was not a concentrated firefight, a counterattack with overwhelming firepower — heavy-caliber stuff from the warbots coupled with 7.62-millimeter fire from the Sierra Charlies. This fire was heavy enough to cut through the thick underbrush. The fifties of the Hairy Foxes were programmed for air-burst in the trees about five meters up, and these shells were antipersonnel shrapnel rounds. Behind them, the 15-millimeter automatics on the ACVs and RTVs kept up their fire over the heads of the deployed Sierra Charlies and their warbots.

The Sierra Charlies laid down such heavy fire that it neutralized that of the Herreronistas.

Back in the Civil War, Rear Admiral David G. Farragut

275

stated a verity of combat: "The best armor (and the best defense) is a rapid and well-directed fire." Battles are won by fire and movement. That's exactly what Curt wanted and why he had acted so quickly to regain the initiative and go on the offensive. In such intense firefights as this one, Curt didn't like to be a sitting duck.

Although he *knew* these things to be true and workable from his own combat experience, his basic instinct for self-preservation and survival told him he shouldn't be doing what he was doing. He fought down the almost overpowering urge to hit the dirt every time a round went past him. But he knew that he couldn't shoot very well from the supine position and he'd be in trouble the instant he tried to get to his feet again. He knew very well that "fire is the queen of battle" and that to win battles you must outshoot the enemy, make him keep his head down, roll over him, and put him out of action as quickly as possible.

It appeared that Lieutenant Kitsy Clinton had read the same book. She pressed her assault vigorously. Curt had trouble keeping up.

The whistle and crack of bullets, the tearing sound of larger rounds going overhead, the screams and warbles of the ricochets, the dust kicked up by glancing ground impacts, the twigs and tree branches ripped off and knocked to the ground—all of these factors added to the confusion. The sporadic small arms fire of the Herreronistas became negligible.

Suddenly, there was no more small arms fire ahead of the Companions. Curt came upon abandoned rifles and submachine guns, discarded equipment, and boxes of ammo scattered among dead and wounded Herreronistas.

To Curt, the dead and wounded Herreronistas he saw weren't soldiers; they were dirty and hungry-looking irregulars with no uniforms, practically no equipment, and armed only with old and obsolete rifles, submachine guns, and a few pistols. This group of Herreronistas wasn't an army; it was an armed detachment of ragtag farmers, *vaqueros, troqueros,* and miners. If Gordo Herrero was indeed their leader, these must be his expendables left behind to ambush the Greys and discourage the Americans by inflicting damage and casualties. But they sure as hell weren't good soldiers and, in spite of the fact that they'd tried to kill him, he felt like he was fighting civilians.

But he'd broken them, and they were running. "Where did they go?" Curt asked on his helmet tacomm.

Kitsy Clinton's breathless voice replied, "They moved to the right. Ran is more like it."

"Alpha confirms," Allen broke in. "I don't have very good sensor data because of the woods, but those targets I'd locked onto have gone up the hill and moved right, heading southward."

"How about the Herreronistas on our left? Anything there?"

"Can't tell. Too much cover."

Curt shifted his attention to his right. A lot of firing was still going on there. Alexis Morgan and her Marauders were either laying down a lot of fire or taking it. "Marauder Leader, this is Companion Leader! Got the sit in hand, or can we help you on your left?"

"Marauder Leader is now pinned down!" Alexis's anxious voice came back. "We were advancing under marching fire when we just ran up against increased enemy fire coming from our left!"

"We just ran those clowns out of their positions!" Curt explained. "We'll wheel right and take them on your flank. Do you have our beacons on your tac display?"

"Negatory!"

"Roger! When you detect us coming in on your left ahead of you, don't shoot at us. When we assault, resume your marching fire!" Curt instructed.

"Uh, yeah! Okay! See if you can take some of the heat off us!" It was obvious from Alexis's tone of voice that the

277

situation had gotten the better of her. This wasn't her first firefight. She'd done well at Bisbee. But the incoming hadn't been as intense as it was in this ambush.

"Companion Alpha, wheel right! Engage the flank of the enemy! Be careful! The Marauders are also on your right, but they're pinned down at the moment," Curt snapped.

"Major, I have new targets moving in from the north!" Jerry Allen reported. "If you go right, they'll be in your rear in five minutes!"

"Roger! Jerry, move forward, give your jeep and a Hairy Fox to Edie Sampson, and let her be rear guard for us. Have her put AP rounds into the trees with her Hairy Fox if she has to. Swing your fire to the right to cover the Herreronistas shooting at the Marauders," Curt told him. "I want you to be right with us. Concentration of force. Sampson stays right with you, too, but she looks to the rear."

Kitsy Clinton had already engaged the left flank of the Herreronistas whose fire had pinned down the Marauders.

Hairy Fox fire was ripping into the trees ahead of them now. "Marauder Leader, tell Ellie Aarts to roll her Hairy Fox barrage to the right!" Curt requested. "We'll be under those air bursts! Why the hell aren't you shooting?"

"We're pinned down!"

"Goddammit, Allie, move your Mary Annes and jeeps forward and advance behind them!" Curt told her.

"Uh, roger! Will do!" A note of confidence suddenly returned to her voice.

It was a matter of move fast and roll over the Herreronistas who were giving the Marauders trouble, then be ready to do a one-eighty and go after the Herreronistas who might be moving south after attacking the rest of the Washington Greys' column. It was tricky timing. Curt had minimal rear guard protection although he knew Sergeant Edie Sampson wouldn't hesitate to shoot if she had to and warn him in the process. He and his Companions had broken the back of the Herreronista ambush now, and the rest of the operation was a rather messy mopping-up activity. The enemy was no longer as dangerous, but the Herreronistas could panic individually and shoot if they hadn't thrown away their weapons already.

The rest of the fight was short. In a few minutes, the remaining Herreronistas firing on the Marauders had broken and run.

"Sampson, any contact?" Curt directed his question to Bravo's platoon sergeant.

"Negatory, Major!"

"Jerry, any track on those targets?"

"Up the hill, Major!"

Curt encountered Alexis coming in from his right behind one of her Marauder Mary Annes. She looked tired, a little scared, and totally whupped. "You okay?" he asked.

She nodded. "Thanks to you."

"Hell, you needed some fire support. That's all we did."

"No, I needed more than that, and you gave it to me at the critical point," she said cryptically.

"We'll talk later," Curt promised.

She merely nodded and started to regroup her company.

Kitsy Clinton wasn't finished fighting. At least, she didn't act that way. "Permission to pursue, Major!" she requested in excited tones.

"Negatory, Lieutenant! Well done! I want to let them run!" Curt informed her. Then, because his style of leadership involved letting his troops in on his secrets, he went on, "I want them to report back to Herrero or his staff, if he has one. They'll claim they were outnumbered and outgunned by the whole Seventeenth Iron Fist Division! Sure as hell, they won't let on that a mere regiment whupped their asses. They'll exaggerate."

"That can work both ways, Major," Clinton replied. "Herrero will either throw in the towel so we can go home, or he'll ambush us in greater strength next time."

He shook his head. "No, Kitsy, this ambush was carried out for another purpose. Herrero must have known that a couple hundred of his irregular riflemen with homemade tinnie bombs couldn't stop what he perceives to be a somewhat different robot infantry regiment. Even if he's read about the Sierra Charlie doctrines in the professional literature—which I doubt he's done if he's running a drug business full-time and just playing soldier on the side—I don't think he really understands what we can do."

"Companion Leader, this is Grey Head! Report!"

"Grey Head, this is Companion Leader! We've broken the Herreronista ambush and chased most of them over the hill to the southeast," Curt replied to his regimental commander.

"Roger, Companion Leader. I watched you on the tac display. Good work! Orgasmic!" the regimental commander replied. "Our birdbot recon shows the ambush force broken up and routed in small groups. Return to your vehicles and let's get damage estimates and assess losses. Curt, what the hell happened to the Marauders on point?"

"They took the brunt of the ambush, Colonel," Curt replied, stretching things a little bit. "The Marauders were pinned down during their counterattack. We wheeled to the right and flanked their enemy." Beyond that, Alexis could give her own report, Curt told himself. He knew what had happened because something similar had occurred in his own past when he first stepped up to company command.

"Roger. Now the bad news," Bellamack told him. "The ambush had a purpose: to delay us and occupy our attention. The Herreronistas picked up truck transportation at Aribabi on the other side of the pass. As soon as we can get reorganized, we've got a real chase on our hands."

"Where are the Cottonbalers? Can they flank them on the right?"

"Negatory! They're just north of Moctezuma some sixty kilometers to our west . . . and behind a mountain range as well." Bellamack paused, then went on. "Return to your vehicles, check for damage and losses, then report to me in person. We've got an answer to the Fredrica matter. That plus what's happened this afternoon may mean we'll want to change our plan . . . and that's where you come in."

CHAPTER THIRTY

"Two old Greys, two new ones," Bellamack said, going over the reports of wounded. "Every damned one of them because they weren't wearing body armor. Two from the Marauders, one each from the Warriors and the Ferrets.

The colonel looked around the gathering of his company commanders and staff inside his OCV. "This isn't a full critique. And I don't chew out an officer in front of the others. Those of you who had wounded know why they go wounded. Either you *must* have your troops wear body armor, or you *must not* allow them outside the armored vehicles until they put it on."

Bellamack paused, sighed heavily in exasperation, then said, "Yeah, I know: This was an ambush and there wasn't time to put on body armor. But I'm not going to micro manage your outfits, so I'm not going to give the unpleasant order that body armor will be worn at all times on the road. I know the weather is hot and humid during the monsoon season here, what with these thunderstorm every afternoon and muggy nights. I guarantee you, I've got no control over the upper air flow coming in off the Pacific Ocean at this time of year to fill the thermal low over the American southwest."

He shrugged. "So. If you want to keep half your troop in body armor while the others rest, that's fine by me; just don't let your people outside the vehicles for *any* reason without body armor. Or you can start training your outfit the way Major Carson has—to wear body armor at all times and get used to it. Major Carson, how many hits did your troops take?"

"Three people hit, Colonel," Curt reported. "No injuries except bruises and contusions under where the bullets hit the armor. Black-and-blue marks. Sergeant Edie Sampson isn't going to be able to wear a topless dress at the Club when we get back . . . at least not for a couple of weeks until that bruise goes away. But the bullet didn't penetrate her body armor."

"Body armor holds down casualties. I rest my case," Bellamack said. "Morgan, how are your two?"

Alexis said quietly, "Platoon Sergeant Patterson took a seven-millimeter in the thigh; Major Gydesen says he'll be back on duty in three days. Sergeant Gatewood had a deflected five-millimeter keyhole through his left arm; he'll be wearing a cast for about three weeks, but he can still carry out all his duties except personal combat. I'll use him as vehicle master if we go dismounted again."

"We probably will; count on that," Bellamack told her. "We're Sierra Charlies; we fight with our warbots. Captain Morgan, did I understand correctly that you were pinned down by the Herreronistas?"

"Yes, sir."

"And all of your company survived with only two wounded?"

"Yes, sir. All of us weren't in body armor. It's rather tough to advance under marching fire when you're not wearing it."

"It takes very little time and money to make a suit of body armor," Bellamack observed. "It takes almost two decades and a lot of money to make a soldier."

"Yes, sir. I've learned my lesson. I should have learned it long ago," Alexis admitted.

"Captain Ward?"

"Colonel, don't lay that body armor charge on the Warriors! We sweated it out along with the Companions! Corporal Tullis was hurt when my Alpha ACV was blown on its side by that homemade limpet mine the Herreronistas rolled under it," Joanne Ward reported, her voice on edge. She was having a little difficulty getting used to Bellamack, and the intimation that she'd exposed her company to risk by not insisting on body armor was almost too much for her. She wasn't going to let Bellamack off the hook easily. "Dislocated his shoulder and wrenched his neck. Major Gydesen tells me he'll be back on limited duty status tomorrow. Sorry about that, Colonel, but there wasn't a whole hell of a lot I could do about that one except wear seat belts like the frigging Air Force . . . and we haven't got seat belts!"

"I didn't have the whole story on Tullis. I'm sorry," Bellamack apologized to her. Ward was a hard and seasoned fighter, and he knew her company, along with Carson's Companions, was the best in the regiment. "Captain Frazier?" he asked the other one of his new company commanders.

"Lieutenant Kirkpatrick took a seven-millimeter through her left side as she was engaged in marching fire," Russ Frazier said quietly. "Doctor McHenry told me he rebuilt her left kidney and she'll be back on limited duty status in four days. She's a new officer; I'm sorry she had to buy it in her first real battle."

"Yes, but she'll live to fight again. And she'll wear her body armor when she does it, as I suspect all Ferrets will," Bellamack said. "Very well, how about equipment? Captain Otis, does your maintenance unit have a list of damaged gear and an estimate of the repair situation?"

Elwood Otis looked at the screen of his portable note board which had been downloaded with the information in his matter maintenance and repair computer. "Headquarters OCV has a busted idler; we'll have that fixed in about an hour because we had a spare. Warrior Bravo ACV has a jammed turret that won't rotate; I have a crew working on that now, but the vehicle is roadable. Companion Leader ACV has a jammed rear ramp hatch; a tinnie bomb distorted the frame, and I'm afraid it's third level maintenance to get that fixed. The vehicle is roadable. Marauder Bravo ACV has major damage to the left running gear and is inop; we'll have to send down a recovery vehicle to pick it up if it doesn't get pilfered to pieces by the locals first. And then I've got a bunch of Robot Transport Vehicles with jammed ramps so the warbots can't deploy — Marauder Alpha Two, Companion Bravo Three, and Warrior Alpha One. The RTVs are roadable but it will take third level repair to open them up and get the warbots out. So that makes us short twelve Mary Annes and six Hairy Foxes that are bottled up and can't be deployed."

That wasn't good news to Curt. It meant that 25 percent of the Mary Annes and 12 percent of the Hairy Foxes weren't available. The short-warbotted units might have to be combined with other platoons, or Bellamack might have to leave them operating short.

"But the worst news is that we lost a Service Supply Combat Support Vehicle with three thousand liters of Jayten turbine fuel that got dumped in the dust when a tinnie bomb holed it," Lieutenant Harriet Dearborn of the supply unit put in. "Our fuel reserves are down by half at the moment, so we can operate all regimental vehicles for another twenty-four hours unless Division can get some fuel down to us by then."

"We're going to need resupply and reprovisioning anyway to get back home," Captain Hensley Atkinson, S-3 Operations, added. "We reach the point of no return tomorrow morning even with full reserves. Either we stop and turn back then, or we have to be topped off to return to the States if we proceed further."

"Work on that with Division staff," Bellamack told her.

"In the meantime, our plans are going to change. I'm going to have to shift some equipment around because of some new elements in the operational equation."

He paused, then went on, "The Herreronistas mounted trucks in Aribabi. They're moving away from us at better than thirty klicks per hour. So I'm going to slim down and go into very fast mobile chase mode. This is something new, and we haven't tried it before. Normally, I don't like to try new procedures in the field under combat conditions. But we've got to try if we're going to carry out our orders. Captain Frazier?"

"Yes, sir?"

"I want the Ferrets to stick with the Headquarters convoy as guard."

"Yes, sir! May I ask if this assignment reflects upon our performance in the recent ambush?"

"It doesn't. You're the newest company, almost rebuilt from top to bottom. I'm going to need my most experienced companies to do what needs to be done from here," Bellamack told him evenly. "I won't be able to reorganize and reassign until I get some further information from the rest of you, because we've got an interesting situation forming here."

There was a heavy silence in the Operational Command Vehicle, broken only by the muffled sound of cool air moving through the environmental system ducts and keeping them all comfortable in the humid heat.

"The United States government has agreed to the stipulations demanded by *Señora* Fredrica Herrero in return for her cooperation," Bellamack announced. "I won't go into details; they aren't important to our mission. I was in the process of conferring with her when the ambush started. She's going to lead us to Casa Fantasma, General Herrero's headquarters approximately a hundred-fifty kilometers south of here in the Sierra Madres."

He passed his hand over a switch on the tactical display

console, and a three-dimensional map of southeastern Sonora appeared on the wall. "We have yet to firm up all the plans on the divisional level, but I've gotten approval for the initial actions of the new ops plan," Bellamack went on, stepping up to the map. "Here's where *Señora* Herrero says Casa Fantasma is located. I can understand its name — Ghost House — because it appears only on certain combinations of multispectral satellite images, the sort of thing you wouldn't normally combine. It's stealthed to certain frequencies of radar, infrared, and visual. It's a hell of a big complex consisting of the house itself plus hidden drug warehouses, aerodyne landing pads, aerodyne hangar bays for maintenance and loading, and even roads."

Another image flashed on the screen, an enlarged multispectral image taken from a recon satellite and recombined in a computer using advanced image-enhancement techniques. It showed a blurry outline of buildings and other structures on a mountain ridge more than 2,000 meters high.

"According to his wife, General Herrero isn't at Casa Fantasma. He's leading the Herreronistas in the field ahead of us. So his headquarters is empty save for a few armed security guards. Drug shipments in and out of Casa Fantasma have been temporarily suspended while Herrero's guerrilla operations are keeping us busy. As a result of my meeting with *Señora* Herrero earlier today, we now know why Herrero did what he did and why the Mexican government allowed the United States to send troops into Mexico . . . at least, if Fredrica Herrero is telling the truth, which is something we're going to find out.

"Basically, it comes to this: Herrero is a Mexican drug lord under pressure from the present Mexican government, so he's trying to bring down the Mexican president and his regime. Ed Levitt's television reports have stirred up a hornet's nest in Mexico City." Bellamack turned to the television personality and remarked, "Thank you, Ed, for

287

doing a good job on this. Your station in Phoenix must be making a mint from selling the rights to your feeds, Ed. I'll expect steak dinners for all when we get back, courtesy KFCB-TV."

"I think that can be arranged. A suitable victory dinner at the Biltmore might be called for," Ed replied casually.

"And thanks for agreeing to keep the Fredrica matter quiet."

"Well, I probably saved her life, so that's worth doing." Levitt remarked. He'd been outraged at first when Bellamack had asked him to put the lid on the Fredrica Herrero story, but now he was beginning to see that it was going to make an even better scoop, depending upon how he played his cards. He'd gained the confidence of this regimental commander now, and as a result he was allowed access to such staff meetings as this one. Ed Levitt had his own plan forming, and he hoped he'd be able to stay out of the regiment's way as he carried it out.

And from what Bellamack started to tell them, it was going to be a very good story indeed.

"We have an AeroBianchi at our disposal," Bellamack went on, looking around the gathering. "It's a deuce-and-a-half. That's twenty to twenty-five Sierra Charlies, depending on how many supplies they take along. Or a mix of Sierra Charlies and warbots. A warbot is roughly two troopers in terms of weight. I want to put a team of Sierra Charlies and warbots into Casa Fantasma. The team's mission will be to take and hold it for twenty-four hours before both the Greys and Cottonbalers mount the external assault on it. I want Herrero to walk right back into a trap with his headquarters already occupied." He paused. "This is not a warbot brainy's sort of mission. But I think the Sierra Charlies can hack it. I'm calling for volunteers. First off, I need an officer to command the mission. I'll let that person get other volunteer officers and NCOs and pick the team from them."

288

Every company commander volunteered by silently raising a hand.

"Well, I sure as hell can't accept all of you as a volunteer commanding officer," Bellamack remarked. "I've got to keep some of you to chase Herrero. No, Russ, you can't go; you've got the job of sticking with the regimental headquarters and keeping the bastards off our ass!"

"Sir, I want it!" Curt snapped. "I ran the show alone in Zahedan; I can do it here."

"You also led the end run in Trinidad and chased across Namibia. You're an experienced chaser," Bellamack observed.

Curt nodded toward Joan Ward. "Captain Ward is a damned good chaser, too. She was on Trinidad and in Namibia. But I'm the only one in the outfit who's conducted an independent operation like this."

"Goddammit, Curt, you're not going to snooker me out of this!" Joan Ward snapped.

Curt shrugged. "Okay, I withdraw my insistent bid. Colonel, I've got to fight alongside Joan, and I don't want her pissed at me."

"The same better go for me, too," Alexis Morgan muttered.

"It does."

Bellamack was silent for a moment. "It's tougher than hell to make a decision like this when everyone has volunteered. But that's why I get the big money and all the perks. Joan, Alexis, you can vent your spleen at me during the next Stand-to. Curt, you've got the job. Pick your people."

"The team will be the Companions," Curt said without hesitation.

"All of them?"

"If they volunteer, and I know them. They'll volunteer," Curt stated with assurance.

"That gives you ten people," Bellamack told him.

"So I'll also ask Captain Morgan and the other members of the Marauders who aren't wounded," Curt told him.

Bellamack nodded his head. "Okay, you've got your team. Eighteen Sierra Charlies. If they accept. Plus five hundred kilos of warbots; probably as many jeeps as you can get to make up the full gross because they're smaller and more maneuverable. Sergeant Nancy Roberts will fly the aerodyne. Fredrica Herrero insists on accompanying you. And I want her to go. She's the only one who knows the place, and she can tell you where to go and what to do once you get there."

CHAPTER THIRTY-ONE

Curt was right. All seventeen members of the Companions and Marauders volunteered for what was tagged "Strike One" because Curt's assault team was a strike battalion or "strike batt."

"I'm not going to micromanage Strike One," the colonel told Curt. "Go in there, take Casa Fantasma, and be prepared to kick Herrero in the ass when we chase him up there." Curt knew the general plan with the Cottonbalers joining up with the Greys west of Casa Fantasma and mounting a massive assault on the Herrero headquarters. But it was the mission of Strike One to get in the enemy's rear and deny him the defenses of Casa Fantasma.

For the rest of the day, Strike One was to stay under cover of the heavy vegetation on the saddle northeast of Aribabi. John Gibbon, S-2, didn't want to take the chance that Herrero might somehow have access to landsat images which, with their half-meter resolution, were perfectly adequate for military purposes. Anyone could pull down real-time landsat photos with a simple antenna made from chicken wire stretched over a wood frame and accompanied by off-the-shelf electronics of the sort that was widely manufactured in Sonora. Security for Strike One was key.

Bellamack bitched about the fact that any peon with some simple hand tools, a few pesos, and some determination could get data of the sort that even he as a regimental commander couldn't access because it wasn't DoD approved and it wasn't on the regiment's TO&E. "When we get back to civilization, I'm going to stretch a few rules and put some of that non-reg gear in our vans," the colonel vowed.

Tacomm frequency-hopping programs as well as code words and unit codes were quickly settled by Bellamack.

Chase Batt Alpha, commanded by Captain Joan Ward and including Frazier's Ferrets, some of the Headquarters Company, and those portions of the Service Company not repairing damaged vehicles, bots, and wounded took off down the road after the Herreronistas. Chase Batt One was trying hard to look like a whole regiment. Bellamack would stay with Chase Batt One.

The road looked better south of Aribabi, and Bellamack chose to press the chase at night. It would confuse the Herreronistas to have the regiment continue its pursuit after engaging in heavy combat during the day. Furthermore, the Americans hadn't chased at night thus far, primarily because of the poor roads. But Bellamack wanted to throw the Herreronistas off-balance now, and he wanted to maintain contact. That was part of the plan.

The departure of Chase Batt Alpha left Curt in charge of the remaining Grey forces in the woods—Strike One plus two Combat Support Vehicles and four maintenance specialists working on damaged vehicles and bots. When Strike One pulled out, the maintenance people would either guard the damaged equipment, roll it south to rejoin Chase Batt Alpha, or return it to Douglas if Division recovery vehicles showed up.

During the time Strike One had to lie doggo in the woods, Curt intended to get everyone ready and to prepare the limited weaponry and warbot support. Since the fighting around Casa Fantasma could be either close-quarters inside or out in the open, the Sierra Charlies could carry their personal choice of Novia 7.62-millimeter assault rifles or the limited-range M26A4 Hornet submachine carbines, plus several hundred rounds of caseless ammo. The jeeps—Charlie Love, Charlie Able, Charlie Baker, Mike Lima, Mike Alpha, and Mike Bravo—were completely serviced and loaded with 7.62-millimeter caseless ammo.

It took most of the day for the command circuitry of the jeeps to be reprogrammed by Sergeants Edie Sampson, Betty Jo Trumble, Tracy Dillion, and Lew Pagan. The six jeeps were all that could be lifted into Casa Fantasma along with the Sierra Charlies and Fredrica Herrero. Even at that, Edie Sampson spent some time stripping the jeeps of some of the equipment useful only in sandy desert climates or in the cold winters of northern Europe.

This disturbed Kitsy Clinton. "Major, I didn't think that stripping bots was really condoned," she remarked to Curt and Alexis when she was called into the planning session. Fredrica Herrero was also there, but she lounged langorously along one of the bench seats and just listened; Freddie had spilled her guts to Curt and Alexis concerning the interior arrangement of her home.

"It isn't," Curt admitted, "but we can use every kilogram we can strip off those humpers. We're over gross for the AeroBianchi."

"My AeroBianchi is in top running condition, and furthermore it's been rodded for better performance at the high altitude of Casa Fantasma," Freddie volunteered.

"Thank you, Freddie, but weight will remain a problem," Curt tried to explain. "I'd rather carry in extra ammo than nonessential warbot components."

But this didn't seem to faze Lieutenant Kitsy Clinton. "Major, the M-thirty-three jeeps aren't industrial bots that can be stripped back to essentials; they've got to function under a much wider variety of conditions."

"Kitsy," Curt told her easily, "for your information Edie Sampson is one of the best bot techs I've known."

"So is Bee-Jay Trumble," Alexis added. "And I know Sampson from my tour in the Companions. Together, those two gals could make an old player piano sound like the New York Philharmonic. Don't worry, Clinton. They've also got two of the best top sergeants in the Army looking over their shoulders. Henry Kester and Carol Head have both been around since B.W."

"B.W.?"

"Before Warbots," Curt explained. "Don't worry, Kitsy. Henry won't let Edie strip anything that could be useful in the sort of combat we'll probably see at Casa Fantasma. Now, the reason I called you into this planning session was to get your inputs. Kitsy, you're fresh out of West Point and Benning. Your personal combat training at the Academy is a little over a year old. I want you to go over what we've done thus far and tell me what we've missed, what we might be doing wrong, and what else we might do to pull this off."

They were in Alexis's Armored Command Vehicle. Curt's was still being worked on. Tech Sergeants Charlie Slocum and Ken Hawkins were cutting away the rear hatch to get the needed jeep out. Edie Sampson had already been over Charlie Love, changed its programming, and done some stripping.

Although all ACVs were ostensibly the same, each had its own little quirks and glitches as if it were an individual person. Curt was still trying to get used to Marauder Leader One, and Alexis was enjoying the fact that she could make her ACV's equipment sing while Curt tended to blunder into program blocks because of minor differences in components and programs. Alexis had entered certain little program enhancements of her own, just as Curt had always done with Companion Leader One. Officers weren't supposed to personalize their computer gear, but it was inevitable and therefore largely overlooked by higher officers.

It had taken most of the memory and display capabilities of Marauder Leader One to create the three-dimen-

294

sional holographic projection of Casa Fantasma. In fact, Alexis had had to tap the Iron Fist Division's computer, Georgie, via satellite relay in order to use some of the algorithms required for the complex task. But the result was a semitransparent image of Casa Fantasma perched on its mountain and surrounded by its complex of hangars, outbuildings, and warehouses. Much of the data had been gleaned from recent satellite images and processed using image enhancement techniques. Fredrica had told Bellamack enough to allow the low-orbit Poker Hand recon satellites to shift their imaging into those portions of the spectrum where they'd have the best look at the stealthed headquarters.

"Me?" Kitsy Clinton suddenly looked about fourteen years old and very surprised. She never imagined that two veteran officers like Curt and Alexis would ever ask for her opinion.

"You," Curt told her and indicated the shimmering hologram of the Casa Fantasma complex. "Here's the situation. This is a rather unusual complex. It's built atop what might be called a dormant volcano. All of its energy needs are met by harnessing geothermal sources under the mountain. So it's energy self-sufficient. The transportation facilities are Swedish-Swiss in style — underground except for the old grassed helicopter pads which are now used for aerodynes. Freddie says they can move a landed aerodyne in under cover in less that fifteen minutes . . ."

"Five minutes," Fredrica corrected proudly. "The Herrero family has spent a lot of money developing and installing aerodyne tug facilities. They can land or launch an aerodyne within five minutes. I'm sure some of those crazy pilots Gordo hires would fly their aerodynes right into the hangars if we let them."

"That would require a pretty big hangar," Curt observed.

"And far more money to build one that size than to

refurbish the old chopper pads with tug facilities," Freddie went on. "You've got to realize that for all its apparent wonder, Casa Fantasma is part of a business enterprise. It was built and maintained by the lowest bidder. It's operated under tight cost accounting principles. But you wouldn't believe my household budget!"

"I'm sure," Alexis said acidly. She didn't probe. It might make her feel decidedly inferior. Poor was the word. An army officer's pay wasn't much, but Alexis estimated that it wouldn't run Casa Fantasma for even a day. Fredrica Herrero lived at a level far above that of Alexis Morgan, and that engendered a certainly amount of jealousy on the part of Alexis.

"Road access comes in from the Yepachic area," Curt went on, indicating the hologram. "It looks like a trail on the satellite images, but it's a well-surfaced wide road that ducks in and out of the trees."

"It's also underground in several places," Fredrica pointed out, "especially where the hills would have been too steep. Gordo's father built the tunnels."

"Most of Casa Fantasma is underground, isn't it?" Alexis asked.

Fredrica nodded. She had braided her long blond hair and pinned it up on her head so it didn't bob when she nodded. Actually, she'd done it to keep it clean; the bathing and sanitation facilities in a Robot Infantry convoy weren't up to her standards, and she longed for a bath and a chance to wash her hair. Pinning it up would help prevent it from becoming dirty before she could get back to Casa Fantasma and proper facilities tomorrow. Then she knew she could let her hair fall again and be properly seductive. This was not the time. Alexis Morgan had already shown her penchant for being overly protective of Curt Carson, but Freddie Herrero was prepared to challenge that under the right circumstances. These, however, were not the right circumstances. Freddie knew she was in

296

the enemy's camp.

"As I told you earlier, most of the warehouse and aerodyne facilities are interconnected by tunnels to allow merchandise to be moved around without taking it outside," Freddie went on.

"Is the house itself connected to the hangar and warehouse complex by tunnels?" Curt asked. "You haven't mentioned that, Freddie."

"Of course, but very few tunnels," she lied. She wasn't going to tip her whole hand. She wanted an escape route if she needed it. But she got up, took a pointer from the horizontal display, and waved it through the hologram. "We have one tunnel to the housing and dormitory complex so that the household help do not have to go outside. Another one runs down to the warehouses. When we want an aerodyne, we usually have it brought up from a hangar and landed on the patio lawn here next to the swimming pool."

"I would think you'd have more access to the commercial side of Casa Fantasma," Curt said, noticing what he considered to be a weak point in the layout.

He was, of course, right. And Freddie knew it. But she didn't reveal her secret tunnels to him. "This part of the complex is our home, Curt," she told him. "If someone needs access, it's available through the passageway to the warehouse complex which, in turn, is connected to everything else. We value our privacy at Casa Fantasma. No sense in offering many access passages into a private home."

"Freddie, you haven't told us where the road comes into the complex," Curt prompted her. He didn't mention that the overall plan called for the Greys and the Cottonbalers to mount their land assault up the road as far as they could penetrate against whatever defenses were left there by that time.

Fredrica showed them with the pointer. "It swings

297

around to the west and enters on the side of the arroyo, where it terminates in the motor fuel storage area and the garage, which is practically right under the service section of the house. Most of our food still comes in by road, and we buy it in quantity and store it in refrigerated lockers under the kitchen area. Because of the ease of moving on our road, it's probably the best defended feature of Casa Fantasma, although the west approaches are the steepest. Anyone trying to come up our road and into our complex that way must penetrate at least three checkpoints at these locations." She indicated them. "Then the entrance on the side of the arroyo is protected by quite sturdy doors . . . several of them. In the past, the family has had several assault attempts come up that road; they've been stopped, of course. But our biggest problem is with the Americans camping out and exploring in the Sierra Madres; they come up the road all the time in their four-wheel drive campers, and we have to turn them back. Diplomatically if we can. Forcefully if we can't."

"What kind of force? How much of it?" Alexis asked.

Fredrica shrugged. "I'm not in charge of that. I understand from my husband that far too many tourists turn up missing in this region . . ." She did indeed know about Casa Fantasma's security facilities, and she also knew what had happened to some rather insistent Americans who wouldn't be turned back because they felt they had the right to go anywhere in the "trackless" Sierra Madres where the country stood on end and wasn't useful for anything except their "back to nature" forays. In fact, she knew where the bodies had been disposed of in the boiling and quite acidic sulfurous underground sinkhole that Herrero's grandfather had stumbled onto while digging some of the initial tunnels back in the twentieth century.

"Now, Freddie, you're going to Casa Fantasma with us," Curt pointed out, making sure she understood exactly what he was saying. "Right with us. Right alongside us.

We're going to put the AeroBianchi down on the patio and take the house itself first; it's the highest structure in the complex, and everything is downhill from it. And I don't like an uphill fight. Now, tell us again where the defenses are for the house. . . ."

"When I left Casa Fantasma," Fredrica began, "the only armed guards left at the house were the twenty-four security guards. They're armed with Mendoza submachine guns. Eight of them are on duty at a time on eight-hour shifts. One mans the main security center with its video cameras and other intruder alerts; that center is located here off the main garage below the kitchen where the tunnels connect the house to the warehouse area. The other seven guards patrol the warehouses."

"Will we be challenged arriving in the AeroBianchi?" Alexis asked.

"Of course, but I'll talk to them by radio during the final approach and provide the necessary passwords." Fredrica didn't know whether or not that would really work. She'd disappeared from Casa Fantasma contrary to the orders of her husband and probably those of the *hermanistas* as well. But she hadn't told Bellamack or Curt about that. She was willing to risk going back without telling them. Revealing the information might cause them to abort the mission.

"Okay, here's the plan," Curt said, aware that it was an extremely trite expression. He explained it in detail, then turned to Kitsy Clinton. "Well, did we miss anything, Kitsy?"

The little lieutenant said nothing for a moment. Kitsy had the feeling that Fredrica Herrero wasn't telling it all. She didn't know why. She'd never met a wealthy and powerful woman like Fredrica Herrero before, and she couldn't figure her out. Fredrica seemed to consider sex the most serious and important thing in the world, something worth spending a lot of time and money on. To Kitsy, military service was the most important thing in the world and sex was a sideshow that was supposed to be fun, not an expensive art form.

Major Carson and Captain Morgan apparently trusted Fredrica and had spent a lot of time and effort on the plan. So Kitsy wasn't about to challenge it even though she didn't think it was the best plan.

She asked herself if she would be willing to participate in it, then realized that she would and rationalized that "the good is the enemy of the best." She'd been taught that a good plan violently executed immediately is better than a perfect plan next week. She also believed, "In war, nothing is impossible, provided you use audacity."

"Major, on the basis of the information you've got, and if Strike One remains flexible enough to handle the unknowns, it will probably work," she replied cautiously.

"They sure as hell didn't teach you at West Point to weasle-word a reply like *that!*" Curt snapped.

"Well, then, we'll *make* it work, sir!" Kitsy fired back.

That was the big salvation of Strike One.

CHAPTER THIRTY-TWO

Lane Hay Lansing III, the United States ambassador to Mexico, was on a hot seat. He didn't like that.

Lansing liked the Mexicans and had been in and out of Mexico City all his life. He wasn't the usual sort of Washington ambassador because he knew the Mexican culture and he understood the Mexican life-style. He would never make the faux pas of saying something or using body language that would constitute a "mistake" to a Mexican. He almost thought of himself as a dual-national with his roots in Boston, his heart in Mexico City, and his life axis being the airline route between the two cities. Washington he didn't totally understand. He'd been picked for the ambassadorial position because of his lifelong banking connections with Mexico and because the Hay and Lansing families had been generous supporters of the presidential aspirations.

Yet here in his first year savoring the plum he'd been handed and living in high style in Mexico City, the whole thing had started to go to worms.

It had started when the secretary of state had dashed in precipitously for the earlier conference with Mexican foreign minister Sebastian Madera y Francisco.

Lansing had never thought that the Mexican government would tolerate nineteenth-century bandits operating on the Mexican-American border. But Mexican president Alvaro was overextended in defending the Guatemalan border and couldn't act quickly or forcefully.

And Lansing could not imagine that the United States would react by sending troops into Mexico under the terms of a long-forgotten treaty originally intended to quash the Apache Indians.

But he knew what was going on in Mexico . . . he thought. Alvaro needed revenues to support the Guatemalan border defense and to continue to pay interest on Mexican debts. *El Presidente* had acted on bad advice from surbordinates and attempted to "legalize" the Mexican drug industry by "legitimizing" it and taxing it. The *hermanistas* obviously wanted nothing to do with that scheme. Their emissaries to the various *hermanistas* drug lords either didn't return or returned in pieces.

It was that rascal Herrero, Lansing knew. Either on his own or acting as the front for the *hermanistas,* Herrero had tickled the tiger by raiding across the Sonora-Arizona border. Lansing suspected that it was the intention of the *hermanistas* to bring down the Mexican government. The scenario was clear to Lansing. The United States was perceived by the Mexican people as an overpowering presence to the north, and the various Mexican power groups wouldn't long tolerate a Mexican president who did not maintain smooth and level relations with the United States.

Lansing had said as much in carefully worded dispatches and reports to Washington, where he suspected they'd been pigeonholed in Old Foggy Bottom. Lansing didn't understand that administrations come and go, but the Washington bureaucracy goes on forever with its own internal agenda. The lack of diplomatic response and the vigor of the military reaction by Washington had surprised Lansing. He *never* imagined such a thing would ever be done by the liberal president he'd helped put into the Oval Office.

But he knew the Mexicans well enough to see that the plan of the *hermanistas* was working. Even trusted aides and confidants of President Alvaro were beginning to scurry quietly about searching for safe haven in the storm and starting activities that Lansing knew were intended to cover exposed portions of personal anatomies. This was the first sign of a governmental collapse. The next one would be the increasing private dissatisfaction of the Mexican army. Lansing doubted whether the powerful Mexican financial interests or even the enormous power of the international banking community could prevail if the situation got as far as public knowledge of the Mexican military dissatisfaction. The republics that were the split-off remains of the old Spanish Empire in the Americas had political ways that were not rooted in English parliamentary democracy.

The ambassadorial seat was getting hotter and reached a new level of discomfort when Lansing was summarily requested in polite diplomatic language to come to the foreign ministry.

Señor Madera was polite but grim as Lansing entered the huge high-ceilinged office through the enormous doors. Once greetings and other amenities were completed, Lansing was invited to sit at the front of the huge desk on the slight pedestal that put Madera slightly above his visitors. Lansing had never noticed the difference in seating altitude before and suddenly recognized it for what it meant. It made him slightly angry, but his commercially bred diplomacy and manners allowed him to keep it inside. Lansing would *never* seat a guest that way. In fact, he was carefully informed by his *charge d'affaires* that the American ambassador *always* spoke with visitors while seated informally on sofas around a coffee table.

"*Mi amigo* Lansing," Madera began, giving the signal that he intended to conduct the discussion in Spanish, which he did. "In view of the abominable conduct of your

303

American troops in Sonora, my government has instructed me to demand that your government withdraw its military forces from the soil of Mexico."

Lansing gave Madera a blank stare and replied in a genuinely surprised tone of voice, "Sebastian, I was not aware that American troops had caused trouble! Can you give me specific information, please?"

"Your army has two brigades of special combat forces moving southward through Sonora."

Lansing knew a little bit about his nation's military forces from a long-ago association with the ROTC in college. "The United States Army has no brigades, Minister. It's organized into regiments and divisions."

Madera shook his head. "Mister Ambassador, our reports are quite accurate. The American military forces are brigade strength."

Madera had signaled that informality had ceased and that this was now a different meeting with formal protocol rules in effect. So Lansing replied with equal formality, "Your Excellency, may I ask how you determined this?"

"I am not at liberty to discuss it. Suffice to say, we have access to high-resolution satellite imagery. And we have an excellent network of observers on the ground."

"And what do these sources report that American troops have done?"

"The brigade moving down the western side of the Sierra Madres Occidental has looted and pillaged the villages it has passed through."

"I can't believe that report, Your Excellency," Lansing replied formally to a man who was otherwise a close friend. He suspected that the reports had been suitably contrived or doctored to cover domestic looting and pillaging that took place after the American troops passed through. He was also convinced that the reports were exaggerating American troop strength; the weaker component of a battle or war always exaggerates because no one will admit to being beaten by anything other than over-whelming force. "American troops have standing orders in this operation—as in all operations on foreign soil—that they are to rely on their own supplies and logistical support; the American government long ago learned that an army attempting to live off the land becomes extremely vulnerable to biological warfare. Our troops are well fed, well paid, well supplied, and thus have no incentive to loot and pillage. In fact, severe penalities are imposed on those troops who engage in any activity that upsets private lives beyond that which is unfortunately the result of battle. I categorically deny the validity of that report, and my government will also deny it. We shall provide proof if desired by your government."

Madera ignored Lansing's response and went on, "Yesterday afternoon, the other American brigade attacked Mexican citizens peacefully engaged in logging and mining operations south of Huachinera. Six Mexican trucks were destroyed and eighty-seven Mexican citizens were killed."

Lansing knew of this from his incoming morning news dispatches. He'd also seen the television coverage of the battle which had appeared on American TV, courtesy of a news team from a Phoenix station which had accompanied one of the American regiments. This coverage had not been broadcast in Mexico, although many Mexicans in outlying areas had undoubtedly picked it up from satellite transmissions. The Mexican government had prohibited its broadcast in Mexico.

Suddenly, Lansing no longer looked upon Sebastian Madera as a friend. In his book, friends do not lie to one another. Madera was now an adversary. Therefore, Lansing told him in a cool, level, but hard tone of voice, "Your Excellency, I know that your president and his cabinet saw the video coverage of the Huachinera battle late last night when it was relayed from Phoenix to various network

305

nodes by Intersat Seven. As a member of the cabinet, you were also present, of course." Lansing had just called the foreign minister a liar, but he didn't wait for the reaction. He forged ahead and said, "My embassay has much the same sort of equipment as your Ministry of Information and Education. So I saw that coverage myself. The American troops were ambushed by several hundred mercenary bandits in the pay of Colonel Luis Sebastian Herrero . . . who, incidentally, is also responsible for the raids at Bisbee and Douglas in Arizona."

It was Madera's turn to be surprised. He shouldn't have been. But even in the twenty-first century, most people were totally unaware of the ubiquitous nature of the communications networks that had girdled the Earth since the 1960s. It would take a long time for everyone to fully realize that the planet was indeed a global village. Only a few pockets of isolation remained. Anything that occurred anywhere in the world could be known by anyone else on the planet provided they knew how to circumvent the "filters" operated by the news media in free governments or by government agencies themselves in totalitarian countries.

Madera recovered his composure quickly and hoped that his astonishment hadn't been evident. "That is the American side of the story. *Cada cabeza es el mundo.* Destruction of Mexican property and taking of the lives of Mexican citizens has occurred. My government herewith demands that your government immediately withdraw all of its military forces from Mexican soil!"

It was patently obvious that President Alvaro had had a complete change of mind. He had tacitly invited American forces to enter Mexico a few days earlier. Now Lansing realized that political and popular pressures had forced the Mexican president to change his policy. Suddenly, American troops were no longer welcome. The United States had been finessed into this Mexican military operation, and the Mexican government was now about to make the

United States into a villain. The hot seat of the American ambassador to Mexico had suddenly become a great deal hotter.

It made Lansing quite uncomfortable. Madera had used him as a stooge and a patsy. Lansing decided that it was time to show backbone. He realized that he was going to have to become quite undiplomatic and begin treating the foreign minister as he would treat a substandard borrower at his bank. This was something that Lansing didn't like to do, but he was capable of it when the occasion demanded it. "Your Excellency, my government's military forces are on your nation's soil under the terms of an old treaty that has not been needed until recently. They entered your country because your government is unable to maintain law and order on your side of the border under the provisions of the Treaty of Nogales. Your government is unable to deal with Colonel Herrero and his private army. Therefore, my government reserves its treaty rights to engage in hot pursuit of Colonel Herrero, to render his private army incapable of future action against my government, and to capture and prosecute Colonel Herrero in the process."

Madera opened a desk drawer. The tension was so high in the room that for a moment Lansing thought Madera might be withdrawing a pistol. But the foreign minister took out a folder and handed it to Lansing. "I request that you forward this formal note of protest to your government immediately. If American military forces do not begin their withdrawal by sundown today, your government is hereby notified that they will be attacked and fired upon by the military forces of my government."

Lansing chuckled as he took the folder but did not open it. "Sebastian," he said informally, "where the hell are you going to get the troops? You and I both know Alvaro has everything committed down south. . . ."

Madera smiled. "We learn things from one another. Although the Army of Mexico is currently operational in the south, President Alvaro has permitted the revival of our state militias. Such a militia now exists in Sonora. It was not mobilized until the current trouble began. Its commanders have been given direct orders by President Alvaro to proceed into the Sierra Madres Occidental with a dual mission: It will locate and destroy the Herreronistas; it will also confront American military units and force them to withdraw from Mexican soil. The diplomatic communication you hold contains this information and a warning to your government to withdraw its military forces lest further death and destruction occur."

Lansing turned the bound document over in his hands and replied, "Are you informing me that Mexico intends to declare war on the United States of America?"

Madera shook his head, still smiling. But it was a forced smile. "Not at this time. My government does not wish to engage in warfare with your government. Therefore, in the document you hold, my government informs your government that it is unilaterally withdrawing from the Treaty of 1882, that the continued presence of American military forces on Mexican soil constitutes an invasion, and that the government of Mexico shall take whatever steps are necessary to defend its soil and citizens. Our military forces will go no further than the border between our two nations. We do not wish to be perceived to be invaders . . . as your government currently is. I shall expect to hear from you later today informing me of your government's decision and plans." Madera stood up from behind his huge desk. "This meeting is over!"

Lansing also got to his feet. In spite of the platform on which Madera and his huge desk stood, Lansing was much taller. For the first time since the conversation began, the American ambassador looked down on the Mexican foreign minister. He quoted a Mexican folk saying: *"El que nada debe nada teme."*

Madera replied with another, *"¿Quién sabe cual será el fin?"*

"Con su permiso, yo me voy."

"Buenos dias, senor." Madera did not say farewell in his usual form. He did not part with Lansing as a friend this time.

Lansing didn't care.

CHAPTER THIRTY-THREE

In the twentieth century, Strike One would have been a straightforward Green Beret, Special Forces, SEAL Team, SAS, or even a commando operation.

In the twenty-first century with its high-technology warbots, super sensors, advanced weapons, and greater reliance on machines than human beings, it was strictly made up of Sierra Charlies, special combat robot infantry.

The AeroBianchi aerodyne came slithering down the canyon in pitch darkness from the north, holding a mere hundred meters' altitude above the undulating, rugged terrain. The commercial aircraft had been highly modified, but its pilot, Sergeant Nancy Roberts, had learned how to use its sophisticated electro-optical systems which permitted nap-of-the-earth flight in total darkness, a necessary capability for a drug-running craft.

And it was necessary because it was ninety minutes before dawn with only the dark outlines of the Sierra Madres around them. Without the EO systems, Roberts could have put the ship into the rocks. But her display panels clearly showed the terrain ahead.

Although she was a very competent pilot, she was only a sergeant in the maintenance unit. Curt wondered why she didn't strike for pilot status. Maybe when this was over, he'd check into her 101 File and maybe see if she wanted to hit for it. Good pilots like her were at a premium.

The 'dyne had lifted off at full gross, and Roberts had

handled it with firm hands and calm demeanor. Even after thirty minutes en route, it hadn't burned off a great amount of J-10 turbine fuel. So it was still heavy.

"Jeez, this humper acts like it can't get out of its own way! Can you get high enough to land at Casa Fantasma?" Curt asked from his position in the right seat.

Roberts nodded her blond curls and smiled. "As long as we don't take bird strikes from the rear, we're fat, Major! Sure, it flies like a truck. Well, it *is* a truck. But we can make three thousand meters if we have to . . . if we have enough time to do it," she admitted. "That's why I'm not going to bounce up to the ridge levels until we're almost there . . . which we are. Whup! There's a radar interrogation! Only place it can come from is our destination. Get *Señora* Herrero up here on the microphone now."

Curt turned in the copilot's seat and looked into the cargo bay behind him, where Alexis and Kitsy were sitting with Fredrica between them. He motioned for Freddie to come forward.

He handed her the microphone. "Someone is painting us with radar," he explained. "What's your procedure? Do they contact you first?"

Freddie shook her head. "No, if I don't call in, they start shooting when we get in range. Robotic Baby Sams mostly. We'll be sitting ducks."

"So push that microphone button and call in, Freddie! Unless you want to get blasted out of the sky with the rest of us!" Curt snapped at her.

"This is my home grounds! Don't . . ." She started to reply harshly, then got herself under control. Bringing the microphone to her large, sensual lips, she said into it, "Ghost, royalty arrives. Xray Charlie. Waiting for confirmation query."

A voice came back through the aerodyne's comm receiver, "Mike Papa. Give me your response."

"Alpha," Freddie said simply.

311

"Sequence complete. Roosting place?"

"Papa Four."

"Acknowledged. Signal for lights when ready."

"*¡Bueno!*"

She handed the microphone back to Curt and told him, "No further communications required."

When Curt raised his eyebrows at this, Frederica said impatiently, "Well, you don't think drug runners chat on an open frequency, do you? By the way, I told them to expect us at Pad Four. We won't be going there. Put this heap down on the patio by the pool as planned."

"Did they sound suspicious?" Curt asked.

Fredrica shrugged. "No, not any more so than usual. This is a common time of day for aerodynes to return from the north. It's nearing the end of the graveyard security shift, and the *mirador* is sleepy and just wants to be left alone, especially since Gordo isn't home and there's practically no business traffic. But if they're awake, we've got them confused. They know it's me. They don't know why I'm coming back."

"Do you think they'll contact Gordo or your uncle?"

"No, not until later in the morning. My husband may or may not have communications with Casa Fantasma. Uncle Carlos Mota probably does, but I'm sure the security guards won't want to risk waking an old man at this hour. He's very nice, but that masks an incredibly violent and ruthless person underneath when something or someone displeases him. The security people know that. We're all right."

Curt slid out of the copilot's seat. "Get in there," he told Fredrica, "and tell Sergeant Roberts where to fly this thing. You know the territory."

As she did so, Curt turned and looked around the central cockpit bubble where the cargo bay of the AeroBianchi was filled with quiet people garbed in dark chameleon battle dress over their body armor. Their faces were smeared

312

with cammy grease so only their eyes gleamed whitely from under their helmet visors.

At 2,000 meters' altitude in the wan hours before dawn, it was cold in the aerodyne's cargo bay. The Strike One personnel were huddled to stay warm.

Curt had let each team member choose a personal weapon. Some preferred to carry the M33A4 Ranger or Novia assault rifle with the greater range and stopping power of its 7.62-millimeter caseless ammo. Others decided it would be more of a close-in fight and opted for the personal weapon of the regimental support troops, the M26A4 Hornet submachine gun with its shorter, lower-powered 7.62-millimeter caseless rounds.

He knew that Edie Sampson also carried her 9-millimeter Beretta pistol, a weapon which Curt considered to be a toy; but Edie liked it and had actually killed with it, so he didn't argue. Tucked into Master Sergeant Henry Kester's belt was the huge M1911A1 .45-caliber automatic pistol, his museum piece and his personal artillery. But both also carried their Novias.

Curt also had his Novia. It had been with him through two previous campaigns; he trusted it and was familiar with it. He'd also taken the precaution of packing a dozen M3 Moldable Plasticex Grenades among the clips of Novia ammo around his waist. Whether Freddie liked it or not, Curt was ready to blow doors and other facilities of Casa Fantasma if he had to.

The six M33 General Purpose warbots, the jeeps, with the 7.62-millimeter machine guns and their low-observable, IR absorbent chameleon paint, hulked in their positions around the bay, their AI computers active but their other systems idling in standby to conserve their power packs. They were loaded with ammo, extra power packs, and J-10 fuel to run their small turbine prime movers. The jeeps weren't the primary forces in this operation; they would be used as point elements entering rooms and going down the tunnels as targets to draw fire and as a fire base with their light machine guns.

It was too noisy to talk in the bay of the AeroBianchi. This was a truck, not a bus, and the cargo bay wasn't acoustically insulated to deaden the turbine and airflow sounds. So he checked the readiness condition of everyone by giving the thumbs up to the seventeen people huddled there. Each of them responded. They were ready. The worst part was now, the waiting.

He felt a hand on his shoulder. Freddie was signaling him. He stuck his head back in the quieter cockpit, and she told him, "Coming over the ridge. About thirty seconds to touchdown. Patio landing spot in sight."

Curt motioned to her. "Come on!"

"What do you mean?"

"We're going out the belly together."

"The hell you say, Curt Carson! There could be shooting!"

"Yeah, the hell I say. If they see you, they're less likely to shoot. Or they'll hesitate about shooting, which will give us time to clobber them. Let's go!" He grabbed her arm roughly and firmly. She tried to resist, but he was stronger. He dragged her down to the belly hatch.

Seeing Curt's motions, the Companions and Marauders of Strike One left their huddled positions and moved over toward the hatch, stooping to keep from banging their helmets on the low overhead of the bay.

There was no external visual view. Only Sergeant Nancy Roberts could see where she was landing the 'dyne. Curt felt the ship rock and wobble as she brought it into hover and began descent. It was a fast letdown, as the plan required, and the aerodyne slammed down onto the patio. The oleo landing legs took up most of the shock, and Curt thought it was probably a damned good landing under the circumstances.

As the turbines began to spool down, Curt heard the

314

sound of bolts being drawn as weapons were cocked and made ready to fire.

The belly hatch fell open as Curt hit the deployment switch. The ladder dropped into position as soon as the hatch was clear.

"Down the ladder!" Curt snapped to Frederica and pushed her into position. She hesitated, but the look in Curt's eyes told her she'd better get down that ladder fast.

As quickly as she was on the ground, Curt grabbed the edge of the hatch, swung through it, and dropped to the ground. He moved quickly, unslinging his Novia and bringing it to the ready. He grabbed Frederica by the arm as he moved away, clearing space for the others to drop out of the hatch as he had done, and dragged her toward the darkly looming mass of the house. The powered loading lift deposited the jeeps on the ground with surprising speed.

The AeroBianchi spooled up and Sergeant Roberts lifted off behind them, clearing the patio. She would take it down the hill toward Pad 4, then jink out of there and return to the moving column of Chase Batt Alpha. Once Strike One had secured Casa Fantasma, Roberts was scheduled to come back bearing additional ammo and a couple of Mary Annes.

No one shot at them as they crossed the patio toward the house. It was a good thing. With Freddie in one hand and his Novia held in his other with its butt against his hip, the only shooting he could have done would have been of the scare variety. He drew confidence from the fact that Alexis Morgan, Henry Kester, Jerry Allen, and the others were behind him. He knew how they fought, and he could trust them.

Since they weren't under fire, Curt took the risk of switching on his helmet infrared headlamp and dropping his night vision visor into place so he could see what he was doing.

315

The clear patio doors were tightly closed and latched. "Open them!" Curt snapped to Fredrica.

"They're locked. I don't have a key," she told him. "And don't try to break the glass. It isn't glass. It's linear polycarbonate. You can't break it."

Curt had counted on something like that and was prepared for it. So was the rest of the Strike One force. Taking an M3 from his waist, he plastered it against the doorjamb. "Live grenade!" he yelled and activated the initiator train.

Freddie didn't exactly understand what he did because it was still semidarkness on the patio and she didn't have an infrared night vision system. "Don't blow up my home!" she shouted.

Curt didn't reply, but merely grabbed her and pulled her off to one side.

The M3 blew the door off.

Gerard, Sampson, and Pagan were through it at once, even before the smoke and dust had cleared. Curt jerked Freddie's arm and the two of them went in behind the sergeants.

The huge living room was empty when Curt looked around with his IR system.

"Deploy as assigned!" he ordered.

The Strike One combat teams, two to three Sierra Charlies, some of them accompanied by jeeps, deployed to their various assignments.

Curt's mission was to get to the central security master station. All Casa Fantasma lighting and power could be controlled there for the other teams. In addition, quick capture of the security center would deny communications and control to the security guards. Alexis and Henry Kester were part of Curt's team. His Charlie Love jeep was also with them.

They dashed down the stairway behind the kitchen and ran down the hallway in the bowels of the mountain.

316

Charlie Love had trouble getting down the stairs as quickly as his human masters, but the jeep quickly caught up with them.

At the end of the hallway was a door bearing a sign in Spanish:

CUARTO CENTRO DE SEGURIDAD
¡PELIGRO!
¡SE PROHIBE ENTRAR!

"Don't go near that door!" Freddie warned as they approached it.

Curt stopped about three meters from it. "Why?"

"I don't know. I've never been allowed in there. But Gordo always told me to stay away from that door," Freddie explained.

"Charlie Love, come forward, go ahead of us, and blow that door down," Curt ordered his jeep.

"Roger!" came the acknowledging words from the jeep's computer-synthesized voice.

When the jeep was less than a meter from the door, a blue-green pencil of light jumped out of a recess in the wall. It hit Charlie Love's side, and the paint began to smoke.

"Back up!" Curt told it. "You were right, Freddie. That's a killer laser! It would have burned a hole right through any of us! You didn't say anything about robot laser defenses!" Which was pretty elegant, Curt admitted to himself, since they could operate with the renewable geothermoelectric energy source of Casa Fantasma and not be limited by an ammo supply.

"I didn't know about them!" Freddie complained.

"Charlie Love, shoot out that laser with a three-round burst, then blow the door!" Curt ordered.

"Roger," came the emotionless warbot voice. The 7.62-millimeter machine gun swiveled.

BRR-UP!

The three rounds left the muzzle so close together that it

317

sounded like someone tearing a box. Then the muzzle swiveled and three more rounds went into the door latch. Moving quickly forward, the jeep pushed the door open.

And was immediately met with a burst of 9-millimeter submachine gun fire.

Charlie Love didn't need to be ordered to shoot back when shot at; that was automatic programming which could be overridden by human voice or radio command if necessary. But the jeep's AI circuits didn't hear a voice command from Curt to hold fire.

BRR-UP!

"Human opponent dispatched," Charlie Love reported dispassionately and unemotionally.

"And *that's* what a warbot is really good at!" Alexis remarked.

Curt was through the door. The single security watchman was dead on the floor, a Mendoza submachine gun alongside him. The band of consoles and video screens was unharmed. Charlie Love was a sharpshooter.

"Charlie Love good warbot," Curt told him.

"Charlie Love good warbot. Thank you," the jeep replied flatly. It was, as Curt had repeatedly pointed out, about like a retarded child as far as mental capabilities were concerned, but it was invaluable in its ability to take incoming and return it with deadly accuracy.

Or killer laser beams that would slice through clothing, body armor, and human flesh in milliseconds but which took far more time and power to burn through composite layered armor.

Curt went immediately to the central control console. All of the labels were in Spanish. "Alexis, I can't read these goddamned control labels. Come over here and run this show," he told her. He didn't yet trust Fredrica to do it, although her trust quotient had gone up a great deal because she'd warned them about the booby-trapped door.

Alexis leaned her Novia against a console and sat down.

318

"Goddamn!" she breathed, looking over the consoles. "A real rocket ship! Oh, boy!" Then she quickly passed her hand over several switches and said to Freddie, "Sweetie, I've got all seven of your security guards on the frequency. Get over here, identify yourself, and tell them to report to their quarters at once." Eight Sierra Charlies under Lieutenant Ellie Aarts were already there, having caught sixteen of the off-duty security guards asleep in their rooms and thus captured them without a fight.

The two guards on the road approach gave up without a fight because they'd been caught flat-footed from behind by Nick Gerard, Charlie Koslowski, and Jim Elliott.

The only guard who put up a fight happened to be in one of the warehouses. He was killed by Mike Bravo, the jeep with Platoon Sergeant Betty Jo Trumble's team, which hunted him down. The underground storage area must have contained millions of dollars of both cocaine and opium. The guard obviously knew the worth of what he was guarding and probably thought that the attacking troops were Mexican *federales*.

Less than thirty minutes after landing on the patio, Alexis Morgan took off her helmet, shook her short curls free, and glanced at all the monitors. "Curt, we've taken Casa Fantasma. I didn't think it would be this easy."

"Yeah, Captain," Henry Kester pointed out, "and now that we've got it, are we ready and able to defend it when Herrero starts heading back here to make his last stand?"

Curt cleared the chamber on his Novia and slung it over his shoulder. "We'll post a watch schedule. Alexis, I'm putting you in charge of the security center here. Re-label these controls in English so you can teach other people how to run it. In the meantime, everyone not on guard duty can break for chow."

Fredrica Herrero looked much relieved. She'd feared a fierce hand-to-hand battle in her house. But her husband had apparently placed far too much faith in his security

319

men and the complex system of sensors, detectors, and booby traps he'd installed. She was glad. She might, she thought, get out of this yet with something more than her hide. She had many valuables sequestered away in Casa Fantasma, things she hadn't had time to get out and take with her when she'd left before. She smiled. "Major Carson, you did such a good job of capturing Casa Fantasma with such little damage that you and your Strike One people are hereby invited to breakfast. Let me scare up my domestic help, and I'll have them whip up a Mexican breakfast of *huevos rancheros* and other delicacies you'll never forget."

CHAPTER THIRTY-FOUR

"Well, that sure as hell beats field rations!" Curt said as he finished off his *hueves rancheros* and *chorizos*.

It was the first time since leaving Diamond Point that any of them had eaten at a table with fresh white linen and napkins.

"First time I've had a Mexican breakfast," Lieutenant Jerry Allen admitted. "It isn't hot at all!"

"Well, Jerry, I've got news for you," Alexis told him. "Real, honest-to-God Mexican food isn't hot or spicy."

"It sure as hell is when you can find it in New England!" Kitsy Clinton explained. "Hot chili peppers and stuff."

"That's just for *gringos*," Alexis explained. "More spices and chili peppers were used long ago before refrigeration."

"Like French sauces," Kitsy said with a nod. "Mostly used to cover up spoiled meat . . ."

Curt had eaten his fill. "Thank you, Fredrica," he told his hostess, deliberately not using her nickname in front of his subordinates on this social occasion. "That was very good."

"I'm glad you were able to carry out this mission without greater damage or killing," Fredrica Herrero replied.

"Sorry that we had to shoot two of your husband's people," Curt apologized.

Fredrica shrugged. "They weren't innocent people; they were being well paid to do a potentially dangerous job and they knew they might be hurt or killed," she replied.

321

Curt had a little trouble understanding Freddie's strange philosophy. When there was more time—if that ever occurred—and the occasion arose where he could ask her privately, it would be interesting to find out about this. But, in the meantime, Curt had work to do, and they weren't out of danger yet.

Shortly before the sumptuous Mexican breakfast, he'd called Colonel Bellamack on tacomm and just barely gotten through enough to report that Strike One had succeeded. Because of the marginal transmission quality, Bellamack told Curt to call in later when Chase Batt Alpha was closer and perhaps had been able to put a tacomm relay on a ridge for better reception with Strike One as well as the Cottonbalers.

He folded his napkin on the table and said to his troops, "We've got three people posted on guard duty. We'll run four-hour shifts as Captain Morgan has detailed on the duty roster I asked her to draw up. I want everyone to stay in Yankee Alert condition. You can take off body armor, but keep it nearby. Same with your personal weapons. Stay inside and out of sight. Fredrica will show you were you can rest and relax. Catch some sack time if you want to. Things could get very intense here, and when that happens I'd rather have rested Sierra Charlies than tired ones. Not if, but when. We've got to anticipate that Colonel Herrero and his forces will probably withdraw to this location, and we want it to be a Big Surprise for him to find us here."

"Major, what if he doesn't come back?" Kitsy Clinton asked. "He could opt to keep this headquarters secret and continue to entice our forces to pursue him deeper into Mexico. His lines of supply and communication are growing shorter, and he's in friendly territory. On the other hand, we're stretched longer and longer . . . and without air support to boot!"

"We face that possibility," Curt replied. "Fredrica, what

do you think your husband will do?"

She shrugged. "I don't know. But I believe he'll return here. This is his headquarters. He has billions of dollars' worth of stock in these warehouses, and the business can't tolerate many weeks of interrupted shipments. Other agents will pick up the customers the Herrero family can't service. So he'll be back. And when he does come back, I want to make certain that everyone understands the nature of my agreement with the United States."

Curt had been briefed on the agreement by Bellamack. He didn't like the idea of letting a drug lord like Herrero go free under the protection of the United States government. But he was a servant of that government and had taken an oath to carry out the duties of his commission, which included the requirement "to observe and follow such orders and direction from time to time as may be required by . . . Officers acting in accordance with the laws of the United States of America." If Colonel Bellamack told him to honor an agreement the United States government had made with another person, Curt had no recourse but to do so or resign.

And he wasn't about to resign. Curt had once known Gordo Herrero as a friend and a classmate, and he'd once loved the woman who was now the man's wife. He wasn't about to act as judge, jury, and executioner because he didn't approve of Herrero's business. Others had those duties. Justice for Herrero would have to come from them or from Herrero's own mistakes.

"For those of you who haven't been briefed in this matter," Curt explained, "the rules of engagement state that you're not to kill or injure Colonel Sebastian Luis Herrero, Fredrica's husband, except in the protection of your own life against deadly force he may attempt personally to use on you. He's to be taken prisoner and treated well. Is there anyone here who doesn't understand that? Are there any questions?"

323

He looked around. The officers and NCOs seated at the table were silent. They understood. They might not have liked it, but they understood it.

"Good! And if Colonel Herrero doesn't come back, we're likely to have the best duty of anyone in Operation Black Jack. Fredrica, I must say that you have a beautiful home here. We'll all do our best to be good guests and not harm it. Anyone who causes trouble will be directly answerable to me." He rose to his feet. "I've got to attempt to recontact Grey Head. Carry on!"

The sun was now well up, and Curt needed to go outside and find the highest terrain for the best tacomm reception. He went through the shattered patio doors, stayed under cover of the overhanging eaves of the house, and eventually worked his way to the top of the little ponderosa-covered knoll on the northern side of the house.

"Grey Head, this is Strike One. How do you read? Over." He spoke into his transceiver once he'd taken the additional step of extending its usually retracted antenna for better transmission and reception.

There was a short pause, and Curt thought for a moment that he wasn't going to make contact. At this time, if Bellamack was chasing according to schedule, the Greys should be about 80 kilometers northwest, while the Cottonbalers, coming down a parallel valley to the west, were about the same distance. That was a long range for a simple tacomm to reach in mountainous terrain such as this. But the regiment didn't have any of the more powerful man-packs that had been reassigned to the Reserves because of the dependence of the Regular Army on the high tech of satellite communications. The C-cubed-I— command, control, communications, and intelligence— needs of the Sierra Charlies were only beginning to be recognized and understood by the Signal Corps. New technology wasn't really needed; old technology could do the job quite well, but it would be a while yet before it could be resurrected and applied.

Faintly and with some buzz caused by frequency hopping right down at the edge of squelch, Colonel Wild Bill Bellamack's voice replied, "Strike One, this is Grey Head. Weak but readable. Been trying to raise you. Over."

"Grey Head, Strike One. We've secured the objective. No casualties. We are prepared for Phase Two. All is quiet here. Over." Curt had resorted to slower and more formal telecommunications procedures such as the use of the word indicating end-of-transmission; it kept the total communications time shorter because each man knew when the other had finished speaking.

"Strike One, Grey Head. Orgasmic! Strike One carrier has returned. We will attempt a second lift for you as soon as feasible. Be prepared for the carrier to return using the prearranged squawk code," the colonel told him, then added, "Be aware that Cotton has encountered Mexican troops. Also be aware that Emilio Orozco could not be located this morning and is therefore presumed to be attempting to rejoin the Herreronistas. Over."

"Grey Head, Strike One. Does Orozco know Strike plan? Over."

"Strike One, Grey Head. We believe he does and we will act accordingly. Therefore, be prepared for Herrero's return. He may leave his Herreronistas in the field and attempt to retake Fantasma with his elite *caballeros*. We may not be able to detect if he leaves the Herreronistas with that unit. So be prepared and report immediately. We'll break off pursuit and push to maximum toward you if you report Herrero at Fantasma. Over."

"Grey head, Strike One. Until you get closer to us, reception is going to be lousy," Curt reported. "I cannot guarantee that I can successfully monitor the freak inside Fantasma. Therefore, I will check in with you again at twelve hundred hours. If I do not check in at that time, you can assume that I'm under cover and defending Fantasma. Over."

"Strike One, Grey Head. Roger. Understood. Grey Head out."

"Strike One out."

Well, with Orozco missing and presumed to be with the Herreronistas, Curt concluded that Herrero would probably return. He didn't think the drug lord would attempt to return by air, not if he knew his headquarters with all its air defenses was already in the hands of Americans. Herrero would come by land, and therefore Curt believed his people in the security room would see this in time and be able to alert Strike One.

He retracted the antenna and descended the knoll to the house.

None of his Sierra Charlies was in the spacious living room. He started to look for someone when a Mexican maid came in. *"¿Major Carson, desea usted un ducha?"*

"No comprendo español, señora. ¿Habla inglés?" Curt replied, dredging deep for what little Spanish he'd picked up.

"Yes," the maid replied. "Do you wish to take a shower? To rest?"

Curt was tired. Exhausted. That sounded good. He hadn't had a bath or shower since he'd left Fort Huachuca many days before. He'd given himself several sponge baths with the limited water supply in his ACV. Now he felt grungy, sticky, and itchy. Suddenly, as he thought about it, it got a lot worse. "Yes, that would be good. *¿Dónde?* Where?" he asked her, speaking very slowly in basic English as he'd learned to do in order to make himself understood in Europe and the Mid-East.

The maid led him down a hallway and through a sumptuous and luxurious bedroom into a bathroom that appeared to a weary, dirty military officer as sybaritic in the extreme. He closed the door, stripped out of his cammies, peeled off his body armor, and discovered that a razor was on the washstand. He shaved, then took a luxurious, long,

326

and very hot shower, enjoying every minute of it. When he was finished, he discovered that the heated towel rack had a warm and fluffy towel ready for him. It was even better than the warm-air body drier of his refresher at Diamond Point because the friction of the towel made him feel good.

The hot shower had also relaxed him. Dressing only in his briefs, he took his cammies, body armor, helmet, equipment harness, and Novia out into the bedroom. It wouldn't hurt, he told himself wearily, to grab a few minutes of sack time. He felt certain other members of Strike One were doing the same. He didn't know a Sierra Charlie who would turn down the opportunity to stretch out and snore off on a soft bed. He had posted sentries.

So he set his tacomm to the alarm-call mode in case anyone tried to reach him, set his watch to wake him at 1130 hours, and stretched out on the soft bed. He didn't stay awake more than a few minutes.

In his exhausted, critically fatigued condition, he became suddenly aware of a warm, soft, and very erotic body next to him.

As he opened and focused his eyes, he learned it was Fredrica. She had nothing very much of anything on, and her long blond hair spread over her shoulders and body like a wispy train. Her abundant Scandinavian breasts pressed against him. As she saw him come awake, she murmured, "It's about time!" And then she kissed him hard.

He tried coming up for air, but she wouldn't allow it. Finally, he pulled away enough to mutter, "Freddie, dammit, this is no time . . ."

"This is the time! And I've waited so long . . ." she said with a moan.

He shouldn't be doing this, but suddenly he didn't care. He wasn't really on duty. He'd ordered the rest of Strike One to stand down and get some rest and relaxation. Still, as their commanding officer, he shouldn't get himself into a compromising situation like this in the face of possible immediate action.

Fredrica wanted her own kind of action. She was strong and fervent and very insistent.

The tension and combat stress welled up within him and discharged itself in the most powerful sex urge he'd experienced in years. And part of it, he knew, must have been this incredibly sensuous woman he'd once loved so much.

It overwhelmed him.

Fredrica overwhelmed him.

It was strong and passionate and violent.

Finally, he lay there and looked at her stunning beauty. "You've changed."

She smiled and snuggled against him. "So have you. You're much more powerful now. . . ."

"Combat does a lot of things to a soldier," he admitted.

"I like what it did to you," she said, stroking his cheek with a long fingernail. "Do you like the change in me?"

He merely nodded. "Herrero must be a hell of a man."

"He is. He taught me a lot. I had to learn to satisfy his strong *machismo*."

"You've changed in other ways, too," Curt told her. "Tell me, how did you rationalize being the wife of a man who provides death-dealing drugs and yet be so opposed to warfare and killing?"

"War kills and injures the innocent. Drugs kill and injure only volunteers who knowingly get hooked," she explained langorously in a very offhand manner, as if it wasn't really important to her at that moment. "It's a matter of choice. War gives you no choice. Drugs do."

"Once you made a choice," Curt reminded her gently. "Was it the right one?"

She hesitated. "Right now, I don't know. I really don't know. You're so much different now. I wonder . . ."

Fredrica didn't have too much time to wonder.

Curt's tacomm squawked.

328

"Goddammit!" he growled. Rolling over, he grabbed the hand unit from his equipment harness draped over the bottom of the bed. "Strike One Leader here!"

"Major!" It was the excited voice of Platoon Sergeant Edie Sampson. Curt came alert at once. When Edie sounded excited, something hot was cooking. "I'm manning security central! We've got indication on all sensors! A major military force has started to assault the eastern side of the complex! Damned if I know where the hell they came from! There ain't a friggin' road out there!"

"Sound Zulu Alert!" Curt snapped and started to get up.

At that instant, three 7.62-millimeter rounds hit the strong transparent plastic of the huge sliding doors looking eastward over the Sierra Madres.

CHAPTER THIRTY-FIVE

The impact of the rifle bullets caused the tough plastic to dimple, bend inward, and vibrate. It produced a sound like someone beating rapidly three times on a bass drum. But the rounds didn't penetrate.

Curt rolled off the bed and began putting on his skin-tight body armor. "Goddammit, what a hell of a time to get caught with my fucking pants down!" he grumbled. In the heat of the moment, he didn't realize the humor in what he'd just said.

"What?" Freddie asked.

"Nothing! Get down! Get under the bed!" Curt ordered her.

"Are you out of your mind, Curt? That plastic door is bulletproof!"

"And do you want to take the chance that the next round that hits it won't be a twenty or fifty that will come right through and blow all to hell?" Curt snapped, strapping on his torso armor and sealing the Velcro seams.

Several more rounds hit the arcadia doors before he got all his armor zipped on and donned his cammies. Slipping into his equipment harness and slapping his helmet on his head, he activated the helmet's circuitry. He had no code words set up. But the Companions knew that in a situation like this, first names would be used as call code names instead. "Edie? Curt! What's the sit?"

330

"Best resolution video I can get this system to cough up tells me there's about two hundred men out there to the east of us," Platoon Sergeant Edie Sampson reported. "Nothing from any other direction. Whoever it is, they've elected to come up the easy slopes."

That made sense tactically, Curt realized. The Sierra Madre Occidental mountain chain was tipped upward from the east. Thus, the eastern slopes were relatively continuous and gentle while the western edge was a welter and maze of vertical cliffs and other steep, broken landforms. Coming up from the west—which is what the Greys and Cottonbalers planned to do—was difficult but the only way that the Americans could approach Casa Fantasma from where they were.

"Lieutenant Clinton here!" came Kitsy's voice. "I've gotten out of the house and have a clear field of view and fire down the slope to the east. Lots of tree cover, but it looks like an assault by at least battalion strength . . . and they're wearing uniforms! They're not dressed like Herreronistas!"

"Kitsy, get the hell back inside the house!" Curt ordered her. "You have no protection out there!"

"Sir, I've got my body armor on! And I've got a good field of fire where I am!"

"And light machine guns? Any heavy stuff?"

"Negatory, Major! Just rifles and submachine guns!"

"What kind of uniforms?"

"Khaki."

"No cammies?"

"Negatory. Khaki."

"Mexican army?" Jerry Allen's voice came through.

"Negatory! Mexican army wears the same style of battle cammies as we do!" It was the voice of Alexis Morgan, who was now on the tacomm net. "Can anyone see well enough to describe the tactics they're using?"

"They look a little rough and ragged" was the reply

331

from Lieutenant Ed Taylor, Marauder Alpha Platoon commander.

"When I put a couple of rounds into them, they scatter and take cover," Nick Gerard reported.

"They're green troops," Curt estimated. "I'll bet they're Sonoran militia. Alexis, get down to security central; I want you to talk to them if the Casa Fantasma system has external audio capability."

"On my way! I didn't think the Mexicans had militias," Alexis replied.

"They do," Curt advised her. "Caught a short paragraph in *The Infantry Journal* last month. The Mexicans just reorganized a militia along the lines of our National Guard because most of their army troops are tied up on the Guatemalan border. My guess is that these are Sonoran militia, and they're still pretty green. So shoot to keep them down. We've got a good defensive position. How's everyone's ammo?"

"Companions are fat," Henry Kester reported.

"The same for the Marauders" was the reply from Master Sergeant Carol Head.

"Put the jeeps outside to draw fire. Sierra Charlies stay inside in the best locations you can find. I'm headed for security central!" Curt told everyone. He called up the Casa Fantasma layout graphics on his visor display so he could find out where to go from where he was, then dashed out of the bedroom, leaving Fredrica Herrero still on the bed looking somewhat confused.

Alexis Morgan was in security central with Sergeant Edie Sampson when he got there. "We've got external audio broadcast capability," Alexis reported.

"Okay, call for their commanding officer, tell him we're American robot infantry troops, request a cease-fire and a parley."

"Roger."

"Strike One, Strike One, this is Curt!" he snapped into

332

the helmet tacomm. "If you can, shoot to make them keep their heads down. I've got to convince their commander that he's taking on American robot infantry, not Herreronistas left to guard this place."

Alexis was talking in rapid colloquial border Spanish into a microphone. She broke off and turned to Curt. "I've told them who we are and asked their commanding officer to meet with you under a flag of truce. I even identified ourselves as the Washington Greys regiment of United States Army Robot Infantry. Let him think we're the whole damned outfit with warbots to boot!"

"Good! That should scare the shit out of him," Curt remarked.

"Major, another target!" Edie Sampson called out and pointed to a video screen. "Vehicle coming up the road fast!"

Curt looked.

It was Ed Levitt's four-wheel-drive television camper.

"Sonofabitch is going to drive right into the middle of a fight!" Curt growled. "Goddammit, and no communication with him!"

As if the TV reporter were reading Curt's thoughts, Ed Levitt's easygoing voice sounded on tacomm in Curt's helmet receiver. "Strike One, this is Ed Levitt! You read me up there in Casa Fantasma?"

"Levitt, this is Carson! Stop where you are! You're driving right into a fight!" Curt told him.

"Roger, I know that! I was out to the east of Chase Batt Alpha last night trying to find an old friend of mine, an *arriero* who knows this country better than any of us. I stopped in an *ejido* and found out that a battalion of Sonoran militia passed through ahead of me. From what little I was told, I guessed they planned to assault Casa Fantasma this morning," Levitt's voice replied. "I tried to get here by some back roads in time to warn you. Looks like I didn't make it!"

"Sure as hell didn't!" Curt told him. "Stop where you are. We've got a firefight going on here!"

"Maybe I can stop it," Levitt said. "If the story I got is right, the unit is commanded by Colonel Joaquin Ortega. He's an old hunting buddy of mine from Hermosillo. So I'm coming up the hill and going to go around the house to the east side. Ortega knows this truck. He won't shoot at me!"

"Okay, do it. We'll try to cover you just in case they decide to shoot at you," Curt snapped. He didn't want to get into a fight with Mexican units. That might escalate an already touchy situation. He'd just as soon try to coop-erate with any Mexican forces who were also out to get Herrero. He turned to Alexis. "You heard that?"

She nodded. "I'll tell Colonel Ortega that his friend Ed Levitt is here and that the two of you want to talk with him."

"Roger! I'm going upstairs and outside. Hope to hell these Sonoran militia riflemen aren't sharpshooters," Curt muttered.

"You've got on body armor," Alexis pointed out.

"Still hurts like hell when a seven-millimeter hits it," Curt said. "Fives I can take, but sevens I don't like." He slung his Novia and ran out the shattered door, down the hall, and up the stairs into the kitchen. There he grabbed a white dish towel and a broom, tied the towel to the handle, and went to the kitchen door.

Well, Carson, you may turn out to be one dumb sonofabitch for trying to stop this, but the worst that can happen is that you get another Purple Heart, which you sure as hell don't need or want, he said to himself.

He carefully opened the kitchen door and stuck the broom handle and white towel out. Then he threw the door open and strode out into the open, feeling totally vulnerable and braced for the impact of a rifle bullet on his body armor.

334

At the same instant he stepped into the open, Ed Levitt's boldly lettered television camper pulled up on the patio. A loudspeaker on its roof bellowed in Spanish with Levitt's voice.

As if by magic, a voice called out in Spanish and the rifle fire from down the slope stopped. Then a man called up the hill, "Señor Levitt! Major Carson! This is Colonel Ortega! I have ordered a temporary cease-fire so we may talk! I'm coming up the hill! Stop shooting!"

"Strike One, this is Curt. Cease fire!" He gave the order into his helmet tacomm.

Levitt got out of the truck, leaving Marge Bogen sitting behind the wheel. Curt had to admit that the man had guts.

Curt joined him at the edge of the patio, where the two of them presented perfect silhouettes against the skyline to any rifleman down the slope.

But if these were Sonoran militia, they were disciplined enough not to break the cease-fire order.

Their commander was also disciplined. In the face of what he must now believe to be enormous firepower from American warbots occupying the Casa Fantasma heights, he strode up the hill through the trees. He also carried a white cloth on the end of a branch and had his Mendoza submachine gun slung over his shoulder.

As he stepped up to the patio deck, Curt rendered him the honor of a salute.

The Mexican returned it. "You must be a West Pointer," he said.

"I am," Curt replied proudly.

"And I graduated from the National Military Academy at Chapultepec," the Mexican colonel said with equal pride. "I am Colonel Joaquin Ramon Ortega of the Sonoran state militia."

"Major Curt Carson, Washington Greys regiment, United States Army Robot Infantry."

The two men shook hands. Ortega turned to Levitt and spoke in rapid Spanish, to which Ed replied in English, "I'm also glad to see you again, Jack. But Major Carson doesn't speak Spanish, only Mandarin Chinese. Might be a good idea to continue our discussions in English.

Ortega shrugged. "Acceptable. It's difficult enough for a military officer to learn one other language, much less the thousands spoken throughout the world. Major Carson, I will be frank in telling you that I did not expect to find the United States Army's Robot Infantry in possession of Casa Fantasma."

"That was apparent, Colonel," Curt replied. "When it became obvious to me that you weren't Herreronistas, it seemed ridiculous for our two units to fight one another. We were sent to Mexico to pursue and destroy Colonel Gordo Herrero and his Herreronista private army. It was not our intention to fight units of the Mexican army."

"How long have you been here?" Ortega wanted to know.

"We captured Casa Fantasma at dawn today."

"How?"

"Vertical envelopment."

"Impossible! The government has not permitted you to use your aircraft in Mexico!"

It was Curt's turn to shrug. "True, and we didn't."

"How can that be?"

Curt heard it first, then looked up and pointed. The AeroBianchi aerodyne plainly bearing the Mexican domestic registration XC-MPA came in over the top of the ridge from the west. The rush of air from the load-lifting craft was too great to permit conversation as Sergeant Nancy Roberts, talking with Alexis in security central, brought it to a hover and touched down on the huge patio. The cargo lift dropped from its belly with two Mary Annes which rolled off once the platform touched the ground.

"I hate to split hairs, Colonel," Curt said, "but we fol-

336

lowed our rules of engagement to the letter. It just so happened that we came into the possession of one of Colonel Herrero's aerodynes. Shall we say that we are rather well supplied and well fortified here in Casa Fantasma? So I say to you again, I don't want to fight you. You and I have missions with a common goal: to capture Gordo Herrero and break up the Herreronistas. When we do that, the Washington Greys and the Cottonbalers will return immediately to the United States."

"You used Colonel Herrero's nickname," Ortega observed. the little Mexican officer still wasn't convinced and was therefore quite wary. "You must then know him."

Curt nodded. "He was a classmate at West Point."

"I see. And you mentioned another American regiment."

"The Cottonbalers, the Seventh Robot Infantry Regiment."

"Ah, yes, so called because of their participation in the Battle of New Orleans," Ortega recalled. "They're in Sonora, too?"

Curt nodded and added for effect, "And other elements of the Seventeenth Iron Fist Division." He didn't say that the only Iron Fist Division element were staff and headquarters units up by the border.

Ortega thought about this. "I presume your operational plan is to chase Herrero back to Casa Fantasma and into a trap, correct?"

"That's right. Join us. We can always use your manpower and firepower," Curt offered.

"My orders from Mexico City said nothing about cooperating with the American Army," Ortega mused. "My objective is to capture Casa Fantasma and eliminate the drug operation being conducted here. But you've already done that. And I, too, do not wish to fight with you about it. Let us make an agreement."

"What do you have in mind, Colonel Ortega?" Curt asked.

337

"Hand over Casa Fantasma to me, and I will then cooperate with you in springing a trap for the Herreronistas. In that manner, I will accomplish my mission, and I can assist you in accomplishing yours."

Curt hesitated, trying to consider all the implications of that in view of the agreement Fredrica Herrero had struck with the American government. Curt would not be able to hand Herrero over to Ortega if the drug lord was captured. He didn't know how he was going to pull off that one. But long ago he'd learned that opportunism was often the solution to a new problem in an operation where a solution wasn't readily apparent.

So he grinned and said to the Mexican officer, "Colonel Ortega, I was hoping that's what you'd say! Let's do it! We'll give Herrero a big surprise when he shows up here!"

Curt didn't know that the entire meeting was being recorded on videotape with a shotgun mike picking up their every word. Marge Bogen was still inside the truck, and she had the tape rolling.

CHAPTER THIRTY-SIX

"Just like being in the colonel's OCV," Alexis Morgan remarked as she glanced over the displays in security central. Ellie Aarts, Edie Sampson, Carol Head, and Sergeant Billy Ed King had made a few minor modifications to the Casa Fantasma security system computers and sensors, added a lash-up patch through a Sierra Charlie battle helmet, bridged some of Ed Levitt's gear into the system, and ended up with something very close to a regimental tactical C-cubed-I display. It wasn't exactly the same, but it would help them do the job of springing the trap on Herrero.

The Greys had also disabled all of the radar, infrared, and visual stealth equipment at Casa Fantasma. The place would now stand out starkly on satellite and airborne recon and surveillance images.

All the designated positions of the Greys and the militia were indicated on the displays, but no one was manning them at the moment. Everyone was in Xray Alert status because the sensor field would provide plenty of advanced warning time.

"What's the latest hot skinny on Herrero?" Curt asked. "Any ETA yet?"

"Last data showed the main body of the Herreronistas up around Guadalupe about thirty-seven klicks northeast," Alexis pointed out on an expanded-scale map. "Tacomm with Grey Head is much improved. They're still in contact hot pursuit, but the roads are a hell of a lot worse than anticipated. The Cottonbalers are starting to move eastward from San Nicholas toward Yecora for the pincer movement."

"You didn't answer my question," Curt pointed out testily.

Alexis threw him a searching glance, decided this wasn't the time or place to make an issue, and replied, "No one knows, but it couldn't be any earlier than tomorrow at the rate they're moving."

"Good! The troops will have some time to rest up," Curt said.

Alexis couldn't resist the opportunity. "Sounds like you could use a little rest yourself."

Curt vented an explosive breath. "Yeah. But in any campaign, there are always more tired commanders than there are tired troops."

"I thought," Alexis said slowly, "that you'd gotten some rest this morning before the Sonorans showed up."

"I did and I didn't."

She nodded slowly. "I know what you mean."

"Huh?"

Alexis passed her hand over a control. A video screen came to life. The video pickup was focused on the spare bedroom where Fredrica Herrero's nightgown was thrown across the bed. She was no longer there.

"I see the security system is also a nifty little spy system," Curt remarked.

"There was no intent to spy, Major," Alexis told him coolly. "I happened to activate that video pickup, saw what was happening, and switched it off. Voyeurism isn't my kick."

"Well, it puts you one up, doesn't it?"

"I'm not keeping score, Major." She paused, then added, "I would say that one deserves at least one last fling with an old flame. And I must admit that she is indeed a beautiful woman. Oh, my, yes!"

"Captain, we'll speak of this later. Not now. Not under potential combat conditions," Curt told her.

"Yes, Major, I suspect we will."

The temper of either officer could have flared but didn't. They were twenty-first-century adults. In addition, their military training and discipline were very strong. Both had emotions. And very strong emotions at that. But they also knew they were in a potentially dangerous situation, facing combat and possible death. Officers and soldiers of an earlier age might not have behaved this way, but they hadn't had the benefit of neuroelectronic patterning and biochemical balancing. A person could not learn how to control warbots with direct neuroelectronic linkage, turning the warbot into an extension of the physical body, without first knowing how to control that physical body and the mind that directed it. The level of training required to operate neuroelectronic warbots in combat was very high and demanded a mentally stable human operator.

Technology hadn't dehumanized twenty-first-century soldiers, but it *had* allowed them to know themselves very well, to control their emotions, and to direct their mental and physical energies toward the task at hand. Since human beings aren't like warbots and can only do one thing at a time, warbot brainies had a lot of training and experience in focusing their energies.

Some civilians called warbot brainies the ultimate realization of the cold, emotionless Prussian soldier of the nineteenth and twentieth centuries. This wasn't the case at all, of course, any more than it had been the case in the Prussian army of Frederick the Great.

Emotions and feelings bottled up inside during combat conditions always erupted later in a grand catharsis. Curt knew this and knew how the release would manifest itself, at least from him.

However, he was beginning to wonder about Alexis Morgan. Company command had seemed to subtly change her. She was no longer his subordinate; she commanded a company alongside his. Something indefinable about her was changing, and Curt couldn't put his finger on it. He wasn't sure he liked what was happening. But then again, it could simply be his male personality looking at a personal relationship. He didn't know. But he did know what to do.

One of the things he'd been taught at West Point was how and when to make a decision. A decision made prematurely with scanty data or data still coming in could often prove to be the wrong decision. A decision made too late often led to the same outcome. The proper time to make a decision was that instant when all the data, the planning, and the other elements suddenly slipped into place to form a pattern or a system.

The fact that Alexis had seen Fredrica and him making love might have blown the whole relationship. He didn't know. The combat situation was still dangerous, and the emotional situation was still highly charged. So it was too early for him to come to a decision regarding Alexis.

But decision-making dynamics did not prohibit advance consideration of all the options.

Curt didn't have time to do that just then. He had other tasks and responsibilities to attend to. People were counting on him.

He checked the displays again. The deployment of the First Tac Batt for the upcoming fight was correct. The Sonoran militia would operate as a support element, although Ortega had been led to believe that his green troops would be at the cutting edge of the fight. Curt's combined forces were in excellent position. Four more Mary Annes had been landed, so he had strong defense and heavy firepower. This gave him concentration and

342

mass in addition to the element of surprise. Because he was occupying a defensive position with good security and intelligence, his situation was a textbook case of strength multiplication.

But he wasn't at all sure that he had the sort of advantage he wanted without the element of surprise. He needed the shock value of Herrero coming home and discovering that Casa Fantasma was in enemy hands.

One of Strike One's disadvantages was that the operation was literally on Herrero's home ground, and Gordo Herrero knew all the little nooks and crannies of Casa Fantasma.

It would be interesting to watch the situation develop as Herrero was chased back into his headquarters.

So he told Alexis, "Carry on, Captain. Set the watch and get some rest yourself. It's likely to get intense shortly." And without waiting for her reply, he left the security control center.

As he climbed the stairs to the kitchen, he heard Fredrica Herrero shouting in Spanish. She was very unhappy about something. So he quickened his pace and burst into the kitchen to find her confronting Colonel Ortega and two of his Sonoran militiamen.

Freddie looked relieved. "Oh, Curt! For God's sake, do something! These louts are looting my home!"

Curt grimaced and said to the Mexican officer, "Colonel, I hope you'll be able to keep your troops under control. Our joint mission here is to catch Herrero, not loot his home, which belongs to his wife, who's cooperating with us."

Ortega looked pained and embarrassed. "Major, I will suitably discipline my men." He motioned to the two militiamen and left.

"Dammit, Freddie!" Curt told her in heated tones. "For God's sake, don't make trouble now!"

"But they were looting my home!" she complained.

"You're not going to be here very much longer anyway," he reminded her. "So if I were you, I'd be gathering up the things I wanted to save. Regardless of what we do now, the militiamen are going to tear this place apart after we leave."

She shook her head in confusion. "I have trouble dealing with that."

"Learn to. It's either your house or your life," Curt told her. "I haven't told Ortega about your agreement with the United States government. I know damned good and well he wouldn't cooperate with us if he knew. He was sent here to capture Gordo and to seize Casa Fantasma. He's going to get Casa Fantasma, but he won't get you or Gordo. He won't be able to score a hundred percent on this mission. So, in the meantime, cool it! You could blow the whole deal!"

She merely looked back at him defiantly.

He was tired. Dog tired. He started to leave the kitchen.

"Where are you going?" she asked.

He looked back over his shoulder. "While we're enjoying this lull, I'm going to try to get some rest. Rest I didn't get this morning. So I'm going to find a room and lock the door!" he snapped.

When he got back to the spare bedroom, he discovered that the door would bolt and latch. So he secured it. This time, in spite of the tight discomfort of his body armor, he didn't remove it or his cammy coveralls. He merely got out of his equipment harness, put his helmet alongside the bed, and stretched out.

Again, his sleep was interrupted unknown hours later, but this time by the insistent alert sound from his helmet.

Curt came awake at once. That sound was etched on his brain. It always meant trouble. And this time was no exception.

When he put on his helmet and activated the tacomm, it was Kitsy Clinton's voice that informed him, "Major, a

Herreronista column is coming up the road. They're still thirteen kilometers away, but we have a make on their images and signatures!"

Curt glanced at his watch, then looked out the windows. It was almost sundown. Huge, white, billowing thunderheads boiled over the mountains.

"I'll be right down! Go to Zulu Alert at once! Get an IR lock on them and stay with them!" he told her. "In the meantime, raise Grey Head, because I want to talk with him!"

Someone had secured the bedroom door from outside. Curt couldn't open it. Freddie in a moment of spite? Or Ortega hoping to keep Curt out of the ensuing fight and take the credit and the spoils? He didn't know who'd done it. He didn't care. Perhaps he could find out later. But right now, he had to get out of there.

So he took an M3 grenade out of his equipment harness, plastered it against the door, activated the initiator, and stepped back while the plasticex blew the door away.

The blast caused consternation among the militiamen who were carefully looting the living room at the end of the hallway. They scattered when they saw Curt. He didn't pay any attention to them, but he'd have a word with Ortega about the conduct of his troops with the Zulu Alert signal in the air.

In security central, Kitsy Clinton was waiting for him. "Major, I didn't have to raise Grey Head. He's on the net and wanting to talk to you in the worst way!"

Curt merely glanced at the displays to ensure that his forces were moving into their positions. All of his Strike One tactical battalion forces were, but the Sonoran militia were lagging. "Kitsy, call Ortega. My compliments, but tell him to shag-ass and get his troops into position! The looting can be left until later . . . if we win this one!" He was aware that he probably had lost the element of surprise in this operation for some unknown reason.

345

"Yes, sir!" Kitsy snapped and went to work. The little lieutenant was surprisingly agile and adept with the lashed-up equipment.

Curt took over the boosted tacomm station his forces had cobbled together to provide greater range and readability than his small helmet tacomm. It was still a lash-up and he could still hear the frequency-hop buzz, but it was a great improvement. "Grey Head, Strike One Leader here."

"Strike One, Grey Head!" Wild Bill Bellamack's voice replied with the characteristic hollow buzz of secure freak-hop communications. "Where the hell is Ed Levitt?"

"He's here with us, Grey Head!"

"When did he get there?"

"This morning before the militia attacked. He helped me get the cooperation of Colonel Ortega," Curt explained. "Problems?"

"Damned right!" Bellamack's voice was angry. "Sonofa-bitch broke his agreement with me!"

"Sir?"

"I let him go to Casa Fantasma on the condition that any video stuff he shot wouldn't be released until this was over! Well, the sonofabitch sent it to Phoenix! The fact that you captured Casa Fantasma was all over the noon news in the States! And what gets on the nets in the States is also picked up here in Mexico!"

"Oh, shit!" was all that Curt could think of to say at the moment.

"Get Levitt in custody and throw away the goddamned keys!" Bellamack roared. "In the meantime, the latest satellite recon data shows a Herreronista column heading your way. I suspect it's probably Herrero himself. He must have picked up Levitt's coverage or was told by someone who did. My guess is that he's coming back to Casa Fantasma to blow you out of his house and get his stock and his wife back!"

346

"That sounds like Gordo," Curt agreed.

"In the meantime, I'm pushing an all-out night attack on the remaining Herronistas at Matarachi," Bellamack told him. "Their strength is reduced because Herrero detached his *caballeros* and headed off to Casa Fantasma with them. So the Herreronistas have lost their leadership. I think we can break them up this evening and come up behind Herrero west of Casa Fantasma later tonight."

"Jesus, Colonel, Herrero is about ten klicks away right now!" Curt reported.

"Can you hold him while I break through to you?"

"Damned right!"

"The Cottonbalers are going to swing east and join me, but I don't think they can link up before I get to your position," Bellamack went on. "They'll be the last reserve if needed. What's your assessment?"

"Herrero will be here in a few minutes, and we'll have to initiate our defense," Curt replied. "I don't have a sit-guess on the strength of his column yet. But we've got Sierra Charlies, Mary Annes, jeeps, and Sonoran militia riflemen here. We're in good defensive positions. The west side of this site is rugged and steep, so he'll have a tough time advancing under fire, and we've got lots of fire to lay on him."

"Very well. Be advised we'll be coming up that road sometime later tonight and certainly before dawn tomorrow. You'll have to hold him until then."

"Roger, Grey Head. Do you have my coordinates in your data bank?"

"Affirmative!"

"When you get within fifteen klicks and can lay some Saucy Cans fire in behind Herrero, let me know. I'll give you firing coordinates."

"Will do! Stand by on this freak!"

"Roger!"

Breaking off the conversation, Curt turned to Kitsy.

347

"Where's Levitt?"

Kitsy shrugged. "I don't know, Major, but I'll give him a holler on the hooter and get him down here."

Levitt showed up before Curt had time to bring his anger to a real boil. But when he addressed the television reporter, his voice was sharp. "Ed, what the hell's going on? Did you release any tapes reporting our capture of Casa Fantasma?"

Ed nodded. "Why, sure. Actually, I didn't release them. I transmitted them via satellite to Phoenix. I've been doing that regularly because I don't want to lose the coverage if the truck should get trashed."

"You had an agreement with Bellamack not to release those tapes!"

"Well, I put a release-hold on the ones I sent from here. They have to hold them until I give them the go-ahead."

"They didn't hold them, Ed," Curt told him.

"What?" It was an expression of amazement from the TV reporter.

"Your coverage of Casa Fantasma was all over the States and Mexico on the nets this noon."

"Those bastards! Those sonsofbitches!" This was the first time Curt had heard Ed Levitt get angry. Usually, the young man was level and laid-back, unruffled and pleasant. "They screwed me to get a scoop!"

"More than that, Ed," Curt reminded him. "Herrero or one of his friends apparently saw it. Herrero must know. He's less than ten klicks down the road right now coming in on us with his *caballeros*. You've blown our security!"

"I didn't mean to!" Levitt was contrite.

"Probably not. I'll give you the benefit of the doubt," Curt told him, then went on, "Never mind. We'll handle that later. Right now, I've got a big problem to deal with. Bellamack told me to detain you, but I don't have the manpower and that's a good excuse because I don't want to jam you in the pokey, which we haven't got anyway. So just

348

stay the hell out of the way. The shooting's about to start. And Herrero is going to be goddamned pushy about this because we've got his home, his wife, and a couple of billion dollars of his business merchandise."

CHAPTER THIRTY-SEVEN

"Strike One, this is Strike One Leader. Hold your fire! We want to let the *caballeros* get good and close before we spring the trap. I don't want them to have a chance to disperse into the forest. Sonora Leader, make sure your men hold their fire," Curt muttered into his tacomm. "Strike One Center, this is Strike One Leader. Data on the tactical display looks outstanding! Good work!"

Curt wanted to run the battle outside, not in the detatched comfort of Casa Fantasma's security command center. So he'd taken up a position with Lieutenant Kitsy Clinton on the military crest of the ridge just above the house itself, a position down off the skyline with a good view of the road.

Over the personally voiced objections of Platoon Sergeant Edie Sampson, who basically had no Hairy Foxes to operate in this situation, he'd assigned the warbot expert to run the command center. She was a good coordinator. And that's what he needed there right then.

The surrounding mountains and forests were falling into the growing gloom of evening. Lightning speared down out of the sky as violent monsoon thunderstorms dumped torrents of rain on the mountains all around them. The air was still hot and muggy even at 2,000 meters' elevation. Curt was uncomfortable in his body armor and clammy cammies. Sweat ran down his face over the cammy grease.

Thank God, Curt thought, *that Ordnance and Quartermaster did a quick-fix on the hot-and-humid problems that bugged us in Trinidad.*

But Medical Corps couldn't do very much about the sweating human body.

The approaching column was driving with no lights at all, not even infrared. But Curt could pick up each vehicle starkly on his helmet display and in his IR binoculars. These seemed to be ordinary Mexican trucks, not stealthed military vehicles.

And they were loud! Ancient vehicles powered by internal-combustion engines, they roared as they came up the road. Mexican truckers rarely maintained such "effete" devices as mufflers. Straight pipes were the rule, an expression of *muy macho*. Few of them had good brakes. Over the sound of roaring engines could be heard the occasional impact of metal on metal as a truck tailgated the one ahead of it. Mexican *troqueros* weren't used to convoy driving. Like the French, in a convoy they simply stopped or slowed down by banging into the vehicle ahead of them.

Curt decided that Herrero either wasn't depending on the element of surprise or, since he knew he couldn't achieve surprise with the trucks, was counting on a less well organized defense that would allow him to blast his way into his home grounds.

"Herrero, you sonofabitch," Curt growled with a grin, "you always were audacious! So I'm going to let your goddamned audacity carry you right into this fucking trap!"

"Excuse me, Major? Did you say something?" Kitsy spoke up from where she was on the ground beside him, presenting as small a target as possible to any Herreronista sensors.

"Nothing, Lieutenant, nothing. I'll tell you later," Curt promised. "But I remember that this bastard Herrero pulled this same balls-out approach during a night maneuver around Fort Montgomery. He hasn't changed a goddamned bit since West Point!"

"The good old 'capture Fort Montgomery and on to Bear Mountain Bridge' exercise! I remember it well," Kitsy replied. "Still a standard tactic night exercise at West Point!"

Pop! One round of small arms fire shattered the evening air and was heard even over the roar of the trucks.

Pop-pop-pop-pop-pop! It was immediately followed by a five-round burst.

Then it became impossible to discriminate between bursts of small arms fire because everyone opened up.

"Goddamn it!" Curt bellowed. "I didn't give the order to commence firing!" He'd wanted to wait about two minutes more to be able to bring the entire column under effective direct fire from not only the Sonoran riflemen but his own Strike One troops with their Novias, jeeps, and Mary Annes.

"The Sonoran militia broke" was Sergeant Edie Sampson's comment in his helmet tacomm.

"Shit, we've lost surprise now! All units, commence firing! Pin them down!" Curt snapped the order.

But it wasn't that easy, and the concentration of fire wasn't as intense as it might have been if everyone had waited another minute or so until the 25-millimeter guns of the Mary Annes could be brought to bear on the whole Herreronista truck column.

The front truck blew up in a fireball of gasoline, that ancient fuel so volatile and explosive in combat. Curt hadn't seen a gasoline fireball before. It shocked him with its violence and glare. It made him glad that less-volatile turbine fuel was now the commonplace vehicle propellant.

The fireball of the explosion and the subsequent firelight illuminated the forward part of the convoy.

The exploding truck set fire to the second one in line because it was following too closely and its brakes weren't that good. It ran into the remains of the first truck and caught fire at once. It began to burn, and armed men quickly piled out, being hit with small arms fire as they did so.

It was a good ambush, but Curt knew it could have been better.

The Mary Annes were making mincemeat of the vehicles they could target. A 20-millimeter round from one of their M212 cannons would go right through one of the old cast-iron engine blocks.

The jeeps with their 7.62-millimeter machine guns were also highly effective.

At closer range, the Hornet and Mendoza submachine guns of the Sierra Charlies and Sonoran militia were also doing their jobs.

"Does anyone see Colonel Herrero in that melee?" Curt asked on the tacomm.

No answer.

If the column had been allowed to get a little closer before it was fired upon, Curt thought that he might have been able to recognize Herrero in one of the trucks. Curt didn't think that Herrero would be in the first truck, the one that had fireballed; at West Point, Herrero had made it a practice of staying the hell off of the point vehicles. When he'd commanded field exercises, he'd ridden three or more vehicles back from the point. Curt didn't think the man's habits had changed. It wasn't that Herrero wasn't macho, but that he was, like Curt, often prudent when he commanded field units.

"Herreronistas are fanning out," Edie Sampson reported. "New data coming up on the tac data loop now. Looks like we've got an element trying to move across the gully to the north and sweep around our right flank."

Curt saw that on his visor display. "Marauder Leader, this is Strike One Leader," he called Alexis Morgan. "Executive Plan Delta! Mary Anne to right flank!"

"Roger, Strike One Leader, we see that here!"

It seemed to Curt that the firing began to taper off.

353

"Strike One all, this is Strike One Leader! Keep up the fire! Ammo's cheap and we've got a lot of it! Ammo's cheaper than losing one of you! Shoot and make them keep their heads down!"

"Major," Kitsy told him, "we're running out of targets, sir."

"The hell you say? Look! About fifty targets heading toward our right flank!" Curt pointed out.

"Yes, sir, and they're in defilade down in the gully. Check the display. The rest of them have flat-out disappeared!"

"Where the hell did they go?" Curt wondered. He wanted to send up a birdbot, but he didn't have one. And he didn't have enough Mary Annes to send a couple of them down the road with Sierra Charlies on a patrol to find out who was where. So he decided to send a fox to catch a fox. He called up Colonel Ortega. "Sonora Leader, this is Strike One Leader. Request that you send a patrol down to the road for recon. We've lost about half the Herreronista force. We don't know where they are."

"Strike One, this is Ortega." The Mexican officer wasn't completely used to American tacomm protocol in English, so he reverted to what was comfortable and easy for him. "If you will lift your fire, I will personally lead the patrol myself!" He didn't say—but Curt knew—that he'd probably have trouble getting green militiamen to go out into the dark unknown on a patrol where they might get shot at. But no militiaman with any sense of the Mexican *la dignitad do hombre* in him would hold back if his commanding officer was out in front and likely to get shot first. There was, after all, a matter of being a man. . . .

"Major, I'd like to take Alpha Platoon down there on recon," Kitsy suddenly said.

"Negatory!" Curt snapped.

"Sir, if it's because I'm a woman . . ."

"Lieutenant, one of the first things I expect you to learn

354

in this outfit is that we are indeed an integrated unit," Curt told her sharply. "Everyone is different, but we depend on each other's differences to make up for everyone's shortcomings. I damned well mean it when I say that in Carson's Companions we don't care about differences in race, color, religion, *or* sex!"

"Yes, sir, I've more than noticed all those differences in the company, but . . ."

"The Sonorans are in their own country," Curt pointed out. "Let them do the recon."

A bolt of lightning speared down out of the southwestern sky. Even in the darkness, they could see that a major thunderstorm was quickly bearing down on them. The wind in the ponderosa pines and junipers picked up and began to blow strongly. Cloud-to-cloud and cloud-to-ground lightning increased. A few sprinkles of rain were interspersed among brief dusty gusts.

"Strike One Leader, this is Ed Levitt," the reporter's voice sounded in Curt's headset. "We've got a nasty monsoon thunderboomer moving in. You're going to get wet outside. I've got some tips on lightning for you."

"Fire away, Ed."

"Get up off the ground."

"What? I thought that's the safest position to be in," Curt said.

"Negative! Stand up, but stay off the ridges and away from trees," Levitt told him. "Try to get into gullies if you can, but watch out for flash floods. If you feel your hair stand on end, it means lightning is about to strike nearby. Drop to your knees and bend forward, putting your hands on your knees. *Don't* lie flat on the ground!"

"Okay, I understand. I want to convert myself from a lightning rod to a sphere on the ground," Curt replied.

"Roger that! Here it comes!"

The storm in the next five minutes was among the most terrifying that Curt had ever experienced. He'd been in

355

many thunderstorms, but never one with this intensity of rain, wind, and lightning. He shut down his tacomm, just to be on the safe side, and told Kitsy to do the same. Within a minute, everyone outside Casa Fantasma was soaking wet. Lightning cracked down from the sky all around them.

Curt saw a figure groping through the downpour and, as it got closer, recognized Master Sergeant Henry Kester. "Major!" Kester yelled over the storm. "Your tacomm out?"

"Turned it off, Henry!"

Kester beckoned. "Thought so! Sampson needs you in security."

"What's up?"

"Colonel Herrero is inside Casa Fantasma!"

"This storm is damned loud, Henry. Did I hear you say that Herrero got into the house?"

Henry Kester nodded.

Curt grabbed Kitsy. "Come on, all of you! Round up all the Companions and Marauders! Get them into the kitchen! Bring the jeeps in, too! If this has turned into an indoor chase scene, we'll need every Sierra Charlie we can get!"

As they were working their way back across the ridge, trying to keep from being hit by lightning, Curt suddenly heard another sound amidst the bedlam of the thunderstorm: storm:

Incoming 75-millimeter shells.

There was no mistaking the warbling, ripping sound followed by the muffled explosion of an airburst Saucy Cans antipersonnel round.

And they came with increasing rapidity.

They were targeted with precision to the northwest and north, down in the gullies and in the area where the Herreronista detachment was trying to flank the house.

"Grey Head," Kester shouted to Curt. "Fifteen klicks

356

west of us. Our Saucy Cans. Boosted self-guided AP rounds. Sampson coordinated the fire support. Passed target data to Grey Head."

The Saucy Cans would take care of the Herreronistas to the north if the Mary Annes didn't get them, and vice versa. They were firing at extreme range and into very gusty weather. Yet they were right on target. *Goddamned good in the middle of a storm!* Curt thought. But the thunderstorm had started to abate, moving off to the northeast. The arrival of Saucy Cans barrage merely provided a proper coda to a weather production of incredible violence.

It was a good thing that most of Casa Fantasma was floored with beautiful, soft-finish Mexican tiles. Curt, Kitsy, and Kester dripped water from everywhere as they entered the house and found their way down to security central.

Alexis Morgan, Jerry Allen, and the rest of the Companions and Marauders were either there or following Curt. They had six jeeps with them. Everyone and everything was wet except Platoon Sergeant Edie Sampson, who looked up from where she was tracking something, grinned, and remarked, "Sierra Hotel! For a change I pulled a shit detail and didn't get wet!"

"What have you got, Edie?" Curt asked her, coming up behind so he could look over her shoulder. "You said Herrero's in the house. Where?"

"Came in a tunnel from what seems to be a hidden entrance we didn't know about down the road. It was unmonitored. It looks like about thirty men. I picked them up when they came into a secure tunnel we knew about," Edie pointed out. She indicated a display showing the video image of several armed men moving down a long passageway toward the camera. One of them pointed his rifle at the screen and fired. The image blinked out because the camera had been destroyed.

Freddie hadn't told them about all the tunnels in the

357

mountainside. Well, maybe she didn't know all of them. "Okay, keep track of him," Curt told her. "We're all going down after him. I want to take Fredrica with us. That might stop Herrero from shooting She needs to tell him about the arrangement with the United States government. Where the hell is she?"

Edie scanned several screen and shrugged. "Don't know."

"I'll go find her," Alexis volunteered. "Ellie, you and Kitsy come with me." Together, the three women left.

Curt looked around. Fifteen wet Sierra Charlies stood around the security central room. "Sampson, ring up Sergeant Roberts and the aerodyne, wherever the hell she is right now. As soon as this storm subsides enough to get in here, have Roberts park the 'dyne down the hill east of the patio deck and be ready to spool up, lift to the patio, and make pickup. In the meantime, the rest of us are going down into the mountain to capture Herrero. So everyone check your equipment. If it comes to shooting, it's likely to be close-in stuff."

Kester hefted his Novia and told the group, "Get your weapons dry, especially the rifle barrels. Make sure you get all water out of the bore. If you fire these high-performance caseless rounds with water in the barrel, your gun is likely to blow up on you. That you can get along without. . . ."

"How about wet caseless ammo?" Sergeant Tracy Dillon asked.

"Don't worry about it. That stuff fires wet or dry," Master Sergeant Carol Head told him.

"Check your supply of grenades," Lieutenant Jerry Allen pointed out. "A plasticex shock wave stuns pretty well in close quarters."

"If your power pack needs a boost, jump-charge it here," Nick Gerard suggested. "We've all got a couple of hours ahead of us. Top 'em!"

"Major, I suggest we leave our equipment harnesses

358

here," Henry Kester pointed out to Curt. "Stuff as many clips and grenades in our pockets as we can carry. Get loose and free and ready to move quickly."

"Orgasmic! Do it!" Curt replied, continuing to watch the images on the display screens. "Edie, where the hell do they look like they're going? Can we cut 'em off at the pass somewhere?"

Alexis, Ellie Aarts, and Kitsy showed up with Fredrica in tow. Alexis said nothing. It was Fredrica who spoke, as usual. "Gordo's in the mountain? Where? What's he doing? How'd he get in?" she wanted to know.

"He's here," Curt told her. "Got in by an entrance down the road you didn't tell us about."

"I don't know anything about that one," Fredrica tried to explain.

"Not important," Curt told her. "Gordo's here and we know where he is. We're tracking him on his own system. We're going down to him. When we find him, Freddie, you've got to get him to listen to you so you can explain the deal to him. Then we've got to shag-ass out of here before Colonel Ortega and the Sonoran militia learn about it." Curt looked around. "Everyone ready? Standard urban interior building procedure. I want a jeep in the lead to take the incoming. Then alternate jeeps and Sierra Charlies. I'll be in Number Three slot with Fredrica. Move it out!"

CHAPTER THIRTY-EIGHT

The tunnel down into the mountain was warm. Cerro Caliente was, after all, a dormant volcano and a geothermal energy source that permitted Casa Fantasma to operate independently of any outside energy supply. But it made the search for Herrero uncomfortable in addition to being dangerous.

Curt and Fredrica followed Platoon Sergeant Nick Gerard and Sergeant Charlie Koslowski with jeep Charlie Able, then Lieutenant Kitsy Clinton and Sergeant Jim Elliott with jeep Charlie Baker. Curt and Freddie were accompanied by Master Sergeant Henry Kester and Curt's own jeep, Charlie Love. Alexis Morgan and her Marauders followed them.

Curt was getting directional commands and a badly degraded tac display signal from Edie Sampson, still in security central. "Edie, if you can't boost that display signal, I'd just as soon not have the mother cluttering up my helmet display," he told her on the tacomm.

"Negatory on the display signal boost, Strike One," Edie's voice came back. "I've got nothing to boost it."

"Then pass me the data verbally, especially when it looks like we're coming up on any cross corridors that should either be guarded or investigated," Curt told her.

"None of those for quite a while, Major. Just keep on your present course."

"How about our intercept? Has Herrero moved too fast?

can we still nail him when he comes into that warehouse cavern?"

"That's an affirmative if he keeps moving as he is now. And he's moving right along. You'll have to step up the pace. You have about fifty meters before entering the warehouse area. When you get there, turn left."

"Roger."

Curt didn't like the idea of possibly encountering Herrero and his troops in the confines of a tunnel. He wanted maneuvering room. The warehouse would provide that. It would also catch Herrero and his *caballeros* coming out of a tunnel and put them at a disadvantage.

"I'm losing your audio signal," Curt reported. "Switch to channel twenty-three and kill the frequency hopping. Working single channel will give us a little better signal-to-noise ratio."

"Channel sixty will penetrate better, Major," Sampson suggested. "That frequency is high enough that the signal will bounce down those corridors like going through a waveguide."

"Roger! Going to channel sixty on the tacomm!" Curt then asked Fredrica, "Freddie, you got any guesstimate where your husband might be going down in these catacombs?"

She nodded her head, her long blond hair flying as they hurried along. "Gordo is probably heading for the Aerodyne Hangar Number Two which is at the end of a short tunnel leading out of Warehouse Seven, which is where we're headed now," she told him breathlessly. They were moving at a jog. At this high altitude, everyone was breathing hard. "My guess is that he'll try to secure the aerodyne hangar, then come looking for me."

"Any aerodynes in that hangar?" Curt wanted to know.

"Yes. Two Delauny-Coanda *Vulturs*."

Those were French tactical strike aerodynes. Curt knew they were fast and deadly, armed with both 20-millimeter

361

rotary cannons and small self-guiding air-to-ground rockets.

Maybe Freddie believes Gordo is going to grab the aerodynes and then come looking for her, Curt told himself, *but if I remember Gordo Herrero, he's likely to spool up those aerodynes and try to hit the house from the rear.*

He ran the scenario through in his mind. His memory of the Casa Fantasma layout indicated that the doors to Hangar Two opened on the northeast. Herrero could blast out of the hangar with two strike 'dynes, hit Casa Fantasma from the undefended east side, and then perhaps attempt a patio landing to pick up Freddie.

Curt didn't think Gordo Herrero would leave Freddie; he suspected that the man really loved this sensuous woman in addition to the fact that Fredrica knew too much about the business. Gordo would try to get her out.

So Curt had to stop Herrero before he could get to the aerodyne hangar.

The only chance of that was to pin him down in the warehouse and get Freddie to talk with him.

But just to cover his ass, Curt called Sampson on tacomm. "Edie, anyone left up there who can run those Mary Annes?"

"Yes, sir! I can!"

"No, you can't! You're stuck with your shit detail, coordinating operations in security central," Curt told her.

"The hell I can't, Major!" Sampson shot back. "I've got command links to them. I can't be with them to monitor them, but I can sure as hell give them orders! Not as positive as direct NE linkage, but we can't do that with Mary Annes anyway."

"Tricky," Curt pointed out. She'd have to run the Mary Annes via radio link without any feedback from them. In short, she'd have to operate them blind.

"However, Major, I can try to monitor their positions and conditions with the Fantasma video system here," Edie went on.

"Okay, Edie," Curt decided, "give it a try. I want you to move two or three Mary Annes off the ridge and down to where they can cover the external door to Aerodyne Hangar Number Two. Can you do it?"

There was a pause while Sampson checked. Curt kept jogging, his breath coming in deep gasps now. He just wasn't used to this high altitude. But Freddie, who lived here, was able to keep up even though she wasn't in the excellent physical condition of the Sierra Charlies.

"Roger, Major, can do! They'll be on station in four minutes!" Edie replied.

"If they see an aerodyne come out of that hangar, they are to open fire on it," Curt told her.

"Understood. I'm moving Mary Annes."

"Your signal's getting bad," Curt told her. "This may be the last communication I have with you for a while. Give me a short count every five minutes; if I can read you, I'll report back."

"Roger, Strike One!" This final response from her was almost lost in the background hiss and hum.

They erupted into the first warehouse area, a cavern that must have covered several hectares with a 3-meter ceiling, all of it hacked out of the bowels of Cerro Caliente. The lighting was subdued; warehouse lighting is usually only that required to allow warehousemen to see their way. Long shadows were cast in the narrow aisles between steel racks containing fiberboard boxes and cartons marked with cryptic symbols and labels. It was a drug storage area, a place where tons of dreamy mind poison rested until it could be transshipped to the United States.

The cases and cartons had no labels other than code symbols or words on them. There was no need to advertise the contents of the boxes, let alone inform some intruder. Herrero's computers knew what each symbol and code word meant, knew what was in each carton, and knew its

363

cost and worth. Warehouse robots could read the code and could thus move drugs in and out without any human being present and thus tempted.

Curt didn't know what was in the various containers. He didn't want to know. If it was cocaine, crack, or any of the opium derivatives, the contents of the warehouse could be worth billions of dollars.

Curt looked to the left. Three fire doors in the long wall indicated where tunnels entered the warehouse.

Edie Sampson hadn't told him which one Herrero would use to enter the warehouse. And he didn't recall the tac display as showing three tunnel entrances along that wall. Again, all of the tunnels in Cerro Caliente hadn't been revealed in the data base.

A meter of open passageway extended between the wall and the rows of shelving. Meter-wide passageways penetrated the rows of shelves in a grid pattern. The aisles were wide enough for warehouse robots to move and operate.

"A Sierra Charlie in every aisle! A jeep in every other aisle! Move!" Curt snapped, beginning a breathless run along the wall.

Before he and Freddie could get to the third door, it slid open and an armed man stepped out, rifle in hand. A look of surprise came over his face, and he raised his assault rifle.

The *caballero* shouldn't have taken the time to bring the rifle to his shoulder. Curt shot from the hip, his Novia putting a three-round burst into the man. The muzzle blast was deafening in the underground warehouse.

Curt wished he'd opted for a Hornet submachine gun for this. It was much better in close-quarter fighting.

"Charlie Love! Get to that door! Shoot anyone in the tunnel behind it!" Curt yelled and pulled Fredrica to the right into an aisle and out of a corridor of fire.

Behind him, the Companions and Marauders with their jeeps melted quickly to the right in among the warehouse

364

shelves.

Charlie Love didn't have time to get in front of the door.
Two other *caballeros,* seeing what had happened to their
point man, didn't step into the open but fired around the
doorjamb at the jeep. Their 5.54-millimeter rounds
bounced off Charlie Love's armor.

The warbot kept right on moving, trying to carry out
what it understood of Curt's order: Cover the door. Its
artificial intelligence really wasn't very bright; its AI computer determined that Curt meant for the jeep to get in
the doorway and fire down the tunnel. It trundled quickly
into position, 5.54-millimeter rounds ricocheting off it. But
when it gained the door opening, someone down the tunnel fired what Curt guessed was an 50-millimeter M100
anti-vehicle/aircraft rocket at point-blank range down the
tunnel.

The rocket's flight time was so short that it hit Charlie
Love right at thrust burnout just before the warhead
armed. Thus, it hit the warbot at its maximum velocity.
Even though it didn't explode or penetrate Charlie Love's
armor, it had enough momentum to pick up the 200-kilo-
gram warbot and knock it backward on its side.

When Charlie Love tumbled, the motion kicked out its
stabilization system. If the warbot had landed in a position
where it could have rolled sideways and come erect again,
it would have realigned its stab system. But it found itself
jammed in between shelving on both sides of an aisle and
couldn't get up. After three aborted attempts to do so, it
simply shut itself off and waited for human help.

"Curt, I'm going over to cover the exit to the hangar!"
Alexis Morgan yelled.

Curt heard her between the sporadic outbursts of gunfire. From the sound, some of his people and some of the
Herreronistas had Hornets and Mendoza submachine
guns. The Novia assault rifles were too powerful for this
enclosed fighting space; their bullets were ricocheting off

the rock walls and plunging into cases and cartons of drug on the shelves. Curt hoped to hell he didn't get winged with a ricochet. His body armor would probably stop it but a tumbling round often hit in a keyhole manner, and that hurt like holy hell.

He didn't have time to reply.

In spite of intermittent small arms fire coming down several aisles, the Herreronistas poured out of the tunnel door and spread out to the right. The Companions were moving through the aisles behind him, taking up positions. He was trying to get off snap shots as Herreronistas dashed across the aisle opening.

Alexis's voice in his helmet tacomm reported, "Exit to hangar secured!"

Suddenly Curt saw Herrero dash in front of him. His trigger finger was a hair away from firing. Instead, he yelled, "Gordo!"

Curt didn't know where Herrero ducked into the warehouse aisles, but from the sound of the man's voice he might have ducked in where Charlie Love had tumbled. He was probably using the downed warbot as cover.

"¿Quién acá? ¿Qué pasa?" Herrero's voice came to them between bursts of gunfire.

"Gordo, it's Freddie!" Fredrica screamed.

"Freddie!"

Another burst of fire echoed loudly through the warehouse.

"Gordo, it's Curt Carson, too!" Curt bellowed in his parade-ground command voice. "Cease fire? Got to talk!"

Three rounds of submachine gun fire plowed into the cartons above their heads. Someone was firing on the sound of their voices.

"Gordo, I've got to talk to you!" Freddie yelled, either not aware of the fact she was giving someone an audible target location or in spite of it.

"I'll cease fire and hold position if you will, Gordo!

366

Curt shouted.

"On your honor, sir?" Herrero's voice came.

"Roger that!"

"Cease fire! Hold position!" Herrero shouted.

Curt yelled the same command.

The warehouse became suddenly quiet. Not everyone was holding the position. Some were slowly moving into a more advantageous location to shoot.

"Carson, how the hell do I know it's you?" Herrero said. He must have been only one aisle over from where Curt and Fredrica were huddled behind a carton of drugs Curt had pulled from the lower shelf in order to provide some protection against wild ricochets.

"Gordo, it's Curt. I *know!*" Fredrica told him. She didn't elaborate on that.

"Goddammit, Gordo, we roomed together on the fourth floor of the First Division in old South Barracks!" Curt reminded him, knowing that few other people would know that bit of trivia from their lives.

"Okay, it's you, Curt. Freddie, are you all right?"

"Yes."

"I've got to see you to confirm that."

"Negatory, Gordo!" Curt broke in. "She's staying here with me. Talk, Freddie!"

"Freddie, are you under duress?"

"No, Gordo, I'm not."

"I don't believe it. I want to see you. And Curt. Stand up and walk to the passageway next to the tunnel door."

"Then you, too, Gordo," Curt insisted.

"Unarmed?"

"Hell, no, but you have my word of honor that my weapon will be slung during truce talk. How about you?"

"Very well, Carson. You have my word."

"Your word? Is it still good? Hell's great balls of fire, Gordo, you're a drug dealer now!" Curt reminded him, wanting to be certain.

367

"With you, yes, my word has been and will be my bond Curt. And do not impugn my personal honor again, sir!"

Curt knew he had indeed offended this former Mexican officer.

He also knew he was taking one hell of a long chance but it was a matter of trusting the honor of a graduate o the United States Military Academy. As such, the two men had been educated as honorable individuals associating themselves with other honorable individuals. Curt knew that not all officers followed the exacting honor code at al times after they left West Point. Utopia hadn't arrived yet

Curt pulled Fredrica to her feet and slung his Novia over his shoulder muzzle-down, in such a fashion that he could bring it to the ready in one smooth motion. He lef it cocked with the safety off.

When the two of them stepped around the end of the rack of storage shelves next to the rock wall, Gordo Her rero was standing there facing them, his Mendoza subma chine gun also slung over his shoulder in the same manner as Curt's Novia.

It was obvious that Herrero was also following the phi losophy, *I trust you, sir, but cut the cards.*

Curt had his hand gently on Fredrica's arm. When she saw her husband, she moved just slightly, and Curt strengthened his grip to keep her from running into Her rero's arms.

"Well, Curt, you're looking just like I remembered you, Herrero said pleasantly but with an edge on his voice.

"Yeah, roomie, but you've put on a little weight," Curt pointed out.

Herrero shrugged. "Trying to live up to my nickname Freddie, are you all right?"

"Of course, Gordo," she told him frankly.

"Curt treating you well?"

"Why shouldn't he?"

The hint of a smile flickered at the edge of Herrero'

mouth. "No reason. He always treated you well. I treated you better, however. Which is why I do not understand why you turned on me, Freddie."

"I didn't turn on you, Gordo," Fredrica maintained. "I told you that I wanted you to forget the sort of senseless warfare you started around Bisbee; you went ahead anyway. I could rationalize the business; I cannot and will not rationalize killing and injuring innocent people by the use of physical force! Gordo, this whole thing got out of control. You became obsessed by it. I want you to be obsessed by me . . . as you used to be."

"We already discussed that. Do you have something else you wish to add, Freddie?"

"Yes. I have arranged with the United States government for asylum and protection of the two of us in America. Curt and his regiment will escort us back to the border. We will go into protected, secure seclusion in the United States — wherever we wish to live — and we've been guaranteed access to our existing overseas bank accounts," Fredrica explained quickly. "This can all be in the past, Gordo. The Mexican government will no longer harass you. The *hermanistas* will be unable to find us, and you won't have to handle the family business any longer. I have an agreement with the United States government; they will honor it. Put down your gun and let's get out of here before the Sonoran militia finds out about this."

A look of total astonishment had come over Gordo Herrero's face as he heard Fredrica's words. He said nothing for a long second after she'd finished. Finally, he merely slipped his thumb under the strap of the Mendoza over his shoulder, shook his head, and said, "No way!"

369

CHAPTER THIRTY-NINE

"Gordo!" Fredrica shouted in dismay. "My agreement is the only way out of this!"

Herrero shook his head again. "Freddie, you know very well that we can *never* be safe from the *hermanistas*. They will track us to the end of the earth and kill us if I accept your agreement with the United States! It may be a year. It may be ten years. But, sooner or later, they will find us. . . . Curt, my old friend, I want to make a deal with you, man to man . . ."

"Gordo, I can't make deals with you," Curt told him frankly. "If you don't accept the offer, I've got to try to capture you, alive if I can. I'm not sure whether I'll have to take you back to the States to stand trial for what you did around Bisbee or if I'll have to turn you over to the Mexican authorities. Either way, I don't like it for different reasons."

Fredrica suddenly glared at Curt.

"Then I will just have to fight my way out of here," Herrero decided. He held out a hand to Fredrica. "Please return my wife to me."

"I can't," Curt said. "Whether she comes with you or takes the United States offer, that's her decision. Freddie, what will it be?"

Fredrica was not prepared to make that decision.

But she didn't have to.

Three shots rang out in the warehouse.

"Clinton, goddammit!" shouted Alexis Morgan. "We're under a cease-fire and stand-firm!"

"Sonofabitch was moving, trying to sneak up on you, Captain!"

"Bullshit! We've got the hangar exit secured! They can't . . ."

"Your word, Curt?" Herrero asked.

But the cease-fire had been broken. Gunfire again broke out.

In the instant of confusion at the start of the firefight, Fredrica suddenly acted.

Curt wasn't expecting it. Later, he cursed himself for trusting the beautiful, sensuous Fredrica.

She reached deep into the plunging neckline of her stylish blouse and drew a pistol from its holster hidden in the deep folds of her full butterfly sleeve. She barely had it clear of her blouse when she pulled the trigger.

She fired it point-blank at Curt.

He took the 9-millimeter round in his body armor on the right side at the bottom of his rib cage. The body armor stopped the slug, but the 125-grain bullet traveling at 350 meters per second—nearly its muzzle velocity—staggered the 100-kilogram man, throwing Curt to his left.

Fredrica ran to her husband.

The two of them wasted no time. In an instant, they disappeared down an aisle together.

Curt staggered on his feet, trying to get his breath because the impact of the slug had knocked the wind out of him.

Henry Kester was suddenly at Curt's side, steadying him.

In the meantime, the warehouse became a maelstrom of gunfire. The confrontation quickly disintegrated into a deadly game of cat and mouse through the maze of passageways and aisles between shelves of drugs worth billions.

371

It took Curt about a minute to get everything back together. By that time, the firefight was almost over. Like most combat situations, it didn't last very long. Most very intense battles between small units are that way. A enormous amount of energy must be expended to sustain the high level of activity, and it doesn't take very long before fatigued people begin to make mistakes. And a mistake in such an intense fight usually means being hit.

The winner is usually the side with the biggest reserves — as Napoleon Bonaparte's chief field marshal Ney once pointed out — but in this case the reserves were physical and psychological.

The herrereonistas were tired. Even though these were the crack *caballero* troops of Herrero's personal guard, they'd been on the run since Douglas. Herrero had audaciously attempted to close on the objective, Casa Fantasma, at night after he'd pushed his *caballeros* on the road all day rather than resting them overnight and striking at dawn. And although they were crack mercenaries, they were up against the highly trained professional soldiers of the U.S. Army's special Robot Infantry, the mixed-force Sierra Charlies who could fight alongside their warbots. The only warbots in the warehouse were the limited M33 jeeps, but they were armored, vulnerable only to such sledgehammer weapons as anti-vehicle/aircraft rockets, and carried the engagement's only light automatic weapons, the 7.62-millimeter M313 machine guns which were deadly in the cramped surroundings.

And Captain Alexis Morgan had sealed off their only known exit from the warehouse.

The *caballeros* wasted themselves in futile attempts to break out into Aerodyne Hangar Number Two.

The Herreronistas began wholesale surrenders when it became patently obvious there was no way they could break through the deadly wall of fire Morgan's Marauders laid down on the exit to the hangar.

372

As the firing petered down to nothing, Curt and Kester slowly and cautiously made their way down long aisles toward the hangar exit. They accepted surrenders of Herreronistas along the way as they encountered them.

The eventual count was fifteen Herreronistas killed, seventeen wounded, and twenty-one surrendered.

But the Sierra Charlies had also taken casualties in the brief but brutal close-in fighting in the warehouse.

As Curt turned his prisoners over to Gerard, Koslowski, and Elliott, he saw Alexis Morgan, flushed and excited as a result of the fight, moving among her Marauders.

Then Curt saw a small form lying on the floor writhing in apparent pain:

Lieutenant Kitsy Clinton.

Jerry Allen saw Kitsy at the same time Curt did. The two of them nearly trampled wounded and prisoners alike getting to her.

Kitsy was curled up in a ball in pain, her face grimacing.

"Goddammit! We left our equipment harnesses upstairs!" Allen swore. "No medikit!"

Curt rolled her over. "Kitsy! What is it? Where did you get hit?" Curt yelled at her.

"Uh . . . Chest! . . . God . . . Hurts like hell!" Kitsy Clinton grunted between breaths.

Curt pried her hands away from her chest. She'd been hit by a submachine gun. Whoever had shot it was good; he'd put two rounds into Kitsy's body armor.

And they had hit Kitsy in her breasts. Both had taken a round.

Kicking a man in the testicles generates intense pain; a woman experiences the same level and intensity of pain when hit in the breasts.

Curt's side was hurting where his own body armor had stopped the 9-millimeter round Fredrica had fired at him. He could only imagine how badly Kitsy hurt.

373

She was suddenly crying. "Oh, my God, it hurts so much!" she gasped.

There wasn't very much that Curt or Jerry Allen could do. Kitsy wasn't really wounded. She'd just been hit very hard in a very sensitive place, and she'd just have to bear the pain until it went away.

Strangely, Curt felt very protective of her. Right then, she seemed so small and so slight and so fragile-looking, an image that she successfully managed to hide behind a brave façade of sprightly, ardent, and animated energy. Now she was hurting. She needed and wanted comforting. She was almost like an injured little waif. Curt held her in his arms and tried to soothe her.

Jerry Allen watched, fascinated. He had sensed his own attraction to the little lieutenant over the past few months, but she had seemed so formidable, spirited, and dauntless that he'd been hesitant to approach her. The essential eagerness of a fresh brown-bar had led him to think she was just like a hundred others he'd known in his own class and since.

Curt felt a touch on his shoulder. "Major, we can't find Herrero and Fredrica." It was Alexis Morgan. She also noticed Curt holding the hurt Kitsy Clinton.

He looked up. "Be right with you." Then he looked down at Kitsy and asked, "Feeling better?"

She nodded and gulped. With the back of a hand that had dirt, mud, and cammy grease on it, she wiped her eyes. "I'll be okay, Major. Honest I will. Godamighty, that hurt. Still hurts."

"Jerry, take over here," Curt told his other lieutenant.

"Sure thing, sir!"

Curt stood up and discovered that his side still hurt. "What the hell, Alexis? Where could Herrero have gone?"

She shook her head. "I don't know. I had that hangar exit covered. I mean *no one* got through that door! I was covering that sucker myself!"

"Which means," Curt muttered, "that Herrero and Fredrica are still in here . . . or they got out another exit, one we didn't know about or weren't watching."

"They sure as hell didn't get to the aerodyne hangar!" Alexis maintained.

"True. Not if you were covering it." Curt keyed channel sixty on his tacomm. "Edie, Carson. You read?"

Surprisingly, Sergeant Edie Sampson's voice came back loudly in his head. "Loud and clear, Major! I've been trying to raise you for the last five minutes!"

"We had a little firefight down here," Curt told her. "Did you see anyone getting out of here?"

"Affirmative! Herrero and his wife skedaddled down another tunnel out of the warehouse," Sampson told him. "I couldn't raise you to tell you, and I lost them when I ran out of video sensors. They must have taken a special private tunnel to a postern of some sort."

"Are they anywhere in Casa Fantasma where you have sensor coverage?"

"Negatory, sir!"

"Keep an eye on the gate they came in . . . back down on the road," Curt suggested.

"Roger, Major. I am. Nothing happening down there now except that the Mexican truckers are arguing with Colonel Ortega."

"What?"

"Seems that Herrero didn't pay his truckers. They're trying to get it out of Colonel Ortega!"

"Well, that should keep him busy for a few hours," Curt figured. "Okay, Edie, do you see *any* other possible escape routes out of here?"

"Major, there are several other warehouses and a couple of aerodyne hangars. I have sensors in all of them. Nothing is happening there," Sampson told him. Then she added, "Herrero must have a priest hole somewhere in this maze. I sure as hell know I would, what with all the drugs

375

and stuff around here! I'd want some way to get out in case of a bust."

"I'll monitor the freak, Edie. Let me know immediately if *anything* shows up!"

"Roger, Major!"

"Damn!" Curt exploded. "Alexis, we're going to have to organize some search parties and probe some of the tunnels leading out of this warehouse."

"Curt, I've spotted six without even trying," Alexis told him. "That means sending only two or three people down each one. Unless we can set up Charlie Love and get it functioning again, we've got only five jeeps . . ."

"And Herrero has a head start on us," Henry Kester pointed out.

"Strike One, this is Edie!" Curt's tacomm sounded in his ears.

"Strike one here! Go ahead, Edie!"

"Aerodyne just departed!"

"Didn't the Mary Annes fire on it?"

"Negatory, Major! It blasted out of a hangar I didn't even know was there, and the Mary Annes are programmed only to shoot at anything coming out of Hangar Two!" Edie Sampson reported. "It's a small, fast sucker! I'm losing radar lock on it already! There! Went full stealth! Not even an infrared return!"

Curt turned and looked at Alexis. "Well, there they go!"

"The big ones got away," Alexis remarked.

Curt shrugged. "We did our job the best we could. I think we broke up this business. Sure as hell Herrero isn't going to be raiding the border towns any longer. And that's what this is all about when you get right down to it."

"So she was your old flame at West Point, eh?" Alexis suddenly asked.

"Yeah."

"A beautiful woman, Curt. I have to admire your taste in women."

376

"I thought you might," he told her cryptically. Then he turned to the Sierra Charlies guarding their prisoners and called out, "Okay, round 'em up and move 'em out! Let's get upstairs, turn these prisoners over to Ortega, and get lifted out of here. It's a long ride back to Douglas! And we aren't wanted here any longer. . . ."

CHAPTER FORTY

"We're going to *stay here*, Colonel?" Curt couldn't believe what the regimental commander had just told him.

"That's right. Fort Huachuca is the new home of the Seventeenth Iron Fist Division," Wild Bill Bellamack told him as he stood looking out the old wood-framed glass window at the ancient parade ground.

"But, Colonel, this post is a low-tech backwater! My God, our computer center is up at Diamond Point! How can we operate hundreds of kilometers from it?" Curt wanted to know.

Bellamack returned to the ancient wooden desk and sat down. Then he told his de facto second-in-command, "Sit down, Curt. As usual, the Army has its own unique little reasons for doing things, and this is no exception."

Curt sat, but he wasn't really comfortable even though an old window air-conditioning unit was blowing cool air into the office. He didn't like the idea of moving out of the twenty-first-century surroundings of Diamond Point into these old wooden buildings more than 100 years old. I had been a suitable temporary camp when the regimen was on guard against the Herreronistà raids, but he didn' think it was a modern Army post.

Generations of Army ghosts must be laughing a him.

"Georgie will remain at Diamond Point," Bellamack ex plained. "How long since you've actually seen Georgie?"

"Well, the computer was first put on line back when we were a neuroelectronic robot infantry unit. The officers got a tour of the installation," Curt recalled. "Lots of rather dull cabinets. But Georgie was right there. . . ."

"So? Since then you've worked with Georgie only by telecommunications," Bellamack pointed out. "This is no different. The current budget situation has required the Army to centralize its computer facilities. Therefore, Diamond Point is being converted into a massive underground computer complex for something new coming down the line we can't be told about yet. Oh, the tech-weenies will let us know in good time, I suppose."

"Is that the real reason, Colonel?"

"No," Bellamack admitted. "When the Army started to close Fort Huachuca permanently under the new 'use it or lose it' regulation, it seems the state's congressional delegation applied some pressure . . . but we're not supposed to know that. So the Iron Fist is going to move to Fort Huachuca and use it."

"Politicians!" Curt muttered.

Bellamack shrugged. "Don't be too hard on them, Curt. If it wasn't for politicians, we'd be fighting all the time."

"I don't follow, Colonel."

"Politics and diplomacy are the greatest inventions of the human race. It's a bumbling and often highly inefficient way to get things done. But they keep most of us from killing the rest of us most of the time," Bellamack observed. "When politics and diplomacy *don't* work, we get called in, which is why in the United States Army we take an oath of loyalty to an institution, not a person or group of persons."

"If I'd wanted to be involved in politics, Colonel, I wouldn't have followed generations of my ancestors into the military," Curt pointed out. "I know we serve the body politic. But, for God's sake, can't they let us do it in a better place?"

"How much of this base have you seen?" Bellamack wanted to know.

"Just these old buildings around the parade ground, the ones we had to try to put back into operation when you fired the civilian contractor."

"Well, Fort Huachuca is a pretty high-tech place," Bellamack told him. "It used to be the headquarters of the Army Communications Command, the Army Electronic Proving Ground, the Army Security Agency Test and Evaluation Center, and the Army Intelligence Center and School. *These* are the buildings from the days of the Apache Wars. Right now, a *good* civilian contractor is remodeling some of the more modern buildings for us, and I think you and your companions will like what you see. In fact, all the Greys will like it, I'm sure. With the thermonuclear threat eliminated by space defenses, we don't have to burrow in the ground any longer. So we'll live like the silly-vilians because, after all, we *are* Sierra Charlies who operate in the field with our warbots, right?"

"Well, that's some good news at least," Curt admitted. "When do we move out of these firetraps and into the new quarters?"

"Whenever they're finished. Don't let the Companions settle into their temporary quarters. But why don't you go over and have a look? Pappy Gratton's people will have data on where your quarters are."

"I'll do that real soon," Curt promised.

Bellamack detected a note of weariness in Curt's tone. "Your company rested up yet?" he wanted to know.

"No, sir. We're beat to the socks," Curt told him. "Acute fatigue in some cases. Chronic fatigue in others. I think the latter in my case. We've hauled our asses all over the world since we converted to Sierra Charlies. I didn't know this planet was in so much trouble. Well, I figure I've done my share to save civilization lately." He wondered why the colonel had called him into his office. Thus far, it had

380

been only an informal chat.

"Hell, want a couple of days in Baja? Go soak up a little sun and surf?" Bellamack offered.

"Not only no, but hell no!" Curt exploded. "I've had all of Mexico I can take for a while! Same for other exotic climes! But I sure as hell lust for a week or two in a Phoenix resort with summer rates. Or Tucson. Or Vegas."

"Make out a leave request. I'll sign it. I'd join you but I don't think I'm the sort of company you have in mind. I remember how horny I used to get after being shot at as a warbot brainy, and it's a lot more intense when your own sweet bod is under fire instead of a warbot's."

"You got it. Sorry, Colonel, but you're not built right." Following hazardous personal combat of the sort they'd just been through, Curt wanted to spend a few days with Alexis. If she wanted to. He wasn't sure right then. "I don't want to go alone. Let me think about it, Bill."

Bellamack didn't object to Curt using a familiar name. The two men had a contract. It had worked in practice. "Whatever."

There was a pause. Bellamack hadn't been regimental commander very long, but the two men had grown to know one another very well in the last few weeks. The colonel sensed that Curt was dead tired, and he thought a little pat on the back would be useful. So he said, "You did a hell of a fine job in the Sierra Madres, Curt."

"Thank you, Colonel, but I don't think so. The big one got away."

"Are you sorry he did?"

"No, not really," Curt admitted. "Gordo Herrero was right. His business associates wouldn't have let him live even if we'd given him quarters on the lower level of Diamond Point or Cheyenne Mountain with maximum security. As it is, *nobody* knows where Gordo and Freddie are. They're on their own. They'll make it or not, depending on what they do and how they do it. It's up to them.

Somehow, that sets better with me than having the United States responsible for their safety . . . and their eventual deaths because security was certain to slip up."

"And I would have difficulty living with that myself," Bellamack replied. "Curt, she was a beautiful woman. Morgan mentioned the relationship you had with her at West Point."

"Oh, she did, huh?"

"Yeah. So I can understand your feelings. You sorry you lost her again?"

Curt shook his head. "Negatory! Freddie would have been a lousy Army wife, and I would have been swinging around in the support branches instead of leading troops in combat like my forefathers did. Quite frankly, I discovered that Freddie really isn't my kind of woman. Maybe I've grown up a little bit since I graduated. Now I like the kind of women we have in the Washington Greys."

Bellamack thought about this. "Yeah, Curt, they are pretty special. And some are more special than others, right?"

"Some. If I could figure them out." Curt had been worried about the changes he'd detected in Alexis. But since Casa Fantasma, she'd been distant. He'd decided he had no special rights over Alexis Morgan; she'd always been her own woman and always would be. She'd always be someone special to him. But if she decided to go her way, Curt wouldn't and couldn't stop her. Maybe that was something he'd learned from Fredrica Nordenskold Herrero, who, in the long run, turned out to be someone quite different than he remembered.

Or had his memories become selective?

"When you find the answer, for God's sake let me know too!"

"Colonel, with all due respect, did you have something specific you wanted to discuss with me?"

Bellamack looked quietly at his senior company com

mander, then folded his hands on his desk in front of him. "Yes, I did. But I found out what I wanted to know," he replied cryptically. "Major, I request that you inspect the resorts in Tucson and Phoenix because I need to know the R-and-R facilities that might be available for regimental personnel. You may take other personnel along as you require for making your inspection. Although you will be on official business, you won't be on duty and you need not observe Rule Ten. I expect a full and complete report in three weeks or so. I'll be pretty busy with administrative duties for the rest of the day, so take this along in case you find need of having an official written order to carry out my request." He reached into the ancient desk drawer and pulled out a blank temporary orders form. Without further comment, he signed it and handed it to Curt. "Any questions, Major?"

Curt looked at the blank signed form, then at his regimental commander. He didn't need to be reminded that Bellamack had given him a direct order. And this form, when fully filled out, would activate an Army credit chit and expense voucher for him. "Not at the moment, sir."

Bellamack stood up. "You're dismissed, Major."

Curt rose to his feet, saluted formally, and turned to go.

"Curt," Bellamack called to his back. When Curt turned, the colonel said, "A report of the facilities is all that's required. I don't want a report of your activities. . . ."

"I understand, sir."

Curt left feeling ambivalent. In a very oblique and very unsubtle manner, he'd have been given a direct order to take some time off, yet it wasn't a pass and it wasn't leave.

Well, he decided, since he'd been given that direct order, he had no recourse except to carry it out.

He went into the next building and up to the day room of the Marauders. No one was there. He called Captain Hensley Atkinson over in regimental ops, who told him that Captain Alexis Morgan had taken the Marauders on a road exercise up to Diamond Point so they could retrieve their personal effects from the old post. The Marauders weren't expected back for five days.

Damn! And Alexis hadn't told him she knew about the change in posts or that she was going to be gone for five days!

Well, he'd make the "inspection" alone if he had to! So he went downstairs to the Companions' day room, entered his office cubicle, and checked the duty roster on his desk's terminal screen. He had planned only minor postoperation cleanup and shape-up duties for the Companions in order to give them some time to recuperate. This was a period in which people could log sack time, get equipment back into shape, make repairs, pull maintenance, and take care of all the little administrative and housekeeping chores that had to be neglected during combat. Curt sure as hell wasn't going to run his people all over the countryside; they'd done plenty of that in Mexico. Lieutenant Jerry Allen could certainly command the Companions for three weeks with Master Sergeant Henry Kester's help. Jerry would have his own company someday, and the experience would do him good.

Curt started to enter the proper items in the duty log that would put Allen in temporary command while he was gone. He rolled the blank, signed order form into the printer so that he could get it filled out.

Three sharp raps sounded at the door.

Second Lieutenant Kathleen Clinton was standing there in a fresh Army Green jumpsuit with belt, garrison cap in hand. She looked fresh and scrubbed and squeaky-clean. Her short dark hair was growing out even more now but still hugged her head.

"Come in, Lieutenant," Curt told her.

"Major, may I have a word with you if you have the time?" she asked in her dynamic and forceful official manner.

384

"Certainly. What's on your mind, Kitsy?"

She came right to the point. "Sir, I request a week's leave."

Looking her straight in the eye, Curt said, "Request denied."

This took her aback. She looked stunned for a moment, then recovered her composure and looked a little bit like a somewhat bewildered plebe. "Sir, I was under the assumption that the company was in a postcampaign recuperation phase. Alpha Company is in good shape, sir! We took no losses in the Sierra Madre operation. With another three weeks' time, Alpha will be ready in all respects for whatever assignment we're given, sir!"

He motioned to a chair alongside the terminal desk. "Kitsy, sit down, please," he asked her gently.

She sat but appeared to remain at attention.

"Do you sit that way because your torso still hurts?"

"No, sir, Major Gydesen says the trauma is gone but I'll be a little sore for a few days yet. I hurt a little when I think about it. I'm going to go to Nogales and have one of those Mexican metalsmiths make me a brass bra. . . ." She suddenly got very serious. "Major, I'd like to apologize for my behavior after I was hit in the warehouse. I . . . I shouldn't have bawled, but it hurt so damned bad! And . . . thank you for what you did, sir. It helped. A lot."

"No apologies are necessary, Kitsy. I'm only sorry the incident didn't qualify you for the Purple Heart. And you don't need to thank me. It's my job to look after you . . . and the other Companions."

"Major, I'd like to reiterate my request for a week's leave," Kitsy pressed the subject again. "If you can't grant me a week, please, I need a couple of days. . . ."

"May I ask why?"

"Uh . . . Sir, it's . . . personal," she admitted with great hesitation and reluctance.

"Operation Black Jack was the first time you were shot

385

at, wasn't it?" Curt suddenly asked.

Kitsy blushed and looked confused. "Yes, sir. And I just need to get away . . . away from you and Jerry. Damn, I didn't expect it would get this bad! I . . . I don't want to bust Rule Ten!" she blurted out with some embarrassment. Then she went on apologetically, "If I stick around here, I'm sure as hell going to!"

"Well, as I told you, your request is denied," Curt told her, then went on after a pause, "unless you decide not to volunteer for a special assignment."

"Sir?"

"I've been ordered by the colonel to spend three weeks inspecting likely R-and-R facilities in Phoenix and Tucson at my discretion," Curt told her in mock seriousness and an official-sounding tone. "My inspection could turn out to be very biased. Therefore, I believe I need to have the female point of view represented in my report. I'm requesting a volunteer. Are you interested? If not, I'll give you that three-week leave. I want your support, but I want to be absolutely fair about this, Lieutenant."

Curt watched while indecision played over her face. This was something totally unexpected to her. Suddenly, she seemed to go all soft and fragile. "Major," she asked in a small voice, "may I ask you a personal question?"

He nodded.

"I told you what my personal problem was. Is it reciprocal?"

"Kitsy, I suspect that if we weren't on duty now with Rule Ten in effect, *neither* of us would be sitting here talking. We'd be in the Copper Queen Hotel in Bisbee. . . ."

She sat there in silence for a moment, then asked, "Major I'm not so sure I *can* volunteer. If we're on official business for three weeks, I don't think I could stand it."

"The colonel specifically told me that this inspection was to be conducted in an off-duty mode. Otherwise, the data might not be valid. And, quite frankly, with you along, I

386

couldn't stand it for three weeks either, Kitsy!" Curt admitted.

"You mean I'm not the only one who feels this way after a fight?"

"Damned right! I was shot at, too. And Fredrica Herrero got to me," Curt told her. "I've got bruises, too— emotional and physical. And it still hurts. Neither of us are medics, but I'm willing to bet we can make each other's bruises go away with three weeks of therapy. At least, I sure as hell would like to try it!"

Kitsy smiled. It was a cute smile. Curt had noticed before that she was petite and trim, but he hadn't noted that she was incredibly cute when she wanted to be—in other words, when she wasn't trying to be an officer and a lady. "Major Carson, you have the damndest way of telling a girl that you care enough for her that you'd like to bed her!"

"Well, Kitsy, you send some strange signals, too," Curt observed.

"This should be made loud and clear then: Major Carson, I'd like to volunteer to assist you on your inspection tour! Can we start right away, sir?"

"No, Kitsy, because I have to teach you something," Curt told her in mock seriousness. "First lesson: When we're off-duty or conversing in private, henceforth you are not to address me by my rank or any honorific. The oak leaves dry up and blow away in the wind of passion and beauty."

"Oh, Curt! How poetic! How schmaltzy!" she said softly with a coy little smile. "What's the second lesson?"

"Well, we'll study the second lesson later, Kitsy."

"I can't wait!"

"You'll have to. Now, get packed."

She stood up, perched the garrison cap at a jaunty angle on her dark hair, and pirouetted slowly before him. "Am I not in uniform and properly attired to leave the post? This is all I need to start with."

"As a matter of fact, Kitsy, you are indeed in uniform and a credit to the Service," Curt admitted with a smile. "But you girls always like to take along a few special things . . ."

"Not this gal! I left everything but my combat gear at Diamond Point. And I am goddamned sick and tired of Army Green and baggy cammies!" Kitsy looked dreamily at the ceiling and went on, "I intend to inspect some Tucson malls with you. I am going to buy lots of little frilly, lacy, dainty, colorful, and scanty feminine things that will turn a strong man into a quivering weakling."

"That's the spirit!"

Impishly, she went on, teasing him, "But not so quivering that he won't be able to take them off me at the proper time!" Then she went mock-serious because there was still a twinkle in her eyes. "I may not be a red-hot bubbling sexpot like Fredrica Herrero, but I have my own inimitable ways! Besides, we need to get good data, right?"

"Right!" Curt turned to the terminal keypad. He entered a rush of keystrokes. The completed order form zipped out, followed by a rental car authorization, a credit chit, and a voucher redeemable for a suitable amount of cash at any bank. He then powered down and got to his feet. "Lieutenant Clinton, you are now officially on inspection duty with me. Lieutenant Jerry Allen has the conn . . ."

"Poor Jerry!"

Suddenly, he wasn't tired any longer. "Jerry can take care of himself. Like the two of us, he's an experienced combat officer. But we're officially signed out, Kitsy. Let's go inspect things!"

"Let's do that, Curt . . . *now!*"

APPENDIX 1

REGIMENTAL ROSTER
OPERATION BLACK JACK

3rd RI "Washington Greys" Special Combat Regiment, 17th Iron Fist Division (RI), Army of the United States:

Regimental commander: Lt. Col. William D. Bellamack

1st Company, "Carson's Companions" — Maj. Curt C. Carson
- M. Sgt. First Class Henry G. Kester

Alpha Platoon — 2nd Lt. Kathleen B. Clinton
- Platoon Sgt. First Class Nicholas P. Gerard
- Sgt. Charles S. Koslowski
- Sgt. James P. Elliott

Bravo Platoon — 1st Lt. Jerry P. Allen
- Platoon Sgt. First Class Edwina A. Sampson
- Sgt. Thomas C. Cole
- Sgt. Tracy C. Dillon

2nd Company, "Ward's Warriors" — Capt. Joan G. Ward
- M. Sgt. Marvin J. Hill

Alpha Platoon — 1st Lt. Claudia F. Roberts
- Platoon Sgt. First Class Corinna Jolton
- Sgt. Vernon D. Esteban
- Corp. Paul T. Tullis

Bravo Platoon — 1st Lt. David F. Coney
- Platoon Sgt. Michael E. Nalda
- Sgt. Thomas G. Paulson

Corp. William P. Ritscher
3rd Company, "Morgan's Marauders"—Capt. Alexis P. Morgan
    M. Sgt. Carol J. Head
    Alpha Platoon—2nd Lt. Everett E. Taylor
    Platoon Sgt. J. B. Patterson
    Sgt. Lewis C. Pagan
    Sgt. Edwin W. Gatewood
    Bravo Platoon—1st Lt. Eleanor S. Aarts
    Platoon Sgt. Betty Jo Trumble
    Sgt. Billy Ed King
    Corp. Joe Jim Watson
4th Company, "Frazier's Ferrets"—Capt. Russell B. Frazier
    First Sgt. Charles L. Orndorff
    Alpha Platoon—2nd Lt. Harold M. Clock
    Platoon Sgt. Robert Lee Garrison
    Sgt. Walter J. O'Reilly
    Corp. Maxwell M. Moody
    Bravo Platoon—2nd Lt. Phyllis B. Kirkpatrick
    Platoon Sgt. Isadore Beau Greenwald
    Sgt. Harlan P. Saunders
    Corp. Victor Jouillan
Headquarters Company—Maj. Wade W. Hampton
    Regimental Sergeant Major—Sgt. Maj. Thomas S. Jesup
    Staff Unit Commander—Maj. Joanne J. Wilkinson (chief of staff)
    Regimental Adjutant—Maj. Patrick Gillis Gratton (S-1)
    Regimental Staff Sergeant—M. Sgt. Georgina Cook
    Regimental Operations—Capt. Hensley Atkinson (S-3)
    Regimental Operations Sergeant—Staff Sgt. Forest L. Barnes
    Staff Sergeants:
    Staff Sgt. Andrea Carrington

Sgt. Sidney Albert Johnson

Intelligence Unit Commander — Capt. John S. Gibbon
   Regimental Intelligence Sergeant — Staff Sgt. Emma
   Crawford
   Intelligence Sergeants —
   Sgt. William J. Hull
   Sgt. Jacob F. Kent
   Sgt. Christine Burgess

Regimental Chaplain — Capt. Nelson A. Crile

Service Company — Maj. Frederick W. Benteen (S-4)
   Regimental Service Sergeant — M. Sgt. Joan J. Stark

Regimental Maintenance Unit Commander — Capt. El-
   wood S. Otis
   Chief Maintenance Sergeant — Technical Sgt. First
   Class Raymond G. Wolf
   Maintenance Specialists —
   Technical Sgt. Kenneth M. Hawkins
   Technical Sgt. Charles B. Slocum
   Technical Sgt. Willa P. Miller
   Technical Sgt. Geraldine D. Wendt
   Sgt. Bailey Anne Miles
   Sgt. Jamie Jay Younger
   Sgt. Robert H. Vickers
   Sgt. Louise J. Hanrahan
   Sgt. Richard L. Knight
   Sgt. Nancy R. Roberts
   Sgt. Robert M. Lait
   Sgt. Gerald W. Mora

Supply Unit Commander — 1st Lt. Harriet F. Dearborn
   Regimental Supply Sergeant — Chief Supply Sgt.
   Manuel P. Sanchez
   Supply Specialists —
   Supply Sgt. Marriette W. Ireland
   Supply Sgt. Lawrence W. Jordan
   Sgt. Jamie G. Casner

Biotech Unit Commander — Maj. Ruth Geydesen

(M.C.)
Biotech Professionals —
  Capt. Denise G. Logan (M.C.)
  Capt. Thomas E. Alvin (M.C.)
  Capt. Larry C. McHenry (M.C.)
Chief Biotech Sergeant — Biotech Sgt. Helen Devlin
Biotechnicians —
  Biotech Sgt. Clifford B. Braxton
  Biotech Sgt. Laurie S. Cornell
  Biotech Sgt. Shelley C. Hale
  Sgt. Julia B. Clark
  Sgt. Marcela V. Jolton

APPENDIX 2

GLOSSARY OF ROBOT INFANTRY TERMS AND SLANG

ACV: The Armored Command Vehicle, a standard warbot command vehicle highly modified for use as an artificially intelligent computer-directed command vehicle in the Special Combat units.

Aerodyne: A saucer- or frisbee-shaped flying machine that obtains its lift from the exhaust of one or more turbine fanjet engines blowing outward over the curved upper surface of the craft from an annular slot near the center of the upper surface. The annular slot is segmented and the sectorized slots can therefore be controlled to provide more flow and, hence, more lift over one part of the saucer-shaped surface than another, thus tipping the aerodyne and allowing it to move forward, backward, and sideways. The aerodyne was invented by Dr. Henri M. Coanda following World War II but was not developed until decades later because of the previous development of the rotary-winged helicopter.

Artificial Intelligence or *AI:* A very fast computer with a large memory which can simulate certain functions of human thought such as bringing together or correlating many apparently disconnected pieces of information or data, making simple evaluations of importance or priority of data and responses, and making decisions concerning

393

what to do, how to do it, when to do it, and what to report to the human being in control.

Biotech: A biological technologist once known as a "medic."

Bot: Generalized generic slang term for "robot" which takes many forms as *warbot*, *reconbot*, etc.

Bot flush: Since robots have no natural excrement, this term is a reference to what comes out of a highly mechanical warbot when its lubricants are changed during routine maintenance. Used by soldiers as a slang term referring to anything of a detestable nature.

Cee-pee or *CP:* Slang for "Command Post."

"Check minus-x": Look behind you. In terms of coordinates, *plus-x* is ahead, *minus-x* is behind, *plus-y* is to the right, *minus-y* is left, *plus-z* is up, and *minus-z* is down.

Down link: The remote command link or channel from the robot to the soldier.

Fur ball: A complex and confused fight, battle, or operation.

Go physical: To lapse into idiot mode, to operate in a combat or recon environment without robots; what the Special Combat units do all the time.

Golden BB: A lucky hit from a small-caliber bullet that creates large problems.

Greased: Beaten, conquered, overwhelmed, creamed.

Hairy Fox: The Mark 60 Heavy Fire warbot, a voice-commanded artificially intelligent war robot mounting a 50-millimeter weapon and designed to provide heavy fire support for the Special Combat units.

Humper: Any device whose proper name a soldier can't recall at the moment.

Idiot mode: Operating in the combat environment without neuroelectronic war robot support; especially, operating without the benefit of computers and artificial intelligence to relieve battle load. What the warbot brainies think the Sierra Charlies do all the time.

394

Intelligence Amplifier or *IA:* A very fast computer with a very large memory which, when linked to a human nervous system by non-intrusive or neuroelectronic pickups and electrodes, serves as a very fast extension of the human brain, allowing the brain to function faster, recall more data, store more data, and thus "amplify" a human being's "intelligence."

Jeep: Word coined from the initials "GP" standing for "General Purpose." Once applied to an Army quarter-ton vehicle but subsequently used to refer to the Mark 33 General Purpose voice-commanded artificially intelligent robot which accompanies Special Combat unit commanders in the field at the company level and above.

KIA or *"killed in action":* A situation where all a soldier's neuroelectronic data and sensory inputs from one or more robots is suddenly cut off, leaving the human being in a state of mental limbo. A very debilitating and mentally disturbing situation.

LAMV: Light Artillery Maneuvering Vehicle, a computer-controlled robotic vehicle used for light artillery support of Sierra Charlie units; mounts a 75-millimeter "Saucy Cans" weapon originally designed in France.

Linkage: The remote connection or link between a human being and one or more neuroelectronically controlled war robots. This link or channel may be by means of wires, radio, laser or optical means, or other remote control systems. The robot/computer sends its data directly to the human soldier's nervous system through small electrodes positioned on the soldier's skin; this data is coded in such a way that the soldier perceives the signals as sight, sound, feeling, smell, or the position of a robot's parts. The robot/computer also picks up commands from the soldier's nervous system that are merely "thought" by the soldier, translates these into commands the robot can understand, and monitors the accomplishment of the commanded action.

Mary Anne: Slang for the Mark 44 Maneuverable Assault warbot, a voice-commanded artificially intelligent warbot developed for use by the Special Combat forces to accompany soldiers in the field and provide light fire support from its 25-millimeter weapon.

Novia: The 7.56-millimeter M3A4 Novia or "sweetheart" assault rifle designed by Fabrica de Armes Nacionales of Mexico. It uses caseless ammo. The version used by the Special Combat units is the M33A4 Ranger made in the United States, but Sierra Charlies still call it the Novia.

Neuroelectronic(s): The electronics and computer technology that permits a computer to detect and recognize signals from the human nervous system obtained by means of non-intrusive skin-mounted sensors as well as to stimulate the human nervous system with computer-generated electronic signals through similar skin-mounted electrodes for the purpose of creating sensory sensations in the human mind—i.e., sight, sound, touch, etc. See "Linkage" above.

"Orgasmic!": A slang term that grew out of the observation "Outstanding!" It means the same thing.

Pucker factor: The detrimental effect on the human body of being in an extremely hazardous situation, e.g., being shot at.

Robot: From the Czech word *robota* meaning work, especially drudgery. A device with humanlike actions directed either by a computer or by a human being through a computer and a remote two-way command-sensory circuit. Early war robots appeared in World War II as radio-controlled drone aircraft carrying explosives or used as targets, the first of these being the German Henschel Hs 238 glide bomb launched from an aircraft against surface targets and guided by means of radio control by a human being in the aircraft watching the image transmitted from a television camera in the nose of the bomb.

Robot Infantry or *RI:* A combat branch of the United States Army which grew from the regular Infantry with the introduction of robots and linkage to warfare. Active RI divisions are the 17th ("Iron Fist"), the 22nd ("Double Deuces"), the 26th ("R.U.R."), and the 50th ("Big L").

RTV: Robot Transport Vehicle, a highly modified artificially intelligent computer-controlled adaptation of a warbot carrier which is used by the Special Combat units to transport their voice-commanded artificially intelligent Mary Annes and Hairy Foxes (which see).

Rule Ten: Slang reference to Army Regulation 601–10, which prohibits physical contact between male and female personnel while on duty other than that required for official business.

Rules of Engagement or *ROE:* Official restrictions on the freedom of action of a commander or soldier in his confrontation with an opponent that act to increase the probability that said commander or soldier will lose the combat, all other things being equal.

Saucy Cans: An American Army corruption of the French designation for the 75-millimeter *"soixante-quintze"* weapon mounted on an LAMV.

Sierra Charlie: Phonetic alphabet derivative of the initials "SC" meaning "Special Combat," the personnel trained to engage in personal field combat supported and accompanied by voice-commanded artificially intelligent warbots.

Sierra Hotel: Shit hot. What warbot brainies say when they can't say "Hot shit."

Simulator or *sim:* A device which can simulate the sensations perceived by a human being and the results of the human's responses. A simple toy computer with an aircraft flight simulator program or a video game simulating a human-controlled activity is an example of a simulator. One of the earliest simulators was the Link Trainer of World War II, which provided a human pilot with the sensations of instrument or "blind" flying without leaving the ground.

Sit-guess: Slang for "estimate of the situation," an edu-

397

cated guess about the situation.

Sit-rep: Short for "situation report."

Snake pit: Slang for the highly computerized briefing center located in most caserns and other Army posts.

Spasm mode: Slang for killed in action (KIA).

Spook: Slang term for either a spy or a military intelligence specialist.

Staff stooge: Derogatory term referring to a regimental or
divisional staff officer.

Tacomm: A portable computer-controlled frequency-hopping tactical communication radio transceiver once used
primarily by rear-echelon troops and now generally used
in a ruggedized version by the Sierra Charlies.

Tango Sierra: Tough shit.

Tiger error: What happens when an eager soldier tries too
hard to press an attack.

Up link: The remote command link or channel from the
soldier to the neuroelectronically controlled war robot.

Warbot: Abbreviation for "war robot," a mechanical device that is operated remotely by a soldier, thereby taking
the human being out of the hazardous activity of actual
combat.

Warbot brainy: The human soldier who operates war robots, derived from the fact that the soldier is basically the
brains of the war robot.

HIGH-TECH WARRIORS IN A
DEVASTATED FUTURE!
C.A.D.S.
BY JOHN SIEVERT

#1: C.A.D.S. (1641, $3.50)

Wearing seven-foot high Computerized Attack/Defense System suits equipped with machine guns, armor-piercing shells and flame throwers, Colonel Dean Sturgis and the men of C.A.D.S. are America's last line of defense after the East Coast of the U.S. is shattered by a deadly Soviet nuclear first strike!

#3: TECH COMMANDO (1893, $2.95)

The fate of America hangs in the balance as the men of C.A.D.S. battle to prevent the Russians from expanding their toehold in the U.S. For Colonel Dean Sturgis it means destroying the key link in the main Sov military route—the heavily defended Chesapeake Bay Bridge-Tunnel!

#4: TECH STRIKE FORCE (1993, $2.95)

An American turncoat is about to betray the C.A.D.S. ultra-sensitive techno-secrets to the Reds. The arch traitor and his laser-equipped army of renegades must be found and smashed, and the men of C.A.D.S. will accomplish the brutal task—or die trying!

#5: TECH SATAN (2313, $2.95)

The new U.S. government at White Sands, New Mexico suddenly goes off the air and the expeditionary C.A.D.S. force must find out why. But the soldiers of tomorrow find their weapons useless against a killer plague that threatens to lay bare to the Soviet invaders the last remaining bastion of American freedom!

Available wherever paperbacks are sold, or order direct from the Publisher. Send cover price plus 50¢ per copy for mailing and handling to Zebra Books, Dept. 132, 475 Park Avenue South, New York, N.Y. 10016. Residents of New York, New Jersey and Pennsylvania must include sales tax. DO NOT SEND CASH.

**TOP-FLIGHT AERIAL ADVENTURE
FROM ZEBRA BOOKS!**

WINGMAN   (2015, $3.95)
by Mack Maloney

From the radioactive ruins of a nuclear-devastated U.S. emerges a
hero for the ages. A brilliant ace fighter pilot, he takes to the skies
to help free his once-great homeland from the brutal heel of the
evil Soviet warlords. He is the last hope of a ravaged land. He is
Hawk Hunter . . . Wingman!

WINGMAN #2: THE CIRCLE WAR   (2120, $3.95)
by Mack Maloney

A second explosive showdown with the Russian overlords and their
armies of destruction is in the wind. Only the deadly aerial ace
Hawk Hunter can rally the forces of freedom and strike one last
blow for a forgotten dream called "America"!

WINGMAN #3: THE LUCIFER CRUSADE   (2232, $3.95)
by Mack Maloney

Viktor, the depraved international terrorist who orchestrated the
bloody war for America's West, has escaped. Ace pilot Hawk
Hunter takes off for a deadly confrontation in the skies above the
Middle East, determined to bring the maniac to justice or die in the
attempt!

GHOST PILOT   (2207, $3.95)
by Anton Emmerton

Flyer Ian Lamont is driven by bizarre unseen forces to relive the
last days in the life of his late father, an RAF pilot killed during
World War II. But history is about to repeat itself as a sinister secret from beyond the grave transforms Lamont's worst nightmares
of fiery aerial death into terrifying reality!

*Available wherever paperbacks are sold, or order direct from the
Publisher. Send cover price plus 50¢ per copy for mailing and handling to Zebra Books, Dept.   132, 475 Park Avenue South, New
York, N.Y. 10016. Residents of New York, New Jersey and Pennsylvania must include sales tax. DO NOT SEND CASH.*